FALLING FOR HER
FRENCH TYCOON

REB

D0765888

FORTUNE'S
TEXAS SURPRISE

STELLA BAGWELL

MILLS & BOON

First Published in Great Britain 2020
by Mills & Boon, an imprint of HarperCollinsPublishers,
1 London Bridge Street, London, SE1 9GF

Falling for Her French Tycoon © 2020 Rebecca Winters
Fortune's Texas Surprise © 2020 Harlequin Books S.A.

Special thanks and acknowledgement are given to Stella Bagwell for her contribution to *The Fortunes of Texas: Rambling Rose* series.

ISBN: 978-0-263-27866-8

0220

MIX
Paper from
responsible sources
FSC™ C007454

This book is produced from independently certified FSC™ paper to ensure responsible forest management.

For more information visit: www.harpercollins.co.uk/green

Printed and bound in Spain
by CPI, Barcelona

FALLING FOR HER FRENCH TYCOON

REBECCA WINTERS

Once again I turn to my oldest son, whom I often call Guillaume, because he's a Francophile like his *maman* and fluent in their beautiful language. Turning to him for information about my favorite place on earth is better than any book. His knowledge continues to stun me. We have the most marvelous conversations and I learn so much. How I love him!

PROLOGUE

NATHALIE FOURNIER RANG Claire Rolon, the best friend of Nathalie's deceased stepsister, Antoinette. The friendship between the three of them went back to childhood.

"Claire?"

"Nathalie! I'm so glad you called! It's been ages."

"Way too long. I'm thrilled you answered. Do you have a minute?"

"Yes. Robert is upstairs playing with the baby while I finish the dishes. Go ahead."

She took a deep breath. "I know Antoinette would have confided in you before she got pregnant two and a half years ago. Is there anything you can tell me about her lover who disappeared on her without explanation? Our family didn't know she'd even been involved with someone until the doctor said she was pregnant. By then she'd sunk into a deep depression."

"Your stepsister was very secretive."

"So secretive she never spoke his name to us and

as she died from infection ten days after her baby was born, we still don't know who his father is," Nathalie lamented. "Now little Alain is fifteen months old and I'm taking the steps to legally adopt him. Before I do, though, I need to try to find his father."

"You're kidding! How could you possibly do that?"

"Hopefully with a little information you could provide." Nathalie gripped the phone tighter. "You probably think I'm crazy."

"Of course I don't."

"You were the closest person to her, Claire. If she said anything, it would have been to you. Any clue you could give me would help. Did she let it slip where or how she met him?"

"She did say he worked at the Fontesquieu vineyard."

Her heart raced. "You're certain of that?"

The Fontesquieu vineyards near Vence, France, were one of the largest and most prestigious, producing the legendary rosé wines of Provence. The land had been deeded to them by royalty centuries ago, and the most coveted vineyard in all Provence was currently run by a titled billionaire. She'd heard stories about the vineyard all her life.

"Yes. Apparently they met at a bistro in Vence where a lot of the vineyard workers from the Fontesquieu estate hang out during the harvest."

"Do you remember the name of it?" Nathalie cried, encouraged by what she'd just learned.

"It was unusual. The Guingot, or some such name, but I don't imagine he would be at that vineyard after all this time. I wish there was something more concrete to tell you. It's not much to go on. I'm so sorry. I think you'll need a miracle."

"Don't be sorry, Claire! The vineyard is the place where I'm going to start looking. One more thing. Did she say what he looked like?"

"Unfortunately not. Only that he was a Provencal and the only man she would ever love."

That meant he'd been a local Frenchman, probably dark haired and eyed.

"You've given me more information than I could have hoped for. Thank you with all my heart."

"Good luck. Let me know if you learn anything."

"I will. You're such a good friend. Thank you for being so honest with me. I know she swore you to secrecy."

"She did, but it's been a long time since then. For Alain's sake it would be wonderful if you're successful."

"Wouldn't it? Talk to you soon."

Nathalie hung up, deep in thought.

At the beginning of the summer, Nathalie had broken up with the man she'd thought she might marry. Guy couldn't handle her bringing Alain into their marriage—he wanted his own child with her.

That's when she'd told him she probably couldn't have children. When she'd explained about having primary ovarian insufficiency, he couldn't handle that news. Guy had said he'd wanted to marry her, but he'd refused to consider adopting Alain. Because she wanted her nephew more than anything, it became clear that marriage was out of the question.

Alain meant everything to her.

CHAPTER ONE

August 31

ADRENALINE GUSHED THROUGH Nathalie as she sped toward the Fontesquieu vineyards of Vence—queen of the cities of the French Riviera, in her opinion. They stretched eye to eye above the blue Mediterranean, row after row of immaculately tended *terroirs* with their healthy grape vines dotting the undulating green hills and summits.

The August afternoon sun had ripened the luscious grapes, filling the air with a sweet, fruity smell as she neared the Fontesquieu estate with its enormous seventeenth-century chateau, rumored to contain twenty-two bedrooms. It reminded her of the book *My Mother's Castle*, made famous by the French author and filmmaker Marcel Pagnol. He'd been born in Provence too and had written some of her favorite books about his childhood memories.

But the Pagnol family's quaint little vacation home in Provence couldn't compare to the one she could see out the window of her trusty old Peugeot. The magnificent chateau had always been closed to the public, but the estate drew artists and tourists from all over the world.

Nathalie couldn't imagine the wealth of a family like the Fontesquieux. She'd been born in Provence and had passed by the vineyard many times, but she'd never enjoyed its scenery more than this afternoon.

With pounding heart, she followed the signs posted to find the tent set up for people seeking temporary work grape picking. After planning this since her talk with Claire a month ago, the day had come for her to get a job that would last only the three weeks of the grape harvest. In that amount of time, she hoped to find the man who had fathered her nephew, Alain, if he was still there. But as Claire had said, it would take a miracle.

When she reached the nearby mobile home park she'd visited earlier in the week, she parked and walked down the road toward a line of people waiting outside the tent in the distance.

Before entering, a man—probably early twenties—with dark blond hair handed everyone an application to fill out. He also gave them a list of items they would need if they were eventually hired. She put that list in her purse and sat down at a small table to fill out the form before getting in line. He eyed her with obvious male interest before it was her turn to enter the tent.

The line moved slowly until there was only one person in front of her being interviewed. That's when she saw the man vetting everyone and stifled a gasp. She wished she had a better description of Alain's father. All she had to go on was that he was a Provencal, which meant dark haired and dark eyed. The man sitting there certainly filled that description, but it could be a coincidence. Was it possible she'd found him?

The breathtaking, late-twenties-looking male could easily be the heartthrob Antoinette had fallen for! Her darling stepsister's now sixteen-month-old child possessed this man's square chin and black hair. He had the same type of build and olive skin.

Thousands of Frenchmen claimed those same qualifications, but this one's piercing black eyes had a distinct look that reminded her so much of her little nephew, Nathalie was astonished. To think, it might be Alain's father sitting there not ten feet away interviewing would-be grape pickers. By applying for this job, she could have found him!

According to one of the people in line, hundreds of workers had already been hired during the week. Today represented the last group seeking temporary employment.

"Prochain?" he said in a deep voice that reached her insides.

Nathalie's heartbeat sped up as she realized she was next in line and needed to follow through. She moved forward to sit opposite him on a chair beneath the tent. The heat of the sun had made the interior uncomfortably warm.

Though he was seated, she could tell he was a tall man, lean in that appealing masculine way. He wore a white shirt with the sleeves pushed to the elbows and as he took the application from her, she noticed a small, pale, café-au-lait birthmark on his underarm beneath the elbow. She had to stifle another gasp because the back of Alain's right calf had the same birthmark.

Maybe it was a coincidence. Millions of people had them, but this was just one more bit of evidence to convince her he could be Alain's father.

Nathalie noticed that he wore a watch and no rings, but that didn't mean he wasn't married. His nails were immaculate. When he looked up, their eyes met and her breath caught.

Heat crept into her cheeks as she got lost in his intense gaze. They were both taking measure of each other while she waited for him to say something. He couldn't have recognized her as Antoinette's stepsister. Nathalie was a blonde. Her stepsister had been a brunette. They came from different sets of parents with different last names.

His virile male beauty stunned her. Her stepsister, who'd been two years older than Nathalie, would have taken one look at him and that would have been it! How well Nathalie understood the instant attraction. She couldn't look away.

He continued to study her features. "Mademoiselle Fournier? I see here you've had no experience as a *vendangeuse*."

"That's right. I didn't know that was a prerequisite."

"It's not, but it's hard labor, seasonal, and the pay isn't that great. Why would a pharmacist from La Gaude apply to do entry-level work like this?" La Gaude, France, was a town a fifteen-minute drive from Vence along the Côte d'Azur, the playground of the world's rich and famous.

She felt those black all-seeing eyes travel over her with a thoroughness that caused her to tremble, and she looked down. He was so gorgeous she was in danger of forgetting why she'd come. For her little nephew's sake, it was vital Nathalie pull this off. She needed to think fast.

"I've lived in Provence all my life and thought that for once I'd use my vacation time to find out what it's like to work in a vineyard as world renowned as this one."

On their website she'd seen one photo of the Duc Armand de Fontesquieu, the gray-haired, eighty-year-old patriarch and CEO. She'd seen no other pictures and realized they had to be a very private family.

Though many vineyards used machinery, some vintners—like the vastly wealthy Fontesquieu family with their many *terroirs*—also hired pickers called *coupeurs*, plus collectors and sorters for the grape harvest *vendange*. It lasted for the first three weeks of September. She'd done her homework.

After a slight pause, he spoke. "You do realize that we have no accommodations for you here."

She raised her eyes to him again. With that comment, she sensed he didn't believe her reason for wanting the temporary work.

Though it was this man's job to vet would-be workers, she sensed he had reservations about her. Obviously the "no previous vineyard work" written on the form bothered him. Naturally anyone could apply for grape picking, but their vineyard would welcome those with experience.

"Yes. That's why I've rented a mobile home at the park down the road from here." Actually she'd come two days ago to put a hold on one until she knew the outcome of this interview.

He gave her a level stare. "Keep in mind you'll have an hour for lunch and quit at four thirty. If you're still interested in working here by Monday morning, report to the tent at six o'clock and the assistant vineyard manager will let you know if you've been hired."

It was all up to this man who would have the weekend to check out her references. He spoke with authority. There was an aura of sophistication about him that let her know he had a position of importance at Fontesquieux and had likely worked here long enough to have met Antoinette at the bistro.

"*Merci*, monsieur." She got up, aware of him watching her as she walked past the people standing in line, and left the tent. The younger man outside giving out applications flashed her a smile, but she looked away and headed for her car, not wanting to encourage him.

When she got behind the wheel, she was still feeling shaky from all the sensations bombarding her. It might be a long shot, but now that she suspected she'd met the man who could be Alain's father, she'd do everything possible to get to know him. When she sensed it was the right moment, she'd show him photos of Antoinette and Alain, including the birthmark. If he was the father, she couldn't imagine him not wanting to see his child.

Of course, if she didn't get hired, then she needed to find innovative ways to cross paths with him, starting tonight. She planned to seek out dinner at the bistro Claire had told her about. Maybe *he'd* be there... Just imagining his handsome features left her breathless.

Having finished the interviews, Dominic Laurent Fontesquieu stopped in the midst of fastening his briefcase full of applications. He couldn't resist taking another look at the Fournier application.

The woman with translucent green eyes and natural silvery blond hair had robbed him of breath. Her deportment and stunning beauty had captivated him. As Dominic studied the particulars on her application, her image swam before him again.

> *Age: twenty-seven.*
> *Home address: La Gaude.*
> *Cell phone...*
> *Email address...*
> *Employed full time at La Metropole Pharmacy.*
> *Driver's license.*
> *Own car.*
> *Bank account.*
> *Covered by social insurance.*
> *Degree in pharmacology from Sophie Antipolis University in Nice.*
> *No experience picking grapes.*

He tapped the paper against his jaw. What was missing here? Only everything else about her life that might answer the question of what prompted her to apply for this temporary work.

This mysterious, gorgeous, educated woman suddenly appears at the vineyard out of nowhere, wanting to know what it's like to help with the harvest for a few weeks?

Dominic didn't buy it for a second. He put the application in the briefcase with the others before leaving the tent, unable to get her off his mind. He was so attracted to her, it shocked him.

Vetting would-be workers was one of his brother Etienne's jobs as director of the vineyard so he usually oversaw the vendange hiring. But he'd been struck down by a nasty flu bug for the better part of a week and their grandfather Armand had rung Dominic's apartment in the south wing of the chateau and demanded that he fill in for his brother.

Little had Dominic known that the most beautiful woman he'd ever laid eyes on in his life would be among the applicants. He'd wanted to catch up with her after she'd left and take her to dinner to get to know her better. But that had been impossible when other people needed to be interviewed.

Frustrated, he headed for his office in a building on the estate behind the chateau. He left the applications for his assistant, Theo, to deal with until Etienne recovered and drove the short distance to the chateau. Once he reached his apartment, he took a quick shower to cool off.

Until today he'd never found a woman whose looks turned him inside out in just one short meeting. In fact he'd doubted if such a woman even existed. But this afternoon, a pair of translucent green eyes had caught him completely off guard.

Throughout the eleven years he'd been away from home in Paris, he'd enjoyed several intimate relationships with beautiful women. But he'd never experienced this instant, intense, earthy kind of attraction to a woman, not even when he'd been a teenager. And he sure as hell hadn't seen a woman like her show up for work at the vineyard before.

After putting on a robe, he went to the kitchen to make himself a sandwich. While he ate, he phoned Etienne with an update and told him not to worry, Dominic would continue to cover for him and told him to get better. After hanging up, he needed a distraction. He turned on the TV to watch the news, but nothing helped get his mind off Nathalie Fournier.

She was on some kind of mission. He was certain of it. Though a pharmacist, maybe she had an ambitious streak and did freelancing undercover for a newspaper or a wine industry magazine to make extra money.

He wished his cousin Raoul was home so they could talk. They were closer than brothers and always confided in each other. But Raoul and his father, Matthieu, the comptroller of the company, were in Saint Tropez at a vintners' conference and they wouldn't be back until Sunday night.

Any conversation would have to wait until Monday. *And then what, Dominic?*

Maybe some politician was paying a lot of money for her to get an exclusive on the vineyard. Was it hoped that her digging would turn up something she could expose concerning the migrants who worked at the Fontesquieu vineyard? No one would suspect her under the guise of a pharmacist, of all things.

He supposed anything was possible and didn't like what he was thinking. Half a dozen ideas of what she might be up to percolated in his mind, as his domineering grandfather was always guarding against trespassers.

Dominic's thoughts turned to his autocratic grandfather who'd been born with a *divine right of kings* syndrome. He felt a bleak expression cross over his features. The austere man's dictatorial personality had forced the whole family to live under his thumb. He'd forced arranged marriages for all his six sons and daughters, and insisted they all live and work together at the massive chateau, determined to keep it all in the family.

Armand had screwed up more lives than Dominic dared count. Under his tutelage, Dominic's own father and mother, Gaston and Vivienne, had put unbearable pressure on him and his siblings to marry certain moneyed, elite people they'd picked out for them. At eighteen, Dominic had refused to be told what to do.

No one in the family— including his parents—had had a good or happy marriage, souring Dominic's taste for the institution. Early on he'd made up his mind to study business and carve out his own future. It had been imperative he get away from the family dynamics to survive. His dreams had gone far beyond being a vintner and he'd left home for Paris under the threat of being disinherited, but he hadn't cared.

He'd begged his brother to go with him, but Etienne

had held back, too unsure to challenge their father and grandfather. Their older sister, Quinette, had already been married off.

Ultimately, Etienne stayed and Dominic had left alone, putting himself through college. After graduation he'd studied investment banking in Paris and, in time, he'd worked for a firm there where he'd made a considerable fortune in investments, coming home only for vacations and various events.

He would have stayed there permanently, but four months ago he'd received a frantic call from his mother that his father was seriously ill with pneumonia and might die. Dominic had intended to return to Vence only temporarily but his grandfather immediately insisted Dominic take over his father's position as funds manager while the older man was ill.

Still hesitant to remain in Vence, it was Raoul, now vice president in charge of marketing and sales for the Fontesquieu Corporation, who'd been the one to beg Dominic to take the job and not go back to Paris.

The two of them had been best friends growing up, always watching out for one another. Over the years they'd always stayed in touch, Raoul visiting Paris when he could. In the end, Dominic hadn't been able to refuse Raoul and so had stayed on while his father was recovering.

He was no fool though. Ever since his return, he'd known his grandfather had an ulterior motive in wanting Dominic to take over the management of funds. Because of a bad year of frost and rain two years ago, the vineyards in France had suffered severe financial losses and even their family had been impacted despite their assets in other businesses.

Dominic knew his father and grandfather were plotting for him to marry Corinne Herlot, who'd bring the fabulous Herlot industrial fortune with her. She'd been at several family parties, but he could never be interested and had planned to leave for Paris by the time the harvest was over.

At least that was what he'd intended *until* today when Nathalie Fournier had appeared. Now there was no way in this world could he leave yet...

Nathalie could hear the sound of jazz outside the swinging doors of what turned out to be the Guinguet bistro. There were people going in and out, enjoying the balmy Friday night air with its hint of fruit from the vineyards. She could well understand the lure this atmosphere had held for her stepsister.

Easing past couples, Nathalie walked inside the crowded establishment filled with small round tables and people slow dancing to the music. In the romantic atmosphere, she realized she hadn't had a date since breaking up with Guy three months ago.

It had hurt that he wouldn't want to take on anyone else's child, whether it was Alain or a child they might adopt after marriage. She couldn't imagine a childless union, but knew that adoption wasn't an option for everyone. She'd hoped Guy would be open to it but he couldn't have made his feelings against it clearer.

She'd learned of her condition at the age of twenty. Nathalie had ovulated only once by then. That was seven years ago. Since that time, she'd ovulated only twice. After what had happened with Guy, her natural worry was that any man she would meet in the future might have reservations about adoption, but she couldn't think about that now. Nathalie knew it had been the right decision to stop seeing Guy and didn't regret it.

Her mind kept going over what had happened to Antoinette. Her stepsister had fallen madly in love with a man she'd met in this very bistro. She'd loved him so much she'd had his baby.

Today Nathalie felt certain she'd met her stepsister's lover inside that tent. One look at him and she'd understood the chemistry. Love at first sight, sweeping Antoinette away. But clearly the fire had been only on her stepsister's part because he'd disappeared on her.

He couldn't have known he'd left her pregnant, could he? After meeting him, Nathalie knew he was the kind of man who could have any woman he wanted. Antoinette had likely been a dalliance for a month, then nothing more.

Now that Nathalie had met him, she feared that if he was Alain's father, he wouldn't want anything to do with a baby he hadn't intended to sire. Nathalie was beginning to think this had been a terrible idea and she should leave this whole thing alone. Alain had a surfeit of love from her and his grandmother. That would have to be enough.

"Mademoiselle?"

A man's voice caused Nathalie to turn around. She'd been admiring some of the paintings of the Fontesquieu chateau and gardens adorning the walls.

"Perhaps you remember me?"

She blinked. "Yes. You were the man handing out applications earlier today."

"That's right. When I saw you walk in alone just now, I thought I'd say hello and offer to buy you a drink. My table is right here."

This was probably how it had happened for Antoinette. Her lover had approached her in exactly the same way. Nathalie had to do some fast thinking. If she accepted the invite, she could at least learn the name of the man who had interviewed her. But she wasn't attracted to this man and didn't want him to misunderstand.

"Thank you, but I only came in to look around."

"You can do that right here." He pulled out a bistro chair for her so she would sit down. Then he took the other seat. "Have you been in here before?"

"Never."

"My name is Paul Cortier, by the way."

"I'm Nathalie Fournier."

"*Eh, bien*, Nathalie, please allow me to order you the specialty of the house, although you may not like it. Guinguet is an acquired taste."

"Guinguet? Like the name of the bistro?"

"*C'est exacte.*" He signaled for a waiter who took their order. "The word comes from the *guinguettes* that were popular drinking places on the outskirts of Paris years ago. They served local sour white wine, a tradition this bistro keeps up."

"Who makes the sour white wine here?"

"The Fontesquieu Vineyards."

"Of course. Your employer."

"That's right. They make enough of it to keep the owner here in business."

"Even though their grapes are red?"

Paul chuckled. "There are lots of secrets about red grapes I'd be happy to explain to you on another occasion. Perhaps on a tour of the winery itself? I'd be happy to arrange to show you personally."

She shook her head. "Thank you, but just so you know, I'm not interested in a relationship with anyone, Paul." It was the truth.

He squinted at her. "At least you're honest."

The waiter brought them each a small goblet of pale white wine. After he walked away, Paul lifted his glass. "Try it and let me know what you think."

Nathalie, who didn't actually like wine, took a sip, then struggled not to make a face.

Paul laughed. "Somehow I knew that would be your reaction. It's not for everyone. But since you'll be helping with the harvest, I thought you'd like a sample. Sort of a christening for you."

She took another sip to please him. "I may not be hired."

"Unless you have a police record, I don't see any problem. Please tell me you don't." He was a charming flirt who never gave up.

She chuckled. "Not as far as I know."

"That's the best news I've had since I handed you an application."

"I guess I'll find out Monday morning if I made the cut. My interview didn't last long since the man saw on the application that I knew nothing about grape picking."

He cocked his head. "Is that true?"

"Yes, but I think it would be interesting to learn."

"It's hard work."

"Ooh. I'm sure there's a great deal to learn and endure." She took one more sip, but knew she could never acquire a taste for it. "Now I hope you don't mind, but I have to get going. When you spoke to me, I had only come in here to take a look around because one of the people in line told me about this place. It was very nice of you to buy me a drink." There was no sign of the striking French god who'd interviewed her earlier.

"I'm sorry you have to go. Let me walk you out."

"That won't be necessary."

"No problem. I'm leaving too." He cleared their way through the crowds and walked her to her car, where she got in.

She spoke to him through the open window. "If I'm hired, we'll probably see each other again."

"I'm planning on it. Otherwise I'll ask my boss why you didn't get the job. He'll go to Dominic for an explanation."

"Dominic?"

"Dominic Fontesquieu. He's one of the family heads who interviewed you earlier today."

What?

"He rarely does any interviewing, but his brother, Etienne Fontesquieu, director of the vineyard, has been ill. If there was a problem with you, Gregoire will get it straightened out with Etienne so you will be hired. You can trust me on that."

"Thank you very much, Paul. *Bonne nuit.*"

CHAPTER TWO

NATHALIE DROVE AWAY with her heart in her throat. Could Alain be the son of Dominic Fontesquieu? A man who came from one of the most prominent, titled families in France?

Had it been an illicit affair on his part that he didn't want getting back to his family? Had he sworn Antoinette to silence because of his name?

Maybe he'd been married and couldn't afford a scandal that would make the news. If he were divorced now, it could explain the lack of a wedding ring. Or maybe he didn't like to wear rings. She wondered if he'd kept his name a secret from Antoinette.

Suffused with more questions than before, Nathalie drove faster than usual, needing answers. Fifteen minutes later, she entered the house and found her mother in the family room watching TV while she worked on some embroidered blocks for a quilt. All was quiet, which meant Alain was asleep.

Nathalie sat down on the couch. "I'm glad you're still up, Maman, because I've got something of vital importance to tell you."

Her mother took one look at her and turned off the TV.

"Please don't be upset with me if I tell you something that might make you angry."

"Why would you say that?"

For the next ten minutes, Nathalie told her about her talk with Claire a month ago and her plan to look for Alain's father. She explained about her visit to the Fontesquieu vineyard to apply for work, and ended by telling her about today's discovery.

"This afternoon I found a man I believe could be Alain's father and learned his name."

Her mother leaned forward. "Good heavens, Nathalie. What do you mean you think you've found him?"

When Nathalie told her what had happened today, her mother jumped to her feet looking startled. "Alain could be a Fontesquieu?"

"Yes. If the man who interviewed me is the one, I can see why Antoinette fell for him. He's...so incredibly attractive, I can't believe it." Nathalie had been mesmerized by him.

"I've never heard you talk this way about a man before."

She drew in a breath. "That's because I've never met one like him in my whole life. It would explain what happened to Antoinette." She cleared her throat. "On the drive back just now, I decided that if I'm hired on Monday, I'll work there long enough to find out his marital status. If he's divorced or single, then I'll approach him. But if he's married and has children, then for the sake of his wife and family, I'm not sure how I'll inform him."

"Oh, Nathalie." Her voice shook. "Darling… You're going to have to be careful without positive proof."

"There *is* proof if you compare the two of them, even without a DNA test. The resemblance is uncanny. And there's something else. Dominic Fontesquieu has the same small birthmark as Alain."

"I'm afraid that still doesn't prove paternity."

"You're right."

Her mother seemed anxious.

"Don't worry, Maman. I promise to talk everything over with you before I make any kind of a move."

"You honestly believe this Dominic could be the one?"

"In my opinion, yes. Just think—if he knew he had a son and wanted him—how wonderful it would be for Alain to get to know at least one of his parents. He's such a treasure, I would think any father worth his salt would give anything to claim him."

"I agree, but I'm afraid to credit any of this because—"

Nathalie got up and hugged her. "Because it would be a dream come true if Alain's father wanted him and they could be united."

Her mother nodded. "But darling, it could be a nightmare if there isn't a good ending to this story."

"I know, Maman. Not every man would welcome that kind of news. I won't do anything until we're in total agreement."

Dominic was already awake at five Monday morning when his phone rang. He checked the caller ID. Something had to be wrong for his brother to call this early.

"Etienne? Have you taken a turn for the worse?"

"*Non, non,* but the doctor won't let me go to work for a few more days. *Desolé,* Dom." His voice still sounded an octave lower than normal.

"I'll be happy to fill in until you're better and will help Gregoire."

"Thanks, brother."

Nothing could have made Dominic happier since he wanted to get to know Mademoiselle Fournier. "Stay in bed and relax. Theo did all the background checks on Friday's applicants and informed Gregoire. No red flags on anyone."

Which meant none on Mademoiselle Fournier, whose image refused to leave his mind. She'd never been in trouble. No parking infractions or car accidents, no warrants out for her arrest. He hadn't really expected anything negative to come up on her but relief had swept through him when he learned she was squeaky clean, even though he still had the feeling she'd come to the vineyard for a hidden reason. He planned to get to the bottom of it.

"That's good considering we need workers," Etienne murmured. "This is a bigger harvest than last year, *Dieu merci.* Such news will make Grand-père happy."

"I'll drive to the tent now."

"Paul will be there to help. Thanks, Dom."

"*Au revoir.*"

After hanging up, Dominic quickly showered and shaved. On his way out the door dressed in jeans and a fresh white shirt, he grabbed a plum and a baguette to hold him over until lunch.

Hurrying to the main garage on the property, he picked one of the trucks rigged with gear to help the workers and headed for the tent at the base of the western *terroirs*. Judging by the temperature outside, it was going to be another hot day, which meant the bulging grapes needed picking now.

Mademoiselle Fournier was in for some hard, menial work. By the end of the harvest he'd discover why she'd really come to the vineyard. With more excitement than he should be feeling, he parked near the tent where Gregoire and Paul were addressing the latest crop of new workers.

Though dressed like the others in rainproof layered clothing and gum shoes to protect themselves from the morning dew, she stood out from everyone else. Her height plus the feminine mold of her body made it impossible for him to look anywhere else.

This morning she'd tied her shimmering hair back at the nape of her neck with a band, revealing high cheekbones and a softly rounded chin. He'd studied the enticing shape of her mouth on Friday and the image had stayed with him all weekend, making him wonder how he'd last until he'd be close to her again.

He parked next to the other two trucks and waited until Gregoire gave final instructions to the workers. One by one they climbed into the truck beds with the aid of ladders. From here they'd be driven to the vineyard needing attention.

At that point Dominic got out of his own truck. He lowered the tailgate and attached his ladder so the last ten workers being ushered by Paul could climb in.

He was happy to see the pharmacist among them and watched as Paul said something to her that produced a smile before she climbed in. Paul was a gossip, the last person Dominic wanted around their new worker. He would make sure that ended fast, he thought as he shut the tailgate.

Gregoire waved to Dominic before driving into the vines. Paul followed and Dominic brought up the rear. When they reached the designated *terroir*, he shut off the motor and walked around to open the tailgate.

After the workers used the ladder to get down, he climbed up and opened the locker. "Before you follow the others, I'm handing out scissors, gloves and knee pads for all of you to use while you work here. For those of you who have done this before, you know the gloves help prevent stains, but it's your choice whether to wear them or not. I presume you've brought water bottles and sunscreen." Everyone nodded and waited their turn.

"At the end of the day, more trucks will be here to take you back to the tent area."

In a few minutes they were ready and followed Gregoire and Paul's groups, lining up and down the rows of grapes to get started. Dominic took a walk along another row, satisfied to see that the trailer had arrived for the collectors who gathered the picked grapes to transport to the winery.

When Paul had to leave to help some of the other workers, Dominic took advantage of the moment to catch Mademoiselle Fournier alone. She was kneeling on the pad and had started cutting grapes. He noticed her gloves stuck in one of the back pockets of her jeans.

"*Bonjour*, mademoiselle."

She looked up in surprise, giving him the full view of her light green eyes. The woman's beauty took his breath away.

"*Bonjour*, monsieur."

"You prefer not to use gloves?"

"Maybe I'll put them on later, but I need to practice without them first to get a feel for the work."

He was surprised as that's what he would have advised. Paul had obviously shown her what to do and already she'd put some grapes in the bucket provided.

"Did you apply sunscreen already?"

"I did at the last minute."

"That's good. The heat is already building. You don't want to get a sunburn before the end of your first day. You'll also likely find you need an over-the-counter painkiller to deal with aches and pains tonight."

An enticing smile broke out on her lovely face. "I brought some just in case. That's very kind of you to be concerned."

"*He*, Dominic."

"*Salut*, Paul." The other man had come back. Dominic still held her green gaze. "Just remember not to kill yourself off today. You'll need your strength for tomorrow."

She smiled. "I appreciate the warning. *Merci*, monsieur."

Dominic nodded to Paul, then walked toward the truck in the distance. On his way back to the office, he ate his snacks, but he'd need coffee. To his relief Theo had already made it for both of them.

No sooner had Dominic poured himself a cup and walked into his private office to get busy than Raoul arrived. All the family offices were in the same building.

"You're a sight for sore eyes, *mon vieux*. Come on in and shut the door."

"I was hoping you'd be here." He'd brought a cup of coffee with him and planted himself on a leather chair opposite Dominic's desk.

"Anything new at the conference in Saint Tropez?"

Raoul shook his head. "The Provencal vineyards seem to be doing marginally better, but it's going to take years before every vintner in France recoups losses from two years ago. *Dieu merci* for the personal investments you've helped me make."

"You're not worried about money, are you?"

"I might be."

"That sounded cryptic."

"Let's just say I'd like you to go over my accounts and let me know what I'm worth. I might need some of it before long."

Dominic sat forward. "I'll look into it before the day is out. But promise me you're not thinking of doing something drastic."

"Like what?"

"I don't know. Like leaving the way *I* did, maybe?"

He knew his cousin's marriage had been in shambles from the start, and that both Raoul and his wife carried a deep sorrow from losing their little girl, Celine, who had died at one month from a bad heart. Dominic wondered how much longer the two could keep up pretensions.

"My greatest regret is that I didn't go to Paris with you years ago. Let's face it, Dom. You were the only one in the family with the guts to get out before being swallowed alive."

"But I'm back now." For how long he didn't know. It depended on Nathalie Fournier, who'd swept into his life on Friday, bringing a beauty and charm that had put some kind of a spell on him. His desire to get to know her had stoked an unprecedented hunger in him, though his cousin didn't know that.

Raoul stared hard at him. "Yes, but you're still free to make your own decisions. Nobody owns you and your life is intact."

"No one owns you, Raoul."

"You're right. I take ownership for my guilt and mistakes with Sabine."

Dom let out a troubled sigh. "As you can see, the tentacles brought me back temporarily."

"The day you came home was my salvation."

"You're mine, Raoul. Whatever you're planning, don't leave."

"Not yet anyway. I need to know where I stand financially before I do anything."

"I'll get busy on it." Something serious was going on with Raoul.

"Thanks. Now enough about me. I hear Etienne is still sick."

"He's finally getting better. I'm filling in for him a while longer, but something odd has come up I want to talk to you about."

"Go ahead."

Dominic told him everything, but didn't reveal the strength of his attraction to the pharmacist. "Am I being paranoid that she's up to something questionable?"

Raoul studied him for a minute. "Being an under-cover freelance reporter is a big stretch from being a pharmacist. But I'd trust your instincts as they're rarely wrong. If you feel something isn't right, then it isn't. What's your plan?"

"I'm going to get to know her."

"After a few days you'll know if she's out for a scoop on the business. It has happened before. Grand-père forced the perpetrators to pay stiff fines and do jail time."

"That's our grandfather." Dominic didn't want her to have to face that type of punishment for trespassing. If that was what she was doing.

Just then, Raoul received a text. After reading it, he looked up. "I've got to get over to my office."

"I'll call you tonight."

"What would I do without you in my corner?"

On that note, he dashed off.

Dominic sat back, pondering his cousin's counsel to follow his instincts about Miss Fournier. He planned to find out what made her tick.

After pulling all the information on Raoul's invest-ments, he did some figures and prepared a form to give his cousin. By afternoon he'd finished his work, so he drove his car back out to the *terroir*. Dominic made sure he'd shown up early enough to catch sight of the woman who was constantly on his mind.

Paul and Gregoire kept moving up and down the

rows to help the workers. At 4:30 p.m. he saw her and several others leave the vineyard, though she walked down the road rather than climb into one of the trucks.

Dominic called to her as he pulled his car alongside her on the road. "Mademoiselle Fournier?"

She swung toward him, her eyes lighting up when she saw him behind the wheel. "*Bonsoir*, monsieur."

"Since I'm on my way back to the chateau, allow me to drive you to your mobile home."

"Oh—thank you very much." It surprised him that without hesitation she climbed in the other side with her backpack.

He started driving at a slow pace. "How was your first day?"

A fetching smile broke out on her flushed face. "You don't want to hear about it."

Her comment made him laugh. "It had to be a change from preparing prescriptions for people."

"Working here with the vines is another existence. No matter how sore I am, it makes you part of this world of living greenery." She had a unique way of putting things that seemed to confirm his suspicions that she could be a writer. She darted him a smile. "How was *your* day?"

Was she trying to get information from him? "You'd be bored to tears." In truth he'd accomplished less than usual and it was all because of the beautiful woman sitting next to him.

"I'm sure that's not true. For my part, I already feel a camaraderie with some of the other workers. The Lopez family next to me is so cheerful."

Dominic remembered interviewing them after she'd left the tent. "It doesn't sound like you're ready to quit yet."

"Oh, no. I'm in for the count."

"Why?" More than ever he wanted an answer to that question.

"I learned as a child that way back when one of your ancestors was titled and given this land. Not very many people can claim a heritage like yours. It made fascinating reading."

All her answers sounded truthful. "Why fascinating?"

"When I was a little girl, I grew up on fairy tales. Your chateau is the embodiment of those painted on the covers of the books I loved. The thought of working in your vineyard sounded intriguing. Is it true your grandfather holds the title of Duc?"

"It's a defunct title." Maybe she was writing an historical account for a publisher and wanted information from the CEO himself. Did she hope for permission from Dominic?

"Even so, it adds a certain mystique from the past that makes you and your family seem out of the ordinary. When I was at the Guinguet, I noticed several paintings of the chateau and sculptured gardens hanging on the walls. It's very cool."

Minute by minute she was enamoring him. Eventually they reached the park. "Where is your mobile home?"

"It's the third one in the second row."

He kept driving and pulled up behind a blue car. Now

that he knew where to find her, he didn't want to let her go. She had a vitality that intrigued him. Much as he wanted to take her to dinner this evening, he knew she was exhausted after her first day.

"Voilà, mademoiselle. Home in one piece."

"Bed is going to feel good tonight."

He could imagine. "I'll see you tomorrow."

"Thank you more than you know."

She got out of the car and he watched her until she waved to him and let herself inside the mobile home. When he was convinced she was safely inside, he backed up and left the park. Tomorrow he had plans for the two of them.

CHAPTER THREE

TUESDAY MORNING NATHALIE woke up at 5:00 a.m. with new aches and pains. Picking grapes was a killer, but she was determined to see this through. Whether he was Alain's father or not, the hope of seeing Dominic again was all she could think about. The man had already captivated her. He had a polish that attracted her to him like mad.

After showering, she hurriedly dressed and tied her hair back, covering herself in sunscreen. After eating breakfast, she packed a sandwich, fruit and water in her backpack, where she'd left the knee pads and scissors. Then she stole from the house.

Right now Alain was still sound asleep. So was her mom, who wouldn't open the pharmacy until eight. She'd hired Denis Volant, another pharmacist from Nice, to help run things while she was undercover at the vineyard. Minerve, the woman who tended Alain, was scheduled to arrive at the house at 7:30 a.m.

Already the air was warm and once again it seemed that it would prove to be a hot day. Nathalie drove along the road to the mobile home and parked her car around the side. After freshening up inside, she left and started walking toward the workers' tent at the vineyard to wait for the truck.

But that meant Paul would be there. Having no desire to encourage him, she changed her mind. As she started out for the *terroir* on foot, she was surprised when a familiar sleek black Renault sedan drove past her.

She glanced at the driver. The sight of Dominic Fontesquieu caused her heart to leap. Everything about him spoke of sophistication and a privileged life most people would never know anything about. It was there in his manner and speech.

He pulled to the side ahead of her on the roadway and got out of the car. In jeans and a pale gray crew neck, his male charisma was devastating. Those black eyes played over her.

"You're still alive," he murmured in that deep voice she loved.

She smiled. "Barely."

"That's honest at least."

"You did warn me."

His hands went to his hips in a totally male stance. "Then I suggest you get in my car now to reserve your strength."

"That's very nice of you, but I don't want to put you out."

"Not at all. I can't allow word to get around that one of our new pickers has been worked to exhaustion after her first day."

She laughed gently. After hoping she'd see him

today, she didn't dare let this precious opportunity get away. "You're a lifesaver. Thank you, monsieur."

"My name is Dominic." He opened the passenger door for her so she could get in carrying her backpack. He'd just thrown her a lifeline to get to know him better.

The interior smelled of the soap he used, teasing her senses. In a minute he'd climbed behind the wheel and they were off to the *terroir* in the distance. "I pass by here several times a day checking on the carriers. If ever you need a ride, just let me know."

Encouraged by the offer, she said, "I might take you up on that since by the end of the day I'm quite sure I won't have enough strength to climb in one of the trucks. You weren't kidding when you said I'd need painkiller."

"The pain will pass."

"I hope so. I've never appreciated the kind of hard work involved. While I was cutting grapes, I marveled to think of all the care needed to keep the vineyard healthy and thriving. No one should complain about the price of wine. Ninety-nine percent of the world has no clue what goes into making it."

He darted her an amused glance. "That's quite a testimonial. What's your favorite kind?"

"I don't have one. I dislike the taste of wine and much prefer to eat the grapes."

A burst of deep male laughter came out of him.

"I know that sounds crazy, especially when you work for a vineyard, but I just don't care for it, and I really despise the sour white wine they serve at the Guinguet."

"You mentioned that yesterday."

Did it bring back memories of being there with Antoinette?

"That's right. One of the workers suggested I go there to relax, so Friday evening I drove there and looked around before driving home. Monsieur Cortier saw me and asked if I'd like to try their famous sour wine." She shook her head. "It was awful. He said it comes from the Fontesquieu winery, but I can't imagine anyone wanting to drink it."

"I don't like it either."

"You're not offended by my frank speaking?"

"Not at all."

Too soon they'd arrived at the *terroir*. Afraid he would realize how much she was enjoying their conversation, she got out of the car. "You saved my life giving me this ride."

"It was my pleasure. I'd like to get to know you better—why don't I come by at noon to take you to the winery for lunch? Since you don't like wine, it ought to be an interesting experience for you to see how the other half lives."

His smile thrilled her. "You'd do that?"

"A man has to eat. I'd rather have company."

"So would I."

Dominic Fontesquieu had a sense of humor and was incredibly easy to talk to. When she'd been hired on here, she'd been intent on finding Alain's father. She'd never expected that she'd meet a man who swept her away with every look and smile. The fact that he could have been Antoinette's lover made this whole situation more complicated. "*A bientôt*, Dominic."

He leaned across the seat. "I'm sorry, I don't recall your name."

Her heart thumped. "It's Nathalie."

"*A bientôt*, Nathalie."

He'd just said he'd see her soon. Once again the sound of that low male voice wound its way to her insides.

A tremor of excitement raced through her as she shut the door and hurried toward the row where she'd been working. Without looking back, she could hear the engine as he drove away. Her hope to spend time with him was coming to fruition much sooner than she'd anticipated.

He'd said he wanted to get to know her better. He wasn't the only one. It shocked her how much she longed to be with him again. For someone of his status, there wasn't an atom of arrogance in him, which made him so appealing she couldn't get enough of him.

Before long the trucks came with the workers and she plunged into her day. But knowing Dominic would be picking her up at noon carried her through the rest of her morning. His irresistible charm had seeped its way beneath her skin and she found herself thinking constantly about him. That was a side effect she hadn't anticipated when she'd considered trying to look for Alain's father.

But therein lay a problem. She needed to learn a bit more about him before she revealed why she'd come to the vineyard in the first place. That meant she had to close off her personal feelings about him because this was all about Alain. She couldn't let it be about her desire for the man himself. She just couldn't!

"Did you know you're talking to yourself?"

She snipped another bunch of grapes in frustration before glancing at Paul. *"Bonjour."*

"How about going out with me after work tonight? I know you don't want a relationship, but can't we be friends at least?"

"Of course, but I'm afraid I have plans."

"Is there a night when you'll be free?"

Nathalie wasn't interested, but didn't want to be rude since he was one of the supervisors here. "Maybe Thursday evening right after work? Get a pizza? I saw a pizzeria near the Guinguet."

He nodded. "Thursday it is. I'll pick you up."

"No, no. I'll meet you there in my car."

She heard him sigh. "Have it your way."

"Thanks for understanding. *Ciao*, Paul."

When he moved on, she got back to work. As for Dominic, Nathalie realized she couldn't allow the situation about Alain to go on much longer before telling him why she'd come.

Nathalie kept checking her watch. When it was noon, she grabbed her backpack and hurried out to the road. Dominic sat in his car waiting for her. She couldn't believe how excited she was to see and talk to him.

He reached across the seat and opened the door for her. When she climbed in, he put her pack in the back, then flashed her a smile that melted her bones.

"You came!" The white crew neck shirt brought out

his olive skin. He was such a striking man with that black hair and all-seeing black eyes, she could hardly breathe.

"As if I wouldn't," his voice grated and they took off down the road.

"I'm so lucky to be whisked away in the middle of the day."

"It's a treat for me too."

Something was going on here. She knew how she was feeling about him, about how she'd felt the moment she'd met him. It was like an explosion going off inside her. If she wasn't mistaken, he was just as attracted and couldn't stay away from her.

Was he the man Antoinette had met? Her conflict was growing. How ironic that Nathalie had hoped to find Alain's father, yet now that she thought Dominic could be the one, a part of her didn't want him to be the man her stepsister had loved.

Before long they approached a chateau that looked older and smaller than the main chateau. There were clusters of cars parked outside. Dominic drove around the back of it. "We'll eat lunch first, then I'll take you on a tour before you have to return to work."

After he'd helped her out of the car, Dominic took her inside a vaulted room with some interesting framed documents and pictures to do with wine. The place was filled with tourists seated at tables drinking wine and enjoying lunch.

Once he'd found them a table in the corner, he deserted her long enough to talk to the aproned man behind the ancient-looking bar. Armed with two bottles of Perrier water and two *croques monsieurs*, he returned.

She took a bite of the melted ham and cheese sandwich. "Mmm. I haven't had one of these in ages. It's delicious. Does every winery offer food like this?"

"Not many."

"The sales must skyrocket after someone has been here."

He finished his food. "That's the idea." His eyes gleamed as he looked at her. "I can get you coffee if you'd prefer it."

"Thank you, but water is much better while I'm working."

"I couldn't agree more. When you're ready, I'll show you around the winery."

"Let's go now. I'd love to see everything possible before I have to get back. I don't want Gregoire to think I'm taking advantage."

"We can't have that." That slow smile made her pulse race.

She held on to her half-full bottle of water and followed him through a door that led to the heart of the building. The huge vaulted rooms filled with machinery and barrels overwhelmed her. The place reminded her of a scientist's laboratory all devoted to producing sumptuous wines that kept the Fontesquieu Corporation one of the top winemakers in the world.

Dominic smiled at her while they walked from room to room. "You're not saying anything."

That was because his native intelligence pretty much staggered her. "I'm too busy marveling over this amazing world. I'm afraid I feel guilty that I don't like wine."

A chuckle escaped him. "Your liver is much healthier leaving it alone."

"I don't think I dare quote you," she quipped, loving this hour spent with him while he explained the wine-making process, overwhelming her with knowledge he'd been learning since birth. He knew so much about everything that it seemed he could go on forever, but it was past time to leave. "I should get back to work."

"I was afraid you'd say that," he whispered. "I'll explain to Gregoire it was my fault that you're late. Come this way."

Dominic led her to another exit not used by the public and they walked around the building to his car. As he cupped her elbow, his touch sent a dart of electricity through her body, making her come alive.

He helped her in before driving her back to the *terroir*. After he stopped, he said, "Since I don't want this day to end, why don't I pick you up after work?"

She sensed he wanted to be with her as much as she wanted to be with him. It was hard to believe this was really happening. "Only if you have time."

"I'll make it," he declared in a firm tone of voice that sent an unmistakable message of his desire to be with her.

"Thank you for lunch and the tour, Dominic. To be shown around by an expert has been a highlight for me I'll never forget." She meant what she'd said and knew she sounded breathless.

"That makes two of us."

He handed her the backpack before she got out of the car. Their hands touched, once again making her feel weak with longing. Nathalie walked to the row where she'd been snipping grapes. When she reached her spot, she finished the bottled water and got busy, counting the minutes until she could be with Dominic again.

When the heat reached its zenith, Nathalie checked her watch. It was four thirty. Quitting time. She gathered up her things, so eager to see Dominic, it was ridiculous. But after reaching the road, there was no sign of his car. Undoubtedly something had held him up because she knew he'd had every intention of coming for her.

Disappointed, she avoided the trucks and started to walk toward the mobile home, anxious to get out of the hot sun. Three-quarters of the way back, she saw the black Renault coming toward her. It shouldn't thrill her to see him, but it did. She was in so much trouble. When she'd followed through on her plan, she hadn't considered being enthralled by the man she'd been searching for.

He stopped and got out. "I'm sorry to be late, but it couldn't be helped."

"Please don't apologize. I know you're a busy man."

In seconds he'd opened the passenger door. This time their arms brushed as she climbed inside, making her acutely aware of him. The AC felt wonderful and she was relieved she didn't have to walk. He made a U-turn and drove them back toward the mobile park.

He pulled up behind her blue Peugeot. "Why don't you go in and freshen up, then we'll drive somewhere for a bite to eat before I bring you back here. Lunch didn't fill me and I'm starving."

"I'm hungry too. Thanks. I'll be out soon."

His invitation opened up a whole evening where she could learn more about his personal life. Totally intoxicated by him, Nathalie slid out of the car and unlocked the door of the mobile home. She hurried inside and took a quick shower. After putting on jeans and a blouse, she brushed her hair.

Her body trembled on the way out to his car because her feelings for him were growing to the point he was all she could think about. She hurried back to the car and got in. "Where are we going?"

"I've ordered us some takeout so you can stay in the car and rest while we eat."

A soft laugh escaped her lips. "Only someone who has picked grapes before would understand how I feel."

He started the car and drove them out to the main road into Vence. "It was my first job. I think I was about four when my *papa* walked me and my five-year old brother, Etienne, to the vineyard and showed us what to do."

She turned to him. "Did you live near this one when you were little?"

In the next breath, he said, "Are you going to tell me that after Paul plied you with sour wine, he didn't tell you who I am?"

Oh, boy. She'd walked right into that one. "No. I was only trying to be discreet. Paul *did* say you were a Fontesquieu, but the last thing I've wanted to do is presume anything and he didn't go into detail."

Dominic didn't respond. Within seconds he turned a corner and pulled up in front of a café. "I'll be right out.

After I get back, you can tell me why you really came to the vineyard for work you don't need."

She groaned inwardly. Nathalie wasn't wrong about his being strongly attracted to her, but it was clear he hadn't believed her reason for being here.

He soon returned with their food and headed toward the Fontesquieu estate once more. After he pulled to a stop and shut off the engine, he handed her cannelloni, salad and an espresso.

"Thank you, Dominic. This smells and looks delicious." But her heart was pounding so hard, she feared he could hear it.

He tucked into his meal before turning to her. "Now, how about telling me what newspaper or wine magazine you're working for undercover?"

Her heart plummeted. "Is that why you showed me around the winery?"

"I took you there because I wanted to be with you, and because I was hungry. But in case you were after a story, I thought I'd show you the inner workings, something not everyone is allowed to see. If you've been hired by a newspaper to find out how the migrant workers are treated at the vineyard, I wanted to give you a favorable impression."

She ate her food, trying to find the right words. Obviously their family had been bothered by infiltrators before. Nathalie couldn't blame him for being suspicious since she didn't meet the profile of the normal picker.

"I'm not a spy, Dominic. Your assumptions are understandable, but they would be wrong about me," she said in a quiet voice. "Is it impossible for you to imagine that I simply want to work here for a few weeks to enjoy a new experience?'"

His black eyes bored into hers, reminding her of Alain. "Yes. Our background check proves you're a full-time pharmacist. If you're truly not here undercover, why don't you tell me the truth about why you chose to work at this specific vineyard for a few weeks?"

She finished her espresso. "This is embarrassing."

"I'm listening." He'd never taken his eyes off her.

"Three months ago I broke up with a pharmaceutical distributor. We met in graduate school in Nice several years ago and continued to see each other off and on. After Christmas I thought maybe he could be the one. But in time I realized we were wrong for each other." Guy's reaction to her being unable to have children had worried her that another man would probably feel the same way. She couldn't help wondering if the man sitting next to her would reject her for the same reason. "Since I'd already arranged my vacation time for a trip we obviously did not end up taking, I decided to do something different that would bring me a little money, not cost me."

"Vintners are noted for paying lower wages," he murmured.

"Nevertheless, I need to save all I can for the future." Now came the lie. "After passing your vineyard, I saw that you were hiring workers for the three-week harvest and thought it would be a fascinating way for me to spend my vacation from the pharmacy.

"I also believed that working with the soil would be so different, it would be cathartic for me. There's nothing like a new challenge." Considering she was doing this for Alain's sake, she hoped lightning wouldn't strike her. "But you would have every right to tell me to walk away now."

"Is that what I'm doing?" he asked in a silky tone.

"No. I'm offering to go." She didn't have enough proof he could be Alain's father to confront him. "If you'll wait long enough for me to get my backpack, I'll return the equipment handed to me. The man running the mobile home park will be glad if I give up mine since there's always a demand for one." She started to get out.

"Wait—" he said, reaching for her arm. She felt his touch to her toes. "You're doing an excellent job, according to Gregoire's nightly reports. Forgive me for jumping to the wrong conclusion about you. It's just that there's nothing my grandfather dislikes more than someone who trespasses on the property for ulterior motives."

"Of course, and you had every right to be suspicious of me when it's clear I'm not desperate for a job."

I'm only desperate for answers.

"That's very generous of you," he murmured. "Maybe you won't believe me, but I'm sorry if I've offended you. Let's hope working with the vines might work its magic for you, even if you dislike the taste of wine." The sudden smile he flashed was enough to reduce her to jelly. "You're not fired, Nathalie."

His ability to admit he'd been wrong made her admire him more than he'd ever know, but she was also filled with raw guilt because she hadn't told him the real reason she'd come. All she needed was a little more information.

"Thank you for a second chance, and for buying me dinner."

"To prove I'm telling you the truth, I'd like to take you on a walk through the vineyard tomorrow evening after you've eaten. You mentioned you'd like to see more of it while we were at the winery. Will your aching joints be able to handle it?"

She turned to him. "There's nothing I'd love more," she whispered.

"Jusqu'à demain soir," he whispered back.

Arriving back home, she climbed out of his car and rushed inside the mobile home, where he couldn't see her breakdown. Nathalie had to face the truth. It had been only a few days, but she'd already fallen hard for him. Love at first sight was no joke. Nothing like this had ever happened to her before.

It wasn't just his dashing dark looks or the background he'd come from. He was a man of extraordinary substance. There was a kind of nobility about him. That's what made it so difficult for her to understand his behavior if he'd had an affair with Antoinette.

If he was the one who'd fathered her child, how could he have disappeared on her stepsister with no explanation? Nathalie needed to learn the truth about him soon and not get carried away by her growing feelings for him.

He'd shaken her with his ability to see inside her and question her motives. She should have told him the truth, but had held back because of too little proof. One thing she knew by now. You didn't play games with a man like him.

Dominic's mind reeled as he drove home.

He'd wanted to believe Nathalie's explanation even though he felt she was still hiding something from him. Why it bothered him so much was a mystery to him. A virtual stranger couldn't possibly be this important to him no matter how beautiful or intriguing.

But the closer he got to the chateau, he knew that wasn't true. He'd been intimate with some attractive women over the years, yet nothing remotely like this had ever happened to him before.

Even if Nathalie was to disappear suddenly and he never saw her again, the fact that he could be swept away by her this fast had changed him in a fundamental way. Nathalie had lit a fire that wasn't going to go out.

It seemed there *was* a woman out there for him, one he wanted to get to know and would do whatever it took to do so. She was an original with a verve and freshness that was a constant delight to him. Her thoughts about everything fascinated him. If he believed in witches, he'd think she'd put him under a magical spell.

Dominic didn't know he could feel this way about a woman. Meeting her had revealed the real reason why he'd reached the age of twenty-nine and still hadn't married. Was it possible he'd unknowingly been waiting for her to come into his life?

He entered his apartment a different man. Needing more coffee, he went in the kitchen to fix it, then called his cousin and gave him the figures he wanted. Silence followed. "Raoul? Why aren't you saying anything?"

"I'm surprised that much money has accrued. It's all because of your expertise. But I'm afraid I may need more than that."

He took a deep breath. "Talk to me."

"When I got home from Saint Tropez Monday night, I told Sabine I was filing for divorce."

Dominic let out a sound, overjoyed for him. "That's the best news I've ever heard."

"Except that you don't know the bottom line."

He frowned. "What do you mean?"

"I can't go into it now. Can you meet me at our usual place Thursday evening to talk?"

"Of course."

"Suffice it to say all hell has broken loose. The family has already heard about it, and it's getting ugly."

"I've got your back all the way. You know what I mean."

"I do. Before we hang up, tell me about you."

"I wish I knew."

"Why do I have a feeling this is about Mademoiselle Fournier?"

He paced. "I was with her this morning, at lunch and after work."

"All in one day? You've got to be kidding me!"

"I know I sound like I've lost my mind. She's not who I thought she was, but I still don't know why she came here."

"And I can tell you're not going to give up until you get answers. I take it she's a knockout."

"You have no idea. I didn't know I could have feelings this fast for another woman."

"That's how it happened with me. One evening while I was checking on the inventory at the Guinguet I met Toinette. As you know, my world changed that night when I called and told you about her. But circumstances forced me to break off with her in order to marry Sabine. I've never been the same since. Thank heaven you're back home and not in Paris because I need to reveal a truth you don't know about yet. I'll tell you on Thursday. For now, I've got to go."

Raoul rang off before a puzzled Dominic could say goodbye. No matter how bad it got, he was thrilled Raoul had decided to get out of his marriage. He'd do whatever he could to help his cousin.

As for his own situation, before any more time passed, Dominic needed to talk to Corinne. He didn't want to put this off any longer. It wasn't fair to her to let her go on expecting an imminent marriage proposal. She was attractive. Dominic knew she'd meet another man, hopefully one who would love her for who she was, whether she came from money or not. She deserved to find true happiness. So did he.

Once he told her the truth and ended any thoughts her parents had put in her mind about marrying him, her pride might be hurt, but it was the only way to handle what their two families had tried to set up.

He had his own life to live. And now that he'd met Nathalie Fournier, he couldn't imagine her not being in his life.

CHAPTER FOUR

"Maman?"

Wednesday evening had come. Dominic would be arriving shortly to show her around the vineyard. It was a beautiful evening and she was going crazy waiting for him so had called her mother to check in.

"Yes. What is it, darling?"

Nathalie had left work to eat dinner and was freshening up in the mobile home. She'd brushed her hair, leaving it loose, and wore a fresh pair of jeans and a yellow pullover. "I'll be home a little later than usual and don't want you to worry."

"That's all I've done since our talk. I don't think it's wise to keep this up. Either walk away now, or tell Dominic Fontesquieu why you're there."

"I will. I just need a little more information and to think everything through. If worse comes to worst and he demands an explanation, I'll tell him the truth. Depending on the outcome, I'll bring him to the house so he can see Alain for himself."

Her mother's sigh was telling. "You could be wrong and it could cause trouble."

"It won't come to that, Maman. When I get home, we'll talk."

After they hung up, her mother's concern ate away at her. Was Nathalie wrong about Dominic having been Antoinette's lover? Of course, the only way to find out was to ask him and hope he'd be honest with her.

But to approach him about such a sensitive matter was daunting. "Did you have a brief affair with a woman you met at the Guinguet during the harvest two and half years ago? If so, then I believe you could be the father of my deceased stepsister's son."

Deep in thought, she was startled by noise outside. He was here. A burst of adrenaline shot through her. She reached for her purse and hurried out the door. Dominic had parked his car behind hers and Nathalie climbed in the passenger side before he could get out.

"Hi," she said, knowing that once again she was out of breath. It happened every time she saw him. He smelled so good and had dressed in a blue sport shirt and khaki trousers. There could be no other man like him in existence.

His black eyes ranged over her, taking in every inch. "You look too beautiful for a woman who's been picking grapes all day."

"That isn't true, but I like hearing it."

"If you'd glance in a mirror, it would remove all doubt."

His words brought heat flooding to her cheeks. "Where are we going to go?"

"I thought we'd take a walk in one of the *terroirs* at

the upper elevation. It overlooks the land down to the sea for a spectacular view."

The male sight before her eyes was so spectacular, she was at a loss for words.

He backed around and drove down the road past the place where she picked grapes. When they came to a crossroads, he turned right and followed another road. It paralleled more rows of healthy vines for a long time, then rose until he pulled over to the side and parked.

"The grapes have all been picked here," she observed.

"That's right. They've turned a few days sooner because of the elevation. The *terroir* you're working on is one of the last that has to be denuded."

She shook her head. "There's so much to learn. Tonight the vines seem to be lined up like soldiers to the horizon. It's an amazing sight. If I were an artist, I'd like to paint the vineyard the way it looks right now. I love it."

"I love your descriptions of everything." The tone in his deep voice filled her with warmth. "This is my favorite spot in the whole vineyard."

After getting out of the car, she let out a soft cry. "I can see why, Dominic. This landscape is like a little part of heaven."

He grasped her hand as if claiming her. They started walking between two rows of vines. A gentle breeze bathed their bodies. "You know what Louis Pasteur once said. A bottle of wine contains more philosophy than all the books in the world."

"Fontesquieu wine," she corrected him. He squeezed

her hand a little harder. "I feel horribly guilty that I don't like the taste of wine."

"But you like the grapes." He gave her a meaningful look. "All is forgiven because you appreciate the vineyard housing the limestone and shale soil that feeds the roots."

A gentle laugh escaped. "Thank you for trying to make me feel better."

"You mean I didn't succeed?" he teased.

"You *know* you did." He had a captivating way about him.

They kept walking beneath a sky full of stars. As their bodies brushed against each other, she'd never known such rapture in her life. At the end of the row, he moved behind her and put his hands on her shoulders.

"Did you know your hair is the color of starlight?"

She could feel his breath on her temple. "Dominic—" His name came out sounding ragged.

A kiss against her neck opened the portals, releasing her longing for him. She turned in his arms and began to kiss his jaw, relishing the feel of his hard, male body. Their mouths slowly came together, seeking and finding what she'd wanted from the moment she'd sat across from him. This was ecstasy. Never in her life had she known this kind of passion.

When he finally relinquished her mouth with reluctance, he said, "Don't you know how dangerous it was to come out here with me tonight?"

His question penetrated deep inside to that spot reminding her they wouldn't be together like this if she weren't trying to find out if he'd been Antoinette's lover. For a little while tonight she'd forgotten.

Shocked by how carried away she'd been, she looked up at him. "Thank you for reminding me. Maybe we'd better go back." Nathalie eased out of his arms and started walking fast, reaching the car first.

He didn't try to catch up with her. While she was a trembling mass of need, Dominic seemed in perfect control driving them down to the mobile home park. He stopped behind her car and turned to her.

"I won't be able to see you tomorrow, but I'd like to see you after work Friday evening if you're free. We'll go to dinner."

Friday evening... That would have to be the night she asked him about Antoinette. "I'll make sure I am." She got out of the car. "I won't ever forget tonight's experience."

With her heart palpitating out of her chest, she rushed inside. The kiss they'd shared had turned her world upside down. To love a man like him, and have to tell him she couldn't have his baby...

After work on Thursday, Nathalie drove to the pizzeria in town and met Paul outside the entrance. They made their way inside and had to wait before being shown a table with menus propped on the red-and-white-checked cloth. She could tell it was a popular place, especially at dinnertime.

After studying the menu, Paul flicked Nathalie a glance. "How do you like your pizza?"

"A little bit of everything except for anchovies."

"Sounds good to me. Anything else?"

"Coffee."

A waitress came over for their order and hurried off.

Nathalie eyed Paul. "Wouldn't it be nice if the Fontesquieu family hired a food catering service that pulled into the vineyard every noon and evening? Think how happy it would make all the workers!"

He smiled. "That's a thought I'll pass on to Gregoire." But not to Dominic or Etienne, either of whom could make it happen.

"I saw clouds gathering this afternoon."

"It'll rain tomorrow."

"I can feel the extra humidity. It ought to make grape picking more interesting."

He grinned. "You mean messy, dirty and wet."

"I guess I'm going to find out."

"Want to go to a film after we eat?"

She shook her head. "I have to get back to the pharmacy where I work and do inventory. That's why I brought my car."

"You're a pharmacist?" Surprise was written all over him.

"By profession."

"But I thought you were on vacation." He looked stunned. "You have to go tonight?"

She nodded. "They need help so I promised to come in."

"Even when you've got a full day's work tomorrow?"

"I can't turn down a promise."

"You're one amazing woman."

Thankfully their food arrived at that moment.

"This pizza is good."

"It's all right," he muttered. "I'd rather we went out for a real dinner."

"Honestly, I'm too exhausted working seven days a week to do anything but fall asleep watching TV. Monsieur Fontesquieu warned me to take it easy so I don't burn out and collapse. Actually, he saw me walking and gave me a lift home the other day. It was very kind of him. If he has a wife who knows about it, I hope she'll understand he was only helping a lowly, exhausted grape picker make her way along the road."

Paul shook his head. "He's never been married."

The unexpected news filled her with joy for several reasons. "I see."

"Not yet, at least. According to Gregoire, who's on close terms with Etienne, Dominic Fontesquieu is on the verge of getting married to a woman with the kind of money most people only dream about."

After hearing he wasn't married, the revelation of impending marriage to a wealthy woman came as a shock. If that was true, how could he have kissed Nathalie like he did last night? Or made plans to be with her tomorrow evening?

Distressed, she wiped the corner of her mouth with a napkin. "Paul, I'm afraid I have to leave." Nathalie pulled some euros out of her purse and put them on the table before standing up. "Stay and finish the pizza."

"Don't forget to wear extra rain gear in the morning."

"I will. See you in the morning. *Merci* for the friendly chat."

Nathalie was tormented as she sped home. After the

kiss they'd shared, she didn't know what to think about Dominic. At least he didn't have a wife or children to consider if he were to learn he'd fathered Antoinette's baby. But if he were getting married soon, he shouldn't have been with Nathalie. Following that thought, the news that he had a son could turn his world upside down.

What was she doing? This couldn't go on any longer.

On Thursday, Dominic had been summoned to the salon of his parents' apartment at the chateau. He knew why.

His father, clearly recovered from his pneumonia, sat on one of the damask couches with his mother, whose stylish black hair showed a few streaks of silver. Dominic's older sister, Quinette, and her husband, Philippe, both serving on the board, had settled on the love seat. Etienne wasn't there because he hadn't shaken his flu completely.

He kissed his parents and sister and nodded to his brother-in-law, but he didn't sit down. "I came as soon as I could. It's obvious you've heard news before I could tell you myself."

"Corinne's mother called me this afternoon to tell me you won't be seeing her anymore."

"That's right, Maman. We've been thrown together at various family parties you arranged, but I never was *seeing* her."

"I simply don't believe it." Her voice shook. "She sounded hysterical. We've all been planning on your marriage."

"I can't help that. I'm not in love with Corinne, and

she doesn't want to be married to a man who can't give her the kind of love she needs."

She turned to his father. "Talk to him, Gaston."

"I tried talking to him when he left home at eighteen. My foolish son has cavorted with Parisian women with no class for too long. His judgment disgusts me."

His chilling pronouncement couldn't disturb Dominic. His father was lamenting all the money Corinne would have brought to the marriage. "I'm aware of that, Papa, but I have to please myself."

His mother's dark eyes filled with tears. "What's wrong with you, Dominic?"

"Maman," his sister remarked. Having been stuck in a bad marriage, she'd begun to see the light and had taken his side.

He smiled at Quinette before he said, "If I ever find the right woman, you'll be the first to know, *ma mere*. In the meantime, if you'll excuse me, I have plans. *Bonne nuit.*"

Now that his parents had let him know they were devastated, he left to meet Raoul at Chez Gaspard, a café on the outskirts of Vence where they could enjoy privacy.

They met there when they needed to talk away from the estate. Tonight there were two households in chaos at the chateau.

Raoul was already waiting for him when he entered and walked to the back table in the corner. The waiter brought coffee Raoul had already ordered for them. Once he'd left, Dominic handed Raoul the financial report.

"Thanks for this." He lifted his dark head and sat forward. "I promised you some new information. As you know, I'd been dating Sabine and made the mistake of sleeping with her once, a mistake I regretted because as time went on I knew my feelings for a permanent relationship with her weren't there. I had to tell her the truth even though it hurt her and I broke it off with her.

"Right after that I happened to meet Toinette Gilbert and found myself in love for the first time in my life. She'd become my heart's desire. We saw each other for a month and I wanted to marry her.

"But out of the blue I got a phone call from Sabine. She told me she was expecting our baby and we had to get married immediately. Her doctor verified it with me.

"I was horrified. Of course, I had to tell Toinette the truth, the most painful thing I'd ever had to do in my life. She said goodbye to me and refused all my phone calls. I never saw her after that. My world had crashed around me."

Dominic could attest to that fact. "You did the honorable thing, Raoul. When I heard you two were expecting, I knew that was the only reason you would have married her, especially after telling me you were in love with Toinette. But what is it I still don't know?"

"I'm getting to that. Only the birth of little Celine helped me to go on. I loved our daughter and was devastated after she died. While I was at the hospital, I talked to the doctor and asked if her heart was the reason why she'd been born a month early. The doctor told me no. Celine had been a full-term baby."

A gasp came out of Dominic. "So the baby wasn't yours."

Raoul stared straight at him. "No. If I hadn't asked the doctor that question, Sabine would have kept that a secret for the rest of our lives. After coming home from Saint Tropez the other night, I decided it was time to tell her I was divorcing her, and I confronted her about the baby that wasn't mine."

"How did that go?"

"She admitted it. Her explanation was that she'd always wanted me, but turned to another man because I'd never proposed."

"*Incroyable.* Did the other man ever know?"

"No," he said in a solemn voice.

"So you've been living with the pain of that lie ever since the funeral."

His cousin nodded. "Because you were in Paris, I didn't want to burden you. Instead I got some professional advice and was warned to put off a divorce until Sabine had recovered enough from Celine's death to deal with it."

A groan came out of Dominic. "How bad are things at this point?"

"Bad. I've been served papers from Sabine's attorney and have been talking with our attorney, Horace Millet."

"He's the best. What is she demanding?"

"Fifty million dollars in damages for lack of affection since she knew from the start I hadn't been in love with her. That was her excuse for being with another man while she waited for a proposal from me. She

claimed she'd wanted marriage to me all her adult life."
He sat back in the chair. "Well, she got it."

Dominic looked across at him. "You could counter-sue because of her lie."

"I could, but we've both been suffering over Ce-line's death. There's been too much grief as it is. I just want this period of my life over. Horace has drawn up papers declaring a legal separation. Since her attorney has indicated that Sabine is refusing to move out of the chateau until the divorce is final, I'm moving out. I've liquidated a few assets to keep functioning before Papa freezes my accounts. Both sets of parents are refusing to accept the divorce and are fighting it."

"Of course they are." And Raoul was too full of in-tegrity to expose Sabine's lie to the family.

"For now I'm planning to live at the Aurora Hotel in Vence until this is over. I'm checking in there after I leave you."

"No, you're not. You're staying with me. I have two extra bedrooms. Both families are trying to take ev-erything away from you. That means I'm not letting you spend money on a hotel. You need to be close to the office."

"I can't do that to you."

"Raoul, if I were in your shoes, I know you'd tell me to move in with you, so let's not waste any more time talking about it. Come on. Follow me back to the cha-teau and let's get you moved in. While we do that, I'll fill you in on what's happening with me. It'll be fun. I've got more space in the apartment than I know what to do with."

"Dom—"

"We share a special bond, right?"

"Oui," his voice grated.

Dominic put some Euros on the table and they left for the chateau. Under the circumstances, he couldn't be happier to have his best friend close.

Within the hour, they'd set Raoul up in one of the bedrooms. His cousin eyed him as they both went to the kitchen for more coffee. "The family will have a collective heart attack when they find out the two bad boys have joined forces, but I could not care less. Have you ended it with Corinne yet?"

"I took care of that last night. When you texted me a little while ago, I was on my way to the parents to be castigated."

"How did that go?"

"According to Maman, Corinne's mother is in hysterics. I know I hurt Corinne for expectations never met, but there were no outward histrionics."

His cousin's dark brow lifted. "Let's change the subject. What's going on with Mademoiselle Fournier?"

"I haven't fired her yet if that tells you anything." Dominic was still shaken by the taste and feel of Nathalie, who'd welcomed his kiss last night with the same urgency he'd been feeling from the beginning.

"Do you still suspect her of something?"

"I don't know," he ground out. "Maybe I'm wrong and she's exactly who she says she is. After hearing about Sabine's lie of omission, I pray to God Nathalie has told me her whole truth by now."

His cousin eyed him with concern. "You sound like a man in love."

Dominic's head reared. "It may have finally happened, Raoul." But he would be in pain until he knew all of her and her heart.

"Does she feel the same way?"

"She hasn't said the words yet, but I know it in my gut." The way she'd kissed him had been proof of that.

Rain fell on Friday. Nathalie's work was wet and messy. She needed to shower and wash her hair after finishing work, as Dominic would be coming by to take her out for the evening.

Learning that he planned to be married soon had shaken her. If he were Alain's father and wanted a relationship with his boy, then how would Nathalie handle it? She was Alain's aunt and they would be sharing him. How was she going to shut off her feelings?

This evening she put on a pale blue short-sleeved blouse and a white skirt with a small blue print. She hadn't worn anything dressy around him. Her hair had natural curl. She brushed it until it swished against her shoulders from a side part, then she put on her leather sandals. Nathalie wore no makeup other than lipstick.

When he knocked on the door, she opened it and sucked in her breath. He stood there wearing a silky black shirt and gray trousers. No man had ever looked so devastatingly gorgeous to her. "Dominic—"

Tonight was her chance to ask him questions about Antoinette. She'd started down this path for Alain's sake and needed to see it through. "Thanks for being on time. I'm hungry again."

He chuckled and backed around. "And here I thought I'd have to wait. You're a constant surprise."

"So are you."

Dominic darted her an amused glance with those gleaming black eyes before they got in the car and headed for Vence. He drove through the town and up into the hills. They wound around to a restaurant with date palms and cypress trees overlooking the breathtaking landscape.

He escorted her inside and they were shown to a table out on the veranda with a sweeping view. The waiter handed them menus.

"Everything's good here."

Nathalie looked over the options. "What's your favorite?"

"Suprême de veau rôti, crème provençale."

"That sounds delicious." She loved veal. "I'll try it."

The waiter came back with coffee and a wine list.

Dominic's gaze held hers as he told the waiter, "We'll pass on the wine." After giving him their order, the waiter walked off.

"I would imagine wine from the Fontesquieu vineyards makes up a good portion of every restaurant's list in Provence and elsewhere."

"My cousin Raoul could tell you all about it. He's in charge of marketing and sales."

"That has to be an enormous responsibility."

"But nothing like the responsibility you have as a

pharmacist. When you make a mistake, it could be life threatening."

She nodded. "That's true."

"What made you choose that for your career?"

Now would be the perfect time to tell him about the family Alain had been born into.

"My parents were both pharmacists. That's how they met and got married. I was born soon after their marriage, then my *papa* died. I never knew him, only my stepfather, also a druggist who was a widower with a daughter. He married my mother. I grew up wanting to be a pharmacist too. After I graduated, they took me on at the pharmacy they owned."

"Sounds like my family."

"In a way." Their eyes held. "My stepfather ran everything until he died several years ago."

"I'm sorry."

"So am I," she whispered. "Since then my mother has hired another pharmacist to help us."

"Do you live with your mother?"

"Yes." And one precious boy.

Their dinner came, interrupting their conversation. She started eating. "This veal is superb. I'm glad you suggested it."

"It never disappoints. Tell me, are you an only child?"

Her heart thudded. Stick to the truth as much as you dare. "No. I just had my stepsister, but she died sixteen months ago of an infection."

"Your family has known a lot of grief," he commiserated. "My parents lost a daughter right after she was born."

"They must have suffered."

"So have you after breaking up with the man you thought to marry."

She sipped her coffee. Since meeting Dominic, she hadn't given Guy a thought. "That has turned out to be a good thing. I can't imagine anything worse than getting married, only to discover you made a mistake. To settle when you already have questions about that person makes no sense to me."

"I couldn't agree more," he said with almost savage conviction. It sent a shiver down her spine.

Taking her courage in her hands, Nathalie said, "Rumor has it you will be getting married soon." She had to find out.

"Paul needs to be careful what he passes on, though it's not his fault what he hears. Marriage was never on my agenda. Otherwise I wouldn't have asked you to come to dinner with me this evening."

Heaven forgive her, but that news meant more to her than he would ever know. If she dared tell him about Alain, and he agreed to take a DNA test to prove paternity, he could be with his son without the complications of a new wife. But only if that was what Dominic wanted more than anything in his life. Alain deserved a father who would cherish him.

Knowing he wasn't getting married prompted her next question. "Why *did* you invite me out this evening, Dominic?"

His eyes narrowed on her mouth, making her whole body go limp. "You can ask me that after our walk in the vineyard?" She averted her eyes. "Because I wanted to." Somehow she felt he'd spoken the truth just now. "Why did you accept, Nathalie?"

Her heart thundered in her chest. "If I tell you the real reason, will you believe me?" They were both circling each other.

"I deserved that."

She was able to tell him one honest truth, though she was riddled with guilt. "Because *I* wanted to be with you too."

Dominic's chest rose and fell visibly, communicating an emotion that appeared to match hers. There was a growing sensual tension between them that couldn't be denied, haunting her more and more.

The waiter came over to suggest dessert. She declined. So did Dominic, who asked for the check. When it was paid, they left and went out to his car.

Nathalie looked up at the sky. "It's still overcast, but I don't think it will rain again tomorrow."

"It won't," he assured her and helped her into the car before walking around.

Once he was behind the wheel, she sent him a covert glance. "If you ever decide to give up being a vintner, you'll make a better weatherman than any meteorologist."

"I wouldn't want the job. They make too many mistakes. Technically I'm no longer a vintner. Not since I left for Paris eleven years ago and went into investment banking."

Eleven years? She blinked. When had there been time for him to meet Antoinette? Had she been wrong about him this whole time? "So you weren't born with grape juice running in your veins?" she teased.

He chuckled. "Maybe, but I was much more interested in what made the world go round. Big business intrigued me."

Nathalie knew there was much more he hadn't told her, but this was a beginning. Before the night was out she might even learn enough to broach the subject of Alain.

CHAPTER FIVE

TWILIGHT HAD FALLEN over the town, giving it a magical look. Nathalie felt like they were the only two people who existed. Instead of driving her straight back to the mobile home, Dominic took her on a long drive around the other side of the vineyard, letting her see the vast property.

"The air smells so sweet, I feel like I'm in a dream. There's a peace here in the vineyard impossible to describe, yet it's alive. Glorious! I read an article on the Fontesquieu website that said there is something special about the manner in which vines in France attach themselves to the landscape. The author suggested that France is where the vines are *supposed* to be."

Dominic nodded. "My family believes as much."

"So do I."

He glanced at her. "When I took you to the winery, I wondered if you'd seen the plaque on the wall right by us."

"I did. It said, 'God planted the best vines on earth here in Provence.' I loved it." She drew in a deep breath. "Seeing all this with you, I believe it."

If the man sitting next to her had been Antoinette's heart's desire, it was understandable that she'd succumbed to him. But more and more Nathalie was beginning to feel that he wasn't Alain's father, and she didn't want this evening to end.

Maybe he was reading her thoughts because he said, "Do you mind if we make a detour to Saint Jeannet before I take you back home? My brother asked me to check on a special shipment of red wine my grandfather has been waiting for, and until Etienne gets better I'm trying to help him. It'll only be ten minutes out of our way."

The question filled her with exhilaration. This would give her more time to be with him. "Tell me about the shipment of red wine, Dominic. I thought you only produced rosé wine."

"We produce everything."

"Even sour wine."

He smiled. "That too."

"Will you tell me what you know about the emperor Charlemagne? I hear there's a story to do with him and red wine."

Dominic chuckled. "One of those stories is purported to have to do with his fourth or fifth wife. She was a beautiful German princess with many gifts and he adored her. When she died, he never remarried. But getting to the point, being a tall proud man with a prominent white beard, he wanted to look his best for her when they were married. Yet there was one problem."

Everything the brilliant man sitting next to her said or did enamored her. "What was that?"

"According to history, he was a big meat eater and red wine drinker. But she didn't like the red stains on his beard."

Nathalie studied the red stains on her own fingers and could well understand.

"Word has it that she demanded he drink only white wine. From then on only white grapes were commanded to be planted on a certain section of the hill. That's when Corton-Charlemagne in Burgundy was born and still continues."

"I had no idea. How fascinating."

"Except that it's partly myth. Other sources say it was Charlemagne's mother who didn't like her royal son looking terrible with those dreadful red stains."

She laughed. "That sounds more realistic."

"Are you ready for this? Some sources say he didn't have a beard. According to scholars, it was customary in the Middle Ages for artists to put facial hair on the rulers, symbolic of their virility."

"Oh, dear—don't tell me that and ruin this picture I have of Charlemagne with his *barbe fleurie*."

It was Dominic's turn to laugh that deep laugh she loved. "Too much authentic research destroys most of our beliefs."

"You're right. It's much more fun to enjoy our own version of life. Since I'm with an expert and we're talking about red wine, please explain about red grapes having many secrets. I cherish the memory of you taking me on a tour of the winery."

His hand reached over to clasp hers, sending waves of longing through her body. Both their emotions were spilling over. "To keep it simple, all grape juice is white. Only the red skins contain a dark pigment. If the juice is separated from the skins shortly after being crushed, it remains white."

"I see."

"If the juice is left in contact with the red skins during fermentation, it becomes that delightful pink color. Left longer, it becomes red wine."

"I'm embarrassed to know so little about it."

He turned to her. "That's because you're not a wine drinker. Those who are show surprise to learn that eighty-eight percent of the wine produced in Provence is rosé. It has a delicious fruity flavor. Some people refer to it as summer water."

Another chuckle came out of her.

"Other drinkers prefer white wine, which is sweeter. Red wine is heavier. But as I explained, our winery produces everything."

During their conversation, she hadn't realized they'd reached the town of Saint Jeannet. He pulled up to a big warehouse before letting her go. He flicked his gaze to her. "I'll only be a minute."

The whole time they'd been talking, she realized she hadn't asked him any personal questions. But after hearing he'd been away from Vence for so many years, she was beginning to think he couldn't have been Antoinette's lover.

It was a lovely night to be out, and being with him was so stimulating to her, there weren't enough hours with him to satisfy everything she was desperate to know. Her whole body tingled from his touch.

He'd returned to the car while she'd been deep in thought. "Let's go."

"Was the shipment there?"

"Not yet. I need to inform Etienne." He pulled out his phone to text him, then started the car and they left for Vence.

"Will your grandfather be upset?"

"I'm afraid he was born in that condition, but he'll live to see another day."

"What's your grandmother like?"

"She's afraid of him and allows him to rule her life."

"Are you afraid of him?"

"Let's put it this way. I learned not to like him or my father." She winced from so much honest emotion. "They have a hard streak that dominates their existence. As soon as I turned eighteen, I left to go to school in Paris."

"Didn't they try to prevent you from leaving?"

"Yes. They told me that if I deserted the family, there'd be no money, no inheritance. That suited me fine. From my bank account I withdrew the pitiful amount of money I'd earned and bought a third-class train ticket for Paris. I slept all the way. When I arrived, I found a job at a warehouse the next day and bunked with some of the workers until I could pay for a semester of college."

"You're amazing!"

"No—only desperate to get on with the life I wanted to lead. At that point, I took out a school loan and got another job as an eighteen-wheeler truck driver. It paid more and I could sleep behind the cab while I had to make deliveries between classes and on weekends."

"Where did you drive?"

"All over Paris and the outskirts. In the process, I made lots of contacts. After a month, I found a rooming house so I could bathe and eat breakfast daily. That's how I lived while I pursued an education in money management. After college I worked for an investment firm."

Dominic was getting to her in ways she didn't think possible. Nathalie knew he had to be a remarkable man, but hearing some of his history told her she would never meet a more extraordinary human being.

"Did your family know where you were?"

"My cousin Raoul knew. That was all that mattered to me. Do you know the sad part of this is that I wanted to have a close relationship with family, but it never happened. My father is made in my grandfather's image, which explains why we don't get along. Both men are driven and cold."

"What about your mother?"

"She's not as cold, but is in lockstep with him over aspirations for their children. You have to do it their way. There is no other."

Her heart pained for him. "I'm so sorry, Dominic."

"It's life, but I don't want to talk about them. I'd much rather focus on you."

He drove swiftly to the vineyard and pulled up behind her car outside her rental. After shutting off the engine, he turned to her. "We'll only need pickers for another ten days at the most. Since the *vendange* is so short a season, I'd like to spend as much time with you in the evenings as possible before you go back to work at the pharmacy. How would you feel about that?"

The question sounded like heaven. Nathalie's mind was spinning with possibilities now that she thought he might not be Alain's father after all. "Maybe one evening I'll provide groceries and cook. Another night you could do the same." During one of their conversations she would ask him straight out if he'd known an Antoinette. After that, anything could happen.

"I'll bring the food for tomorrow's meal."

"Um. That sounds perfect."

She undid her seat belt. "Thank you for a lovely dinner and drive. Learning about red grapes has made me feel more legitimate as a grape picker. Good night."

To her surprise, he got out and walked her to the door. "I wish you didn't have to go in." The next thing she knew he'd cupped her face in his hands and lowered his dark head to kiss her. She'd been wanting this all evening.

The feel of his mouth on hers sent rivers of warmth through her body, but his kiss didn't last long enough. She moaned when he stepped away far too soon for her liking.

"*A demain*, Nathalie." His voice sounded husky.

After letting her go, he walked to his car and drove off. She waited until he'd disappeared before getting in her car to drive home. Her legs had turned to mush. Tomorrow evening couldn't come soon enough.

On Saturday Dominic drove into town for groceries, then went to his office to do work until it was time to drive to Nathalie's. The sun had shone all day and warmed everything. On the drive over, he talked to Raoul.

"Just giving you a heads-up that I'm spending the evening with Nathalie."

"If you want to bring her here, I'll go to the hotel."

"Thanks, but it's not necessary. To be honest, I wouldn't take her to the chateau. Too many eyes. For the rest of the harvest we're having dinner at her place and taking turns cooking meals."

"Cooking."

"That and other things." Dominic chuckled. "You'll have my kitchen to yourself. Nathalie's no longer in a relationship with the man she thought she would marry. Within another week, I'm going to know a lot more about her."

"Do you still feel she's not being completely honest?"

"Unfortunately, yes. But I have to believe it's something I'll be able to handle."

Raoul sobered. "I hope so for your sake."

So did Dominic, who could see her coming up the path. "Talk to you later." He hung up and got out of the car. Whether she wore her silvery-gold hair tied back or loose, she was a vision.

"Imagine meeting you here," Nathalie teased with a smile.

"I've been imagining it since I left you last night."

She blushed and opened the door to her rental. He followed her inside with the groceries. "I'll be out in a minute," she said before disappearing into the back.

"Take your time while I put things away and get our

meal started." He'd bought items for his own version of *salade niçoise* with fresh fish and rolls.

By the time she'd emerged in a sleeveless pink blouse and khaki pants looking enticing, he'd prepared café au lait and handed her a cup from the kitchen counter.

"Um…" She took a sip. "Fabulous. You're going to make someone a wonderful wife one day." She always said something unexpected that amused him.

"Our dinner is waiting."

"I know. I can smell the tuna aroma from here." She walked over to the table in the little dining area and sat down on one of the chairs. "This salad is a work of art. You're spoiling me rotten!"

He wanted to do more than that.

They both ate with relish. Being with her made him feel like a light had been turned on, illuminating a world he was seeing only for the first time. "I detect red stains on your fingers."

"Me and Charlemagne," she teased. "They're unsightly, but I don't like wearing gloves. I can't do as effective a job with them on."

"You and a lot of workers."

A laugh escaped her lips.

"Wouldn't you know one of the sons in the Spanish family working by me told me there's a place called the Guinguet that has a live band on Sunday night. Everyone goes there. I pretended I didn't know."

He smiled into her eyes. "I went there a few times in the past myself." *Was that true?* Had he met Antoinette there? When? "I presume this Casanova intends to take you."

"He knows I'm not interested."

Dominic finished his roll. "That's two down in a week. How come I'm still standing?" The desire to make love to her was going to consume him before long.

A glint entered her gorgeous eyes. "Because *you* didn't ask me to go to a place where they serve sour wine." With that clever remark, she started to clear the table. "While I clean up, you're welcome to watch TV."

"I'd rather help you." He was determined to find out what she was hiding and handed her more dishes as she loaded the dishwasher.

She darted him a glance. "Do you mind if I ask you a personal question?"

"Not at all."

"Paul said you were filling in for your brother, Etienne, because he'd been sick. What is *your* official position in your family's business?"

Why did she want to know that? He felt he was getting closer to her secret. "As I told you earlier, I went to Paris and studied investment banking. After graduation I worked for a firm there before I came home four months ago because my father was ill. As it turns out, I've been deciding on the investments the company makes. In other words, I took over my father's job as funds manager."

"I see. Another huge responsibility that takes brilliance," she murmured. "You have to be an accountant whiz too."

"That's part of it. You wouldn't be looking for a career change, would you? Are you after an administrative job and need an in?"

She flushed. "No. I enjoy my work. But I do a lot of thinking while I'm out picking grapes. So much goes into running a family business like yours. It's overwhelming to me. You have to know everything about soil, grapes, weather conditions, and that's just for starters. There's hiring and payroll. I think about the equipment you need.

"Someone has to have the incredible expertise to make wine. Another person has to know how to distribute and advertise. A man like you has to make life-and-death decisions about money. When and where to invest. It all blows my mind."

Dominic stared into her eyes. "Where has all this come from?"

"I didn't realize until my stepfather died how much went into his buying the pharmacy and making it thrive. He had to learn so much to go into business after having worked for someone else. There were nights when he was up until late working on everything. I never understood what he went through." Her eyes glistened with unshed tears. "Now my mother has the load."

"One you share."

"I'm trying. Working on the vineyard has opened my eyes to so many things. We've only had to consider hiring one pharmacist to help out. But we have to provide insurance and make sure we can afford to pay another wage."

"It's a fine line at times."

"It certainly is. Your family has to hire hundreds of workers at harvest time, not to mention your regular employees. Every application has to be vetted. You carry a huge burden in order to pay your employees and deal with all the ups and downs. I can't tell you how much I admire a family like yours that has kept their business solvent for hundreds of years. You have an unmatchable work ethic."

While she'd been talking with such heartfelt emotion, he heard her cell phone ring. "Excuse me a minute, Dominic." She pulled it out of her pocket and checked the caller ID. "It's my mother. She probably wants to know how soon I'll be home tonight."

"You're leaving?"

"I always go home at night." That piece of information came as a surprise. "I'll call her back."

If that was true and she never stayed here alone at night, the news pleased him. "In that case I'm going to leave now so I don't prevent you from driving home too late."

She looked up at him. "You'll come tomorrow evening?" she asked in a throbbing voice. Those light green eyes beseeched him. "I'll make the dinner."

His breath caught. "Try to keep me away. *Bonne nuit*, Nathalie." This time he gave her a long, hard kiss, then bolted for the door, not daring to stay any longer.

The more she'd talked to him tonight, the more he'd been ensnared. No other woman he'd known had shown her kind of sensitivity and understanding of his family's unique work. The well-heeled type of women in his family's world weren't interested in much more than his overall financial worth.

But his fear that it could be a front was ripping him apart. Was it possible she'd seen Dominic somewhere and planned to work at the vineyard to get close to him? The thought pained him when he wanted to pull her down on the couch and start kissing the daylights out of her. Hell and hell.

CHAPTER SIX

SUNDAY MORNING, NATHALIE left home earlier than usual to buy groceries. She drove to Vence and put everything in the fridge before reporting to the vineyard.

Dominic must have wondered what was wrong with her to go on about his family. She hadn't been able to help it. If Alain truly was his son, then he belonged to a remarkable man with an amazing history.

Her mother wanted her to give up on this. It was wrong to date Dominic when she was holding back this huge secret that could backfire. Nathalie knew her mother was right, but since he'd admitted he'd been to the Guinguet in the past, that placed him where Antoinette could have met him.

Here she'd been thinking Dominic hadn't been the one involved with her stepsister, but this new information threw her. The one thing she had to do now was find out *when* he'd been to the bistro. Had he gone there after returning from Paris during one of his visits home? Once she knew if the timing fit, then she'd break her silence.

As soon as four thirty rolled around, she left the vineyard under a semicloudy sky and hurried to her temporary home. She wanted to get there first and make herself presentable.

Relieved that she didn't see his car outside, she rushed in and took a quick shower. After she'd put on a green skirt with a lighter green blouse, she brushed her hair and caught it back with a light green scarf.

He still hadn't come when she started the chicken crepes and prepared a strawberry and cream dessert. By five thirty she started to worry. The thought of him not coming caused her more misery than she should be feeling for this man.

While she was making coffee, she heard a knock on the door. She hadn't heard him drive up. With her adrenaline gushing, she rushed to open it. "Dominic?" she cried.

"I'm afraid not."

Oh!

She'd just come face-to-face with a man who bore such a strong family resemblance to Dominic in looks and coloring it was unbelievable. She reeled and clung to the door.

"Mademoiselle Fournier?"

"Yes?"

"I'm Etienne Fontesquieu."

She'd already guessed as much and was stunned. He had Alain's eyes too!

"My brother asked me to stop by in person since he couldn't reach you on the phone."

That's right. She'd turned it off so it wouldn't wake Alain this morning. Her body was shaking. "Please, come in."

"I'd better not. I'm getting over a cold." She could hear it. "Dominic wants you to know he's been unaccountably detained and is aware you've gone to a lot of trouble to make dinner." She'd been living for tonight. "He asks your forgiveness and will get in touch with you."

Dominic...

"That's very considerate of you, especially since you're not well."

"I sound worse than I am."

"Please let your brother know I understand. Thank you."

"Thank *you* for doing such a good job for us. Gregoire tells me you've caught on fast. I'm impressed. Have a good evening."

He turned and walked back to his silver Mercedes. From a distance, his tall, lean silhouette reminded her of Dominic. She let out a troubled sound. Good heavens—had she gotten it wrong and *Etienne* had been Antoinette's lover?

Nathalie shut the door and sank down on the couch in shock. If she'd met Etienne first, she would have thought *he* could be Alain's father. At this point she was convinced she'd lost her mind.

After this experience she'd lost her appetite too.

What if Dominic's distrust of her had prompted him to send his brother here to check on her and find out what she was up to? Maybe Etienne didn't trust her either. Once she'd gathered her wits, she put the food in the fridge.

After driving back to La Gaude, she flew into the house. "Maman?"

When there was no answer, she tiptoed to Alain's room. Her mother was looking down at him in the crib. When she saw Nathalie, she put a finger to her lips. Nathalie went back to the living room to wait.

In a minute her mother walked in. "What's wrong? You sounded upset when you called out."

"I am. I met Dominic's brother, Etienne, today." Nathalie launched into the reason why he'd stopped in to see her. "They share an amazing family resemblance. Alain could be Etienne's son."

A small cry came from her mother. "That does it, Nathalie. You've got to give this up. I think you should quit your job at the vineyard before you do something that will cause irreversible damage. You're tampering with other people's lives. It's something that is out of your hands. Don't you see what is happening?"

"Yes." Meeting Etienne had thrown her completely. Worse, she'd fallen for his brother, a man who was still a mystery to her and could have been Nathalie's lover. "But as I told you last night, I learned Dominic had been to the Guinguet several times in the past. I need to find out when. Tomorrow night I'll ask him if he ever met a girl at the bistro named Antoinette."

"He'll demand to know why you want that information."

"At that point I'll tell him that she was my stepsister and died before she told me the name of the man she loved. She'd kept it a secret, and I wanted to know why. Then I'll add that I decided to follow a few clues that led me to the Fontesquieu vineyard."

Her mother's worried expression didn't change.

"Maman, if Dominic continues to deny all knowledge, I'll believe him and ask him if his brother might have known Antoinette. I promise I won't say anything about the baby."

"Nathalie? He's too intelligent not to figure that out."

She folded her arms to her waist. "For Alain's sake I have to find the truth if I can. Do you really wish I would give this up?"

"Yes, but I know you won't and suspect you're more than attracted to Dominic. Am I right?"

She lowered her head. "I'd give anything if I weren't."

"It's going to get worse the longer you keep seeing him."

"I know. But it's a risk I'm still willing to take for Alain's sake. Thanks for supporting me. I love you."

She kissed her mother and went to her bedroom. After putting in a wash, she packed some more clothes and finally went to bed exhausted. The next morning, she left for Vence after having packed her lunch. She also turned on her phone.

Dominic filled her mind to the exclusion of all else. The knowledge that he'd be coming over tonight made it difficult to breathe. Nathalie stopped there first to get her backpack. The walk to the vineyard didn't take long.

She'd just reached the next row to start cutting grapes when her cell phone rang. Her heart leaped when she saw Dominic's name on the caller ID.

She put down the scissors. "*Bonjour*, monsieur."

"*Bonjour*, mademoiselle."

His distinctive voice melted her insides.

"Would you please let Nathalie Fournier know I'll be arriving tonight with our dinner? I owe her one after not showing up last evening." He hung up before she could respond.

His call brightened the already beautiful day. She hardly noticed the work she had to do. When she left the vineyard at four thirty, she came close to a run in her excitement to see Dominic again. She'd brought a summery dress in a small floral print on white to wear this evening. Even if he didn't believe her reasons for coming to the vineyard and all this was about to come to an end, she wanted to look her best.

Nathalie had been listening for his distinctive knock that came as she was brushing out her hair. She hurried to open the door. Tonight he wore a silky claret-colored shirt and tan chinos. He carried a grocery bag.

"Well, if it isn't the mysterious monsieur!"

His black eyes were alive. "I hope mademoiselle is ready for coq au vin straight from the chateau kitchen."

"Hmm. After Guinguet Fontesquieu, do I dare try it?"

His deep laugh rang out to delight her. "I don't know. I'll eat first. If I don't expire, you'll know it's safe. But I need to be invited in."

"You don't need an invitation."

"I'll remember that." He walked through to the kitchen while she shut the door and followed him. His gaze traveled over her. "You look lovely tonight."

You look incredible. "Thank you. I've set the table and the coffee is ready. We can eat whenever you want."

"You know me. I'm hungry now. Let's dig in while

it's hot." He pulled the ingredients from the bag and they sat down to enjoy what turned out to be a fabulous meal. "How went another day in the life of our latest *coupeuse*?"

She laughed. "Backbreaking, as if you didn't know. I'd much rather talk about your day." Hopefully she could ply him with enough questions to learn the truth.

Once again Dominic had to ask himself why Nathalie seemed so interested in *his* day. "In truth I've been counting the hours to be with you. I'm sorry about yesterday."

"It doesn't matter."

"Of course it does. That's why I asked Etienne to come in my place and make my apologies in person. He texted me around six and told me all was well, adding, 'She took my breath. How did you manage that, Dom?'"

Heat crept into those beautiful cheeks. "I realized something important had held you up."

"Yesterday I had a phone call from my cousin Raoul. After living in a tumultuous marriage, he's decided it has to end and has asked his wife for a divorce, *grâce à Dieu*. He should never have married her."

"How sad."

"I had to help him with some important business. You have no idea of the turmoil he's been through."

She breathed deeply. "More and more I'm relieved I ended it with Guy. Your cousin's situation reminds me of what I avoided by not marrying him."

Dominic wanted to believe her. He put down his coffee cup. "Raoul is my best friend and always has been. Over the last couple of years I've seen him so unhappy. His wife is making demands. I'm trying to help him. We didn't get back from Nice until ten."

"He's lucky to have you."

"One of these days his nightmare will be over. In the meantime he's rooming with me in my apartment at the chateau."

"Where does your cousin usually live?"

"In the other wing of the chateau."

She blinked. "I know it's massive, but you *all* live there together?"

His brows lifted. "A horrifying thought, isn't it?"

"Only if you want to be private."

Dominic smiled at her. "That's why I lived in Paris for as long as I did."

"But you came home once in a while."

"Yes, for visits and vacations. If I decide to stay in Vence, then the day is coming when I'll buy my own home. Raoul is planning to do the same thing. It's just as well they're separated until they go to court and a settlement is made."

"I feel terrible for him. Did they love each other before they got married?"

"He'd been seeing her, but hadn't proposed marriage though both their families wanted it desperately. One night he met a girl and overnight fell deeply in love with her, wanting marriage. But then came the news that Sabine was pregnant.

"Raoul had only slept with her once and regretted it before breaking it off with her. But hearing the news about Sabine's pregnancy, he had to end his relationship with the woman he loved. At that point he did the noble thing and married Sabine. Sadly their baby died a month after she was born. He buried his heart with his little girl. Since the funeral there's been an emptiness in him that worries me."

"I can't imagine so much pain."

Their eyes held.

"You're not a Fontesquieu," Dominique murmured. He noticed her shudder.

"Would you believe Etienne was pressured into his marriage at around the same time? He should have married a girl he was crazy about, but the family didn't consider her good enough to marry and wouldn't hear of it."

She shook her head. "Does that mean he's also on the verge of divorce?"

"It could happen, but they have a little girl, Sophie, to think of."

She pushed herself away from the table to retrieve dessert from the counter.

"I shouldn't have unburdened myself to you. You're far too easy to talk to."

"Please don't say that. Your worries help me forget my own." She brought the two *tartes aux pommes* to the table and sat down. "I'm curious about something. Since you all live at the chateau, are your offices there too?"

Was it natural curiosity on her part? Even if she had a hidden reason for asking the question, it made him chuckle. "No. Maybe you haven't seen the big modern office building behind the chateau. We each have our own suites."

Her eyes smiled. "But you never really get away from each other. Togetherness has to be the reason your family's business has risen to such heights."

Something was going on in her beautiful head. Nathalie had a charm about her that was tying him in knots. He needed to put distance between them this evening. Whether he discovered her reason for coming to the vineyard or not, he couldn't be around her much longer before he took her in his arms and made endless love to her.

"I've enjoyed tonight more than you know, but I have some business to take care of and need to get going. Let me clear the table first."

"No, no, Dominic. You brought this wonderful food and I've loved it. I'll take care of everything else. Tomorrow evening I'll provide the dinner."

"I'd like that, but I have an even better idea. As your employer, I'm giving you the day off tomorrow to spend it with me. How would you like to cook in the galley on my cruiser? It's docked in Nice. We'll leave in the morning and enjoy a full day and evening on the water together. It's a beautiful sight watching the sun go down over the Mediterranean while we swim and eat." Tomorrow he'd break her down.

His suggestion lit up her whole expression. "That would be incredible."

"Then we'll do it. Don't bother to get groceries. We'll buy them in Nice."

She walked him to the door. "I won't be able to

sleep." He'd had close to none since he'd met her. Dominic was besotted by her. "Thank you for everything."

"Pick you up here at eight in the morning. Bring your swimming suit."

"I'll be ready."

He gave her a swift kiss before striding to his car. It took all the self-control he possessed not to crush her against him. Tomorrow everything was going to change.

Nathalie had trouble getting to sleep that night. Dominic's story about what had happened to his cousin had sounded so much like what had happened to Antoinette, it had shaken her. Maybe she was losing it and tried to put it out of her mind.

The next morning her heart pounded out of rhythm when Dominic arrived at eight. He'd dressed in a blue pullover and white cargo pants. It should be a sin for a man to be so devastatingly handsome and marvelous. For today she didn't want to think about anything but being with him, and wished she could thrust her guilt aside. Of course, that wasn't possible.

She'd showered and changed into white shorts and a short-sleeved lavender top. After catching her hair back with a clip, she was ready and walked out the door with her overnight bag. He helped her into the car and they reached Nice in a half hour under a sunny sky. What perfect weather!

She turned to him. "Shall we have steaks tonight?" He'd stopped at a grocery store and they hurried inside to find what they wanted. "The rest we can get in the deli."

He nodded and reached for several baguettes to go with their meals. Before long they left for the pier where he kept his white thirty-foot cruiser with a black stripe. Everything was state of the art. This was a world most people could only dream of. Yet she couldn't forget he'd left it for a decade or longer to pursue the life he'd wanted. As far as she was concerned, he was a Renaissance man.

They both carried a bag along the dock. He got in the cruiser first with the groceries, then helped her in, but didn't let her go. "I've been waiting to do this all the way here. I need to kiss you. Really kiss you."

"Dominic—" Unable to help herself, she threw her arms around his neck hungrily and met that male mouth she'd been longing to taste again. Swept away by rapture, she lost track of time and never wanted to let him go.

Someone let out a loud whistle from another boat that reminded her they weren't alone. She eased herself away from Dominic, whose black eyes were glazed with desire. "I'm taking you to a place where we can be strictly alone." He handed her a life preserver and helped her put it on. "Let's go below and put away the groceries. After I show you around, we'll get going."

He pointed out the bedroom and bathroom on the lower deck. They wanted for nothing. Nathalie hadn't known joy like this in her whole life. To think she'd ever thought of marrying Guy. Being with Dominic had transported her to another dimension of living.

Yet the chateau, the cruiser, all the trappings of a privileged life had nothing to do with how she felt when she was with him. He'd brought her alive. They could be stranded on a desert island with nothing but each other and she would have felt she'd found paradise. That was when she knew for certain she was in love with him.

They went back up on deck, where he undid the ropes and they cast off. "I'd like to take you to a place I love to go when I have time. Have you ever been to Les Calanques de Cassis?"

She shook her head. "Even though I've lived on the French Riviera all my life and went to the university in Nice, I've only heard of them. My friends didn't have boats." The Fontesquieu family lived a different life than 99 percent of the world.

"Then you're in for a fabulous treat. They're magical coastal inlets," he spoke with excitement. "Great cliffs of limestone that form mini fjords with sandy beaches. We'll find one for ourselves."

"I can't wait."

"We'll head there now."

When they'd reached the buoy, he opened the throttle and they sped toward the open sea. She'd had some good times in her life, but nothing like the experience she was having now with a man who was perfect to her.

She walked over to the side to take in the incredible sights along the coast. Soon they were passing Antibes. She wheeled around. "I've been there to see the Picasso museum, but I never saw the town from the water. It's all so breathtaking."

"To be honest, I prefer the sight standing a few feet away from me on those fabulous legs. You're rather breathtaking yourself."

She laughed in delight. "Keep it up, Dominic. Every woman loves to hear flattery like that."

"You're not every woman and it's not flattery."

Nathalie turned away and clung to the side of the boat. No. She was one of the small percent who couldn't have children. The pain of that knowledge had run marrow deep since meeting him.

Before long they passed Cannes with its profusion of glittering yachts and a Mediterranean beach that drew film stars and sheiks from all over.

"I miss you, Nathalie. Come and sit by me."

In an instant she moved to sit across from him and studied his chiseled male features through her sunglasses. There was never a more beautiful man born. "This is heaven for me."

He looked back at her through his own sunglasses. "I'm trying not to think about my life without you in it. The day you applied for work, my world changed."

"So did mine," she answered honestly. "I've been so happy." It frightened her that in coming to the vineyard, she'd met the man who'd changed her life for all time.

Today she selfishly wanted to put every thought out of her head except to enjoy every single second of this precious time with him. Depending on where the conversation led this evening, it might never come again.

"Do you miss the pharmacy?"

What pharmacy? Her mind was so far away from any thoughts except for him, she was a total mass of unassuaged longings only he could satisfy. She smiled. "What do *you* think?"

He grasped her hand, threading his fingers through hers. "I think I'd like to sail away with you and never come back."

Don't say things like that, Dominic.

It wasn't possible. She couldn't allow herself to imagine a life with him. "That's a tempting thought, but not realistic." She stood up. "I'm going to get us some sodas. I'll be right back."

He watched her leave. Whatever she was keeping from him had made her squirm, but he wasn't worried. Dominic wouldn't let things alone until he'd gotten the truth out of her. There was no way he'd be taking her back until all was exposed.

Two hours later they'd come in sight of Les Calanques. He headed for his favorite channel.

"Oh, Dominic—I've never seen anything so fabulous in my life! It's like entering a canyon of sheer cliffs with a fairy-tale backdrop. The white of the limestone with the blue sky above is out of this world."

He knew she would love it as he drove his boat in and headed for the sandy little beach at the end. It wasn't quite noon yet. Any boaters would probably come out later when it was warmer. For now they had this piece of paradise all to themselves.

After cutting the motor, he laid anchor and looked over at her. She'd already removed her life jacket. "How soon can you be ready for a swim?"

"Right now." She flashed him a smile to die for and took off her clothes to reveal a jade-colored bikini beneath. He came close to having a heart attack before peeling off his own clothes down to his black swimsuit. She beat him to the transom and jumped in the water.

He heard a shriek and laughed. "It'll warm up."

"Now you tell me!"

Dominic dived off the boat and swam under the water, catching her around those fabulous legs. They played for a while until he couldn't take it any longer and dragged her to the warm sand. Pulling her down next to him, he said, "You thought you would get away from me, but I'm telling you right now I'll never let go."

She lay there breathing hard with the sun bringing out the gold threads of her silvery-gold hair. "With those light green eyes, you look like a goddess who has enchanted me."

"This whole day has been one of enchantment."

He plunged his hand into her hair, which had come undone. "I want you, Nathalie. More than any woman I've ever wanted in my life."

"I want you too," she confessed, running her hands over his shoulders. He began to kiss her, starting with her throat, then every feature of her face until he found her mouth. Desire consumed him as she responded with an abandon he could only dream about. They were on fire for each other.

"I can't believe I had to live this long to meet you."

"I know. I feel the same way," she murmured against his lips. "You're too good to be true. I—" She paused because they could both hear voices and laughter. "Oh, no. Someone has found our spot."

Damn. She'd been about to say something that could

have been important for his peace of mind. "Come on. Let's swim back to the boat and fix a meal. Hopefully they'll go away after a while."

He helped her to her feet and they ran into the aqua-colored water, anxious to get away from the encroaching world. By the time they'd climbed on board the transom with their bodies free of sand, the other boat had reached the small beach.

"You shower first, Nathalie. I'll get lunch."

"Tonight I'll make dinner." She grabbed her clothes, but he didn't let her go until he'd given her another kiss that made him crave a thousand more. He would need a lifetime and beyond to be with her and still never have enough.

Soon they were at the galley table away from prying eyes, eating a deli salad and rolls. She'd put her shorts and top back on.

"How long have you had this cruiser?"

"I bought it five years ago. It provided me a safe place when I came home for visits."

She cocked her head. "Safe?"

"I needed my space."

"Away from the chateau. Of course."

Nathalie's pulse started to race. This was it. "Was there a special woman in your life, Dominic? Either here or in Paris? You know what I mean."

Tell me the truth, her heart cried. She needed answers now.

His eyes narrowed on her face. "Not enough to get married. No blondes with shimmering hair like yours.

The Fontesquieu men haven't had the best luck when it comes to marriage, but I live in hope."

It sounded less and less like he was Alain's father. Her mind shifted to Etienne. What if Alain was *his* son? The damage that knowledge would do to his already unhappy marriage would be disastrous considering he already had a child.

Whoever had gotten Antoinette pregnant had been the love of her life. But no matter how tragically hers had ended, Nathalie was beginning to realize she didn't have the right to interfere. Her mother had been right. She'd been so obsessed with finding Alain's father, she hadn't considered what new nightmares she could be creating.

Her eyelids smarted. She couldn't keep this up anymore. After she'd finished eating, she got up from the table and took her dishes to the sink.

"Dominic? It's getting busy. Since we no longer have this place to ourselves, why don't we head back to Nice. Somewhere along the way I'll fix dinner and we can watch the sunset. What do you think?"

For an answer, he finished clearing the table. "What's bothering you? Up until a minute ago, we were communicating. Don't tell me it's nothing." He put his hands on her shoulders.

At his touch, she trembled. "This is all moving too fast."

"Fast or not, it's happened," he whispered into her hair. "I don't want what we have to be over. Not ever." He slid his hands down her silky arms before turning her around. "I need you, Nathalie. You're all I can think about."

"Please let me go," she begged, but he didn't listen and found her mouth. *"Dominic—"*

"You want me too. I know it."

In the next breath, she surrendered to a force she couldn't control. She couldn't get close enough to him. For a few minutes, the world disappeared while they tried to satisfy their hunger. All she knew was ecstasy with this unforgettable man who filled her arms and heart.

But when he started to move her toward his cabin, she found the strength to break free of him and braced herself against the counter. "We can't do this, Dominic." After the passion that had enthralled her, she was in literal pain trying to avoid his touch.

He struggled for breath. "What do you mean?"

"I—I never meant for this to happen," she stammered. "It's all wrong."

"How could it possibly be wrong? We both felt an attraction during the interview. It's been building every second since and you know it. I've never felt this way about another woman in my life! Nathalie? Look at me."

"I can't."

"All along you've been hiding something from me. Tell me what it is."

"I don't dare."

"I knew it!" he bit out, and raked his hands through his hair in frustration. "Why are you so terrified? Help me understand."

"I shouldn't have applied for work at the vineyard. It was a mistake, and now I'm paying for it. Forgive me for the trouble I've caused you. I never meant to hurt you when you've been so wonderful to me."

"What in the hell are you talking about? Have you run away from a husband I don't know about and you're hiding at the vineyard, afraid he'll find you?"

"No!" she cried, shaking her head.

"Are you working for some editor to get information about the family business? You can tell me the truth."

"No! No one is involved but me."

"Involved how?"

"I can't answer that. Would you please let me go, Dominic? I'm begging you."

"Whatever this is, we can fix it."

She backed away from him. "The only solution out of this is for us to stop seeing each other. Let me honor my contract to pick grapes until the harvest is over."

He drew in a harsh breath. "How could I possibly stay away from you now? Deny it all you want, but our feelings for each other aren't going to fade. Before you came into my life, I'd decided this experience would never happen to me. Then you showed up in that tent. I could no more walk away from you for good than stop breathing!"

"Don't say that!" Tears trickled down her cheeks. "You mustn't."

"Why? Let's hear the truth. Are you dying of a disease and don't want to tell me?"

Not a disease, but I can't give a man children.

"I promise it's nothing like that," she cried.

"*Bon.* I'll drive us back to Nice. But this isn't over."

After cupping her wet face in his hands and kissing her breathless, he left the galley. She heard him race up on deck. Then he was back with her life jacket. He tossed it on a chair, then took off again. In another minute he'd started the motor.

The long journey back was pure agony for her. She cleaned up the galley before going up on deck. He said he didn't want dinner. What she'd done to him was tearing both of them apart.

By evening he'd deposited her at the door of the rental. He didn't try to kiss her again before she went inside. When she heard him drive away, she wanted to die, but there was a reason she hadn't told him the truth tonight.

She still didn't have proof that either brother was Alain's father and didn't dare probe further since she could be wrong and hurt everyone. It didn't matter that she'd had the best reason in the world for doing what she'd done. She'd gone way too far and her feelings for him needed to be cut off for good.

She'd ventured where she shouldn't have and would suffer for having given in to her guilty longing for him. It had to end now before she did damage to two men who had no comprehension of why she'd come to the vineyard to work.

Knowing that she was doing the right thing, she drove back to La Gaude at full speed. When she entered the house still in tears, she found her mom on the phone with Nathalie's *tante* Patrice, her mother's sister, who lived in Nice with her husband and family. Alain had already been put to bed. Her mother took one look at her and ended the conversation.

"You're so pale, it alarms me. I'm almost afraid to ask what's happened."

Nathalie sank down on the chair. "I spent the whole day with Dominic and had a chance to confront him. But I couldn't do it because I have no proof that either brother was involved with Antoinette. He knows I've been holding back." She wiped more tears off her cheeks.

"I was afraid of this," her mother murmured.

"I'm too involved with him, but it's not too late. If I give up the job in the morning and never see him again, no one but you and I will know anything."

"Does Dominic know you're quitting?"

"No. He'll find out after the fact."

Her mother got to her feet. "I can tell how much he means to you. If he feels the same way—and I suspect he does—he's not going to stay away from you."

"I know him. He'll come to the vineyard tomorrow to get the truth out of me. But I won't be employed there or living in the mobile home."

"Which means he'll come here."

"I hope not, but I'll have to face that moment if it happens. I'm going to go to bed now and get up extra early to take care of what I have to do. Get a good sleep, Maman." She kissed her and hurried to the bedroom, but there'd be little sleep for Nathalie.

She got up at the crack of dawn after a restless night and drove straight to the vineyard, praying there'd be no sign of Dominic. She waited in her car until she saw Gregoire. No one else was there yet. He'd just arrived in his truck. She got out with the equipment she'd been given and ran up to him.

"Gregoire? Forgive me, but an emergency has happened at my home and I can't work here any longer."

He frowned. "I'm sorry."

"So am I. Here are the things I was given to start work." He took the items from her. "You've all been so nice to me. I can't thank you enough for taking me on. I hope you find a replacement without too much trouble. Say goodbye to Paul. He was a great help."

Gregoire gave her a perplexed nod before she ran back to her car and headed for the mobile home. She'd never cleaned things so fast in her life, hoping against hope that Dominic wasn't around and wouldn't see her car. When she'd finished, she drove over to the manager's office and turned in her key.

Once back in her car, she left the vineyard. She'd cried so many tears last night in bed, she didn't know she had any more in her. But she was wrong and could barely see her way home to La Gaude.

CHAPTER SEVEN

DOMINIC HAD BEEN struggling to get some work done in his office when Etienne unexpectedly walked in at lunchtime. He looked up. "Hey, bro. You're looking better."

Etienne frowned. "I wish I could say the same thing about you. From where I'm standing, I'd say you've come down with that wretched flu."

"I'm afraid I've got something much worse." He hadn't slept all night trying to work out what was going on with Nathalie.

"Then you're not going to like my news."

"What do you mean?"

"I just received a message from Gregoire at the office and came over on the double to see you."

"What's wrong?"

"Mademoiselle Fournier showed up at the vineyard early this morning and told him there was an emergency at home. She said she couldn't continue to work at the vineyard. After thanking him for everything and handing over her supplies, she drove off. I just called the manager of the mobile home park. He said she cleaned her home and dropped off the keys early. That was it."

Dominic jumped to his feet, feeling as if he'd just received the final blow to the gut. He rubbed the back of his neck, incredulous that she would actually quit. But last night her panic had been real. He should have foreseen her flight.

"Thanks for telling me, Etienne."

"I'm sorry to bring you this kind of news. It's obvious this woman is important to you."

"More than you know."

"Is there anything I can do?"

"Thanks, but no. I appreciate everything you've done. I've got a decision to make."

He nodded. "Call me if you need to talk."

His brother walked out, leaving Dominic standing there stunned. He'd felt her fear on the cruiser and realized he couldn't get anything out of her. It had propelled her to take flight this morning. Needing to channel his energy, he reached for his phone to call her, but all he got was her voice mail. No surprise there. He asked her to call him back, but knew she wouldn't.

After telling Theo he'd be gone from the office for the rest of the day, he drove to the chateau to change into casual clothes, then left for La Gaude.

When he reached the town, he turned on the GPS to find the La Metropole Pharmacy and parked near the front. He didn't know if she'd be working there today, but this was a place to start.

After parking the car, he entered the pharmacy that had a number of customers. One man stood behind a counter waiting on people. Dominic looked around until he spotted a striking older blonde with a slender figure who had to be Nathalie's mother. She was talking to a customer in the back. There was no sign of her daughter. That meant Nathalie was probably home.

Dominic walked back out and drove to the address on Olivier. She lived in a very modest, soft-yellow Provencal *bastide*. A red car had been parked in front. Around the side he caught sight of her blue car. His heart skipped a beat. He walked to the front door and knocked.

There was no response so he knocked again. Maybe she'd seen him from one of the front windows and intended to ignore him. After another minute he turned and headed for his car, defeated for the moment.

"Dominic? Wait!"

He wheeled around in time to see her hurry toward him wearing a colorful top and jeans. Her hair flounced around her shoulders. "I didn't realize you were out here." Her normally beautiful skin looked mottled from crying.

"I received alarming news today to hear you'd quit your job and given up the rental. Gregoire told Etienne it was because of an emergency at home. I tried to reach you on the phone. When I didn't hear from you, I came to see if you were all right."

"I'm fine, and I'm so sorry about everything. Now they have to find a replacement for me." She sounded full of remorse.

"They already have, but you and I need to talk. I'm not going to take no for an answer."

She nodded. "Just a minute while I grab my purse. I'll be right out."

His world had just gotten a little better while he waited to help her in the car. She returned and he drove them into the hills. He parked on an overlook shaded by more olive trees and turned off the engine.

"I planned to phone you later today because I owe you an explanation, Dominic."

"How about starting with the truth. Why did you quit?"

"I had a good reason."

"Convince me."

She moistened her lips in a nervous gesture. "After your brother left the other evening, I didn't like what was happening to me."

"What do you mean?"

"The news that you wouldn't be coming for dinner disappointed me much more than it should have."

"That's a bad thing?" he asked in a husky tone.

"It is for me. I never dreamed that working at the vineyard would mean I could be attracted to another man. I felt it was best to leave and still do."

Dominic had been listening. "Nathalie… You and I have experienced *coup de foudre*. It makes no sense that you're trying to put distance between us when we know we're both on fire for each other. That kind of attraction is so rare I still haven't recovered and know you haven't either. Which means there's something else you can't or won't tell me. I'm not going to leave you alone until you do."

She'd been looking out the window, then turned to him with a sober expression. "I came to the vineyard because…because I'm looking for someone."

That's what all this was about? He took a deep breath. "A man or a woman?"

"A man."

He didn't like the sound of that. "Obviously it's someone who's important to you."

"Yes."

Ciel. "How important?"

"So important I've gone overboard looking for him and am regretting it."

"You mean you wish we hadn't met."

"I didn't say that," her voice trembled. "But I've been guilt-ridden over applying to work at your vineyard in order to look for him."

"Why did you think to come to our vineyard of all places?"

"Because at the beginning of the summer I learned he worked at the Fontesquieu vineyard. I planned to take my vacation around the harvest so I could apply for work. By some miracle, you hired me."

The revelation racked him with pain. He studied her profile. "Did this man disappear?"

"Yes, as if he'd been wiped off the face of the earth."

Dominic's brows furrowed. "What does he look like?"

She let out a troubled sigh. "All I can tell you is that he's a Provencal."

That meant he was probably dark haired and dark eyed. At this point Dominic was shattered. "If you were in a relationship at the time he disappeared, did you contact the police?"

"No. He wouldn't have gone off like that if he'd wanted to be found."

Nathalie... "Yet you're still looking for him."

"Yes. I—I just wanted to know why he disappeared." Her voice had faltered again.

She'd been in love with him! *That* was why she hadn't married the guy she'd met in pharmacy college. "If you find him, what will you do?"

"The question is no longer relevant. I've given up trying to find him. That's why I quit my job at your vineyard. There's no place else to look and I've decided to let it go."

He slid his arm along the back of the seat, refusing to let this alone. "I take it your guilt over what has been happening between us is the reason you don't want to go on seeing me."

She nodded without looking at him. "I can't have a relationship with you."

"Why? Deep down do you still hope to find him one day?"

"If only to have closure."

There were degrees of pain. "If you'll tell me his name, I can run a search by my vintner sources and possibly find him."

"I would never ask you to do that, and couldn't anyway because he never would use his name. He was so secretive I'm convinced he was hiding who he really was. I wish I knew the reason. He was around for a month, then he was gone for good."

Dominic rubbed his jaw, tortured by everything she'd revealed. "But in that time he made a lasting impression."

"Yes."

"Nathalie… How long ago did he disappear?"

"It's been two and a half years."

"That long?" He was incredulous.

She nodded. "That's why it's absurd for me to keep looking. For all I know he's been in another part of the world all this time."

But at this point Dominic was frozen in place.

Two and a half years ago, Raoul had been forced to break off with Toinette.

Was it possible? Raoul was a Fontesquieu… All the men in their family were tall and dark. Provencal. That's how Nathalie had described him.

No…

Dominic didn't even want to think it. But what if by a stroke of fate, Nathalie *had* been the woman Raoul had adored, and she had used a different name with him?

Why would she be looking for him now? She knew he'd had to marry another woman. Did she come to the vineyard to find out about his life because she'd never been able to let him go in her heart?

If it was true, Dominic was haunted by the thought that Nathalie had loved his cousin and had been looking for him. He knew Raoul had never forgotten his love for her.

Dominic's eyes closed tightly for a minute when he considered yesterday when he'd started kissing her again in the galley. If she hadn't stopped him, they might have ended up making love all night long. *Bon Dieu.*

Until he'd had a certain conversation with his cousin

tonight and ascertained the truth, he needed to take her home *now*.

"Dominic? I know that what I've revealed has shocked you."

You mean crucified me. "That's one way of putting it, but I'm glad I have the truth at last and will drive you back to your house."

"Thank you. I hope you can forgive me."

"There's nothing to forgive. The vineyard is grateful for the excellent work you've put in. Pretty soon those red stains will be gone." He started the car and took her home.

She opened the door and jumped out the second he pulled up in front of her house. "Whether you believe me or not, I've loved every moment we've spent together." There were tears in her voice. "I'll never forget you, Dominic."

Those throbbing words would stay with him all the way to Vence. "*A bientôt*, Nathalie."

He'd rebelled against saying goodbye to her. But if she and Raoul had been lovers... His cousin would soon be free of Sabine. He and Nathalie could finally be together.

Raw pain clawed his insides as he drove to the estate and hurried inside his apartment. He and his cousin were going to have the talk of their lives. For the first time in his, he felt like death.

But Raoul texted him later and told him a problem had come up at work and he'd had to drive to their warehouse in Saint Jeannet. He wouldn't be back until the next evening.

It was just as well since Dominic needed to calm down before he talked to his cousin. He didn't want them to have been lovers.

Dominic couldn't bear it.

Nathalie had been staying home for the rest of the week to take care of Alain while her mother ran the pharmacy with Denis. It gave Minerve some time off. Next week Nathalie would go back to her routine at the pharmacy.

She adored her nephew and played with him to her heart's content. He would be her baby one day, the only one she would ever have. She would spend the rest of her life giving him all the love she could while she loved Dominic in silence. There was no man in the world like him.

If he was the one Antoinette had fallen for, Nathalie understood why she'd told Claire he was the only man she would ever love. Nathalie couldn't imagine loving another man either.

On Saturday morning she took Alain to the local park as usual and walked around with him, holding his hand. His little giggles while they fed the ducks in the pond delighted her. When she could tell he was tired, she took him home for lunch and a nap.

While it was quiet, she phoned Claire to tell her everything that had happened. "I quit my job." She'd also said goodbye to Dominic, but she didn't confess her feelings for him to Claire. That would have to remain her secret.

"I know you had hopes, but I can't say I blame you."

"You and Mom were right. I have no proof. But I want to thank you with all my heart for your help."

"Oh, Nathalie. I was happy to give you any information I could. What are you going to do now?"

"Start adoption proceedings for Alain."

"How wonderful!"

"I'm his doting, would-be mother. After it's official, I want him to start calling me Maman and we'll all live together with my mother. He loves his *grand-mère*."

"Antoinette was lucky you're there for her son. I miss her."

"So do I. One day I'll bring Alain by to meet you. Thanks again for everything. Talk to you soon."

"I'd love that. Au revoir, Nathalie."

They clicked off, but she was restless and went to her room to take a shower. As she was getting dressed in a skirt and blouse, she received a text. Maybe it was her mother. She reached for her phone on the dresser.

Dominic.

The blood pounded in her ears as she read it.

I have some information you've been wanting. If you're interested come to my office between five thirty and six today. You can pick up your paycheck at the same time. If you don't come I'll have it deposited in your bank. Dominic—

She let out an agonized groan. To hear from him now when the separation had been so excruciating for her… What information did he think he'd found for her when she believed either he or his brother could have been the man involved with Antoinette? Or not. Did she dare break down and walk through fire in order to be with him again?

While she stood there in utter turmoil, that fluttering organ she called her heart gave her the answer. Fool that she was, she answered back. I'll come.

Having done that, she rushed around to get ready and left the house after her mother got home at three.

She battled fear and excitement all the way and felt feverish by the time she drove onto the estate. The road led around the magnificent seventeenth-century chateau. Seeing his home in all its glory up close brought back the conversation she'd had with Dominic about his family.

The big modern business building beyond the chateau and sculptured topiary trees looked out of place. She studied the cars parked in the lot on the side. The black Renault and silver Mercedes caught her eye immediately.

On trembling legs she got out of her car and entered the door of the main entrance.

A well-dressed, attractive receptionist seated at a desk smiled at her. "*Bonjour.* Can I help you?"

"Yes." She could see Dominic's name on the door to the right. "I'm Mademoiselle Fournier. I was told to pick up my paycheck in Monsieur Dominic Fontesquieu's office."

"*Très bien.* I'll let him know you're here."

A few seconds later the door opened. The tall, dark Frenchman she loved with all her heart and soul stood there dressed casually in jeans and a tan sport shirt. Every inch of him was so arresting, she felt inundated with longings, but lines marred his handsome face and she noticed a certain pallor. Maybe he'd caught his brother's flu.

"I'm glad you could make it. *Entrez*, Mademoiselle Fournier."

He'd never been this formal with her. "Thank you."

Nathalie stepped inside, but came to a sudden halt. She'd thought Dominic would be alone. Out of the corner of her eye, she saw another tall, dark-haired man standing near the desk wearing a blue business suit. He was on his phone.

After he hung up, he turned in her direction. She let out a tiny gasp, unable to trust the sight before her eyes. This man reminded her of Dominic and Etienne. With his coloring and those familiar features, he had to be *another* Fontesquieu! Incredibly he had a look of Alain, as well. Now she really knew she was losing it.

His smiling black eyes looked over her with male interest. "Dom? Aren't you going to introduce us?"

Dominic didn't answer. What was going on?

"I'm Nathalie Fournier." She spoke up to ease the sudden tension. "And you?"

"Raoul Fontesquieu."

Dominic's cousin! The one going through the painful divorce. "It's very nice to meet you, Monsieur Fontesquieu."

"I hear you did an excellent job of picking grapes while you were here. Not everyone has a knack for it."

"I don't know about that, but thank you."

He walked over to Dominic and patted his shoulder. "We'll talk later at home."

That's right. She remembered his cousin had moved in with Dominic while getting his divorce.

Raoul flashed Nathalie another glance. "It's a pleasure to meet you."

Dominic walked him to the door. After his cousin left, he turned to her, but he looked like a different person. The lines around his compelling mouth had disappeared, but he didn't say a word to her, making her uncomfortable.

"Dominic, I wouldn't have come if I'd known you were busy."

"I asked you to come. My cousin only dropped by for a minute."

"Why are you staring at me like that?" She didn't understand.

"Because you're even more breathtaking than when we swam in the lagoon."

So was he. She swallowed hard. "You said in your text that you had some information for me I've been wanting."

Nathalie heard his sharp intake of breath. "You don't have to believe me, but until just a little while ago I thought I might have found the man you've been looking for. But my source was mistaken."

"I believe you because I know you wouldn't make that up."

"Thank you for that," he said in a thick-toned voice. In the next breath, he walked over to his desk and handed her the envelope with her paycheck. She put it in her purse.

"How are things going with your cousin?"

"It's a waiting game until his court date. His wife is fighting to stop the divorce."

"That's awful."

He grimaced. "Other things are worse, like not being able to see you anymore. Are you really planning to go through your whole life putting your personal life on hold while you wait to find the man who disappeared without a trace?"

Don't.

"I—I shouldn't have come and need to get home." Her voice faltered. "Thank you for the check." She started for the door.

"Just know that when you leave, there's a man here who's aching for you. That ache isn't going to go away."

She knew all about the pain he was describing. Nathalie hurried out of the building to her car. The situation had become impossible.

To add to her turmoil, there was the shocking realization that Raoul Fontesquieu could have been Antoinette's lover. The thought wouldn't leave her alone.

On the way home, she went over the conversation with Dominic when he'd told her about Raoul's unhappy marriage.

"I'm so sorry. Did they love each other before they got married?"

"He'd been seeing her, but hadn't proposed marriage. Both their families wanted it desperately. One night he met a girl and overnight fell deeply in love with her, wanting marriage. But by then Sabine was pregnant.

"Raoul only slept with her once, but he did the noble

thing and married her. Sadly he had to cut everything off with the girl he loved. Then their baby died. He buried his heart with his little girl. Since the funeral there's been an emptiness in him that worries me."

"I can't imagine so much pain."

"You're not a Fontesquieu."

The same looks ran in some families. Sometimes it was astounding. The Fontesquieu men were incredibly handsome in a similar way that made them unique. But she had to be realistic. Although Alain had many of their traits, he might not belong to any of them and probably didn't.

It was imperative she put all this behind her for good.

What her family needed was a vacation. They hadn't been anywhere since her stepfather died, and ought to go someplace far away with Alain.

When she arrived at the house to discuss it with her mother, she discovered Tante Patrice and Oncle Tommaso had dropped in for a visit. They were playing with Alain. He laughed so hard he got the hiccups.

Nathalie loved their extended family and got into the mix, spending a wonderful evening with them. She caught up on their news about her two cousins who were married and had children. One of the little girls named Angelique had just had her second birthday. She and Alain could play together.

After a while they talked about Nathalie's plans to adopt Alain. He would be her life from now on.

CHAPTER EIGHT

SUNDAY MORNING, AFTER being awake most of the night, Dominic got showered and dressed. He and Raoul went out for breakfast and talked. Very soon now his trial date would be set with the judge.

Afterward they went house hunting for Raoul, who had no desire to return to his apartment at the chateau once he was divorced. They found several possibilities. As they drove on, Raoul said, "Let's find one for you too, Dominic."

He frowned. "If I were getting married, I'd do it in a shot."

"Since I know you're head over heels in love with Nathalie Fournier, I don't understand why there's an *if*. Dom—I've poured out my soul to you. Now it's my turn to listen while you tell me what has you gutted."

"I finally learned the truth. She's in love with a man who told her he worked in our vineyard, but he disappeared on her two and half years ago. They were only together a month. Nathalie came to our vineyard trying to find him. She didn't know his name, but she described him as Provencal." He flashed his cousin a glance. "Because certain pieces of information fit, I thought it might be *you*."

Raoul let out a strange sound. "So *that's* why you called me into your office just minutes before she showed up? You thought she was the woman I'd loved?"

"I thought it could be a possibility and she'd used another name with you."

"Well, now that you know I'm not the one, why aren't you with her right now?"

He shook his head. "Until she finds this man and has closure, she refuses to be with me."

"Closure is different from being in love. It's been over two and a half years since she last saw him!"

"Then how do you explain why she quit work at the vineyard?"

"Because she has fallen in love with you, but you've been her employer. She's probably nervous about getting involved. I saw the way she looked at you. After the vibes I got from you two yesterday, I can promise you she couldn't still be in love with that other guy.

"Come on. Take me back to your apartment so you can go after her and break her down. Don't lose the woman who makes your life worth living. She'll most likely be home."

Raoul had been talking to a desperate man. His advice made so much sense, Dominic dropped his cousin off and left for La Gaude under a warm noon sun. Before long he turned the corner onto her street.

The red car he'd seen in front of her house the other day was gone. He saw Nathalie get out of the blue car parked at the side of the house. Her long shapely legs emerged first. She wore navy shorts and a sailor top.

He pulled to a stop, not wanting her to see him yet.

Next, she opened the rear door and reached for a little boy maybe the same age as Etienne's daughter, buckled in a car seat. She kissed his black curls several times before putting him down so he could walk. The child reached for her hand.

That trusting gesture caused Dominic's throat to swell with emotion.

Her son? He was staggered by the fact that Nathalie was a single mother and hadn't been able to admit it to him.

Dominic wondered how she'd been able to handle being away from her little boy during the harvest. She said she lived with her mother, who was also a pharmacist. No doubt Nathalie had hired someone to take care of him while she'd been working at the vineyard.

As for her picking grapes, it explained why she came home every night instead of staying in the mobile home. No wonder she'd come looking for the man who'd made her pregnant. With her stepfather deceased, she and her mother were her son's only support.

All of these thoughts ran through his mind. Yet he wondered why she'd waited until this summer to look for the man who'd changed her life.

Not about to give up, Dominic pulled out his phone and texted her.

Nathalie? I'm out in front of your house. When I came to see you just now, I watched you take a little boy inside with you. Is it his father you're looking for? I would like to talk to you and see what I can do to help. When will you be free?

A minute later she responded.

I'm putting him down now. It may take a half hour.

At least she hadn't said no.

Then I'll grab lunch for both of us and come back.

He drove to a bistro and picked up some food for them. When he returned, she came out of the house having changed into jeans and a blouse. She looked good enough to eat.

"Do you have to stay out in front?" he asked after she'd climbed in the car.

"No. My mother is home today."

Good. "In that case I'll drive us to that overlook we went to before."

He felt her cast him a covert glance. "I can't believe you came." There was a tremor in her voice.

"As you can see, I'm unable to stay away from you." Dominic drove up into the hills and parked the car under the same olive tree. "I bought us some meat pies and coffee." He reached in back for their lunch and they both started to eat.

"Thank you. I don't deserve how good you are to me."

"I'd like to do a lot more for you if you'd let me."

"Dominic—I never planned to be with you again, but

now that you've seen Alain, I can't keep the truth from you. Over sixteen months ago my stepsister had a baby."

"Your *stepsister...*"

He groaned as unmitigated joy streamed through him. Her stepsister had been the one in love with this mystery man. Everything was finally starting to make sense.

"Yes. She adored him and named him Alain. But ten days after he was born she died of a staph infection."

"I'm so sorry that happened to her." He studied her profile. "How hard that had to have been for you and your family."

"You have no idea."

"I'm sure I don't." He leaned closer. "You've been such a good listener I want to hear whatever you're willing to tell me."

Nathalie smoothed a strand of hair behind her ear. "She was an elementary school teacher. One evening she and some other teachers from her school went to the Guinguet, a place I'd never heard of. I was working in Nice at the time and learned all this from her best friend, Claire, who lived across the street from us."

At the mention of the Guinguet, Dominic's heart began pounding like a jackhammer.

"Apparently it was love at first sight for her, but she kept him a complete secret from our family. According to Claire, her affair lasted a month, then he suddenly stopped meeting her. Two months later she went to the doctor and found out she was pregnant. I remember that she was in a terrible depression throughout her pregnancy and refused to talk about the man she'd loved."

"Incroyable," Dominic murmured.

"She refused to give our family any information about the man and insisted we never talk about him again. She begged us to leave the whole subject of Alain alone."

"But you couldn't do that." How he loved this woman!

Nathalie looked at him with tear-filled eyes. "I honored her wishes until the beginning of this summer after I broke it off with Guy. When I told him I was going to adopt Alain, it changed our relationship. He didn't want to bring her son into our marriage. For that and other reasons, I said goodbye to him."

Grâce à Dieu.

"Oh, Dominic, Alain is so adorable and it seemed so terrible he didn't have a mother or a father, I couldn't bear it. So I thought that before I started adoption proceedings, I'd at least try to find my stepsister's lover, as he has a right to his child.

"That's when I called Claire to gather any information she could give me. All she said was that he was a Provencal, had worked on your family's vineyard and Antoinette met him at Le Guinguet. At that point I started wondering about the man she'd loved. Knowing her, he had to have been someone exceptional. Maybe something serious had happened to him and he couldn't let her know why he'd stopped seeing her. He left before she learned she was pregnant so he never knew he was a father."

All the time she was talking, Dominic was fitting

two and two together so fast, his thoughts were running away with him.

"I'm pretty sure she'd met a married man who'd wanted an affair and forced her to keep quiet about it. Since none of us knew the truth and never would, she asked our family to put the questions away and simply love Alain. I know now it was wise advice. I'm through looking."

"Nathalie—" He was trying to control his emotions. "Now that I know the truth, then there's no reason we can't go on seeing each other."

She averted her eyes. "I couldn't. Please don't ask. If you wouldn't mind driving me back home now, I promised my mother I wouldn't be long."

Beyond frustrated, he started the car and they left for her house. "Is it because of the man you'd planned to marry, your feelings for him prevent you from wanting to be with me?"

"You know I don't have feelings for him any longer or I wouldn't be this involved with you, but I'd rather not talk about it." He could feel her separating herself emotionally from him.

In a minute he turned the corner and pulled up in front. "What will it take for you to agree for us to be together? I didn't make up what happened when you melted in my arms on the sand. I need an answer I can understand."

"I'm…frightened to tell you."

What?

"Am I some kind of monster to you?"

"Of course not!" she cried.

"Nathalie—" He'd reached his limit.

She turned a pained face to him. "How would you feel if I told you I thought my stepsister had either had an affair with you, or Etienne."

"Say that again?" Surely he hadn't heard her correctly.

"My nephew looks so much like all of you, it's uncanny."

"Do you have a picture of him?"

She nodded and pulled one out of her wallet. His heart almost failed him when he examined the black-haired cherub up close. She'd spoken the truth. "I can't believe it," he murmured. "Alain is a double for some of the baby pictures of me and Etienne. Talk about look-alikes." He handed it back to her. "It's remarkable."

"I couldn't believe I'd met two men in one family who could possibly be his father. Then came another shock when I met your cousin in your office. He shares the same looks with you and your brother. I never saw anything like it. After you told me his marital history, I—I've wondered if Raoul could be the one," she stammered.

This was unbelievable! "You're right. Your stepsister's son has a remarkably strong resemblance to all three of us."

Her eyes beseeched him for answers. "Who would have thought?"

He swallowed hard, trying to digest everything. "I only saw Alain from a distance earlier."

"He has that same lustrous black Fontesquieu hair. You should see his piercing dark eyes in person. All three of you could claim him. When I first met you, *you* fit the description my stepsister had given Claire. You worked on the vineyard and I couldn't help but think you could have been with her."

Dominic was dumbfounded. "All this time we've been together you've thought *I* could have been her lover...?"

"At first it seemed more than plausible, but I never expected to become involved with you. That first day you took my application, I could see you written all over Alain. He has a birthmark on his leg. I saw the same one on the underside of your forearm and thought you could be the one. It's the only reason I returned on Monday to see if I'd been hired."

"You noticed that?"

"Yes. But then on the cruiser you told me about the women in your life you enjoyed, but didn't marry. I deduced you probably hadn't been with her. But you can't imagine my guilt over being attracted to you when I thought she could have been with you and had your baby."

"I'm still trying to take this in." He was incredulous.

Nathalie stirred restlessly. "You did admit you'd been to the Guinguet several times."

"So you thought that's where it all started with me."

She nodded. "I lived in hopes of getting closer to you and learning all I could first. But then my world was turned upside down because your brother, Etienne, stopped by the mobile home. You have no idea what meeting him did to me. After you told me your brother had loved another woman before his marriage, but the family thought she wasn't good enough for him,

I thought… Well, you know what I thought. Couple that with my meeting your cousin, and I couldn't go on with my plan."

A man could take only so much. "Do you have a picture of her?"

"Yes."

"May I see it?"

She hesitated before opening her purse. After pulling out her wallet, she handed him a photo.

He took a look at it. "She's very attractive, but I've never seen this woman in my life."

A hand went to her throat. "This whole situation is hopeless."

Dominic's heart almost failed him. Exasperated, he said, "Nathalie? Why didn't you just come out and ask me the first time we were alone?"

She shook her head. "How could I have dared do that when you were a perfect stranger? After Paul told me that you and Etienne were both members of the Fontes-quieu family, not mere employees, that made my fear worse. Then I met Raoul. In my own way I *did* infiltrate, and you knew something was off."

"True, but you could have handed me this picture. I could have asked them if they'd seen her or knew her without telling them my reasons."

"You're right. But to tell you the whole truth would have seemed like an accusation, especially if you and the others were innocent of being with her. You could have lied to protect yourselves. I wouldn't have blamed you."

Her reasoning made a bizarre kind of sense.

"I thought… Oh, what does it matter? All this time

I've been functioning under a premise that's way off. I'm so sorry."

"Nathalie—" he said, but she interrupted him because she was beyond listening.

"My mother wanted me to leave everything alone, but I was so certain I was right. You must think I'm a fool." She opened the car door.

"Wait—"

"It's no good. We still don't have answers and I'm not going to ask Etienne or Raoul anything. That's why I stopped picking grapes. This has to be goodbye, Dominic."

Before he could credit it, she slid out while he was still holding the photo, and ran toward the house. Dominic didn't try to stop her. Tonight it was more important he get answers. Whatever the outcome, his whole life and hers were going to change.

He left for Vence and drove straight to his office. Theo had already gone home. Dominic phoned Etienne.

"We need to talk. Can you come to the office now?" Dominic had decided to question his brother first.

"Give me a half hour."

"You've got it."

They clicked off. If by any chance Etienne had been with the woman in this picture, then his brother needed to know. Dominic had been in Paris and wouldn't have known if his brother had gotten involved with Nathalie's stepsister.

While he waited, he took care of some business Theo had left for him. Before long Etienne walked in. "What's going on? You sounded ultraserious."

"That's because it could be. I have something to show you. Maybe you should sit down."

"That bad?" Etienne remained standing with his hands on his hips.

"Have you ever seen or known this woman?" Dominic handed him the two-by-three colored photo.

Etienne's dark brows furrowed before he studied it, then shook his head. "She's a beauty, but I never saw her in my life. Who is she?" He handed the photo back to him.

For his brother's sake and his own, relief swamped Dominic. "You're not going to believe what I have to tell you." For the next little while he related everything Nathalie had said, right down to the birthmarks.

His brother whistled. "Mademoiselle Fournier believes her stepsister got pregnant by a Fontesquieu?"

Dominic nodded. "She swears the boy could belong to any one of the three of us."

"You've seen him?"

"She showed me a picture. It could have been one of us when we were that age."

They stared at each other. "Well, it isn't you, and isn't me. When was this supposed to have happened?"

"According to Nathalie, their affair took place two and a half years ago."

Etienne's eyes narrowed. "That's when Raoul got married. Are you thinking what I'm thinking? People have often said they think we're all brothers."

"I know," Dominic murmured. "As late as yesterday evening I thought it was possible Nathalie had been involved with Raoul because I didn't know about her stepsister. Naturally, when I introduced them, they didn't know each other. There's only one thing to do. Show Raoul this photo."

"Agreed."

"If this is the woman Raoul fell in love with, then his life is going to get a thousand times more complicated."

"When are you going to talk to him?"

CHAPTER NINE

MONDAYS WERE ALWAYS busy at the pharmacy. Nathalie went in at nine and waited on customers with a quick break for lunch. Her mom stayed home to take a breather from work. Nathalie told Denis to go home early and she would close up at seven, her one late night during the week. It was time she did her part.

The last customer left the pharmacy a few minutes after seven. Nathalie locked the door and was walking to the rear of the store when someone knocked on the front door.

She turned and walked back, thinking it was the customer who'd just left. But it was Dominic! Her heart plummeted to her feet.

"Will you let me in for a minute, Nathalie? I have something important to tell you."

Help. "No, Dominic. I've already said goodbye to you."

"It can't be goodbye. I've found your nephew's father. We need to talk."

What?

She knew Dominic was honesty personified. That

meant he'd shown Antoinette's picture to his brother and cousin. Which one had recognized her? Nathalie pressed a hand to her heart, unable to believe this was happening.

"Where can we go now that you've closed for the night? I'll follow you."

She didn't dare go anywhere alone with him. Better to stay right here with the lights on. She unlocked the door. "Come in."

"Thank you."

There was no one more appealing to Nathalie than Dominic. Tonight he'd dressed in a business suit and tie. No doubt he'd come from some kind of meeting. She looked uninspiring in a white lab coat over a dress, no makeup and her hair pulled back to the nape. But right now that wasn't important.

"Which one of them recognized her?"

He studied her features. "Raoul."

"So *he* was the one?"

Dominic nodded. "I asked him to tell me if he'd seen or knew this woman, then I handed him the photo. He took one look at it and paled before asking me how I came by it. That's when I told him you'd been looking for the man your stepsister had loved, but I didn't tell him there was a baby."

"Oh, Dominic—" She hugged her arms to her waist, hardly able to contain her emotions.

"He remembers her telling him she had a stepsister and can't believe it's *you*! He wants desperately to talk to you anywhere, anytime you say."

Her eyes met the burning blackness of his. "I want that too," her voice trembled.

"You have no idea how eager he is and will do whatever you suggest."

She shook her head. "That's wonderful!"

"*He's* wonderful. You've only met Raoul for a moment, but you don't know him yet. There's no better man in this world."

Nathalie had difficulty swallowing. "Obviously my stepsister felt the same way or she would never have gotten involved with him. Where would he prefer to meet?"

"That's up to you. You could come to my apartment since he's living there with me."

She moistened her lips nervously. "When would be a good time?"

"As soon as you can make it. Since I told him, he's been so anxious to talk to you about your stepsister, he hasn't been able to settle down."

"I've been in that state since I learned she was pregnant." She drew in a breath. "Is he free this evening?"

"Yes. I could drive you there and bring you back."

"That wouldn't be a good idea. Give me a minute to freshen up, then I'll follow you to the chateau. After my talk with your cousin, I'll drive home because I have to help with Alain."

He nodded. "So be it."

"I'll see you out and lock the door, then let myself out the back door."

Dominic left the pharmacy while she rushed to take off her lab coat and run a brush through her hair. After texting her mother that she wouldn't be home for a while, she put on lipstick.

Her mom wouldn't believe it when she heard the news that Alain's father had been found. Nathalie could hardly believe it either. Finally Nathalie locked up and followed the black Renault to Vence.

It gave her a strange feeling to park outside one of the entrances to the chateau, knowing she would be entering the home of the man she loved with all her heart and soul.

He unlocked the door that led upstairs to his private suite of rooms. The elegance of the sumptuous chateau wasn't lost on her as they walked down a hall lined with paintings.

When he opened the door at the end, his cousin stood there in the salon waiting for them in a sport shirt and trousers. Raoul was the tall, striking Fontesquieu her stepsister had given her heart to. Naturally, Dominic had alerted his cousin that they were on their way.

Raoul stared at her for a full minute after she walked inside. "You and Toinette might be stepsisters, but you share one similarity. She is a raving beauty too."

Nathalie was so overwhelmed to have found him, her eyes filled with tears. "You called her Toinette. That was my stepfather's nickname for her too."

His handsome features softened. "When I met her, she introduced herself as Antoinette Gilbert. I shortened it." Raoul held the photo in his hand. "This is the only remembrance I have of her. May I keep it?"

"Of course. We have hundreds at home."

"If you two will excuse me, I'll go in the other room."

Raoul turned to Dominic. "Are you kidding me? Stay! You're the reason any of this is happening. Please sit down, Nathalie."

She sank down on one of the leather couches. Nathalie could tell a man had been living here. All the masculine touches proclaimed Dominic's more modern abode. He sat next to her.

Raoul found a chair and cleared his throat. "Whether you believe me or not, I want you to know that your stepsister is the only woman I've ever loved in my life. We knew how we felt about each other by the end of that first night we met at the Guinguet."

The same thing had happened to Nathalie by the time she'd left the tent that first morning. Meeting Dominic had changed her life forever. She could fully relate.

"Before I'd met her, I'd been seeing a woman named Sabine Murat. We slept together once, but I knew deep down I didn't love her the way I should, and I ended things. Soon after, Toinette came into my life. I felt I'd been reborn and wanted to marry her on the spot. Then came the nightmare when Sabine phoned and said she was carrying my child."

Nathalie nodded. "Dominic told me."

"The worst moment in my life came when I had to tell Toinette the truth."

"She'd been so deeply in love with you, no wonder she went into depression."

Pain was written all over Raoul's face. "Toinette heard me out, then said goodbye to me and I never saw her again. I tried phoning her many times so we could talk, but she didn't answer. Of course, I couldn't blame her. No one could overcome such a cruel reality."

Tears trickled down Nathalie's cheeks. "Since then Dominic told me you've lost a baby."

"Yes. I loved our little Celine, but I found out recently she wasn't my daughter."

"Oh, no—" Nathalie cried.

"It's in the past and I'm getting a divorce."

Nathalie shared a worried glance with Dominic. "Raoul—there's something vital you need to know. It's the only reason I've been looking for you."

"What is it?"

"Antoinette died of a staph infection over sixteen months ago."

Raoul went white as a sheet. Dominic rushed over to him, but he shot to his feet. "She's gone?"

"Yes."

He rubbed the back of his neck, looking totally shattered.

"She's buried in La Gaude. But what's more important right now is the fact that she had *your* baby before she died."

Raoul staggered backward. "*My* baby?" The man had received too many shocks.

"Yes."

"I—I can't believe it," his voice faltered.

Nathalie smiled. "He looks like you, but he also resembles your two cousins."

"*He?*" Raoul cried.

"Yes. Alain is almost seventeen months old now. My stepsister named him that before she died. My mother and I have been raising him since my stepfather died."

"Toinette called our son Alain?" Suddenly the pain on his face gave way to joy, answering the most vital question for her. "That's a name in my family's line. We talked about having children."

Nathalie stood up with a smile. "Well, you got your wish. I have no proof he's yours, not without a DNA test. But here's a picture of him."

When she handed it to him, he took one look and sank back down on the couch with a low sob before studying it.

"I'm going to leave now, Raoul, and give you a chance to think about everything." She needed to get away before she broke down in tears too.

"Please don't leave yet, Nathalie."

"I have responsibilities at home. Dominic knows how to get in touch with me when you're ready. I'll see myself out."

She might have known Dominic would follow her to the car. After she climbed inside, she started the engine before looking up at him through the open window. "I pray I've done the right thing. A man has the right to know he's a father."

He reached in to brush the tears off her cheek. His touch sent a quiver through her body. "Equally true, a son has the right to know his father. Because of you, that's going to happen."

Dominic's words sank deep into her soul.

"You've done something so courageous and honorable, my cousin will be down on his knees to you when he sees the boy he and your stepsister created out of love." She felt his breath on her mouth before he gave her a brief kiss.

She lowered her eyes. "You should go back in. He needs you."

"Nathalie—"

She heard his cry, but couldn't remain there. After putting the car in gear, she headed for the entrance to the estate. The touch of his mouth remained with her all the way home. How wonderful it would feel to be able to give him a son or daughter...

Twenty minutes later she reached the house. Her mother had already put Alain down for the night. Nathalie found her cleaning the high chair and putting things away.

"Maman?"

She lifted her head. "Where have you been?"

"At Dominic's apartment in the Fontesquieu Chateau. It's a long story. He came to the pharmacy at closing time, and now I have news."

"What is it?"

"I gave Dominic a picture of Antoinette from my wallet. Neither he nor Etienne had ever met or known her. Then he showed it to Raoul Fontesquieu, his first cousin who's vice president of sales and marketing. I met him at the vineyard a few days ago. Raoul also resembles his cousins."

"You mean all three men look alike?"

"To an incredible degree. Right now he lives with Dominic while he's going through a bitter divorce. He took one look at the photo and confessed he'd been in love with Antoinette and would have married her but for impossible circumstances. I'll tell you about them later."

Silence surrounded them. "Is this the truth?"

Nathalie nodded. "Then I told him he had a son named Alain and showed him a photo. Though a DNA test would be needed for proof, he sounded and looked so overjoyed, his reaction thrilled my heart. But I left to give him time to absorb the news.

"He's had a shock, especially to hear that Antoinette had died. I have no doubt we'll be hearing from him before long, unless another impossible circumstance happens that prevents him."

A light entered her mother's gray-blue eyes. "He really loved her?"

"With every fiber of his being."

Her eyes filmed over and the two of them embraced. "Darling, this means you don't have to feel guilt over how much you care for Dominic."

Nathalie grasped the back of the nearest kitchen chair. "But I do."

"What do you mean?"

"Maman—I fell for Dominic when I believed he and Antoinette had been lovers. Knowing she was my step-sister didn't stop me from kissing him and wanting to be with him all night. That was wrong."

Her mother shook her head. "But look what has happened because you were so anxious to find Alain's father. I believe you were guided."

"Maybe. But there's something else. You know what it is. I can't have children. The doctor told me it would take a miracle. I love Dominic with every fiber of my being. He says he loves me, but I can't give him a son or daughter. After what happened with Guy, I—I don't know if I could handle it if it changed Dominic's feelings for me. I'm frightened, Maman."

"But, darling—"

"I don't want to talk about it. *Bonne nuit.*"

"Can you believe I have a son?" Raoul stood in the apartment a different man since hearing the revelation.

Dominic eyed his cousin. The news had made new men out of both of them. Nathalie no longer had to feel guilty now that she knew he and her stepsister had never been involved. As for Raoul, he had a whole new reason to live. "It's the greatest news you could have been given."

"I'll have to keep this quiet until my divorce is final."

"I agree."

"Would you talk to Nathalie and ask her how soon I could see Alain in private?"

His pulse raced. "I'll call her right now and find out what can be arranged. Even if she's in bed, she'll understand the urgency."

"What would I do without you, Dom?"

Feeling euphoric, he patted his cousin's shoulder before pulling out his cell phone. With the whole truth revealed, nothing could keep him and Nathalie apart now. His pulse raced when she picked up on the third ring.

"Dominic?"

"*Dieu merci* you're home safely. I needed to hear your voice and am calling for my cousin. How soon can he see his little boy? Considering Raoul is in the middle of a divorce, it should probably be someplace away from your home where he won't be seen."

"I can understand that. How soon could he come?"

"Tomorrow. You set the time and the spot."

"There's a park I take him to not far from the house. It's at the Place des Canards. We could meet tomorrow around noon by the pond with the ducks. Afterward I'll take him home and leave for the pharmacy."

"Does your mother know what has happened?"

"Yes. I've told her everything. She believes this was meant to be."

His eyes closed tightly for a minute. "You're an angel, Nathalie."

"I'm anything but."

She was still struggling with her guilt. He had plans to help her with that. "Raoul agrees with me. *A toute à l'heure.*"

Tuesday morning they both cleared their schedules to be gone from the estate at noon and left for La Gaude in Dominic's car. En route, Raoul asked him to stop at a store where he could buy a toy. He soon came out with a bag that contained a little blue-and-white sailboat like the one Raoul owned.

Using the GPS, they found the Place des Canards and parked along the side of the road near the pond. He couldn't miss Nathalie's gleaming hair, which she'd left loose today. In those jeans and frilly blouse, her feminine figure took his breath away.

Alain formed a contrast with his black curls. Today

she'd dressed him in a navy short-sleeved romper with small red-and-white horizontal stripes.

They got out of the car and approached slowly so they wouldn't startle him. She saw them first and smiled. *"Bonjour."*

That brought Alain's head around. Up close Dominic could see why Nathalie had believed her nephew looked like their family. In person the resemblance to the Fontesquieux was absolutely uncanny. One day he'd grow to be a tall, dark-haired duplicate of his father.

"Alain?" She picked him up so Raoul could get a good look at him.

Raoul eyed him in wonder. "He has Toinette's cheeks and mouth." The moment he spoke in an awe-filled voice, Alain squirmed. His eyes, black as poppy throats, darted toward the pond.

"I've brought something for him, Nathalie." He pulled the little sailboat out of the bag.

She smiled. "Oh, look, Alain."

When the toddler switched directions again, Raoul handed him the toy. "Here's a *bateau* for you."

"Can you say *bateau*, sweetheart?" He started turning it around in his hands. "You'll have to play with it when you're taking your bath."

Between the way she loved her nephew, and the incredible sight of seeing father and son meet each other for the first time, Dominic's heart was melting on the spot.

"Look, Alain. *Canards!*"

As she pointed to some that had come close to the edge, Alain pointed too. *"Cans."*

"Yes. Lots and lots of them. And now you've got this *bateau."*

"Bat!" he burst out, causing all three of them to chuckle.

Her eyes met Raoul's. "He knows about eight words. So far all of them are one syllable."

Raoul grinned. "What does he call you?"

"Nat."

"And your mother?"

"Gran."

"I'm anxious to meet her."

"She feels exactly the same way." Nathalie lowered Alain to the grass. "Let's walk over to the bench where we left our bag and feed the *canards."*

Alain toddled alongside her in his sandals, clutching his toy. He had a lean build like his father all right. Anyone at the park would think father and son were enjoying the sunshine with Nathalie. Once more Dominic thanked providence that she'd never been with his cousin.

She pulled out a bag of wheat grains provided by the park. Raoul took some and threw them near one of the ducks. It was eaten immediately. That prompted Alain to do the same thing.

While the two were happily occupied, Dominic walked over to Nathalie and put his arm around her shoulders. "This is a moment my cousin will remember all his life, and you're the reason for it."

She lifted those light green eyes that were filled with

spiration to find him. Thank heaven for the woman in you who was willing to pick grapes on enemy territory to achieve a result like this. My heart almost stopped beating when this exquisite woman handed me her application. I haven't been the same since."

"Mine almost stopped too," she admitted. "I couldn't believe I was looking at the man I thought could be Alain's father."

Dominic sucked in his breath. "Raoul lost his raison d'être when he had to give up Antoinette and then lose his child, even if he found out Céline wasn't his. You don't know it yet, but learning he has a son has made him feel reborn. He'll praise you forever for what you've done."

They could hear Raoul's chuckle before Alain came running back to Nathalie and wrapped his arms around her legs. She smiled down at him. "Did you have fun?"

Raoul followed with a smile that filled his handsome features with happiness. "I want to see him every day."

"I *want* you to," Nathalie cried with excitement.

"I could come every lunch hour."

"That would be perfect! Minerve, the nanny who takes care of him while my mother and I are at the pharmacy, could plan to meet you here. She drives a red car. We'll tell her about you. If you come here tomorrow at noon, I'll take off work so you can meet her.

He's already seen ___ ___ ___ "I don't know how to
for him tom ___ you for what you've done, but I'll find
a way."

Ra___

"After close to seventeen long months it's been my
joy to unite you at last. Now if you'll forgive me, I can
tell he's hungry. I need to take him home."

"Understood."

Dominic watched his cousin hunker down to look
at Alain close up. The love in his black eyes was alive.
"I'll see you tomorrow, *mon fils*."

Nathalie put the sailboat in her bag, then picked
up Alain and waved to them. Alain copied her. Raoul
walked with her and helped put Alain in his car seat.
After Nathalie drove off, Raoul strode to Dominic's car
with an illuminated expression of joy.

When he climbed inside, he turned to him. "Tell me
I didn't dream this up. It's like having a part of Toinette
back. Tomorrow I'll talk to Nathalie about a DNA test. I
already love him in a way I didn't know was possible."

That was the way Dominic felt about Nathalie.

"I'm beyond happy for you, Raoul. That rose-colored
villa with the swimming pool we saw is looking better and better. I can see a little boy and his father having fun out there with a bunch of colored *bats*." They
both laughed. "Why don't we stop by the Realtor on
our way home?"

"You're reading my mind, Dom. I want to put in an
offer before anyone else takes it off the market. Sabine

plans to wipe me out, but no matter what, I have a son to love and raise. Because of circumstances, I've missed out on Toinette's pregnancy and seventeen months of Alain's life. Never again. There's no way I'm letting the divorce rob me of another second to be the father my son needs."

While Dominic waited for him outside the realty office, he texted Nathalie.

I have to see you tonight. Will you be at the pharmacy?

Her answer wasn't long in coming.

No. I'll be home.

That was good news.

I'll come by your house and pick you up at seven. No excuses, Nathalie. Alain's existence changes things for all of us. One way or another we're family now.

This was only the beginning.
She texted back.

You're right. Let your cousin know that tomorrow Maman will come to the park too so she can meet him.

Raoul would be thrilled.
He texted her again.

Parfait! A demain, ma belle.

* * *

Ma belle…

Dominic had never used that endearment with her before.

Nathalie looked down at Alain, who'd just fallen asleep in his crib holding the *bateau*. Too much was happening too fast, but it was the result she'd wanted, even if she hadn't realized it until now.

Today the world had shifted. There'd be no adoption. Alain belonged to Raoul. At the pond, his rightful *papa* had claimed him. In a millisecond, he had become a true Fontesquieu. Nathalie knew in her heart her stepsister would be overjoyed to see her son and the man she'd loved together forever.

But now Nathalie had to make a drastic decision about what to do with the rest of her life. Her mother had done the heavy lifting after Alain had come into their lives. She would always want to live near her grandson and Raoul.

The question for Nathalie was how to get through the rest of her life when she would be Alain's *tante* from now on rather than his adoptive *maman*. She and her mother would have to help Raoul with the transition once Alain went to live with him. But Dominic and Raoul were closer than brothers. Dominic would always be around. Nathalie couldn't imagine how that would work.

She couldn't bear the pain of living this close to Dominic's orbit. Though they hadn't made love, it was what had been in her mind and heart that counted. She'd pushed thoughts of Antoinette away when she'd been

a new in. arms. If he had thoughts of marriage, she
ning into him. Nathalie owned La Gaude and start
when he learned she couldn't give
enough money to rent an apartment. She should be liv-
danger of run-
ing on her own now anyway. It would have to be close
enough to still be able to visit her mother without difficulty. They could plan times together when Alain would
be there with her.

For the rest of Tuesday afternoon, Nathalie got on the
computer to look for jobs available for pharmacists in
the greater Provence area. Before her mother returned
from work, she'd found an opening at a privately owned
pharmacy in Menton, a city of twenty-five thousand on
the French Riviera. The hour's drive from La Gaude
would be perfect. They needed a pharmacist full time
and the pay sounded good.

Nathalie applied for it online. She believed her
mother and Denis would get along just fine without
her, and they could always hire another pharmacist to
help out.

Knowing she'd done this much to plan out a new future for herself helped Nathalie to find the courage she'd
need to face Dominic with the truth about her condition
when he came by for her this evening. It was time to get
ready. She'd watch for his car and hurry outside. One
day her mother would meet Dominic, but not tonight.

CHAPTER TEN

DOMINIC PULLED UP in front of the Gilbert home. Today the stakes had changed. Their lives were about to be transformed forever.

Even before he shut off the engine, Nathalie came walking out to his car wearing a stunning gold-on-green print dress. His breath caught at the shape of her gorgeous figure. Her hair caught the fire of the setting sun. No other woman matched her beauty inside or out.

He leaned across the seat and opened the door for her. She climbed inside, bringing her delicious floral scent with her. "Thank you, Dominic." She wouldn't look at him.

Without telling her his plans, he drove down the street.

"Where are we going?"

"I'm taking you to Vence. There's something I want you to see. It won't take long."

"I'd rather we didn't. Can't we stay here? All I want to know is if your cousin is truly happy."

He darted her a glance. "You already know the answer to that question. But tonight I don't want to talk about Raoul. You and I have other business that's only important to us."

"No, we don't!" she cried, turning to look out the passenger window.

"That's what you think."

"I only agreed to see you in order to work out arrangements for Raoul."

"Tonight I want to talk about us." Since he could tell she was attempting to shut him out, he turned on the radio to a soft rock music station. It didn't take long to reach Vence.

He wound around to a street on the heights of the city with a panoramic view of the sea. The modern white villa peeking out from the cypress trees had appealed to him while he'd been house hunting with Raoul. Five bedrooms, three thousand square feet and a swimming pool. Everything that had been missing while he'd lived in a massive old chateau most of his life apart from those years in Paris.

Dominic pulled up in front and shut off the engine.

"Why did you stop here?" He heard that panic in her voice again.

"This villa is for sale. I'd like to know what you think of it."

"It's lovely, but it has nothing to do with me."

"It could have everything to do with you once we're married. I've been inside and think it would be the perfect home for us and the children we're going to have."

She suddenly buried her face in her hands. "I could never marry you, Dominic."

He reached across to caress her shoulder. "I could never marry anyone else. I'm madly in love with you."

"A marriage between us isn't possible."

"Give me one good reason why."

Her head lifted abruptly. She turned to him. "Because I can't give you children, and just now I heard in your voice that it's what you want most."

Pain rocked his body. "On the cruiser you said you weren't dying of a disease or anything like it."

"I'm not, but I do have a condition. It's called primary ovarian insufficiency. By twenty years of age, I'd only had one period. Amenorrhea is the name for it. The doctor put me through a series of tests. Since that time I've only ovulated twice and I'm twenty-seven. I'm one of the five to ten percent of cases that happens to younger women. It means pregnancy will pretty well require a miracle. You don't want to marry me."

"Nathalie—"

"There's nothing you can say to make me change my mind. Right now I'm in so much pain, I can't be around you. Please take me home."

Devastated that she could be this tortured, he had no choice but to drive her back to La Gaude. There had to be a way to reach her, but it wouldn't be right now. He needed to come up with a plan. Silence filled the interior all the way back to her house.

When he drove up in front, she turned to him. "What I wanted to tell you when I came out to the car earlier was to please ask Raoul to deal with me and my mother from now on. There's no reason for you to act as the go-between any longer. You've had more to deal with than any man should have to."

"Doesn't it matter to you that I fell in love with you and wanted to do whatever I could to be with you?"

"That's because you're the most decent and honorable man I've ever known." Her voice trembled. "You were always wonderful to me even when you suspected I'd applied for work with ulterior motives. Just look what I did, Dominic. I suspected three men of being Alain's father and tried to prove it. Who does something like that?" she blurted in pain.

Dominic grasped her hand in exasperation. "How can you say that when you brought about the miracle that restored your stepsister's boy to his birth father?"

She shook her head. "It doesn't matter. I'm so honored you would want to marry me, but you deserve a woman who can give you children." She eased her hand away, then opened the door.

Talk about agony.

"I'm sure we'll see each other accidentally from time to time over the years. I have no doubt Alain will get to know you and love you. Between his father and you, he'll have the greatest role models in the world to learn from. It's so much more than I could have hoped for when I started down this slippery slope."

Dominic watched her get out and disappear inside the house. If another miracle didn't happen fast…

He drove back to the chateau needing help before he drowned.

CHAPTER ELEVEN

THE MEETING AT the park on Wednesday was an emotional one for Nathalie. Her mother had been bowled over by Raoul, who'd come alone to meet her and Minerve. They planned to go to the hospital on Thursday at noon for the DNA tests. It wouldn't be long before Alain became the newest official member of the Fontesquieu family.

Nathalie was thankful Dominic had gotten the message and didn't accompany his cousin. She couldn't have handled seeing him today.

This time Raoul had brought a little toy car for Alain, bringing a smile to his adorable face. The two of them proceeded to throw more food to the ducks. Already Nathalie could tell a bonding was taking place between father and son.

When her mother and Minerve started walking Alain to her mother's car, he didn't want to go. He'd been having too much fun with his *papa*.

Raoul helped him in the car seat, then asked Nathalie to stay for a minute after they'd driven off. "Before you go, there's something else we have to talk about."

Nathalie knew what it was. Her heart sank. "I'm sorry, but I've got to get to the pharmacy. Denis is alone right now."

"Can you give me five minutes? This is an emergency."

"If you mean Dominic—"

"You know I do," he interrupted her. "He came home last night a shattered man. You can't do this to him. Your fear about being unable to have children is unwarranted when it comes to Dominic."

"You don't know that. The man I thought I would marry couldn't handle it."

"You don't know Dom. He loves you, and your rejection of him without giving him a chance to tell you how he feels about your condition is crucifying him. In time it's going to crucify you. I know what I'm talking about. If you shut him out, you're making the worst mistake of your life."

She switched her gaze to him. "What do you mean?"

"I had to tell your stepsister the truth when I found out Sabine was pregnant. There was no altering the outcome. I felt like a monster who didn't deserve happiness. But your situation is entirely different. Let Dom tell you what's in his heart. More than anyone in the world, I want him to be happy. He adores you, Nathalie."

Raoul's words rang so true, the tears coursed down her cheeks.

"I couldn't fix my situation, but you have every chance to find happiness with Dom. Just let him in. I'm begging you. I also believe in my soul Toinette was urging you on to find me."

"You can honestly say that?"

"As God is my witness. Dominic was the conduit. Don't you think she's been in heaven suffering because she refused to tell your family about me?"

Her heart leaped. Was that true?

"You've been an answer to prayer and I'll spend the rest of my days being the best father I can be to our child. I've been given a second chance to redeem myself, all because of you. I love you for what you've done for me and Alain, Nathalie. You were there for him all that time. His wonderful aunt."

By now she was sobbing.

"Before you leave, remember there's another man out there who loves you body and soul. Don't be afraid. Have faith in his love for you. If you don't, that would be the real tragedy. Dom told me it was love at first sight for the two of you. That good old *coup de foudre*. It caught me and Antoinette too. The four of us are a lot alike."

She nodded. They definitely were.

"Don't you think it's time you let Dom out of his prison? He's the reason my miracle happened to me. I'm pleading with you not to let him spend another night in hell. That's where he was last night. I know because I was with him and felt utterly helpless to comfort him. He's waited twenty-nine years for a woman like you to love him."

Nathalie kept wiping her eyes. She wanted to believe him.

"I have one more piece of good news. My court date is in ten days. When it's over, then I'm taking a needed

vacation so my son and I can be together twenty-four/
seven. I've put money down on a house for us."

He and Dom had both been house hunting. The
knowledge sent another thrill of excitement through
her body.

Raoul gave her a hug and left for his car on a run.

Nathalie drove to the pharmacy in a daze. Last night
she'd filled out an application to be a pharmacist in
Menton in order to put distance between her and Dominic. But Raoul had said so many things she couldn't
dismiss, she had difficulty concentrating at work. When
it was time to close the pharmacy, she went out to her
car and headed home at top speed.

As soon as she walked in the house, she saw her
mother and Alain sitting on the living room floor playing with his building blocks. Nathalie got down with
them.

Her mother smiled at her. "Today Raoul called you
an angel. I agree. Your desire to find him means our
Alain is going to have a wonderful life with his *papa*.
He told me everything about his heartbreaking choice
back then. I have real compassion for him considering
the kind of family he's come from."

"I can't blame him either, Maman." She put another
block on Alain's.

"Antoinette could have looked all over and never
found a man more exceptional. He's so crazy about
Alain already, it's extraordinary. I can only think of one
other besides your father who's his equal."

They stared at each other. "You mean Dominic."

"You know that's who I mean. You never gave up

and he never let you. If that isn't love, then I don't know anything."

"You know a lot."

"Then stop worrying you can't have children. We've been through a lot of sadness and grief over the last two and a half years. It's time we filled this house with real happiness. Finding Raoul is just the beginning."

Nathalie got to her feet. "Do you have Raoul's phone number?"

"Yes. He gave me his business card with his cell phone number. It's in the kitchen on the counter."

"Thanks." She tousled Alain's curls before walking in the other room. Once she'd put the number in her own phone, she texted him.

Do you know where Dominic is tonight?

Raoul answered back so fast it took her by surprise.

Dom and I have a meeting with Etienne at the Tour de l'Est. There's been a problem with the latest batch of wine. We'll be on our way in a minute. I'll keep you posted.

In her mind's eye she knew the location of the Tour de l'Est. It was a massive round tower on the property. In her readings she'd learned that the land deeded to the Fontesquieux contained some battlements from the fifteenth century. Since they'd cleared out the old weapons and munitions from the east tower, its eight-foot-thick walls with rooms on four floors had been used to store their wine.

Now that she'd found the courage to talk to Dominic, she groaned to think he wasn't available.

She sent another text.

Thanks. Please don't tell him I asked about him.

In came his response.

Your secret is safe with me.

The blood hammered in her ears as she made the decision to drive to Vence tonight and take a look at the tour. Maybe she'd be able to catch him. After putting on one of her favorite dresses, she hurried into the living room.

"Maman? I'm leaving for the vineyard. I might be late."

Her mother smiled at her. "I hope you are. That man has brought a light to your eyes that has never been there before."

She took a quick breath. "I love you, Maman." Nathalie leaned over to kiss them both and raced out the front door.

Dominic had just left the office for the Tour de l'Est with Raoul in his Jaguar when he received a call from their grandfather.

Raoul darted him a glance. "Aren't you going to get it?"

"No. The old man's furious because I ended it with Corinne. All that money could have come to the Fontesquieu treasury. I don't live in the same universe as our *grand-père*."

"Does anyone?"

Nathalie had shown Dominic what life had to offer if you were lucky enough to meet your soul mate. He hadn't believed such a thing existed until she'd entered his world. In the short time he'd known her, she'd taught him what it was to lay down your life for someone you love. In her case, her stepsister's son. She'd risked the unknown with nothing to go on but a hope and a prayer of uniting a father and son.

Tears stung his eyelids. She might not want to be with Dominic right now, but he had to have faith that in time she would change her mind. They were meant to be together whether she could have his baby or not. He felt it to the very depths of his being. Otherwise there was little sense to life.

Raoul drove them past the winery where they could smell the fermentation before reaching the tour. A dozen cars and trucks filled the parking area. They got out and walked inside the double doors of the old battlement.

"Hey, bro." The two of them entered the vaulted conference room on the ground floor. Etienne was already there talking with a group of storage workers and managers. "Where's the fire?"

Etienne handed them each a bottle of wine. "It's always a fire with Grand-père. He insisted the three of us meet. Sorry you had to come. These bottles have undergone six rackings over thirty-day intervals and still have a problem. Take a look."

Dominic examined his. "You're right. The wine has failed to clear."

"As I indicated on the phone, it's definitely nonspecific. I don't think any bacterial contamination is at work. In my opinion it will probably clear, but it may take up to a year or so."

"Unfortunately Grand-père doesn't want to wait that long." Raoul had checked his bottle. "He's always in such a damn hurry. There's one thing we can do right now."

Dominic nodded. "Arrange for the wine to be moved. Store it in a cooler place for several weeks. All that's required is a drop in temperature of ten degrees. If nothing changes, we'll come up with plan B."

"That's the route I'd go."

"Then we're all in agreement." Etienne gave the group instructions and they left. He walked back to Dominic and Raoul. "I'll let the old man know what we decided as soon as I get home so he won't have a fit. Sophie's come down with a cold. I need to spend some time with her before bed. Thanks for coming. See you later."

After he left, Dominic stared at his cousin. "Pretty soon you'll be able to tell everyone about your son and you'll be putting him to bed in your new house. Just think. When Alain grows up, he might become a wine expert like you."

"He might hate the wine business."

"Maybe he'll become a pharmacist like his grandfather Gilbert."

"True. I can promise you one thing. I'll allow Alain to find his own way in life, whatever it is."

"You think I don't know that?"

Raoul nodded. "The divorce can't come soon enough for me. How about we go to the Guinguet before we go home? That's where I met Toinette and want a night to reminisce."

Just the mention of it reminded Dominic of his conversation about red wine with Nathalie. Everything reminded him of her. He couldn't deal with any more pain. "I don't know, Raoul. I'm lousy company."

"I'll take your lousy company over anyone else's. Come on. We could use some noise and music." They walked out to the car in the cooler night air. The beginning of the harvest had brought Nathalie with it. Now the grapey fragrance meant the harvest was almost at an end and the fruit was being turned into wine. The thought of it being over with her was untenable. He wanted her so badly, he was in agony.

Soon they arrived at the bistro where many of the Fontesquieu employees hung out. Unfortunately, Nathalie dominated his thoughts. His cousin had the right idea to keep him occupied until he went to bed. But nothing could be done about the empty nights.

"Tonight calls for a celebration." Raoul called the waiter over. He ordered some tapas and their best rosé wine. Dominic had never seen him so jubilant. After such a tragic marriage, he understood his cousin's euphoria. But he hoped the family wouldn't get wind of anything until after the divorce was final. One word about Alain could bring new pain to Sabine and make things uglier.

In a few minutes their waiter came to the table with their order, but he also placed a small goblet of white wine in front of both of them.

Raoul shook his head. "I didn't order this."

"It's compliments of *la blonde exquise*. She's over at the bar."

They both turned around. Dominic almost went into cardiac arrest to see Nathalie walk toward them in a filmy violet dress, holding a similar goblet. His gaze collided with the jewel green of hers.

"Welcome to the Guinguet, messieurs. I thought you might enjoy the special Guinguet wine made by the famous Fontesquieu family. I'm buying this evening. It's an acquired taste to be enjoyed for a very important occasion. You two fine-looking specimens appear to be able to handle its unique flavor."

She leaned over to click each of their goblets with hers. "Here's to a harvest with unexpected bumper crops. Our family historians will be forced to add two new names to our family trees. *Salut.*"

"Nathalie!" Dominic cried as her words sank in.

She smiled into his eyes. "Drink up, *mon amour.*"

He watched her put the goblet to her lips before he had the presence of mind to drink his. For the first time in his life, the sour wine tasted like ambrosia.

With a secret glance, Nathalie wordlessly acknowledged Raoul's departure from the bistro. Then she slid into the chair he'd just vacated. After she fed Dominic a tapa, she ate one. Suddenly Dominic reached across the small round table for her hands, grasping them for dear life.

"What happened since the last time you claimed you couldn't be with me?"

"Your cousin spoke to my heart. He said there was a man out there who loved me body and soul. To quote him, 'Don't be afraid. Have faith in his love for you. If you don't, that would be the real tragedy.' I knew it was true and came as fast as I could to find you."

Dominic's black eyes burned with love for her. "Let's get out of here. I need to hold you so I can believe this is really happening."

He got up and pulled her to her feet. Still gripping her hand, he drew her through the crowd to the outside of the bistro. "Where's your car?"

"Around the corner."

"How did you know I was at the Guinguet?"

"I followed you and Raoul from the tour after I'd texted him earlier. He told me you would be there."

A painful squeeze of her hand told her how happy that had made him. They were both out of breath when they reached the Peugeot. "Mind if I drive?"

"I want you to. I'm shaking too hard to get behind the wheel."

Dominic helped her in, then hurried around and got in the driver's seat. He had to adjust it to accommodate his long, powerful legs. She handed him the keys. Within seconds he'd started the engine and drove out to the street.

Nathalie didn't care where they were going. She

clung to his hand, dying to get in his arms and stay there. As he drove them to the heights of the city, she knew where they were going. The moon shone down on the beautiful site of the white villa surrounded by the dark cypress trees.

"I've bought the place, so it means we're private here."

"You already did?"

"Yes. No matter how long it took for you to come back to me, I wanted it for us."

"Darling—"

He pulled into the driveway and drove up to the side of the villa. In the next breath, he turned off the car and reached for her. "Do you have any idea how long I've been waiting for this? I'm only going to say this once. We'll adopt as many babies as we want when we decide it's right. What matters is that we'll be man and wife. Do you hear me?"

"Yes, darling."

He lowered his mouth to hers in an explosion of needs they'd had to repress.

She moaned aloud. "Dominic... I love you so much you can't imagine," she cried, giving him kiss for kiss until they were devouring each other.

Time became meaningless as they attempted to appease their hunger, but the fire kept building. Over and over again their passion engulfed them. He was such a gorgeous man in every way, no amount of love she could shower on him would ever be enough. Every touch of his hands and mouth ignited her senses.

From the first moment she'd looked into his eyes at

the interview, he'd brought her alive. Until then she'd been in a deep sleep, but no longer. He was the answer to her existence.

"You're the most beautiful thing to come into my life, *mon tresor*," he murmured, kissing her with abandon. "I'm so crazy in love with you, I don't know how long I can wait for our marriage."

"I feel the same way and never want to be apart from you again."

He cupped her face in his hands. "Let's have a wedding as soon as possible with your mother as witness."

She fingered his luxuriant black hair. "What about your family?"

"I'm afraid we'll have to leave them out of it. Tell me you understand."

"Of course I do," she cried without hesitation. Eleven years away from his family was explanation enough.

"You're incredible," he cried, kissing her with increasing hunger.

"Tomorrow I'll tell Maman we're getting married right away."

"How about Sunday, four days from now?"

"If only we could."

He kissed the base of her throat, then her mouth. "I know a justice of the peace whose funds I've managed on the side since my return from Paris. Andre Godin is now a wealthy man. When I ask him to marry us at your house, bypassing the usual waiting time, he'll do it."

She hugged him harder. "I'm convinced you can do anything you wonderful, wonderful man." Nathalie could cry for joy over what was happening.

He gave her another long, hard kiss. "I'm thinking that while we furnish the villa, we'll stay at a hotel in La Gaude so you're close to Alain during the transition and can go on working at the pharmacy."

"Maman will love that."

"When Raoul's divorce is final, we'll have a big party for all our families and friends. Whether my family shows up or not will be up to them. After that we'll take a honeymoon. For now it will be enough to be your husband."

It sounded like heaven on earth. Beyond words, Nathalie covered his mouth with her own. Again they were lost in the thrill of knowing they would become one in just a few days. Nothing else mattered.

"I know you need to get home," he eventually whispered against her lips. "I'll drive us to the chateau for my car and follow you home."

"I'll be fine."

"Let me be the judge of that. You're the most precious thing in my life. If anything were to go wrong now, I wouldn't survive. Do you hear what I'm saying?"

"Yes. Oh, yes!"

CHAPTER TWELVE

ON THE RIDE home from La Gaude, Dominic made a few important phone calls and constructed a list of all the other things he had to do before Sunday. Near midnight, he let himself in the apartment so euphoric over the miraculous outcome at the Guinguet, it took him time to realize Raoul wasn't there.

Eager to share the news of his impending marriage with his cousin, he texted him. Within a minute his phone rang. He clicked on. "Raoul? I just got home. Where are you?"

"I've been in Nice, but I'm back on the estate. See you shortly." He clicked off fast.

His cousin didn't sound at all like himself. Raoul's jubilance of earlier had vanished. Worried about the change in him, Dominic went to the kitchen to make them coffee. They had a lot to talk about.

"Dom?"

"In the kitchen."

His cousin walked in. "I can't tell you how happy I am for you, Dom. I knew Nathalie would come around."

"You had a lot more faith in her than I did." He put

their coffee on the table, but when he glanced at Raoul, he saw a man in pain. "Sit down and tell me what's wrong."

"Horace contacted me after I left the bistro and told me I'd better come to his office in Nice because there was a problem."

"Has Sabine demanded more money?"

"She's demanding that the two of us go to counseling to try to save our marriage, claiming she still loves me. Her reason is that with professional help we could start over again."

Dominic sat back in the chair. "Counseling? That doesn't sound like Sabine."

"No. It sounds like both sets of parents have gotten together to try to stop the divorce. Hell, Dom!" He shot to his feet, raking a hand through his hair. "No amount of counseling can make me love Sabine. That's what I told Horace."

"Does he know about Alain?"

"Not yet."

"What's he going to do?"

"Respond with my answer to the judge. But Horace imagines she'll come back with possibly a hundred million dollars in damages since our family has billions. Horace said he'll hammer out the best settlement he can."

"Whatever the judge decrees, you know I'll help."

"You're the best, Dom, but it's my problem and I'll have to solve it. One good thing did come out of tonight's meeting. He's still asking for the same court date that was set."

"Good. For Alain's sake you need to be divorced ASAP."

A glimmer of a smile broke out on his face. "So when are you two getting married?"

"This Sunday."

He shook his head. "When you make up your mind about something, there's no stopping you. How can I help?"

"You already have. Nathalie told me your talk with her reached her heart. None of this would be happening without you. We're going to have a ceremony at her house with her mom and Minerve. That's it. Andre Godin will officiate. And within less than two weeks your divorce will be final."

"God willing, Dom."

"Nathalie Durand Fournier, do you take Dominic Laurent Fontesquieu to be your husband in sickness and in health? Do you vow to love and cherish him for all the days of your life?"

She couldn't believe this moment had come. Her heart was so full of love for Dominic she really did have trouble breathing. With those dark eyes and hair, and wearing an elegant dove-gray suit, he was so gorgeous it didn't seem possible she'd won the love of this man.

"I do," she cried softly.

With a smile, the judge turned to Dominic. "Dominic Laurent Fontesquieu, do you take Nathalie Durand Fournier to be your wife, in sickness and in health, always watching over her, loving her and protecting her for as long as you both shall live?"

"I do," he answered in a thick voice.

"Then by the power invested in me, I now pronounce you man and wife. What God has brought together, let no man put asunder. You may now kiss your bride, Dominic."

Her new husband pulled her into his arms and kissed her with such hunger her legs started to tremble.

When he finally let her go, the judge said, "You may now present each other with rings."

Dominic drew a diamond ring out of his jacket pocket and slid it home on her ring finger. It had a dazzling sparkle as she took the gold band from her little finger and put it on his ring finger. The engraving said *Mon Bien Amie*.

He kissed her deeply again before relinquishing her once more.

The judge beamed at them. "It has been my pleasure to marry a man I've highly esteemed for years." He gazed at Nathalie. "How I envy him."

She felt the heat rise into her face. "Thank you, Your Honor."

He shook Dominic's hand, then said a few words to her mother before leaving the house.

"Oh, darling." Her mother ran to her and they hugged. "It was a beautiful ceremony and you look so lovely."

"So do you, Arlette," Dominic murmured. "Now I know where Nathalie gets her fabulous looks." He gave her a hug.

Alain made some noises that caused them to turn around. He was getting restless. Minerve had been holding him during the short ceremony. Nathalie's mother reached for him so Nathalie could hug Minerve. She'd been a part of their family for a long time.

"I'm so happy for you, Nathalie." On a whisper, she said, "If he were my husband, I don't think I'd ever be able to let him out of my sight."

"I won't if I can help it."

Dominic hugged Minerve. "Thank you for supporting us and for being so good to Raoul. You've made all the difference while he's been bonding with Alain."

The older woman's eyes filled. "This has been a happy time for all of us. I hope his divorce is final soon. I know he wants to show off his son to everyone."

"It'll happen before long," Nathalie chimed in. She looked at her mother. "Now we're going to leave, but I'll be at the pharmacy in the morning as planned."

"It doesn't seem right that you can't go off on a honeymoon, but I understand what's at risk here."

After knowing how difficult Raoul's life had been when he'd met Antoinette, her mother knew it was vital everything stay secret for a while longer. None of them wanted anything to go wrong at this point.

Nathalie gave Alain a kiss and hug, then hurried out the door with Dominic carrying an overnight bag.

The Soleil Hotel was only two minutes away from Nathalie's house. That was good because Dominic couldn't last any longer before he got his bride all to himself. She looked a vision in a white silk and lace wedding dress that came to the knees of her shapely legs.

He parked the car and walked her inside to their room

down the left hall. Each room had a balcony that overlooked La Gaude. Earlier that morning he'd procured the card key and had arranged for flowers to be put on the dresser and table.

Once inside their room, he lowered their overnight bags to the floor and caught her around the waist from behind. "You're trapped now, *ma belle*. There's no escape."

She whirled around, her green eyes burning with love for him. "I have news for you, *mon amour*. I told Minerve I'd never let you out of my sight and I meant it."

Slowly he unpinned the gardenia corsage he'd given her. After he'd unfastened the buttons of her wedding dress, she slipped out of it while he removed his suit jacket and tie.

"I love you, Dominic. You'll never know how much."

He studied her exquisite features, taking his time. "We have all day and night to show each other I can't wait any longer."

"I don't want to wait," she cried.

He picked her up in his arms and carried her through the sitting room to the bedroom. Once he'd followed her down on the bed, he lifted a lock of hair to his lips. "Do you know you have strands of gold and silver? You're like a princess come to life with your hair splayed around you. And you have a perfect mouth. When we met in the tent, I couldn't take my eyes off you. You beguiled me."

"You enchanted me." She kissed his jaw. "When I left the tent, I wasn't the same woman who'd gone in. I didn't know a man like you existed."

"By some miracle we've found each other. I swear I'll love you forever, *mon coeur*." Burning with desire for her, he lowered his head to kiss her seductive mouth. At the first touch he was gone. Her response enraptured him, sending him to a different world where all that mattered was to love and be loved.

The sun was going down by the time Nathalie became aware she was lying against her husband's rock-hard body. Dominic's legs had trapped hers and his arm lay across her hip possessively. No woman on earth would ever know this kind of joy because there was only one Dominic. Being loved by him made her feel immortal.

Nathalie wanted to know his possession again and started kissing him. They'd married a lot sooner than many couples, but that was part of the fascination of loving him and learning new things about him.

"Nathalie," he murmured. Suddenly he'd come awake and pulled her on top of him. "No man ever had a lover like you. To think you're my wife!" He started to kiss her again, filling her with rapture.

The room had grown dark by the time they came awake again. She eased reluctantly out of his arms. "It's almost ten o'clock, Dominic. We haven't eaten all day. You must be starving. I'll call for room service."

While she reached for the house phone and put in an order for meat crêpes, crème brûlée and coffee, he'd gone in the other room for their bags. When he returned, he was wearing a striped robe, and he answered the door to bring in their food.

They ate in bed. She faced him. "I've never been this happy in my life. If my stepsister hadn't loved Raoul the way she did, we would never have met. The thought of that…" She couldn't finish.

"I don't like to think about it either, so we won't." He moved the tray to the floor, then pulled her into him. "I've been so impatient to make you my wife we haven't talked about the practicalities of being married."

She raised up on her elbow. "You sound worried."

"In a way I am. Your mother lost your stepdaughter, then your stepsister. Soon Alain will be living with his father. Today I took you away from her. I want both of you to be happy."

Tears stung her eyes. She was married to the most remarkable man in the world. Nathalie flung her arms around him. "I love you for thinking of her and caring about her. There's no one like you, but La Gaude isn't that far away from Vence. We'll work things out."

"What if she moved to Vence? I'd help her get into a house near our villa. She wouldn't have to work anymore and could have time for friends as well as being a grandmother. Raoul's house is only two streets away from us. I'd like to be there for her and offer support if the idea appealed to her."

She shook her head in disbelief. "You're so generous and amazing. What did I ever do to deserve you?"

"I keep asking that question about you. The women who've been in my life have been so different from you. There's nothing shallow about you. You're an exceptional woman in every way, Nathalie. It means you've had exceptional parents. I see the way you are with Alain. The love you've shown him is a revelation."

"He's easy to love," she said in a broken voice.

"The day I saw you get him out of your car, he reached for your hand. I thought he was your son. There was a tenderness in the way you treated him. It was a defining moment for me where you're concerned and brought tears to my heart. I knew at that moment I loved you desperately."

"Oh, Dominic." She half sobbed and clung to him. "Do you know when I knew I loved you forever? I was telling you about the man I was trying to find. And even after you thought I loved him, you offered to help look for him because that's the kind of unselfish person you are. You even said you'd talk to your vintner friends. You don't know what that did to me. That day, like all the others with you, will live in my memory."

"Nathalie—"

He caught her to him and started making love to her again. Far into the night he swept her away. She couldn't believe it when morning came. He was already awake, kissing her so she'd wake up.

"It couldn't be time to go to work!"

"I'm afraid it is."

"I can't leave you."

"You think I want to let you go? But we'll have tonight. I'll pick you up at five."

"I can't bear to leave you, but I have to. I'd better hurry and shower."

"Go right ahead. Of course, I'd be happy to help

you." His grin turned her heart over. "But it might make you late for work by six or seven hours."

Blushing from head to toe, she grabbed the robe he'd taken off and ran to the bathroom to get ready. Within ten minutes they were both dressed and walking out to his car.

En route to the pharmacy, she clung to his hand. "If this is the way it's going to be from now on, I can't do it. Leaving your arms this morning has been agony."

"How do you think I feel? I'll be in my office all day watching the clock until it's time to come and get you. My assistant, Theo, will tell me to go home because I'm worthless. This is why we're going to need a honeymoon soon."

"Where will we go? I don't know if I want it to be far away. Traveling to get someplace will take time away from lying in your arms."

"Then we won't go anywhere. We'll just stay home and go out on the cruiser for weeks on end. We'll explore the other sites of Les Calanques to our hearts' content." He'd pulled up in front of the pharmacy.

"Do you promise?"

He caught her to him and kissed her long and sensuously. "Anything you want."

She kissed his jaw before getting out of the car. "There's nothing else in life I want but you."

"In that case, be ready to leave Vence right after work. I'll pack for you."

Her eyes lit up. "What have you got planned?"

"You'll find out."

"Dominic—"

"I've cleared it with your mother."

He drove off, taking her heart with him.

When Dominic drove up to the pharmacy at five, his brand-new wife came running out. His heart leaped at the sight of her. Once in the car, he reached for her and kissed her with abandon. But too many onlookers caused him to relinquish her mouth.

"Let's get out of here." He started the car and merged with the traffic. "Where are you taking me?"

"To the airport. We're flying to Paris on my private jet."

Paris?

"For how long?"

"Two days. We'll eat dinner en route. I own an apartment there where we can be private and make plans for our future."

She let out a squeal of joy. "I feel like I'm in a dream."

"Before I met you, I didn't believe in dreams and planned to go back to Paris."

Nathalie gazed at him in alarm. "When?"

"Once the harvest was over. My father has recovered and I had no desire to remain on the estate any longer. In fact, the morning I had to help do Etienne's job at the tent, I was already making plans to leave for good. And then you sat down in front of me, and every coherent thought left my mind but one. *Who was this gorgeous creature who'd come out of nowhere?* Suddenly the idea of leaving Vence held no appeal. That was longest weekend of my life waiting for Monday to roll around so I could talk to you. Until I saw you, I'd been holding my breath for fear you'd changed your mind and wouldn't come."

She leaned closer and put her hand on the back of his neck. "There was no chance of that, *mon amour*, not after meeting the most exciting man to ever come into my life. Whether you were Antoinette's lover or not, I knew I had to see you again and get to know you no matter how brazen I was. I had no willpower where you were concerned."

He reached for her hand and kissed the palm. "We were meant to be, Nathalie. Whatever life has in store for us, we'll face it together." They'd reached the Nice airport and he drove to the private jet section where his jet stood on the tarmac.

Dominic looked into her eyes. "Are you ready?"

"I was ready the moment our gazes collided beneath the tent," her voice trembled. "It was like falling into space, and you were there to catch me. Don't ever let me go."

"As if I could. You're my heart."

"And you are mine. Forever."

* * * * *

FORTUNE'S
TEXAS SURPRISE

STELLA BAGWELL

A big thank-you to animal shelters and the devoted
workers who give our needy furry friends a
special home.

Chapter One

A cold north wind swooshed past Stephanie Fortune as she stepped through the glass door of the Rambling Rose Pediatric Center, but the tiny baby bundled in a heavy blue blanket was snug and warm in her arms as she carried him down a short corridor and into the busy day-care center.

As she made her way through a large room filled with shrieks of laughter and squeals from a group of preschool children, a few of the busy staff members glanced in her direction and waved. Stephanie waved back and continued walking until she reached a wide door that led to an area designated for babies under twelve months of age.

After a short knock, the door swung wide and Alaina, a middle-age woman with a kind face, greeted her with a cheery "good morning" and immediately followed it with a disapproving eye on her thin jacket.

"Young lady, how long is it going to take you to remember you're living in Texas now, not Florida? You're going to freeze without a proper coat!"

"I haven't had time to buy any winter clothing. Besides, most of the locals tell me that spring comes early to this part of Texas. And as long as little Linus is warm and comfy that's all I care about."

Stephanie flipped the blanket off the baby's head and smiled lovingly down at the four-week-old boy. According to his pediatrician, Dr. Green, the baby had been born three to four weeks early. But thankfully, his birth weight had been enough to keep him out of neonatal care.

"It wouldn't be good for his mother to come down with a cold," Alaina said. "You might give him the sniffles."

Unfortunately, Stephanie wasn't Linus's real mother. No one in Rambling Rose, or points beyond, seemed to know where Laurel, the biological mother, had gone after she'd walked into the pediatric center and left the infant with a nurse at the front desk. Since then, Stephanie had been the boy's foster mother, and with each passing day she was beginning to regard the baby as her own son.

"I never get a cold," Stephanie assured her, then bent down her head and pressed a kiss to Linus's smooth forehead. He smelled of baby oil, powder and the formula he'd nursed only minutes before she'd made the drive into town. The scents, along with the warm weight of his little body tucked into the crook of her arm, comforted her. "And as long as Linus's mother is missing, I'm going to give him the best care I can."

"I'm sure you get tired of people asking, but have you heard any news about her?" Alaina asked.

Mixed emotions swirled inside Stephanie as she studied Linus's little pug nose, bow-shaped mouth and dark blue eyes, which were not yet developed enough to focus on much more than movements directly in front of his face. Like everyone in Rambling Rose, Stephanie hoped Linus's biological mother was alive and safe. On the other hand, she'd wanted a child of her own for a long, long time, so ever since she'd suddenly been given the chance to be a foster mother to Linus, she'd felt like her life was a dream come true. Yet, each day she had to force herself to remember that Linus didn't actually belong to her. It would be a year or more before she might get the chance to adopt him legally, and before that happened, Laurel might have a change of heart and show up to claim her son.

"No news at all," Stephanie said, answering the woman's question. "Dr. Green believes she could be suffering from postpartum depression or maybe even some sort of psychosis. But she wasn't his patient, so he's only guessing."

"Well, you're doing a wonderful job with Linus," Alaina assured her, then held out her arms for the baby. "And from what I hear you're doing a bang-up job at the Paws and Claws Animal Clinic. Frankly, I don't know how you handle both. Every time I pass the new building, the parking lot is overflowing with vehicles."

Stephanie handed over Linus and a heavy diaper bag to Alaina. "The animal clinic is very busy," she agreed. "And today is spay-and-neuter day, so we'll be even busier than usual." She glanced at a large clock hanging on the wall. "Which means I'd better be going."

Stephanie gave Linus a goodbye kiss, then hurried out of the day care. As she drove to Paws and Claws Animal Clinic, she thought about the millions of other mothers who had to leave their children at day care while they worked at a job they either loved or simply endured to help pay the bills at home.

Thankfully, Stephanie loved her job as a veterinary assistant and she didn't have to worry about making her paycheck stretch to cover essentials. She realized there were some folks around Rambling Rose who assumed she'd inherited her wealth because her last name was Fortune. But that wasn't entirely the case. She'd worked hard to acquire her college education and later support herself in her chosen profession.

In less than five minutes, Stephanie arrived at Rambling Rose's animal clinic and rescue facility. The new sprawling building that housed Paws and Claws had been built by her three brothers, who owned and operated Fortune Brothers Construction. The modern structure of white brick and brown trim was a far cry from the cramped space of the old clinic that had served the community for many years. So far, Dr. Neil and the whole staff were enjoying the updated treatment rooms and a waiting area large enough to accommodate the daily influx of patients.

Stephanie entered the building through a back entrance and went straight to a small break room to stow her jacket and handbag in a locker. As she turned the dial of the combination lock, an excited female voice sounded directly behind her right shoulder.

"Stephanie! Oh, wow, are you going to be extra glad you came to work early this morning!"

Stephanie turned away from the block of metal lockers to see Monica, a young woman who worked in the clinic's bookkeeping department. From the animated look on her face, something unusual was going on.

Combing fingers through her long, windblown red hair, Stephanie said, "I'm always extra glad to be at work, Monica. What's so different about today?"

"Because he's in the waiting room! With his dog! It been ages since he's been in the clinic and now— finally—he's back!"

Stephanie refrained from rolling her eyes as she pinned a name tag to the thin black sweater she was wearing with her blue jeans. At twenty-seven, she'd had far too many dating disappointments to let herself get excited over a man.

"He?" she asked with casual indifference. "Who is this man that's got you all gaga this morning?"

"Acton Donovan! His family owns a ranch not far from town. And believe me, Stephanie, there's no other man in Rambling Rose like him! He's cute and sexy and adorable and—"

"Whoa!" Stephanie held up a hand. The only kind of guys Stephanie had been able to find were those who'd been more concerned about their own personal wants and needs, but Monica didn't need to know that. "There's no such man that you're describing. He'd be too good to be true. And I have work to do."

She started out of the break room with Monica stalking her heels. "All right, you don't have to believe me," she said under her breath. "You'll see for yourself when Dayna brings him and his dog back to an examining room. So be prepared. That's all I can say!"

Stephanie cast her an indulgent smile. "Don't worry, Monica, I won't faint at the sight of Mr. Hunky."

"Stephanie, when it comes to men, it's like you're from another planet!" With an exasperated grunt, Monica hurried on past Stephanie and disappeared through a door to the accounting office.

Stephanie walked on toward the examining rooms, then stopped in midstride as she saw the door to the waiting room open and Dayna usher in the next patient, which, in this case, was a long-haired dog that appeared to be a mix of cocker spaniel and Australian shepherd. She was thinking how adorably cute the dog was when the owner suddenly appeared through the door, and for one ridiculous second her breath caught in her throat.

This had to be the dream man Monica had been raving about. Dressed in faded denim, dirty cowboy boots and a chocolate-brown Stetson, he was young, with a tall, lean body that could only be acquired through hard, physical labor or hours at the gym. And somehow she couldn't see this cowboy stepping his booted feet onto a treadmill or any other piece of gym machinery. No doubt those long, muscular thighs straining against his jeans had developed from hours of straddling a horse. Not a stationary bike.

"Oh, there you are, Stephanie." Dayna walked up to Stephanie and handed her a manila folder with the dog's file. "I'm taking Seymour and his owner to Exam Room 2."

Stephanie glanced over the tall blonde's shoulder to where the cowboy was standing patiently with the leashed dog. As soon as he spotted Stephanie glancing in his direction, he tipped the brim of his hat and grinned.

Oh, Lord, for once in her life, Monica might have been right. This man's looks were lethal!

Clearing her throat, she turned her attention back to Dayna. "Is Dr. Neil ready to see patients? It's a quarter to eight. I thought he'd be starting surgery already."

"Neutering and spaying is on hold for an hour or two. Dr. Neil is running late this morning—some sort of emergency at home. And we have several walk-ins already waiting. Until the doctor gets here I thought you might deal with the less serious patients."

"I'll do my best," Stephanie told her.

With the folder pressed to her chest, Stephanie stepped past Dayna and headed to the exam room. While she waited for the patient and his owner to arrive, she refrained from fidgeting with her clothes or hair. Stephanie had never been one to primp or worry about her appearance and she wasn't about to start just because she was going to meet the sexiest man in Rambling Rose.

She was plucking gloves from a box on a work counter when the door opened and Dayna ushered the man and dog into the examining room. Stephanie instantly felt the oxygen being sucked from the space around her. Either that or her lungs had forgotten how to function.

"Stephanie, this is Acton Donovan," Dayna said, introducing the cowboy. "Acton, this is Stephanie Fortune. She's Dr. Neil's right-hand man."

He cleared his throat and shot another lopsided grin in Stephanie's direction. "Excuse me, Dayna, but she, uh, doesn't look like a man to me."

Dayna glanced at Stephanie's pink face before she turned a suggestive look on the cowboy. "It's just like you to notice, Acton," she said drily. "Stephanie is Dr. Neil's number-one *assistant*. She'll take care of you—I mean, she'll take care of Seymour."

Dayna left the room and after the door had clicked closed behind her, the long, tall cowboy looked at her, his expression a bit sheepish. "Guess you can tell Dayna thinks I'm a pest."

"You two know each other?" Stephanie asked.

"Oh, sure. We went to the same school. Except that she was a few grades ahead of me. She thought I was a pest then, too."

"Oh? Why is that?"

One of his broad shoulders rose and fell and Stephanie's gaze automatically dropped to the front of his shirt. The blue-denim Western shirt molded to the muscular shape of his chest and torso, and for one brief second Stephanie wondered what he looked like beneath the tough fabric.

He chuckled. "I was a bit naughty back in my younger days."

He wasn't exactly old now, she thought. And even from the distance of a few feet, she could see there was a mischievous twinkle in his sky-blue eyes.

Deciding it would be best to drop the subject, she cleared her throat and walked around the examining table to where the spotted black-and-white dog was sitting close to Acton's leg.

"So what brings Seymour to the clinic today?" she asked. "Is he not feeling well?"

"He's having scratching fits. And I can't find a flea or any kind of insect on him."

As though Seymour understood the two humans were discussing him, he looked up at her and whined.

Before Stephanie approached the dog, she asked, "Is he friendly?"

"He's never bitten anyone, but he can have a nasty temper. He snaps at me whenever he wants to remind me that he's the boss. And he isn't good around strangers, and that includes Dr. Neil."

Stephanie wasn't put off by his words of warning. Most cats and dogs wanted to be friends. When they did lash out it was out of fear and the instinct to protect themselves. "Well, I have an idea that Seymour is a very smart guy and he knows I'm going to help him feel better. Don't you, Seymour?"

With her palm upward, she allowed the dog to sniff her hand. Immediately his bushy tail began to thump against the tiled floor. "What a sweet boy," she crooned, then gently stroked his head.

Acton pushed back the brim of his hat and rubbed a hand across his forehead. "Holy smoke! What did you do to him?"

"Just told him I was his friend," Stephanie replied.

She gave the dog another rub between the ears, then patted the end of the examining table. "Would you like to sit up here, Seymour, so I can take a look at you?"

The dog promptly walked over, stood on his hind legs and rested his paws on the edge of the table. Stephanie put her hands beneath his hips and lifted the dog onto the stainless-steel surface.

"Well, if that isn't the damnedest thing I've ever seen!" Acton exclaimed. "I normally have to man-handle him up there and hold him down while Dr. Neil takes care of business. Look at that traitor! He's actually enjoying this!"

Stephanie took her eyes off Seymour long enough to look at his owner, then promptly wished she hadn't. Now that he was standing only an arm's length away from her, she was bowled over by the vivid blue of his eyes and the tanned, masculine angles of his face.

He wasn't one of those pretty boys, she thought. No, there were too many little imperfections about the man to put him in that category. Like the unruly way his sandy blond hair curled around his ears and down the back of his neck, the faint white scar that marked one brown eyebrow, the way the bridge of his nose was a bit too sharp and the jut of his chin overly stubborn. But, dear heaven, put them all together and he had enough sex appeal to knock any woman off her feet.

After drawing in a deep breath, she suggested, "Perhaps you should try a different tactic. Like allowing him to choose to obey rather than forcing him into it."

The eyebrow with the scar arched upward and his reaction had Stephanie wondering if any woman ever dared to question him.

"I could give him an hour to choose to jump on that table and he'd still be sitting on the floor giving me the evil eye. You've put some sort of spell on him. Do you practice magic tricks or something?"

Stephanie turned her attention to the dog, and after checking his vitals, she began a visual inspection of his eyes, nose, teeth and coat.

"I can assure you I haven't put Seymour under any kind of spell. And, no—I'm not a magician. I don't even like magic."

"Uh, what about cowboys with unruly dogs?"

The flirtatious tone of his voice warned her not to look up, but she couldn't stop herself. The boyish grin on his face was worse than charming—it was downright sinful.

"I don't know any cowboys with unruly dogs," she said stiffly.

He laughed. "You do now."

His laughter was infectious and Stephanie had to press her lips tightly together to prevent herself from smiling back at him.

"I only met you five minutes ago. I don't know you."

"Well, we've been properly introduced. And in my case, what you see is what you get."

She didn't plan on getting anything from this man, except a bundle of rattled nerves. Which was so unlike her. She'd been around all sorts of good-looking men before and never experienced this kind of hot, shivery feeling. It was ridiculous.

"I see. No pretense or subterfuge with you," she said as she lifted back one of Seymour's ears to look inside.

"That's right, Miss Fortune. I'm one-hundred-percent genuine."

When Stephanie had first moved to Texas, she'd quickly learned that people put the *Miss* in front of a woman's name to show respect. Especially when they were speaking to an elder. But the way Acton Donovan said "Miss Fortune" made it sound downright provocative.

"That's nice to know," she replied.

She finished with Seymour's left ear and moved to the right. Across the examining table, she heard

Acton release a long sigh. Whether he was tired, or impatient, or simply bored with her, she couldn't guess.

He said, "If it's any help, he's constantly scratching underneath his neck and his belly."

"What sort of food do you give Seymour? The dry chunks?"

He named a certain brand. "Fed him that ever since he was a tiny pup. That's been four years."

"I've never heard of that brand."

"Get it at the feed-and-grain store where we buy our cattle cubes and everything else we need on the ranch."

She vaguely recalled Monica saying the Donovans owned a ranch north of town. No doubt he was experienced in dealing with large animals like cattle and horses, she thought.

"What color is the food?"

"Excuse me? I didn't know food needed to be color-coordinated with the animal that eats it."

She shot him a droll look. "It's better to be free of food coloring. Some animals are allergic, including dogs."

"Oh. Sorry. Guess that's why you're the doc's right-hand man—I mean…woman. You know a hell of a lot more than I do."

Frowning, she turned her focus back to Seymour.

He shuffled his feet. "Sorry again. I meant to say

heck. As for Seymour's food, it's just plain brown. You think what he eats is making him scratch?"

"If the food doesn't have colored pieces, it's probably fine. But I'm fairly certain he's having an allergic reaction to something. Which could be one thing or many things." She parted the fur on the dog's throat. "See? He has these irritated patches of skin in several places on his throat and underbelly."

Acton lifted his hat from his head and leaned in for a closer look at the dog, which put his face not far from the pretty vet assistant. Immediately, Seymour bared his teeth and gave Acton a warning growl.

"You damned turncoat! I'm not going to touch Miss Stephanie, so just quit your growling."

Stephanie straightened away from him and the dog. "Is this his normal behavior?"

He looked up at her and grinned. "No. He's just acting this way because he's smitten with you and jealous of me. He doesn't want me to get close to you or touch you. See, let me show you."

He reached over and placed his hand on Stephanie's arm, which promptly caused Seymour to erupt in a barking, teeth-gnashing fit.

She swiftly jerked away her arm and stepped back. "I really don't have time for this sort of... demonstration. And I honestly think you ought to leave the room so I can give your dog the treatment he needs."

Up until a few minutes ago, when Dayna had introduced the two of them, he'd never seen Stephanie Fortune. Not here in the clinic or anywhere around Rambling Rose. She didn't exactly have a Texas drawl, nor did she have a Louisianan lilt to her voice. Which meant she'd migrated here from much farther away.

He'd heard about some rich folks by the name of Fortune moving into the huge mansion on the outskirts of town. He'd also read a few articles in the local paper about Fortune Brothers Construction building the pediatric clinic and this animal clinic, but he'd never met any of the family. Acton couldn't imagine this woman being one of them, anyway. Why would someone who belonged to such a wealthy family be working in an animal clinic, handling mutts like Seymour? No, Stephanie must be from a different bunch of Fortunes, he decided.

"Okay, Miss Stephanie, no more demonstrations. I'll be good." To convince her, he moved a few feet away from Seymour and the examining table.

She darted him a wary glance, then let out a long breath and stepped tentatively back to the dog. "Just be sure you stay where you are."

Acton tried not to grin at her, but she looked so darn pretty, with a bright shade of pink splashed across her cheeks and her blue eyes flashing, that he couldn't help himself.

"I won't move a muscle," he promised. "Even if a honeybee flew in here right this minute and landed on my nose, I wouldn't even swat it away. But then, if a honeybee really did fly in here it wouldn't land on me, anyway. It would go straight to you."

A suggestive line like that would normally catch any woman's attention. Apparently Stephanie Fortune wasn't just any woman. Instead of glancing at Acton, she kept her focus firmly on Seymour.

"That's a bunch of nonsense," she said as she continued to part Seymour's long hair and examine his skin.

"Makes plenty of sense to me. Bees go straight to honey and I can tell by the way Seymour takes to you that you're sweet."

She shot him a droll look. "I'm sorry, Mr. Donovan, but this flattery you're throwing at me won't do a thing to lighten your vet bill."

He let out a good-natured groan. "And here I was trying my best to get a free visit this morning. Oh, well, Seymour's worth it."

She stroked the dog's head, then turned to the cabinet, where Seymour's medical file was lying open. As she started writing on one of the pages, she said, "That's good to hear. A loved pet is always a healthier pet."

Acton could've told her that the same went for a

man, too. But he kept the comment to himself. She didn't appear to appreciate his brand of flirting. Which might mean she had a husband or a steady boyfriend.

He'd noticed her left hand was empty of a wedding ring or anything resembling one. But given the nature of her work, she might not wear one while she was dealing with animals. He hoped his assumption was wrong. There was something about the pretty redhead that made it impossible to tear his gaze away from her. Even if she wasn't noticing a thing about him.

While Acton was carefully studying the graceful curve of her waist and hips, she suddenly walked over to the door and partially stepped into the hallway. She must have signaled for Dayna to join her because after a brief moment, Stephanie reentered the room with the other woman right behind her.

"It looks as though Seymour is suffering from allergies," Stephanie explained to Dayna. "And from Dr. Neil's notes, he's treated the dog before with shots."

"So what now?" Acton asked. "Can you give him the medicine he needs or do I need to wait around until Dr. Neil gets here?"

Stephanie looked at him. "I can give him what he's been prescribed before. Or you can wait until Dr. Neil comes."

"And at this point, we don't know when that might be," Dayna interjected.

"I'll take my chances with you, Miss Fortune." He winked at her. "Seymour obviously trusts you."

The serious expression on her face never wavering, she turned to Dayna and instructed her as to what sort of medications she needed for the dog.

"I'll be right back with them," Dayna said, then warned Stephanie, "But while I'm gone don't listen to a word Acton says. He's a wolf disguised in cowboy clothing."

"Aww, Dayna, don't be telling Miss Fortune scary stuff like that. I'll never get her to like me."

"Ha!" Dayna laughed and gave him a backward wave as she hurried out of the examining room.

With Dayna gone, Acton glanced at Stephanie, but her attention was riveted on Seymour. What did a man have to do to get a smile out of the woman? Stand on his head or walk on his hands? Maybe she just didn't like cowboys. The thought bummed him out more than he cared to admit.

"Dayna is joking," he said. "I'm not really a wolf. See? I don't have fangs, at all."

To his delight, she looked up at him and he gave her an extra wide smile to show his teeth.

"I'm quite certain you're not a member of the *Canis lupus* family, Mr. Donovan," she said primly.

He shook his head and wondered why he wanted Stephanie Fortune to notice him. Not as Seymour's owner, but as a man. She wasn't his type at all. He liked fun girls who naturally smiled and laughed. This woman was as serious as a judge.

"No one calls me Mr. Donovan. I'd be pleased if you'd just call me Acton. And if I knew what a *Canis lupus* was, then I might know what you're really thinking about me, uh, being a wolf."

To his surprise, the corners of her mouth lifted with something like amusement. "*Canis lupus* means *dog wolf.*"

"Oh. That's good. Because I'm as gentle as a little pup."

She looked as though she was about to reply to that when Dayna suddenly stepped back into the room carrying a needle, a syringe and a fat jar.

Before Seymour had a clue what was happening, Stephanie had already pulled up the skin on the back of his neck and injected him with the medicine.

"Amazing. Purely amazing," he said with disbelief. "I'd have to chase Seymour all over the county to do that." He looked at Dayna and winked. "Does she put spells on all the animals who come to the clinic?"

"Ninety percent of them," Dayna agreed. "She has the touch."

Stephanie opened the jar of ointment and began to swipe it on the worst of the raw spots on Seymour's skin. "Do you think you can do this twice a day? It will help stop the itching and heal the skin."

"We'll probably end up in a wrestling match, but I'll try."

"Any amount you can manage to put on him will help." She put the lid back on the jar and jumped the dog off the examining table. "Seymour is ready to go home. If he doesn't seem to be improving in a couple of days, then we'll need to see him again."

She handed Seymour's leash and the jar of ointment over to Acton, and with the dog walking alongside him, he followed the two women out of the examining room and back to the waiting area, where a payout counter was located next to the check-in desk.

"Don't wait so long to come see us again, Acton," Dayna said. "We can always use a smiling face around here."

"I have a feeling I'll be back soon." He glanced around to see Stephanie squatted on her heels, giving Seymour a goodbye hug. Too bad he wasn't a dog, Acton thought.

Leaving the dog, she stepped forward and handed an itemized bill to the young woman behind the counter, then turned and extended a hand to him.

He wrapped his hand around hers and was totally enchanted by the incredibly soft skin pressed against his, and the gaze of her deep blue eyes connecting with his. Acton could've stood there until the cows came home. Unfortunately, she had other ideas.

Easing her hand from his, she stepped back. "It was nice meeting you, Acton. I'm glad you brought Seymour to the clinic to be treated. He should feel better soon."

Feeling unusually tongue-tied, he stuttered, "Uh, sure. It was nice meeting you. And thanks for taking care of my dog."

She turned and walked away, but not before the tiny smile on her face smacked Acton right in the middle of his chest. *What in heck was going on here?* he wondered. First she had Seymour eating out of her hand and now he was feeling like a moonstruck teenager.

"Will that be cash or card, Acton?"

The question failed to register with him. He was too busy watching Stephanie leave the waiting area with an older woman toting a cat carrier.

"Acton! Do you think you can beam yourself back to earth?"

Forcing his attention back to the counter, he stared blankly at Sheri, a young woman he'd known since their kindergarten days.

"Sorry, Sheri. Did you say something?"

Sighing, she gave him a smile that would've melted a lesser man's bones. "How do you want to pay your bill today? With cash or card?"

Mentally shaking himself, Acton dug his wallet from the back pocket of his jeans. "Card. How much is it?"

The amount Sheri quoted caused him to whistle under his breath and he glanced wryly down at Seymour. The dog was grinning happily and thumping his bushy tail. Yep, Acton thought, the dog was still under Stephanie Fortune's spell.

"Seymour, I'm not so sure you're worth this," he said. "But I guess I'll keep you."

He swiped the debit card, then punched in his PIN. After he'd placed it back in his wallet, he leaned casually against the counter.

With gamine features and short black hair, Sheri was cute, but in his opinion, not anywhere near as pretty or classy as Stephanie.

"So when did Miss Fortune come to work for Paws and Claws?"

Sheri handed him a receipt. "Before our new clinic opened. She had lots of experience back in Fort Lauderdale, Florida, working with animals, so Dr. Neil hired her right off."

"Hmm, Florida," he mused aloud. "Wonder how she happened to come to Texas?"

Surprised, Sheri asked, "Are you saying you don't know who she is?"

Acton frowned. "Am I supposed to know her?"

She rolled her eyes. "Acton, you really ought to get out of the barn more often. It means Stephanie is one of *the* Fortunes. It also means that she's way out of your league, cowboy."

"Maybe in your mind, Sheri. But I might have other ideas about that."

Grinning at the shocked look on Sheri's face, Acton stuffed the receipt in his shirt pocket and led Seymour out of the clinic.

Chapter Two

"It was more than obvious the cowboy liked you. The way he was looking at you…" Dayna's words ended on a wistful sigh. "If only he would look at me that way, I'd be walking around on a cloud."

Stephanie glanced at her coworker as the two women moved from one kennel to the next, checking on the cats that had been spayed and neutered earlier in the day.

"He? Who are you talking about?"

Dayna rolled her eyes to the ceiling. "Oh, come on, Stephanie. There's only been one hunk of a man stroll into the clinic today. I'm talking about Acton—

the dreamy cowboy. You know! Blond hair, sparkling blue eyes and a grin that turns my knees to mush."

"Oh, him." Shaking her head, Stephanie turned her attention back to the cats. "If you think the man had any interest in me personally, you're totally confused. Anyway, he's obviously a flirt. And I seriously doubt he discriminates by age or looks. He wouldn't have acted any differently if I'd been an eighty-year-old grandmother."

"Oh, puh-leeze! If you believe that nonsense, then you're thinking has gone haywire." Dayna frowned in disbelief. "Didn't you think he was cute and sexy? The whole staff is still going gaga over him."

Stephanie reached into the kennel and rubbed a finger gently down the middle of the head of a calico cat. She loved animals and had ever since she'd been old enough to know what they were. The job she'd held back in Fort Lauderdale had been at an animal clinic such as this one, only larger. She'd enjoyed working there and had been hesitant about giving it up to move here to Texas. But her three brothers had assured her she wouldn't have any trouble finding an equally worthwhile job. And they'd been right. So far, working for Dr. Neil had been a real pleasure.

As for having a man in her life, that was an entirely different matter. She'd been burned too many times to let a young hunk like Acton Donovan turn her head.

"Okay, I'll admit the guy was super cute and

sexy—in a boyish way. Rather young, though," Stephanie told her, then cast a curious glance at the other woman. "Does he, uh, have a steady girlfriend?"

Dayna laughed as though her question was the funniest thing she'd heard in a long time. "Let me put it this way—Acton has a steady stream of girlfriends. In the plural sense." She named several different young women who'd recently brought their pets to the clinic. "Those are a few of his castoffs."

Somehow that tidbit of information didn't surprise Stephanie. The man had reeked of charm and sexiness. He probably had a bevy of women knocking on his door. Which made the idea of him being interested in Stephanie even more ridiculous and her more determined to forget him. Her last boyfriend, the one she thought she wanted to spend the rest of her life with, had been a playboy. Only Stephanie hadn't known it until her heart had become involved. Then she'd found out the hard way that he was seeing other women on the side.

"I see," she said thoughtfully. "So I guess you'd say he's a playboy in boots and hat."

"That's one way of putting it. But I'm sure every woman who goes out with him likes to believe she's the one who can settle him down—turn him into a husband and daddy," Dayna told her.

Stephanie couldn't picture Acton Donovan settling down in the near future or even years from now.

And she figured any woman who tried to transform him would only be asking for heartache.

"Well, the guy seemed nice enough. But I'm not interested. Not only is he too young and too much of a flirt for my taste, but there's only one man I'm interested in. My little man, Linus. He's my main focus right now."

"That's well and good. But you might not always have Linus in your life. Even if his mother never comes back, there's a dad out there somewhere."

That thought was something Stephanie tried not to dwell on. "That's the reality I live with every day, Dayna. Although, Laurel told my sister-in-law, Becky, that the baby's father was totally out of the picture."

"Yes, that's what this Laurel woman said. But can anyone really believe her? What kind of woman gives birth to a baby and only days later, leaves it at the front desk of the Rambling Rose Pediatric Center?"

Stephanie moved on to another kennel with Dayna following close behind her. "From what everyone who was at the ribbon-cutting ceremony at the center says, Laurel seemed perfectly fine when she went into labor. But who knows? She was just a stranger passing through. She could've made up the part about the father. All I know is that I love the little guy like he's my own. And right now I'm concentrating on him. I'm just not interested in dating anyone."

"Well, I'll say one thing," Dayna replied. "If you

can resist Acton, then I'm going to start calling you Lady of Steel."

Stephanie laughed. "Come on, it's almost closing time. We'd better make sure everything is ready to shut down before Dr. Neil locks the doors for the night."

Later that evening, Acton was cleaning up the mess he'd made cooking his supper when he heard a knock on the front door.

After drying his hands on a dish towel, he walked through the small house where his grandparents used to live and peeked through the curtain covering the paned window on the door.

Seeing his oldest brother, Shawn, standing on the porch, Acton pulled open the door.

"What the heck are you doing knocking?" Acton asked him. "You know you can just open the door and come on in."

Shawn, who was similar to Acton in coloring, but a bit taller, cast his brother a droll look. "And walk in on you and some lady in a lip-lock or something worse? No thanks. I'll keep knocking."

Up until a couple of months ago, Acton had lived in the big ranch house with his parents and two brothers. But then his father, Ramsey, had decided that his own mother, Hatti, no longer needed to be living here alone and had practically ordered her to move into the big house. Seeing the chance to have a place of his own, Acton had promptly made the move.

Stepping into the living room, Shawn gestured to the apron tied around Acton's waist. "What are you doing, anyway? Don't tell me you're trying to cook."

Acton closed the door behind him. "I'm cleaning up my mess. And who are you kidding? You know I'm a pretty darn good cook. When it comes to making great dishes, Grandma Hatti is a good teacher. I made spaghetti. Want some?"

"No thanks. I had a burger in town. But I will take some coffee. Got any made?"

"No. But it'll just take a minute to get some brewing."

The two men passed through the living room, down a short hallway, then into a small kitchen decorated in red, green and white.

Shawn pulled out a chair at a round pine table and sank into it. "Actually, I didn't come by to beg for a cup of coffee. I came by to tell you that Dad has decided to work the herd in the northwest corner in the morning. He wants to be loading the portable pens by daybreak."

"I hope he doesn't plan on doing all three hundred head in one day," Acton said. "Has he hired any day help?"

Shawn shook his head. "He said if four grown men can't handle the job, then he needs to get rid of some cattle."

Acton groaned as he spooned coffee grounds into a filtered basket. "Sounds like we're in for a long day tomorrow."

"That's why I stopped by. To make sure you didn't have something else planned."

"Like what?" Acton took a seat at the opposite end of the table. "I show up every day for work, don't I?"

"Well, you've been known to get distracted by a pretty face." He eyed Acton's ragged blue jeans and old gray T-shirt. "You're not going out tonight?"

Acton frowned. "On a date, you mean?"

"Yes. Like you and a girl," Shawn said drily.

"No. I wished I was," Acton admitted. "But I wasn't sure the girl would agree to going out with me. So I didn't ask."

Shawn's eyebrows piqued with curiosity. "Don't tell me you ran in to a woman who actually resisted your charm."

Acton grunted with wry humor. "She resisted me, all right. To be honest, I don't even think she liked me. She was polite enough. But I think that's because it was her job."

"Hmm. Do I know this lady?"

Acton shrugged. "I doubt it. She's moved here from Florida and works for Dr. Neil at Paws and Claws as a vet assistant. I took Seymour there this morning to get something done about his scratching."

"From Florida..." Shawn mused. "What's her name?"

"Fortune. Stephanie Fortune."

Shawn let out a disbelieving groan. "Oh, dear brother, now I understand why you didn't get to first base with her. She's probably one of the Fortunes that moved here a few months ago. You know, the ones who moved into that mansion on the outskirts of town. I think they call it the Fame and Fortune Ranch or something. Other than a few horses, I don't believe there are actually any livestock on the place. But you know how city folks are. They own a few acres in the country and get the idea that entitles them to call it a ranch."

"Oh, so that's what Sheri meant when she said Stephanie was one of 'the' Fortunes," he remarked. "Obviously these people are rich."

Shawn shrugged one of his broad shoulders. "Well, it appears so. Fortune Brothers Construction is the company that finished the pediatric center and the animal clinic. Now they're working on some other properties in town. So apparently, they have money. And I heard tell that they're related to the famous Fortune family in Austin."

Seeing the coffee had finished dripping, Acton rose from his seat and poured two cups.

"I have some pecan pie. Want a piece?"

"Don't tell me you baked a pie," Shawn told him. "I won't believe it."

"Ha! Grandma was pretty good at teaching me

how to cook, but she wasn't that good. The pie came straight out of the bakery in the grocery store."

"In that case, I'll eat some."

Acton cut two pieces of the dessert and carried everything over to the table.

Once they were both eating, Acton said, "Dr. Neil wasn't at the clinic this morning so Stephanie treated Seymour."

"Bet that was a wrestling match. No wonder she wasn't interested in you, after she had to deal with that rowdy dog of yours."

"Wrong, brother. Seymour was a perfect gentleman. He took to Stephanie like…well, I never saw anything like it. She could have told him to walk across the exam room on his hind feet and he would've done it for her."

"Hmm. That's a first. Frankly, it surprises me that this Fortune woman was working in a place like Paws and Claws. Dealing with sick and wounded animals all day isn't exactly what I'd consider a glamorous job."

"Stephanie doesn't seem like the glamorous sort. But she sure is pretty. And she didn't act uppity. Just a bit disinterested—in me."

"Aww, my poor little brother. He finally met a female he couldn't charm out of her shoes," Shawn teased. "Sounds like trouble ahead for you."

Acton frowned at his brother. "Trouble? A sweet

little thing like Stephanie couldn't cause trouble. Not with me."

Shawn snorted. "Maybe in another five years you'll learn about women."

Acton let out a short laugh. "Like you're an expert on females? Cows, maybe. But not pretty women."

"Well, I have sense enough to know that a woman, pretty or homely, isn't going to ever be serious about a simple cowboy. Men like us can't offer a woman riches."

"Not all women want riches," he retorted.

Shawn's response to that was a dry laugh. "Dream on, brother."

Acton thought as he sliced off a bite of pie. "I guess this Fortune family must have tons of money. From a distance, that house of theirs looks impressive."

"I wouldn't call it a house. It's a mansion."

"Well, by Texas standards, it's not the biggest or the best. But it's hardly a shack," Acton joked.

"I can bet you one thing," Shawn said. "Stephanie Fortune's kitchen doesn't look like this one. I doubt she's ever so much as cooked herself an egg."

Acton could've told his brother he wasn't looking for a cook, but he kept the remark to himself. He didn't want Shawn or any of his family to get the idea that he was looking for one special woman. Their parents had already been hounding their three sons to settle down and give them more grandchildren.

Acton said, "I think I recall reading an opinion piece in the paper about Fortune Brothers Construction. Some of the folks in Rambling Rose aren't too happy about these fancy new buildings and shops they're planning for the town."

Shawn shrugged. "You know how some of the older townsfolk are. They're not keen on change. Especially the progressive kind. Frankly, I think it's good to make improvements."

"I get that part of it," Acton acknowledged. "But I agree with the old folks about not wanting to turn Rambling Rose into some sort of tourist attraction. Hell, pretty soon it will be against the law to ride our horses down Main Street."

Shaking his head, Shawn snickered. "Acton, since when have you ridden your horse down Main Street? Not since us three brothers decided to ride in the rodeo parade and that was five years ago!"

Acton carried his empty plate over to the sink, then refilled his coffee cup. "I'm only using that as an example of how things are changing around here."

"Well, if you want to get to first base with Stephanie Fortune, then I suggest you don't bring up the subject of her brothers' plans for a ritzy hotel."

Acton glanced at his brother. "A ritzy hotel? For real?"

"That's what I'm hearing. But you can hear anything at the Crockett Café."

The old eating establishment had been a fixture

in Rambling Rose for as long as Acton could remember. When he and Shawn and their brother Danny had been small boys, their father would take them to the café on the weekend as a special treat for doing their chores. All three would get milk shakes. The kind that was handmade with real ice cream and so thick you had to eat it with a spoon. The café still made handmade milk shakes, but now that Acton and his brothers were all grown men, it wasn't the same.

"A ritzy hotel in Rambling Rose," he murmured, thinking aloud. "Don't reckon that will ever work. But you can bet I won't tell Stephanie Fortune my opinion on the subject—if I ever get the chance."

Finished with the pie, Shawn pushed aside his plate and cast a taunting grin at Acton. "How do you plan on seeing her again? You going to take Seymour back for a special checkup?"

"If he doesn't improve I'm supposed to take him back. Damn dog, I don't think he's scratched once since I got him home. So I doubt I can use him for an excuse."

Clearly amused, Shawn said, "You can always gather up the barn cats and take them in for their yearly shots."

"Dad always takes care of that chore," Acton said, then snapped his fingers with sudden dawning. "I know. I'll take Elizabeth and Ryan by Paws and Claws. The clinic always has a few cats and dogs to be adopted and the kids love to look at them."

Elizabeth, age seven, and nine-year-old Ryan were their older sister's kids. On some evenings, after Acton was finished with his ranch chores, he'd drive over to Gina's house and take the kids out for burgers or pizza. Gina often accused Acton of spoiling her children, but to tell the truth, he probably enjoyed the outings as much, or more, than the kids.

"Oh, how low can you stoop, Acton? Using your own niece and nephew to snag the attention of a woman," Shawn taunted jokingly.

Frowning now, Acton walked back over to the table. "Look who's talking. I don't see you making any headway in the love department."

Shawn's eyebrows shot up. "Love? Don't try to tell me that's what you looking for."

Acton could feel his face growing hot and he figured he looked like a sun-ripened tomato. Damn it, there were times Shawn could make him feel like he was sixteen years old again.

"Well, what if I am?" He tossed the question at his big brother. "Is there anything wrong with that?"

The goading look on Shawn's face turned empathetic. "No. Nothing wrong at all. Except that maybe…"

His words trailed away and Acton couldn't let it go at that. In spite of the teasing and bantering that went on between him and his brothers, Acton valued their thoughts and opinions.

"Except what?" Acton prodded him to answer.

Shawn shrugged. "That maybe when you really start looking for a woman to love, you should start with someone in your own social sphere. Just my opinion, little brother."

If Acton was being totally honest, he'd probably admit that Shawn was right. Wanting to date someone out of his league was one thing, but getting serious about her would be downright stupid.

"Don't worry. I'm not hearing wedding bells in my head. That's not going to happen for another ten years, at least."

Shawn chuckled. "I won't tell Mom and Dad. They have the idea that you moved down here to Grandma's house because you have marriage on your mind."

Acton let out a loud burst of laughter. "Seriously? Who would I be marrying?"

Shawn pretended to think. "Well, you've been seeing the little blonde who works at Reddick's Ranch Supply on a fairly regular basis."

Acton's laughter quieted to a chuckle. "Marietta? I've already put the brakes on dating her. She's too much of a party girl."

His comment caused Shawn to stare at him in comical disbelief. "Too much of a party girl? For you? Is that possible?"

"It is when she's partying with more than me."

"Oh."

"Yeah. Oh. Which is no big deal. We didn't have

a serious thing going. And I sure didn't move down here to Grandma's house because of Marietta. I moved to give everyone more space in the big house."

"Oh, I thought you moved because you were tired of everybody treating you like the baby of the family. That you wanted to prove you can take care of yourself."

Acton slanted him a perceptive glance. "Maybe that, too, big brother."

Stephanie softly hummed a lullaby as she gently rocked Linus and watched the last of the formula in the bottle drain away. In spite of the baby being born a bit early, he was thriving. This past month his cheeks had rounded and his arms and legs had grown fleshier. She'd even noticed that his gaze was trying more and more to focus on her face.

Incredibly, Stephanie had ended up being Linus's foster mother by sheer happenstance. When Laurel had staggered into the ribbon-cutting ceremony in the throes of labor and shouted for help, Stephanie's sister-in-law, Becky, who happened to be a nurse, and Dr. Green both rushed to the frantic woman's aid. The next day, after the news had spread that she and the baby were safely settled in a hospital in San Antonio, everyone had believed that was the last they'd ever hear of the incident.

But a couple weeks later, Laurel had walked into the pediatric center, handed over the baby to a nurse and declared she couldn't handle being a parent. Later, they'd found a note on the baby stating his rightful home would be found at Fortune's Foundling Hospital.

Neither Laurel's behavior nor the note had made any sense. And to make matters worse, none of the local foster families had been able to take in the infant they'd initially called Baby L. Stephanie, however, had.

Her brothers, Callum, Dillon and Steven, had been surprised. They'd always known she was a nurturer with a soft heart. However, they had been stunned to learn that she'd already gone through the process of being fingerprinted and background-checked in hopes of adopting one day.

They had all wondered why their lovely sister needed to adopt a child when she could give birth to one of her own. Stephanie hadn't bothered to explain her reasons. They might not want to admit it, but all three brothers knew the answer to that question. Over the past few years they'd watched her suffer through several short-lived relationships, none of which had even gotten close to true love or an engagement ring. She didn't want to wait to start a family at the end of her childbearing years. She wanted to have children while she was still young. And hopefully, later on, she might be fortunate enough to find a man who would truly love her.

"Linus, you might be the only baby I'll ever have

a chance to hold and cherish," she whispered down to the sleeping boy.

His lips had gone slack around the nipple, and as Stephanie carefully eased the bottle from his mouth, emotional tears stung her eyes. She'd been told that in a year's time if neither parent showed up to claim the boy, she might have a chance to adopt him. But a year was a long time. Anything could happen between now and then.

She rose from the cushioned rocker, then carried Linus over to a hooded bassinet and was tucking a warm blanket around him when a knock sounded on the door of her suite at the Fame and Fortune Ranch.

After crossing the large space that served as a living room, she opened the door to find Steven, her oldest brother, holding a large covered tray.

"Room service," he said cheerily. "Hungry?"

She pulled the door wide and gestured for him to come in. "I was about to come down to the kitchen to see if there was anything to eat. What's all that?" she asked, gesturing to the tray. "I thought Manny was taking the night off."

He carried the loaded tray over to a green leather couch and placed it on a glass-and-wood coffee table. As Stephanie followed her brother, she thought she caught a whiff of pizza.

"Callum treated the construction crew this evening and there was so much food left over I brought some home."

"This is nice, Steven. Thanks for thinking of me."

"When you didn't come down to dinner, I thought I'd better check on you. Is everything okay?"

For a long while in their family, Stephanie had been the only girl and her four older brothers had been very protective of their little sister. And even though a set of triplet girls had been born into the family four years after Stephanie, the guys still went out of their way to shield and care for her. Maybe because they thought that, due to her bad luck at love, she might never have a husband to love and protect her.

She smiled at Steven, while hoping that the tears that had stung her eyes a few moments ago were no longer visible. "Sure. Everything is fine. We had a hectic day at the clinic and it was later than usual when I finally picked up Linus from day care. So I've been playing catch-up. By the time I took care of my pets, Linus was yelling that he was hungry. So I put supper on hold."

Steven chuckled. "I'd be flat on the floor if I'd been that busy today."

She gave a wry laugh, then took a seat on the couch. "Join me?"

"I'll sit for a minute. But I can't stay for long. Callum is on a conference call and wants to talk with me afterward."

"Callum is really excited about his projects. I think even more so now that Becky and the children are in his life." She was happy for her brother; he'd found a wonderful single mother of twins who'd given him an instant family. She glanced slyly at her brother. "Is seeing him so happy giving you any ideas to become a family man?"

Steven shrugged. "It'll take more than Callum's grinning face to get me to the altar."

Stephanie pulled the linen cloth from the tray to expose a wide array of food, ranging from hot wings and pizza, to macaroni and cheese and chocolate cake.

"No salad?" she asked teasingly.

Steven chuckled. "Sorry. The guys ate all the salad. There wasn't a drop of it left."

"I'd be willing to bet there wasn't a drop of it to begin with," she said drily.

He laughed. "Construction workers need more than rabbit food for their dinner." He glanced around him. "Speaking of rabbits, where is Orville?"

"Look behind you. He finally managed to charm Violet and Daisy into sharing their bed."

Steven glanced behind the couch to see Stephanie's Siamese cat and yellow tabby snuggled in a large basket. Wedged between the two felines, a brown-and-white domestic rabbit snoozed contentedly.

"Ha! They must have decided Orville was just a strange-looking cat. I'll say one thing—he's one lucky rabbit to have you adopt him. Did you ever find out how he happened to be roaming around the clinic parking lot?"

Stephanie shook her head as she placed a pair of hot wings on a small paper plate. "No. We figure someone just didn't want him anymore and put him there hoping the clinic would take care of him. It's so sad, too, because Orville is a real sweetheart."

"Every needy creature is a sweetheart to you." Steven settled back against the couch and crossed his ankles out in front of him. "Stephanie, sometimes I think you'd take on a small zoo and a dozen kids without ever batting an eye."

Smiling wanly, she shrugged. "What would I be doing if I wasn't taking care of Linus, my pets and the animals at Paws and Claws?"

"Anything you wanted. You might actually have time for a personal life."

Trying not to grimace, Stephanie reached for a piece of cheese pizza. "If you're talking about me getting myself a man, there's no need for you to worry. I've decided the best thing I could ever do for myself is cross marriage off my list of lifelong endeavors."

Steven hardly looked pleased. "You're twenty-seven, intelligent, beautiful and, most of all, loving. But you want to hide away and waste yourself just because you've dated a few losers."

Stephanie ate a bite of pizza before she bothered to reply. "Not only were they losers, they were users and jerks, too. Let's face it, I wouldn't know a good man if he wore a sign around his neck."

"If he has to wear a sign around his neck to let people know he's good, then he probably isn't."

She let out a brittle laugh. "No need to worry, Steven. Linus keeps me happy."

Her brother left the couch and walked over to the bassinet where Linus was sleeping peacefully. Gazing down at the baby, he said, "You're very brave, Stephanie, for taking on this little fellow with so much uncertainty surrounding him."

Leaving her plate on the coffee table, she walked over to where he stood and slipped an arm through his. "I'm hardly brave."

He looked at her. "Don't suppose you've heard any news about the mother?"

"No. It's like her trail has vanished."

The cell phone in his shirt pocket suddenly chirped to signal a new text message had arrived. Steven glanced at the phone. "Callum is finished with his conference call. I'd better go see what he's stirring up next. We've just put the finishing touches on The Shoppes at Rambling Rose."

"Poor you," she said with a grin. "The building never stops."

"Wait until he hears I need to hire more carpenters," he joked. Then he planted a kiss on the top of Stephanie's head and started out of the room.

"Thanks for the food," she called after him.

He gave her a backhanded wave and shut the door behind him.

Stephanie's attention returned to the baby, and as she gazed down at Linus's quiet features, her heart overflowed with warm, maternal love. Would she ever have a child of her own? A man to love?

Love.

These days she rarely allowed herself to dwell on the fleeting emotion. But after meeting Acton Donovan this morning, she'd been feeling totally out of character.

True, she wasn't good at judging the quality of a man, but even she could see he was far from her type.

So why had she continued to think of him throughout the day? Why was she thinking of him now?

Because no guy like him had ever flirted with her? Of course, she'd had men hit on her before, but most of them had been sleazy or unattractive, or just downright obnoxious. But Acton had been none of those things. He'd been cute and rather sweet, and she'd gotten the impression that he was a nice guy. With a dog like Seymour, he had to be nice, she thought.

There you go, Stephanie, judging a man by his dog. That's a brilliant deduction. It's no wonder you've had your heart broken a dozen times. Before long you'll be saying the denim shirt he was wearing made him look dependable and trustworthy.

The mocking voice in her head made her turn

from the bassinet and return to the tray of food sitting on the coffee table.

She couldn't let thoughts of a young, happy-go-lucky cowboy elbow their way in on her common sense. And yet, she couldn't help but wonder what it would be like to have Acton Donovan sitting next to her on the couch, sharing this little supper with her.

Chapter Three

Two days later, with Elizabeth and Ryan safely buckled in the backseat of his truck, Acton was driving to Paws and Claws with one thing on his mind—seeing Stephanie again.

"Why do we have to go to the animal clinic first, Uncle Acton?" Ryan asked. "I'm hungry now."

Elizabeth made a smirking face at her big brother. "You're always hungry. And you can eat any ol' time. We're going to look at the cats first. Mom says if I see a cat I like I can bring it home. 'Cause we don't have Tinker anymore."

"She didn't say that!" Ryan insisted, correcting her. "She said maybe."

"You're lying! She said yes! Not maybe," Elizabeth countered.

"Okay, you two, if you don't be nice to each other, I'm going to turn the truck around and take you both home," Acton warned. "There won't be any cats or burgers or anything else for either of you."

The interior of the truck went silent and a glance in the rearview mirror showed the pair exchanging stunned looks.

"Okay," Ryan mumbled. "If Elizabeth will be nice, I will be, too."

The girl pursed her lips together, and for a moment Acton thought she was going to reach over and bop her brother over the head, but then she smiled to signify all was forgiven.

"I'll be nice, too," she promised.

"I'm glad to hear it," Acton told them. "Because I want you two to be on your best behavior."

"How come?" Ryan asked.

"Because you're supposed to be well-behaved and I have friends at Paws and Claws. I don't want them thinking my sister has raised a pair of heathens."

Puzzled, Elizabeth looked at her brother. "What's 'heathens'?"

"Aww, Lizzie, you know. It means somebody like Mikey Walters."

Elizabeth nodded as though that explained everything. "Oh, so a heathen is a bully and a creep."

"That's one way of putting it," Acton told her, while trying to keep a straight face.

He wheeled the truck into the parking lot of the new Paws and Claws building and after giving the kids one last list of rules to follow, ushered them through the front door of the facility.

With only an hour to go before closing time, there were only two patients left in the waiting room. Both were leashed dogs, who appeared as bored as their owners.

Carla, a young woman with brown hair wrapped into a ballerina bun, waved from behind the check-in desk. "Hi, Acton. Can I help you?"

With a hand on each child's shoulder, he nudged them forward. "This is my niece and nephew. They'd like to look at the cats you have up for adoption."

The attractive receptionist shot him a dazzling smile, while at the desk down from her, Sheri was loudly clearing her throat.

"Dayna might be free at the moment," Sheri said. "Want me to call her?"

Before Carla could make any kind of response, Acton asked, "What about Stephanie? Is she around?"

"She is," Carla said. "But she's assisting Dr. Neil out back with a large animal. A bull with a bad horn or something."

Acton couldn't imagine delicate Stephanie any-where near a bull. But she'd probably put the same charming hex on it like she'd used on Seymour, he thought.

He was about to tell Carla that they'd wait for Stephanie when the door leading back to the examining rooms suddenly opened and a big burly man with a crumpled straw hat and muddy boots entered the room with Stephanie following close behind him.

"There she is now," Carla said. "If you and the kids would like to wait—"

"We will," Acton said before she could finish, then guided his niece and nephew to the nearest couch.

Once the man had dealt with his bill and was leaving the office, Acton hurried the kids over to where Stephanie remained at the checkout desk.

As soon as she spotted him, she smiled and Acton felt something in the middle of his chest melt like a chunk of ice on a hot sidewalk

"Hello, Mr. Donovan," she said, her gaze encompassing the children standing next to him. "Who are your friends?"

Acton nudged the children slightly forward. "This is my niece, Elizabeth, and my nephew, Ryan."

The smile on her face deepened as she politely shook hands with both children. "Hello, I'm Stephanie. I took care of your uncle's dog for him the other day."

Ryan grinned naughtily. "You mean Seymour? Bet that was a big dogfight."

She arched an eyebrow at Acton. "This boy must spend a lot of time with you."

Acton chuckled. "Everyone says he takes after me. Much to my sister's disappointment."

"Uncle Acton is going to take us to eat. But we want to see the cats first," Elizabeth told her. "The ones that people can take home with them."

Stephanie glanced at Acton again and as he looked at her lovely face, he realized that somehow during the last two days, he'd forgotten just how vibrant her eyes were and how her hair was the color of a red-gold sunset.

"You want to adopt a cat?" she asked him. "That's wonderful."

"Uh, well, not me. I mean, I love cats. I think they're super. But Gina—that's my sister—has promised the kids they can have another cat. The cat they had went missing."

Realizing Ryan was tugging on his sleeve, he looked questioningly down at the boy.

"What about the dogs, Uncle Acton?"

Acton shot Stephanie an apologetic smile. "Sorry. He wants to see the dogs, too. But if you're too busy—"

"Not at all. Dr. Neil just finished with his last patient," she assured him. "You three, follow me."

With Stephanie leading the way, they walked to a room located near the back of the building.

"This is what we call our cat room," she said as she gestured for them to step inside.

"That took some real original thinking," Acton joked.

The room was filled with scratching poles, gym sets and other feline furniture. Stuffed mice, small rolling balls and other toys littered the floor.

"Well, I suppose it could be called the feline room."

"Wow! This is cat heaven, Uncle Acton!" Elizabeth exclaimed. "May I go look in the cages?"

"Of course," Stephanie told her. "But I wouldn't try petting the cats that are running lose. Sometimes they get frightened of strangers and scratch."

"I won't," Elizabeth promised, then rushed over to a cage where a calico mother with a litter of four was housed. Ryan followed close on her heels.

Acton said, "Thank you, Stephanie. This means a lot to the kids, especially Lizzie. She cried for days over her missing Tinker."

"Aww. I can only imagine. I have two cats, two dogs and a rabbit. If any one of them went missing, I'd be devastated."

Surprised, he looked at her. "After working here all day, you go home to five pets? You must really love animals."

"I do love them. When I was a child I couldn't have pets because of my mother's health issues. Since then I've made up for it." A tentative smile played at the corners of her lips. "So how is Seymour? You didn't bring him with you today, so I'm assuming he's doing better."

Acton nodded. "I don't think he's scratched once since I took him home. Yesterday he helped us round up cattle, so he was a happy dog. Today he's resting."

A look of interest brightened her face. "Seymour is a working dog?"

"Why, sure. You don't think I'd keep a mutt like him around just for the company, do you? Damn dog would just as soon snap my hand off as look at me."

She responded with a soft laugh and the sweet sound nearly knocked Acton off his feet.

"What's so funny about that?" he asked, while savoring the fact that he'd somehow managed to make her laugh.

"You thinking Seymour is cranky. He knows how you feel about him. That's why he treats you like—"

"A dog," Acton said, finishing for her. Then he grinned to soften his words. "That's okay. He and I understand each other. And I wouldn't trade him for anything."

"Uncle Acton, come look at this cat! He has stripes that go sideways!" Ryan called out. "Can we have him?"

"But I want this white one!" Elizabeth interjected as she gazed into a separate kennel. "Her ears have black on the tips. She's beautiful!"

Acton glanced at Stephanie. "I think I hear an argument coming on."

"Perhaps their mother would let them have both?" Stephanie suggested. "It would be good for the cats to have a companion."

He contemplated the idea for a moment before he said, "I have a feeling you could talk Gina into it. If I get her on the phone, would you mind speaking to her?"

"I'd be glad to," Stephanie told him.

Acton pulled out his cell phone and punched in his sister's number. To his relief, she answered after the first ring.

"Gina, there's a very nice lady here at Paws and Claws who'd like to speak with you," he told her, then immediately passed the phone to Stephanie.

While the two women discussed the cats, Acton went over to the children. So far, neither had given an inch as to which cat they wanted to take home.

"Uncle Acton, why should Ryan get to choose? He didn't even want to look at the cats. All he's been talking about is dogs!"

"Well, I like dogs, too," Ryan said, attempting to defend himself. "But Mom won't let me have one until we get a yard fence. So a cat would be the next best thing."

Acton rubbed a hand on top of each child's head. "Okay, kids, no arguments, remember?"

They both nodded soberly and Acton kept his smug smile to himself.

"I got a little surprise," he announced. "Miss Stephanie is on the phone right now trying to talk your mother into allowing you both to have a cat. How's that?"

"Oh, that's cool!" Ryan exclaimed.

Elizabeth jumped up and down. "Wow, wow! Triple wow!"

Both kids were hugging Acton's waist when Stephanie walked over and handed him the phone. From the stoic look on her face, he had no idea how the conversation with Gina had turned out.

"So what's the verdict?" he asked.

Stephanie suddenly encompassed all three of them with a happy smile. "She's agreed to letting you have both cats. Only because I told her that you two looked like responsible children who will take proper care of your pets. Am I right?"

"Yeah!" Ryan answered enthusiastically.

Her little features suddenly serious, Elizabeth said, "We're responsible, Miss Stephanie. We're not heathens."

Acton watched Stephanie's mouth fall open just before she covered it with her hand. Whether she was shocked or laughing at Elizabeth's remark, he couldn't tell. He hoped it was the latter.

"Uh, that's a new word she learned," Acton explained.

Turning away from the children, Stephanie dropped her hand, and he was immensely relieved to see she was smiling.

"I wonder where she might've heard it."

The shrewd look on her face very nearly made Acton laugh, and he suddenly realized that Stephanie Fortune was a whole lot more than a pretty face and a shapely figure. Just being in her presence and listening to her soft voice was a pleasure he'd never quite experienced before.

"They're seven and nine years old, and I still haven't learned that they pick up on everything I say," Acton admitted, then gestured toward the caged cats. "I realize it's nearly closing time for the clinic. It might be better to come back tomorrow evening to pick up the cats. That way I can take the kids to the pet store and buy whatever supplies they'll need."

"Sounds good," she said. "I'll have Sheri fill out the adoption papers tomorrow and meanwhile we'll tag both cats so that no one else can take them."

Acton explained the plan to the kids and though they were initially disappointed that they couldn't take the cats with them this evening, neither put up a fuss.

"Does this mean we can go eat now?" Ryan asked.

"I don't want to eat," Elizabeth said. "I want to go to the pet store."

Acton shook his head. "No pet store tonight. We're going to eat."

The girl suddenly looked at Stephanie. "Will you come eat burgers with us, Miss Stephanie? It would be more fun if you would come, too."

Stephanie looked awkwardly over at Acton and his heart skipped a hopeful beat. Did he honestly have a chance in talking her into joining them?

"I wasn't invited," she told Elizabeth.

Tilting her head to one side, the girl said, "I'm inviting you."

"Yes, and that's very nice. But your uncle hasn't invited me. And I—"

"I'm asking you now," Acton interrupted. "Would you like to join us? We're only going down the street to the burger place. The one with the kiddie playground in the front. That is, if you don't have other plans."

For a long moment she appeared to consider his offer, then a slow smile tilted her lips. "Actually, the only plan I have is to go pick up my baby."

Stephanie expected her announcement to surprise Acton, but his friendly expression didn't change. Still, she couldn't help but wonder what he was actually thinking. That she was an unwed mother or a divorcee with a child, or even a widow?

It didn't matter what he was thinking, Stephanie scolded herself. Acton Donovan was just a guy offering her a hamburger, not a red-hot affair.

"You, uh, have a baby?" he asked. "As in a little human baby? Not an animal baby?"

Stephanie couldn't hold back her laughter. "Linus is a real little human baby. He's a month old and I'm his foster mother."

He smiled. "Foster mother? Oh, that's, uh, great. Real great!"

Great for her, or Linus, or the both of them? Stephanie wasn't sure what he meant, but at least the news that she had a baby, even on a temporary basis, hadn't sent him running out the door.

"Yes, well, I really need to pick him up before I could join you three. Unless a baby would bother you," she added, while carefully trying to gauge his reaction. If Linus wasn't welcome, then she'd decline his invitation.

"Bother me? Shoot, no!" He gestured to Elizabeth and Ryan. "I've been around these two since they were a day old. I'm an old hand with babies."

Honestly? He looked more like he was an old hand at creating babies rather than caring for them, Stephanie thought. But she could be wrong about the man. And it wasn't fair for her to be judging him without really knowing him.

She pushed back the cuff of her thin sweater. "It will be a few more minutes before the clinic closes and I can pick up Linus from day care. Elizabeth and Ryan might not want to wait for me."

"We don't mind," Ryan said.

Elizabeth bounced joyfully on her toes. "We won't eat without you, Miss Stephanie. Promise!"

The grin on Acton's face said he didn't mind waiting, either, and the idea that he might actually want Stephanie's company made her feel light hearted and foolishly romantic.

"The kids want you to join us and so do I. Waiting isn't a problem. We'll meet you there."

"Okay. I'll see you there."

He gathered up the children and ushered them out of the cat room. As the door shut behind the trio, Stephanie felt like she'd just encountered one of those Texas whirlwinds she'd heard about. Had she just agreed to a date with Acton Donovan? The gorgeous hunk that made the whole staff at Paws and Claws swoon?

No. It isn't a date, Stephanie. It's sharing some fast food with new friends. A man like Acton will never want a real date with you. So quit daydreaming. You have work to do.

Galvanized by the taunting voice in her head, Stephanie hurried down the hallway to where Dayna was straightening shelves in the supply room.

The woman gave her a sly look. "Sounds like you made a score with Acton."

"What?" Stephanie blurted.

Had her coworker already heard that Stephanie was meeting Acton later? She hoped not. She was hardly ready to start fielding off a bunch of silly questions.

"The cats," Dayna explained. "Acton told us the kids are adopting two of the cats. Good job, Steph."

Stephanie felt a blush sting her face. "I really had nothing to do with that. The cats sold themselves."

Dayna hardly looked convinced. "Carla said when Acton and the kids first came in he was purposely asking for you. Wonder why?"

Stephanie refused to make a big deal over Acton's attention. Especially when she knew his interest would quickly wane. "Probably because he thinks I have some sort of mystical powers with animals."

Dayna laughed. "You do."

Relieved that Dayna accepted her theory, Stephanie quickly changed the subject. "Are all the patients cleared out?"

"Dr. Neil finished with the last one a few minutes ago," Dayna answered. "Let's finish tidying up so we can get out of here."

It took Stephanie another thirty minutes to finish her work at the animal clinic, pick up Linus and drive back to the fast-food restaurant.

When she stepped inside the busy eatery with the baby tucked safely in her arms, she was acutely aware of her stained work jeans and limp hair. She didn't need a mirror to tell her she looked washed out, even though she had taken the time to swipe on a bit of pale pink lipstick.

She was glancing around the room, trying to spot Acton's brown Stetson among the sea of heads, when Elizabeth and Ryan raced over to meet her.

"We're sitting over here by the window," Ryan told her. "Uncle Acton is saving our table."

Elizabeth grabbed Stephanie's elbow as she stared up at the bundle in her arms. "Is that Linus? Can we see him?"

"Wait until we sit down," Ryan scolded his sister.

Elizabeth stuck her tongue out at him, but didn't argue.

Stephanie patted the girl's head. "It's okay. You can see Linus as soon as we get settled," she promised.

Grinning from ear to ear, the girl skipped ahead of them to the booth, then gestured to the side of the table where Acton was sitting.

"You can sit there, Miss Stephanie. By Uncle Acton," she said.

Before Stephanie reached the booth, Acton stood up and reached for the baby. "Here. Let me hold the little guy while you take a seat."

Acton hardly seemed like the daddy type. Yet here he was with two young children and offering to help her with the baby. *Could Dayna and the others be wrong about the man?* she wondered.

She handed the baby over to him, then slid onto

the smooth bench seat. "Thanks for your help," she told him. "And I'm sorry you had to wait so long."

"No problem." Still standing, he peeled back the blanket covering Linus's face and peered down at the baby. "Hey, he's cute as a button."

Stephanie said, "I think so, too."

Grinning, he gazed at Linus a moment longer, then gently handed him down to Stephanie.

"Okay, it's time to take orders. Who wants what?" He glanced at Stephanie and winked. "And don't be bashful. Order anything you want."

From you or the menu?

The naughty thought came out of nowhere, shocking Stephanie with its implications. She wasn't setting her eye on this handsome cowboy. Not in the least!

Thankfully, the children diverted her attention as they gave him their complicated requests. Once they were finished, Stephanie followed with her choice of a fish sandwich and fries.

Acton left to go put in their orders and Stephanie comfortably positioned Linus in the crook of her arm. Across the table, Elizabeth and Ryan leaned eagerly forward to get a closer look at the baby.

"Boy, he's really tiny," Ryan said, then wrinkled his nose. "Reckon I was ever that little?"

"Probably," Stephanie told him.

"His eyes are open," Elizabeth said. "Can he see us?"

"Yes, just not in the same way you and I can see," Stephanie explained. "He'll be able to see you better when he gets a few weeks older."

Elizabeth's head tilted curiously to one side as she regarded Stephanie. "Uncle Acton said you were a foster mother. Is that like our mother?"

The child's innocent question sent a pang of regret through Stephanie. "Not exactly. But I love and care for baby Linus just like she loves and cares for you two."

Thankfully, that explanation seemed to satisfy the girl, and before any more questions could be asked, Acton returned to their table carrying a tray laden with food.

After taking a seat next to Stephanie, he passed the food around the table and helped the kids situate their meals and drinks.

Stephanie was thinking how good he was with the children when he asked, "Would you like me to hold Linus while you eat? It's kind of hard trying to hold your food with only one hand."

"Thanks, but I'm used to it," she told him, while secretly surprised that he was being so thoughtful. Was this guy too good to be true? "I have a carrier in the car, but I prefer holding him. And he seems to like it better this way."

"Well, if you get tired just let me know," he told her.

For the next few minutes as they ate the casual

meal, the children plied her with questions about the cats and other animals that she helped treat.

Stephanie enjoyed their chatter. But it wasn't enough of a distraction to draw her attention from Acton. With his tall, lanky frame sitting only inches from her, she could practically feel the heat exuding from his body and smell the faint masculine scent emanating from the green plaid Western shirt he was wearing.

"We're finished eating, Uncle Acton," Ryan suddenly announced. "Can we go to the playground?"

Acton glanced toward the glassed-in area designated for children's play. "Okay. But be sure and watch out for your little sister. And don't be picking on any of the other kids."

Ryan looked properly insulted. "I'm not like Mikey Walters."

Acton waved the kids on and they wasted no time racing to the playground. Once they were gone, the table seemed incredibly quiet.

Acton slanted her an apologetic look. "I know they're noisy, but they're basically pretty good kids," he said.

"I think they're lovely. Do you spend much time with them?"

"Probably more than I should. Gina constantly accuses me of spoiling them. I just like to make them happy."

"So you like children? Or just your niece and nephew?"

Now why had that question come out of her mouth? She wasn't sizing him up for fatherhood, or anything close to it.

He nodded. "I've always liked kids. Probably because my brothers say I'm just a big kid myself. And I guess that's partly true. I like to have fun. But they forget that I'm a grown man now."

He was definitely that, Stephanie thought. At least, on the outside.

Linus squirmed and she glanced down to see he was chewing on his fist. "So are Elizabeth and Ryan the only niece and nephew you have?"

"My two older brothers are still single—like me." He gestured to Linus. "It's probably none of my business but how did you happen to be this little guy's foster mother?"

She pulled a bottle out of the diaper bag she'd carried with her and offered it to Linus. He latched on with a hunger that made her smile.

Glancing at Acton, she said, "I'm surprised. I thought everyone around town had heard about the baby being left at Rambling Rose Pediatric Center."

Acton's mouth fell open. "You mean Linus is *that* baby?"

"So you did hear about it?"

He nodded. "Mom was talking about the incident at dinner one evening. Anytime something happens involving a baby she gets all teary-eyed. You know how women are."

"Yes, I know," she said, finding it an effort to keep a straight face. "In case you failed to notice, I am one."

Ruddy color washed over his face. "Oh, damn. Sorry, Stephanie. I wasn't thinking. I mean, I've noticed. I've definitely noticed you're a woman."

She smiled at his flustered apology. "I couldn't help teasing you a bit," she said. "As for me fostering Linus, I just happened to be the first eligible person that was available to take him. And I'm very glad I was. He's a joy to me."

"So what about his parents? Mom said the mother ran off and can't be found?"

"That's true. After she left the baby at the pediatric center, she disappeared. How or why, no one seems to know."

"I assume the authorities are trying to locate her?" he asked.

Stephanie sighed. "Well, it's all a bit complicated. You see, there's a thing called the Safe Haven law that legally protects a parent from leaving a child at a safe house. Which, in this case, was the pediatric center. So that means they can't track her down for child abandonment. But if the mother is considered ill or in danger they can search for her."

Nodding, he said, "Sounds as though the law officials have to walk a fine line with this sort of case."

"Exactly. But so far there's been no news from anyone regarding Laurel's whereabouts."

He shook his head with dismay. "That's tough. So what now? Are you going to keep on being Linus's mother?"

Nodding, she said, "If his biological mother shows up, naturally that will end my role as Linus's foster parent. If she's never located, I'd love to legally adopt him."

"What about the dad? He has to be somewhere—unless the guy is dead."

Stephanie grimaced. "From what the mother implied, the man wasn't a part of their lives. Even so, I think there's an effort being made to find him, too. Just in case he might want to make a legal claim of Linus. But locating him might prove difficult. Laurel didn't share any valuable information about the man."

"What a loss. For both parents."

Acton obviously considered a baby to be a precious blessing, which was more than Stephanie could say for the guys she'd dated. Most of them would have bolted at the sight of a baby. Was she beginning to see a sign hanging around Acton's neck with the word *good* written on it?

"Well, for now I'm going to do my best to make sure Linus knows he's wanted," she said.

He sipped his cola, then shifted around on the

seat so that he was facing her. "I'm glad you agreed to have dinner with us, Stephanie."

"I'm glad, too." Without even trying, Acton lifted her spirits and reminded her that she needn't be serious all the time. "On weekdays my brothers often work late, so usually I'm eating alone. It's nice to have company."

"So you live with your brothers," he mused. "How does that work out for you?"

"It's good. Our house is spacious enough for me to have my own suite of rooms. Which is especially nice now that I have Linus. That way we don't disturb my brothers."

His blue eyes were studying her keenly and she figured he was thinking she led a boring life. And compared to his, it probably was.

"It's good that you have your own space. I'm just now learning what that's like."

"You don't live on your family's ranch?" she asked.

"I do live on our ranch, the Diamond D. Just not in the big ranch house. A couple of months ago I moved into my grandparents' old house. You see, Grandmother Hatti has had a few health issues. Nothing serious, but she's not quite as spry as she used to be, so my parents persuaded her to move in with them. I moved out so that she could have my room and everyone wouldn't be so crammed in."

"That was generous of you."

She watched his lips take on a guilty slant.

"Not really. I got the whole house to myself. Unless Shawn or Danny—my brothers—get the bright idea to move in with me. And I don't think that's going to happen."

"You like living on your own?"

"Most of the time. Other times I miss the hustle and bustle in the big house. And to be honest, I'm not fond of cleaning up after myself. But I try to keep things tidy."

"Who does your cooking?"

He tapped a finger against his chest. "I do all my own cooking. In fact, I'm the only one of my brothers who knows how to cook. Just to prove it, I'll fix supper for you one night. As long as you don't ask for gourmet dishes. I'm not into that kind of stuff."

Supper at his place? With no one else around? That would be a risky temptation—for her. For him it would probably be no more than having a friend over to share a meal. "I might take you up on that... someday," she told him.

Seeing Linus's mouth had gone slack around the bottle's nipple, Stephanie placed the baby on her shoulder and gently rubbed his back until he burped.

"Who does your cooking?" he asked.

Though it shouldn't have, his question caught her off guard. Mainly because she didn't like admitting that her family had Manny, the ranch's caretaker who also did most all the cooking. It bothered her to think the people of Rambling Rose might look down on the Fortune family for being so wealthy.

She said, "We have a great guy who cooks for the family. Which is a good for me. I've never been very good in the kitchen. The best I can do is a couple of Cuban dishes. That's what I liked to eat when we all lived in Fort Lauderdale. Since we moved here I've fallen in love with Tex-Mex food."

As she talked, she'd noticed the look in his eyes hadn't changed to boredom. He still appeared to be actually interested to hear about her life. The idea definitely warmed her. Most of her past boyfriends would've already turned the conversation back to themselves.

"There's nothing better," he agreed.

He plucked up a leftover fry and dipped it into a pool of ketchup. Stephanie found herself studying his hand, with its long tanned fingers. When she'd shaken hands with him the day he'd brought Seymour to the clinic, she'd felt hard calluses on his palm. Now she wondered how it would feel to have that work-worn palm rest against her cheek. To have it slide over her bare skin. To have it—

"Do you like living here in Texas? In Rambling Rose?"

The questions pulled her out of the erotic trance and she prayed he wouldn't notice the wave of heat rushing to her face.

Clearing her throat, she said, "I love it. Rambling

Rose is just the right size. Not too big or too small. And I especially like the people."

To her surprise, he reached for her hand and folded it inside his.

"I hope that means you like me, too," he said gently.

Stephanie's heart couldn't seem to decide if it wanted to skip or do a wild jig.

"I... Of course I like you," she finally said. "And your little niece and nephew, too."

His eyelids lowered while the corners of his lips curved into a sexy grin. Just looking at his face so close was causing heat to roar through her like flames in the wind.

Oh, Lord, she needed to free her hand and put some sensible space between the two of them. But how was she going to do that without looking like a prude?

Stephanie's dilemma was suddenly solved as Elizabeth and Ryan came rushing up to the table. Acton released her hand and turned his attention to the kids.

"We want ice cream, Uncle Acton," Elizabeth said. "Can we have some?"

"It's 'may' we, Lizzie, not 'can,'" Ryan corrected her as though he was an expert on grammar.

The girl crossed her arms against her chest as she sneered at her brother. "Know-it-all! You ask for the ice cream! And if we don't get it, it'll be your fault!"

With a covert wink at Stephanie, Acton said,

"There's no cause for this kind of commotion. You both ate everything you asked for, so I'm going to say yes."

He pulled out his wallet and handed a bill to Ryan. "You're in charge of the money, Ryan. But let Elizabeth order whatever she wants. The money that's left over you can split evenly between you. Okay?"

"Yeah!" Ryan exclaimed.

Elizabeth gave Acton's neck a huge hug. "Thank you, Uncle Acton!"

The two kids took off in an excited rush and Stephanie gave him a pointed smile. "I think Gina has a point about you spoiling them."

His grin was shamelessly guilty. "You're supposed to have fun when you're a kid. Come to think of it, you're supposed to have fun when you're a grown-up, too. Are you having fun yet, Stephanie?"

Without thinking, she burst out laughing. "I'm having loads of fun, Acton."

And as the sound rolled out of her, she realized it had been a long while since she'd felt this carefree. And even longer since she'd enjoyed the company of a man.

Chapter Four

The next afternoon, after the clock had passed regular school hours, Stephanie began watching for Acton and the children to show up at Paws and Claws to collect the cats. But as the closing hour neared without any sign of the three, she began to wonder if Gina had changed her mind about letting the children adopt the cats.

Which would be disappointing for two reasons. She wanted the cats to have a real home. And she wanted to see Acton again. It was that simple and that complicated.

Last night, after she and Linus had gone home, she'd spent hours thinking about the man. And today, she'd been trying to convince herself he was just a friend. The problem with that was she'd never felt like this toward a friend.

Knowing her history with men, her brothers would surely advise her to forget about Acton. A young lothario wasn't what she needed in her life. Especially now that she had Linus to consider. Yet it felt so good and right to be with him.

Pushing the swirling thoughts aside, she walked over to a large kennel where a brown-and-black shaggy dog with a cast on his leg was watching her with pleading eyes. Several days ago, the poor thing had been struck by a vehicle and a Good Samaritan had brought the injured dog to the clinic. Thankfully, Dr. Neil had managed to successfully operate on the leg and so far the dog was recovering at a rapid pace.

"Hi, Buddy," she said softly. "Ready to try for a little walk?"

Dr. Neil had prescribed the dog three short walks a day and because he'd not yet had his third excursion today, Stephanie attached a leash to the mixed breed's collar and allowed him to step out of the ground-level kennel.

Wagging his tail with excitement, Buddy, a name the clinic staff had given him, let out a happy bark and Stephanie took a moment to rub his head.

"What a champ you are," she said to the dog. "Let's walk down the hall and show everyone how good you're doing."

They left the rehab room and started down the long hallway that led to the waiting area. Along the way, Leonard, an older man who'd been a longtime assistant to Dr. Neil, stopped to give Buddy an encouraging pat. "He's going to get along fine on that leg. Are you going to adopt him, Stephanie?"

Stephanie let out a good-natured groan. "You know me, Leonard. I already have a small menagerie. But my dogs live outside and their fenced-in yard is plenty big enough to accommodate a third. And I confess—I'm getting a soft spot for Buddy."

"Hey, Stephanie, you have a visitor."

She looked around to see Dayna and Acton standing at the far end of the hallway, but his niece and nephew were nowhere in sight.

"Excuse me, Leonard, I need to speak with this person."

Leonard peered down the hallway. "That's Acton Donovan," he stated.

"You know him?" she asked.

"Been friends with his family for many years. Fine folks. They raise some of the best Brangus cattle around these parts. Tell him I said hello. I better run. Dr. Neil is waiting on me."

Leonard hurried away and Stephanie urged Buddy forward. By the time she reached Acton, her heart was pounding and not from the exertion of the walk.

She didn't understand why, but seeing the man again was like looking at blue sky after a rainstorm.

"Hello, Acton."

"Hi, Stephanie. Sorry I'm running late."

They were smiling at each other, a fact that Dayna was clearly taking note of.

"No problem," she assured him, then asked, "Didn't Elizabeth and Ryan come with you?"

He shook his head. "They both forgot they had after-school projects this evening. They made me promise to pick up the cats for them. I've already filled out the necessary papers and paid the fees."

"I'm happy for the cats. But I'm disappointed that Elizabeth and Ryan couldn't be here. I was looking forward to seeing them again," she said.

He chuckled. "After putting up with those two last night, I'm surprised. They can wear on a body's nerves."

Picking up on his comment, Dayna cast a shrewd gaze from Stephanie to Acton. "Last night? What happened with the kids last night?"

"Just a hamburger, that's all," he said.

That's all it had probably been to him, Stephanie thought dismally. To her it had been a special evening. It had given her the opportunity to see Acton in a totally different light than the one Dayna and the other female staffers put him in.

Thankfully, the other woman turned her attention to Buddy, who was standing obediently at Stephanie's side.

"Look at you, Buddy. You hardly have a limp now.

Next thing we know you'll have that cast off and be chasing squirrels."

Stephanie explained to Acton how Buddy had wound up at the clinic and ended it with Leonard's idea that she adopt the dog when he was well enough to go home.

"I really think you ought to take him, Acton," she suggested. "It would be good for Seymour to have a friend."

The suggestion caused him to laugh. "Seymour have a friend? He'd try to tear Buddy's head off!"

"Poor Seymour. You're underestimating your dog," Stephanie told him.

Acton laughed again. "Listen, I made the mistake of letting Seymour watch *Lassie* reruns. Now he thinks he's just as good an actor as that famous collie. All the nice behavior he shows you is just a big performance. He's actually Cujo in disguise."

Stephanie couldn't stop a giggle. "Oh, stop it, Acton! That's horrible!"

"Horrible is right. I can't turn my back on the monster," he said, then added with a mischievous wink, "Only kidding. Seymour is a loyal mutt. Most of the time."

Sobering her laughter, Stephanie said, "If you're ready to collect the cats, I'll help you. But I need to finish Buddy's walk first."

Dayna promptly reached for Buddy's leash. "You

two go on," she said coyly. "I'll be happy to take Buddy on the rest of his walk."

Dayna and the dog turned and headed back down the hallway. Stephanie cast Acton an apologetic look.

"I apologize for Dayna's little insinuations. She has this silly idea that you like me."

"What's silly about that? I do like you."

Clasping her hands in front of her, Stephanie let out a long sigh. "Dayna means a different kind of like. And it's embarrassing. So please just ignore her."

His eyebrows arched upward until they very nearly disappeared beneath the brim of his hat. "It's embarrassing for you to be associated with me?"

"No! That's not what I meant. I was afraid all her sly innuendoes were embarrassing you."

Clearly amused, he said, "I'm twenty-five years old, Stephanie. I suppose by most standards that's young. But I'm past the age of being easily embarrassed. And for your information, I'm feeling rather flattered that she's linking you to me."

Stephanie decided she should've never started this conversation. The more he talked, the worse it got.

"I'm glad you feel that way," she told him, while trying not to melt with pleasure at his compliment. She'd be a fool to let herself swoon over a man who had the reputation of being a cowboy Casanova.

"Well, that's that," he said a few minutes later as he shut the back door of the truck. In the carriers that were safely positioned on the floorboard, the two cats were howling in protest.

"You're probably going to hear plenty of meowing the whole trip," she warned. "But they'll quiet down once you get them to your sister's place."

Acton rubbed his palms down the thighs of his jeans and wondered why he was suddenly feeling nervous. He'd never felt anxious about asking a woman to spend time with him. Stephanie shouldn't be any different. But she was different, he realized. Not because she was a sister to the high-rolling Fortune brothers. But because she was sweet and sincere and being around her made him feel good.

Did that mean he was falling in love with her? Acton didn't know. He'd never been in love before. But he did know that the warmth she evoked in him was like nothing he'd ever felt before.

Rubbing her hands up and down her arms to ward off the chill of the February wind, she said, "Well, I'd better get back inside."

"Before you do that I, uh, was wondering if you'd mind riding over to Gina's house with me? To get the cats settled in," he explained. "I won't mind waiting out here until you get off work."

Her lips parted with surprise and Acton found himself staring at them, imagining how they would feel against his.

"Oh, I don't know, Acton," she said in a doubtful tone. "Linus is at day care and—"

"I won't keep you that long. Promise." He used his forefinger to make an *X* across his chest. "I'd really like for you to meet my sister. The kids have been telling her all about you. I think she's getting the idea that you're some sort of princess."

She let out a little laugh and Acton felt something deep inside him go as soft as pudding. He couldn't deny it was a joy to hear her laughter and see her smile. She needed to do it more, he thought. With him.

"Your sister is definitely in for a surprise," she said.

"Then you'll go with me?" he asked.

As she considered his invitation, Acton watched her wrestle with the long strands of hair being whipped about by the wind. Today she was wearing a pair of dark jeans and a canary-yellow blouse that buttoned down the front. The bright color made her red hair stand out even more.

From the time he'd entered his teens, Acton had taken extra notice of pretty girls, and down through the years, he'd ogled plenty of them. But he'd never stopped to appreciate all the tiny things that made them attractive. With Stephanie, every minute detail caught his attention. What did that mean?

"I suppose I could go," she finally answered. "But I can only stay for a few minutes. I don't want to leave Linus at the day care any longer than necessary."

"That's fine. That's okay," he said happily, then gestured behind her to the building. "You go on and finish your work. I'll wait for you out here with the cats."

She glanced at her watch. "Give me ten minutes."

As she hurried back into the clinic, Acton realized he'd give her all night, just to spend five minutes alone with her.

Oh, brother, he was sicker than a calf at weaning time, he thought. And if he didn't man up soon and get over this constant urge to be with Stephanie, he was going to end up being some kind of whimpering sap.

Acton's sister, Gina, lived in a rambling redbrick house on the north edge of town. The yard was perfectly landscaped with shrubs and rose bushes, while most of the house was shaded by the huge, spreading limbs of a live oak tree.

"This is nice," Stephanie said as he pulled to a stop in the driveway behind a white family-type SUV. "And the roses growing near the house are blooming like it's the middle of June instead of February."

"I guess from living in Florida you're used to a mild climate," he said.

She nodded. "I am. Before we moved here to Texas I thought I'd be moving into cold, snowy winters. I had all these plans to buy furry coats and dress boots. Then I find out the temperature hardly dips low enough to cause a frost. So I ended up not buying any heavy clothing."

"Sometimes the weather surprises us with sleet or freezing drizzle," he said. "But let's not hope for that. During those storms it takes a heck of a lot of work to make sure the baby calves have enough shelter."

Stephanie glanced over at him. He was such a laid-back, fun guy that sometimes she forgot he worked the serious job of ranching. She didn't know all that much about raising cattle, but enough to know that taking care of large herds of cows and calves couldn't be easy.

He parked the truck, then helped her step to the ground. After they'd collected the cats from the back, they walked to the concrete porch that ran halfway across the front of the house.

Acton rang the doorbell, and within a few seconds, the door opened and Stephanie found herself looking at an older, female version of Acton. The tall blonde with shoulder-length hair and bright blue eyes smiled warmly at her.

"Hello," she said.

Acton wasted no time in stepping up and wrapping a hand around Stephanie's arm, as though she belonged to him. The thought left her feeling ridiculously feminine and even a bit cherished.

"This is Stephanie Fortune, sis. She kindly offered to help me deliver the cats to you. She's an animal expert so you can ask her anything about taking care of them."

Smiling, Gina pushed the door wider and made a sweeping gesture with her arm to usher them inside.

"An expert? Wow! For Acton to put you on that kind of pedestal you must be good."

Stephanie waved off the woman's compliment as they entered. "I'm hardly an expert. But I have worked as a vet assistant for the past six years. After that length of time you do learn a bit."

"I'm sure you've learned more than a bit," Gina said. She paused in the middle of a large, comfortable living room, then clasped her hands out in front of her. "So should I simply let the cats loose here? The other cat we had—Tinker—was very frightened when we first brought him home. It took days to get him to come out from under the bed."

Stephanie nodded. "That's not unusual. But maybe we can do something to help these two get acquainted more easily. Do you have a small room you can shut off? One without too many things they can hide under?"

Gina thought for a moment. "The mudroom. There's nothing in there except the washer and dryer, a set of sinks and a dirty-clothes hampers."

"That sounds perfect," Stephanie said. "Cats feel more comfortable in a small space and they'll be more likely to let Ryan and Elizabeth come near them. Once they get fully acquainted with you and the kids, you can let them have free rein of the house."

Acton shot his sister a confident grin. "See, I told you she was an expert."

There was a note of pride in Acton's compliment and it touched Stephanie in a way that took her by surprise.

Jeff, one of the first guys she'd dated in college, had thought her job as a veterinarian assistant was little more than cleaning cages and litter boxes. When she'd tried to explain that she actually helped treat the animals, he'd laughed as though she couldn't possibly be smart enough for such a job. In the end, she'd shown Jeff exactly how smart she was by dumping him.

On the other hand, Acton was often praising her, and though most of what he said was probably little more than mild flirtation, she felt he was being genuine when he talked about her experience with animal care.

Gina gave her brother a calculating look. "Yes, I can see. She's smarter than you are."

Acton groaned. "Oh, sis, don't go telling stuff on me. I'm already having a hard enough time trying to make Stephanie like me."

With a shake of her head, Gina smiled pointedly at Stephanie. "Don't believe a word this guy tells you. It's all lies."

Acton glared at her. "Gina! You're breaking my

heart. Just see if I help you paint that damned garage again!"

Laughing, Gina hooked an arm affectionately through Acton's and tugged him toward an open doorway. "Come on, baby brother, I'm only teasing. Let's take care of these cats and then you and Stephanie might like some coffee and cookies. I just took them out of the oven."

A few minutes later, after Stephanie helped Gina set up makeshift beds and litter boxes, and the cats were exploring their new digs, they all returned to the kitchen.

"Sit at the bar or the table. Any place you like," Gina told Stephanie. "Make yourself at home. Acton always does."

"Thank you," Stephanie told her. "I can only stay a few minutes. I have to pick up my baby at day care."

At a white farm table, Acton pulled out a chair for Stephanie, then sat next to her.

Gina carried two cups of coffee over to the table. "Acton told me that you were fostering the abandoned baby. I admire you, Stephanie. Especially since the whole situation is uncertain at best."

After taking a careful sip, she said, "No matter what's going on with his parents, Linus needs to be mothered. To be honest, I hope his real mother is alive."

"So sad to think of any mother leaving her baby

behind. I can't remember anything like this ever happening in Rambling Rose."

She placed a plate of cookies in front of Stephanie and Acton, then took a seat at the end of the table.

"Is Jack still at work?" Acton asked as he reached for a snickerdoodle.

Gina explained to Stephanie. "Jack is my husband. He works for a heating-and-cooling company."

"And repairs appliances on the side," Acton added.

"Jack was called to the high school gymnasium. There's a basketball game tonight and the heat in the locker rooms went on the blink. He'll probably show up about the time I have to leave to pick up the kids. Hopefully, he won't let the cats out. I'd better send him a text and warn him before he gets here."

"That's not a bad idea, sis."

Gina leaned back in her chair and eyed Stephanie with open curiosity. "So the Fortunes who've been building the fancy things around town are your brothers? I work as a secretary for a real estate agent so I hear if a new roof goes on a barn. Your brothers have already made a huge mark in Rambling Rose."

Nodding, Stephanie said, "My brothers dream big. And they want to build big things for Rambling Rose. I realize not everyone around here is happy with what they're planning, but they truly want what's good for the town."

Gina's smile held more understanding than Stephanie expected.

"Change of any kind always makes waves," she reasoned. "You shouldn't worry. These things have a way of working out."

"I hope you're right."

Gina said, "Until Acton told me about you, I didn't realize the Fortune brothers had a sister."

Stephanie was surprised that he'd mentioned her to his sister. She'd certainly not brought up the subject of Acton to her brothers. Only because she couldn't say the word *man* without all three of them going into long lectures about getting her heart broken for the umpteenth time. She wasn't keen on being reminded that she was a loser in the romance department.

She said, "Callum, Steven and Dillon are my brothers who make up Fortune Brothers Construction. And there's Wiley, another brother, still living back in Florida. I also have triplet sisters, Ashley, Megan and Nicole. They're still in Fort Lauderdale, also, but I think they're strongly considering moving here to Rambling Rose."

"You're from a big family," Gina remarked. "And triplet sisters—that's amazing! I can't imagine dealing with three at once. Ryan and Elizabeth are two years apart and they're a handful. Just ask Acton."

Stephanie looked at him and smiled. "I think he handles them quite well."

Acton smiled back at her and suddenly some sort of invisible force arced between them. Except for the two of them, everything in the room seemed to fade away.

If it hadn't been for Gina clearing her throat and disrupting the moment, Stephanie would've continued to stare at Acton like a moonstruck fool. Instead, she managed to shake away the dazed feeling and turn her attention back to the other woman when she asked a question.

"Are your sisters anything like you?"

"Not really," Stephanie answered. "They're four years younger than me and have a totally different mind-set. And they're much prettier."

"That couldn't be possible," Acton said.

Blushing now, Stephanie shook her head. "Has your brother always blurted out this kind of thing?"

Gina laughed and the sound reminded her of Acton's laughter. It was an easy, happy sound and Stephanie had no doubt the Donovan home had always been a warm and loving place.

"As long as I can remember he's been this way. Grandma Hatti calls him the charmer of the family. Though, I have a few other choice names for him," she teased. "With Acton being the baby of the family, he's always gotten away with murder."

Acton feigned an innocent look. "What can I say? I didn't tell my parents to quit having kids after me."

Gina said, "I'll be honest, Stephanie—most of my friends are curious about what that mansion you call home looks like on the inside. We're Texans and we've seen lavish before, but not here in Rambling Rose."

Stephanie shrugged. "It is luxurious. But to be honest, I don't need that much space. And I'm not a fancy person. But my brothers wanted the place and they convinced me to go along with them. The part I like about it is that I have plenty of room for my pets. Two dogs and two cats and a rabbit."

"And she's going to adopt another dog with a cast on his leg," Acton added.

"You have more energy and patience than I do," Gina said with a laugh.

On a nearby counter, Gina's cell phone pinged and she left the table to check it.

"That's probably the kids texting to let me know they're ready to be picked up. Just wait until you have older children, Stephanie. Most of the time, you'll feel like a taxi driver."

Stephanie rose from the chair and carried her cup over to the sink. "It was very nice meeting you, Gina. Let me know if you have any problems with the cats. I'll be glad to help."

Gina reached over and gave her a brief hug. "I hope we can be friends, Stephanie."

"I'd love that," she told her. "Perhaps you could bring the kids out sometime and let them play with my cats and dogs? I'll show you my part of the house."

"Now that's an invitation I won't let you forget," Gina promised.

They told Acton's sister goodbye and once they were in his truck, headed back to Paws and Claws, Acton surprised her by bringing up the subject of Gina visiting the Fame and Fortune Ranch.

"That was nice of you to invite my sister out to your place. We've never really brushed shoulders with anyone like you, Stephanie. She'll enjoy seeing how you live."

From the corner of her eye, she studied Acton's profile. Did he really see her as someone that different from him? The thought hurt her. One of the things that had drawn her to him in the first place was the fact that he hadn't made a big issue of her being a Fortune, or having money. But now she wondered if he was actually like all the other guys she'd known—eyeing her as a dollar sign instead of a woman with normal wants and needs.

"Yes, I live in a fancy house. But that doesn't make me different, Acton. I live just like other women my age in Rambling Rose."

He arched his eyebrows in question and glanced at her. "What is your age?"

"Hasn't anyone told you that it's a no-no to ask a woman her age?"

Amusement crinkled the corners of his eyes and mouth. "My dad warned me a time or two, but I don't always follow his advice."

That was hardly a surprise. Everything about him shouted rebel.

She said, "I've hardly reached the point of being ashamed to reveal my age. I'm twenty-seven."

"Well, to be frank, Stephanie, I don't know of any twenty-seven-year-old women who live as you do. You've already told me the ranch caretaker also does the family cooking. I'll bet you have house-keepers, too."

He made it sound like having hired help was a crime. "That's right. We have people to come in and help with the cleaning. And a groundskeeper, along with a man to care for the horses and stables. But none of that means I'm a spoiled girl. That is what you're getting at, isn't it?"

His laugh was a sound of disbelief rather than one of humor. "*Spoiled* is the last word I'd use to describe you, Stephanie. I can see you work hard. And just so you know, I'm not looking to be your friend because you have money."

Stephanie had heard that before. Not in those exact words, but close. And for years, she'd chosen to believe them. Every woman needed to be wanted just for being herself. But after a few humiliating at-tempts at romance, she'd learned how naive it was to blindly trust a man. Men were out to get whatever they could from her. Both physically and monetarily. Yet in spite of those hard lessons, she desperately wanted to believe Acton was different from the jerks who'd strolled in and out of her life.

Deciding it would be best to keep things light between them, she teased, "No, you're looking to be my friend because you think I'm an expert with animals—especially a dog named Seymour."

He laughed. "How did you ever guess that was my ulterior motive?"

By now they had reached the Paws and Claws parking lot. Acton braked the truck to a stop next to Stephanie's car, then surprised her by reaching across the console for her hand.

As his fingers wrapped around hers, there was a glint in his eyes that gave her the impression he was going to lift the back of her hand to his lips.

The idea caused the breath of air she was trying to draw in to lodge in her throat, but she did her best not to cough or sputter. No matter if she fell over in a dead faint, she thought—that would be better than letting him know he'd thrown her senses into a major earthquake.

"I saw a flyer on the bulletin board in the waiting room about a Valentine's fund-raiser for Paws and Claws this coming Friday. Are you going to be helping with the event?"

Caught off guard by the unexpected question, she stared blankly at him. "The fund-raiser? Oh, uh, yes, the whole Paws and Claws staff will be contributing in some way. It's going to take place downtown

in The Shoppes—that's the old Woolworth's building my brothers just finished restructuring. Dr. Neil
hopes the function will raise a ton of money to off-
set caring for stray and orphaned animals. Why do
you ask?"

Even as she spoke, all her attention was on her
hand in his. If he continued to hold her hand, it was
going to combust into flames, she thought wildly.
The heat from his fingers was racing up her arm
and, she feared, straight to her face.

A lopsided grin curved his lips. "It's a good cause.
I thought I might volunteer to help. If that's okay
with you."

His thumb began to move gently against the back
of her hand and Stephanie felt goose bumps erupt
over her forearms. How could the simple touch of his
hand make her feel hot and cold at the same time? It
was downright scary.

Forcing herself to breathe, she said, "You don't
need my permission to volunteer. All help is welcome."

His fingers tightened around hers, and though she
couldn't be sure, she thought his face was a fraction
closer to hers than it had been a moment ago.

He said, "I don't want to make you feel awkward."

Puzzled, she asked, "Why would I feel awkward?"

He shrugged. "Well, Dayna already thinks the two
of us are a couple. And I can see that bothers you."

It bothered her because they weren't a couple.

And they had no business trying to be, she thought gloomily. She wasn't his type and he was…well, he'd be another heartbreak for her.

"What Dayna or anyone else thinks hardly matters," she said. "As long as it doesn't bother you, then it doesn't bother me."

A wide smile exposed a set of beautiful white teeth and Stephanie found herself wondering how it might feel to have them gently nipping her skin, her lips. He'd be a generous, giving lover. Somehow she knew that.

"I'm glad you feel that way, Stephanie. So I'll be around to help. Just send me a text to let me know when the work starts."

"I don't have your number."

"Yes, you do. It's on Seymour's chart."

Seymour. That dog had put her life into upheaval, she thought.

"Okay. I'll text you."

She eased her hand from his and turned to climb out of the truck, but he caught her by the shoulder and gently urged her back around.

"Not so fast," he said gently. "Before you go I want to thank you."

Before Stephanie could guess his intentions, he leaned forward and pressed a kiss to her cheek.

Her heart pounding, she stared wondrously at him. "What are you thanking me for?"

The smile on his face disappeared and for the

first time since she'd met him, a serious expression took its place.

"Just for being you, Stephanie."

Without even trying, he made her feel special. But common sense told her she couldn't take him seriously. He'd only end up breaking her heart.

A lump in her throat, she pulled her hand from his and scurried out of the truck before he could notice her eyes were filled with tears.

Chapter Five

Stephanie was sitting on the couch, changing Linus's diaper, when the door opened and Becky stuck her head inside.

"Knock, knock. Can you stand a bit of company?" she asked.

Happy to see Callum's wife, she motioned for her sister-in-law to join her. "Come in, Becky. I'd love company."

The pretty brunette entered the suite and walked over to the couch, where Linus was lying on his back, kicking his arms and legs as Stephanie fastened the disposable diaper in place.

She said, "He's definitely grown since I saw him

a few days ago. Aww, and look at those eyes, they're sparkling. What a cutie!"

Stephanie tugged the navy blue onesie back in place and snapped it together. "I'll let you watch him, while I go dispose of his dirty diaper," she told Becky. "He's too young to roll over yet. But you never know."

"Sure. I'll be glad to keep an eye on the little man."

Stephanie carried the diaper to an airtight plastic container in the bathroom, then returned to the living area, where Becky had taken a seat on the cushion next to Linus.

"I took him in for a checkup today," she told Becky. "Dr. Green said he's healthy. Thank God for that. By the way, I didn't see you there. Were you not working this afternoon?"

"I was. I must've been on my lunch break."

Stephanie nodded as she sat in an armchair. "Probably so. I had the appointment scheduled on my lunch hour so I wouldn't miss work."

"You have a fire in the fireplace tonight," Becky noted. "It feels great."

Stephanie followed Becky's gaze over to a small fireplace that stretched across one corner of the room. Her cats, Violet and Daisy, were stretched out near the hearth, while Orville sat observing the flames from a safer distance.

"I'll be so happy when this wintery weather

moves out," Becky remarked. "I've been bundling up the twins and keeping my fingers crossed that they don't catch cold."

"Where are the twins? Don't tell me Callum is chasing after them."

Becky laughed. "Actually, he is. When I left them in the den, he had both girls in his lap and was attempting to read them a story about a horned toad and a dragonfly. If that last more than five minutes, I'll be surprised."

Stephanie chuckled. "It still surprises me to see Callum putting himself in daddy mode."

Sighing, Becky covered Linus with a light blanket. "To be honest, I still have a hard time believing he really wanted me and the girls as his ready-made family."

"Callum loves you and the twins more than anything," Stephanie assured her. "But my little ready-made family?" She nodded at Linus. "Well, that's a shaky matter."

Becky's expression was empathetic. "I guess it would be pointless to tell you not to worry."

Stephanie sighed. "Linus might be the closest thing I'll ever have to having a child of my own."

Becky groaned. "Stephanie! You make it sound like you're going to be a spinster."

"I'm sure Callum has told you stories about some of the men in my life," she said bitterly. "I've picked some real losers. Actually, I've given up on picking.

I've decided the best choice for me is to forget about a husband and try to adopt as a single mother."

Shaking her head, Becky said, "Callum explained that's why you were already eligible to be a foster mother for Linus. You'd already had a background check done in order to adopt."

"I realize that shocked them. I hadn't mentioned it before because…well, it's such a private decision and I thought they would disapprove."

"Honestly, I don't think any of them disapprove of you adopting a child. But they do frown on this idea of yours to remain single."

Stephanie snorted. "That's very funny. Anytime I mention dating someone, all I hear is discouragement."

"They believe you deserve real love. That's what they want for you."

Love. Ever since Acton had walked into Paws and Claws with Seymour trotting along beside him, she'd thought far too much about that one particular emotion.

"Actually, Becky, I have met someone that makes me think about things like love and babies and even marriage. But he's all wrong for me. So I'm trying hard not to think about him—and everything that I'm missing."

Becky suddenly scooted to the edge of her seat. "Who is this guy? If he's making you dream about love and marriage, then he can't be all wrong."

"Oh yes, he can," she said glumly. "Among other things, he's two years younger than me. How can I take a twenty-five year old man seriously?"

"So? That's just a number. I've known twenty-five-year-old men who were more mature than forty-year-olds."

"Perhaps. But he's good-looking. Too good-looking, if you know what I mean. Women go gaga over him and rightly so. Trouble is, I think he enjoys the attention. From what I hear he's dated plenty of them."

"A playboy, huh?" She shook her head. "What's his name? I might know him."

Stephanie should've never started this conversation, but Becky was the closest thing to a sister she had here in Rambling Rose. As for her triplet sisters back in Florida, Ashley, Megan and Nicole had never understood Stephanie's reluctance to jump into the dating scene with both feet. No big deal that she'd had a few bummers, they often told her. Unless she kept trying, she'd never find a good man.

When Becky asked the identity of her mystery man again, Stephanie knew there was no getting around it. "Acton Donovan," she replied. "I think his family owns and operates the Diamond D Ranch."

Becky's lips formed an *O*. "The Donovans. Sure, I know them. Gina brings her children into the pediatric center. I can't say that I've ever had any personal dealings with the men of the family. Although, I've seen them around town. They're all good-looking. And all still single, I think. I heard one of the nurses I work with say she'd like to date Acton, but as far as I know that never happened."

"From what I hear, there are plenty of women around town who'd like to date Acton. And the last thing I want to do is stand in line."

Frowning, Becky left the couch and walked over to the fireplace. "Have you actually met Acton?"

What would Becky think if she told her that the man had kissed her on the cheek yesterday? Warn her that she was playing with fire? "We've had a few meetings at the clinic. He's flirty, but fun and nice. He's offered to help with the fund-raiser Friday night."

Glancing over her shoulder, Becky smiled at Stephanie. "If that's the case, he can't be all bad. Do you think he's interested in you?"

Linus began to whimper and Stephanie went over to the couch to pick up the baby. As she positioned him against her shoulder, she said, "The girls on the staff have the idea that he likes me. I find that hard to believe. I mean, yes, I think he likes me—as in like as a friend. But I'm fairly vanilla, Becky. This guy can have rocky road...if he wants it."

Chuckling, she said, "Don't sell yourself short, Steph. Vanilla might be his favorite flavor."

She walked over to the couch and reached her arms out toward Linus. "Let me hold the little guy.

With the twins being toddlers I've almost forgotten how tiny they were at Linus's age."

Stephanie handed the baby over to her, while thinking Becky was one of the strongest, most resilient women she'd ever known. Shortly after she'd learned she was pregnant, her husband had been killed in a car accident. Since then, she'd raised the two babies alone. Until she'd met Callum and they'd fallen in love and married a few short weeks ago. Now Callum was the twins' father and loving every minute of it.

With Linus in her arms, Becky sank into the rocker and used her toe to push the chair into motion. While she rocked the baby, Stephanie walked over to a large plate glass window that overlooked the back portion of the property.

The Fame and Fortune Ranch was equipped with a huge swimming pool and a stable full of gentle riding horses, plus many other amenities that made life easy and pleasurable. It was a home that most people could only dream about, and because of this lavish place, Acton seemed to think she had everything she could possibly want. But she didn't have any of things she'd always truly wanted. Like the love of a man, or children to nurture and call her own.

She looked over at Becky. "You never did give me your opinion about Acton Donovan," Stephanie said. "Do you think he'd be trouble?"

"Aren't all men trouble?" She laughed before her

expression turned serious. "Just remember, Steph, I thought my chance for happiness was gone and I believed Callum was all wrong for me. Now look. We're married and very much in love. Anything can happen, even when it looks impossible. So I'm saying you'd be foolish to rule out Acton. Not before you give him a chance."

Acton might not want a chance with her, Stephanie thought.

And if he did? Was she brave enough to open her heart to him?

Acton spent the whole day helping his father and Shawn tag and vaccinate calves. The job was time-consuming, not to mention exhausting, and by the time they called it quits, it was too late to drive into town and see Stephanie at Paws and Claws.

Which was probably a good thing, Acton decided, as he drove the bumpy pasture road that led back to his house. If he didn't quit showing up at the animal clinic, Stephanie was going to start wondering what his intentions toward her really were, and Acton wasn't sure he could truthfully give her, or himself, the answer to that question.

Yes, he enjoyed being with her, especially two days ago when he'd picked up the cats. Everything about her turned him on. But the more he was learning about Stephanie Fortune, the more he worried that Shawn was right about her being out of his league. In the end, what could Acton really offer her?

The idea of her moving out of that palatial mansion and into his old two-story house, with its linoleum floors and wooden screen doors, was laughable. No woman in her right mind would sacrifice all that just for him. And Acton would do well to remember that.

Five minutes later, he reached the modest, white-clapboard house he called home. Seymour was waiting as Acton parked the truck beneath a live oak. The dog followed him onto a screened-in back porch, then into the kitchen.

Inside, the dog walked straight to his feed bowl and stared impatiently at Acton.

He stripped off his dusty chaps and denim jacket, then tossed them across the back of a chair. "Look, Seymour, one of us has to do some work around here. And I don't punch a time clock, so get over it."

The dog let out a single, demanding bark.

With a shake of his head, Acton went over to a corner pantry, where Seymour's food was stored.

"And you're not getting canned food tonight," he told the dog. "You ate it all and I'm not driving into town for more. Besides, the dry stuff will be better for your waistline. I'm surprised Stephanie didn't say you were fat!"

The dog whined and Acton stared at him in dismay. Surely the canine didn't know he was talking about the vet assistant who'd made his itching go away. Seymour was smart, but he wasn't human.

Acton poured a full bowl of food and was about to search the refrigerator for something to feed himself when the cell phone in his pocket dinged with a message.

Expecting it to be Shawn or Danny, he was surprised to discover the text message was from an unknown number.

Would you like to help me with a little baking this evening at my place? I'm making cookies and cupcakes for the fund-raiser.

Stephanie was inviting him to her house? He'd never expected anything like this!

Acton rapidly typed in a one-word message. When?

Whenever you can get here. I'll watch for you.

He replied that he'd be there shortly, then tossed the phone onto the cabinet counter and stomped a jig in the middle of the kitchen.

"Oowwee! Seymour, this is the best day of my life!"

Clearly unimpressed, the dog looked at him.

"Well, the second-best day," Acton told him. "I

keep forgetting the very best day was when I got you, old buddy. Just don't tell Stephanie I said so."

He raced out of the kitchen and straight down the hallway to the bathroom. As he stripped off the rest of his work clothes and stepped into the shower, he thought how shocked Shawn would be when he heard Stephanie had invited Acton to the Fame and Fortune Ranch.

But not clearly not as shocked as he was.

With Linus cradled in her arms, Stephanie met Acton at the front entrance to the house and guided him back to the main kitchen she shared with her three brothers.

"I'm surprised you agreed to this, Acton. Like I told you before, I know very little about cooking or baking. And Manny, our cook, is off tonight." She gestured to an array of ingredients and mixing bowls she'd laid out on a large work island in the middle of the room. "Do you think you can help me figure all this out?" she asked, letting her eyes look at him squarely for the first time tonight.

Dressed in faded jeans and a dark green shirt that contrasted with his light-colored hair, he was far more tempting than any cookie or cupcake they might make.

"I think I can," he told her. "After I get used to feeling like I've stepped into a palace. This place is incredible, Stephanie." He didn't bother to hide his amazement as he turned in a full circle, staring in awe at the endless rows of cabinets, tall, beamed ceilings, rich tiled floor and the most up-to-date appliances on the market. "Seymour wouldn't know what to do in this kitchen. When I left, he'd finished his supper and was lying on a braided rug in front of the gas range. This room would probably scare him."

Laughing, Stephanie carefully placed Linus in a padded carrier sitting at one end of the work island. As she fastened a safety belt across his middle, she said, "It's just a kitchen to me. I'll show you my part of the house later if you'd like—after we get the treats for the fund-raiser baked."

He continued to glance around as though he still couldn't believe what he was seeing. "I'd like that. Except I can't tell Gina. She'll be jealous that I got to visit this place before she did. Are you and Linus the only ones here?"

"No. Callum and his wife, Becky, and their one-year-old twin girls are in their section of the house. Steven, my oldest brother, usually works late with his construction crew, so I don't know if he's home yet. Dillon is in his office. I should say the office he uses here in his part of the house," she explained. "He spends most of his time on the phone conferring with the triplets on a design for the restaurant that they're planning in Rambling Rose."

He looked at her with faint surprise. "Rambling Rose is getting a new restaurant? If it's anything like this kitchen, I'm not sure the regular folks around town can afford to eat there."

Stephanie shrugged. "I purposely stay out of their business. Because it's a polarizing subject to the townspeople. If I made a point of openly siding with my brothers, some people might choose not to use Dr. Neil just because I work there."

He said, "In other words you prefer to remain neutral."

"Exactly."

He leaned over her shoulder to peer at Linus, and Stephanie breathed in the clean scent of his aftershave. If she turned slightly, her lips would almost be level with his and all she would need to do was lean in... But the man wasn't here for kissing, she told herself crossly. He was here for baking.

"Hey, Linus. When are you going to get big enough to eat a cookie?" he asked in a soft voice. "Do you even have a tooth yet?"

The gentle way he interacted with Linus never failed to surprise Stephanie. It also endeared him to her as nothing else could. "He doesn't have a tooth yet," she told him. "Maybe in another couple of months."

"He sure is cute. I've never seen him cry. Does he cry often?"

"Rarely. He's a happy baby."

He shook his head. "Ryan squalled all the time.

And Elizabeth yelled. I don't know how Gina came out of their baby years with any sense left."

He moved away and as Stephanie tried to regain her breath, she reached for a white bib apron. While she tied it on over her long dress printed with green and red flowers, he said, "I was surprised you invited me here tonight."

She glanced up at him and hoped he couldn't read the emotions she was feeling at seeing him again. Joy was pouring through her and curving the corners of her lips into a permanent smile. "I think I surprised myself by asking you over."

He smiled back at her. "I'm glad you did. And, by the way, you look very pretty. I've never seen you in a dress before or with your hair pinned up like that. The only thing you need is a magnolia in your hair and then you'd look like a tropical goddess."

Blushing, she said, "How do you know what a tropical goddess looks like?"

"Oh, I've squired plenty of them around Rambling Rose," he joked.

"I'll just bet." She laughed, then gestured to the work island. "What do you say we get to work and start with the cookies?"

"Sounds like a plan to me."

For the next few minutes, Stephanie read off the cookie recipe while Acton measured the ingredients into a large mixing bowl.

After he'd stirred everything together to make a

stiff dough, Stephanie read the next step. "Chill the dough at least an hour before rolling and cutting."

"Rolling and cutting? I've never rolled and cut," he said with a shake of his head. "I thought you spooned it onto a metal sheet and baked it."

"Well, I've never done this before," she admitted. "So I don't know what will happen if we skip that step. But I don't really have time to wait for the dough to chill. Let's do it your way. If they don't turn out, I'll cheat and go by the bakery. If I do, Sheri and Dayna will never quit teasing me, but that's okay."

He chuckled. "So you're not going to admit to them that I made these cookies?"

"Um, no. I'd never hear the end of it. For a lot of reasons."

A few minutes later, Stephanie was placing the freshly baked cookies onto a cooling rack and Acton was reading over the cupcake instructions, when her three brothers sauntered into the kitchen.

Deep in conversation, they didn't notice Acton and Stephanie at the work island. When they did finally spot them, they stopped in their tracks and stared at Acton as though he'd just stepped off a UFO.

"Stephanie! You're baking?" Steven asked.

The shock on her brothers' faces was almost comical.

"With a little help," she admitted. Then she took Acton by the arm and urged him toward the three men.

"Acton, these are my brothers. The tall dark-haired one on the left is Callum. The one in the middle, who thinks I'm a disaster in the kitchen, is Steven. And on the right with the sandy blond hair, that's Dillon. Most of the time he's the quiet one of the three."

Acton politely shook hands with each man. "It's nice to meet you all," he said.

Callum's skeptical gaze vacillated between his sister and Acton. "It's nice to meet you, too, Acton. We hope."

Hope? Oh, Lord, Stephanie thought, this curt attitude from her brothers was the last thing she needed right now.

"Stephanie hasn't mentioned you before. Are you a new boyfriend or something?"

The question came from Steven, who as the oldest of the siblings, had always considered himself the boss. He was frowning with disapproval. Which was ridiculous, Stephanie thought. He didn't know Acton. And he certainly shouldn't be judging him by his appearance.

"You're jumping to conclusions, Steven. Acton is just a friend. You don't need to start interrogating him."

She glanced at Acton and was suddenly struck by a wounded look in his eyes. Had her brothers' attitude offended him? Or had her comment about him being just a friend put the shadows in his eyes? Either way, she felt sick and helpless at the same time.

"I don't think Acton is someone we need worry about," Dillon said bluntly.

"Worry?" Acton repeated blankly as he studied the three men. "I don't get this."

"You'd get it if you knew all the losers that Stephanie has dated," Steven told him. "None of whom deserved our beautiful little sister. So just make sure you don't give us something to worry about."

"Steven!" she practically shouted at him. "I don't need this or deserve it! And neither does Acton! I'd appreciate it if all three of you would please get out of here and leave us alone."

His face grim, Steven walked out of the kitchen with Dillon following after him.

Pausing, Callum said, "We're just trying to protect you, Stephanie. That's all. We don't have anything against Acton."

"No," she drawled with sarcasm. "You just doubt my judgment. That's all."

Furious, she turned her back on her brother and waited until she'd heard the door close behind him before she turned a mortified look at Acton.

"I'm so sorry, Acton. I'm sorry for their behavior and sorry that I put you in this situation."

Letting out a long breath, he sat down on a wooden stool at the island. "You should've warned me about your brothers. If a person is expecting to be insulted, then it's not quite so bad when it does happen."

"They weren't insulting you. Not personally."

His short laugh told her exactly what he thought about that. "You could've fooled me. Do they always behave like jerks to your friends?"

Wishing she could melt into the floor and disappear, she walked over to him. "They didn't used to act like a trio of jackasses. But now...well, they're very protective of me. Because I... like they said, I've had some real stinking boyfriends in my life. And they're tired of seeing me end up on the losing end."

He frowned and his head moved slightly back and forth. "So they don't want you to date? Is that the problem?"

"Oh, they want me to date. They even want me to get married—eventually. But not before they make sure my man meets their expectations."

"Hell, that's like having three dads around trying to run your life. You're twenty-seven, Stephanie. You're old enough to choose your own man."

Her gaze dropped to the floor. "You're right. But so far I've been terrible at choosing. Or maybe I'm just not special enough to attract a good man."

His forefinger suddenly slipped beneath her chin and she sniffed as he lifted her face up to his.

"You're wrong, Stephanie. You're a special

woman. In so very many ways. You've just been unlucky in love, that's all."

She couldn't stop her eyes from misting over. Not to mention the fact that the touch of his finger on her chin was making her tremble all over. "You really think so?"

His smile was so tender that it made her heart hurt with longing.

"I know so. Because I've been unlucky in love, too. I understand what you've gone through."

Her lips parted with surprise. "You? That's not possible. I'm sure you have all kinds of women knocking on your door. And I can't imagine any one of them throwing you over for someone else."

He dropped his hand from her face, then speared his fingers through the dark blond curls falling near one eye. "Oh, Stephanie, sometimes I think you are far younger than me. Finding someone who fits you just right, who won't hurt you for any reason, who'll stand beside you through thick and thin—that's not an easy thing to do. I haven't managed to get it done...yet. Each time I think I'm getting close to finding that kind of woman, I've been disappointed. Big-time disappointed."

She placed her hand on his forearm, and as she did, their eyes met. The intimate clash caused her heart to skip a beat, and when she finally managed to speak, her voice sounded as if she'd just woken from a deep sleep.

"A few minutes ago, I'd wished that my brothers had never walked in here. And I'm still darned annoyed with all three of them. But now I'm almost glad. Otherwise, you might never have shared this with me. And it... I guess what I'm trying to say is that it makes me feel much closer to you. I hope you think that's a good thing."

A soft light glowed in his blue eyes. "I think it's good and great and every other stupendous adjective."

Laughing lightly, she leaned forward and kissed his cheek.

"What was that for?" he asked while rubbing his cheek with the tips of his fingers.

"It's my turn to thank you. Just for being Acton Donovan. And for not judging me by my brothers' behavior."

"You're very welcome, Stephanie. Now what do you say we start on the cupcakes? The sooner we get them baked, the sooner we can do a taste test."

"A taste test? Hmm. That's probably a good idea. If we bomb with our baking efforts, then I'll be forced to go to the bakery."

His grin oozed confidence. "With the two of us working together, we can't fail."

Chapter Six

Nearly an hour and a half later, after the cupcakes were cooled and frosted and the cookies packed away in a plastic storage container, Stephanie made coffee, then filled a basket with a thermos and a few of the sweets.

With Acton carrying Linus, and Stephanie toting the basket of goodies, she guided him to a wide foyer that connected a separate wing to the main section of the house. As they walked along, he noticed most of the hallway was made of plate glass. Beyond it, he could see footlights outlining a path through a perfectly landscaped courtyard.

When they reached a carved wooden door, she

opened it and gestured for him to enter. "This is my personal space," she told him. "I guess you'd call it my home within a home."

As she closed the door behind them, Acton gazed around the large, open area. The space was furnished as a sitting room, and though it was elaborate, it had a much homier feel than the monstrous kitchen they'd just left.

"Do you let the dogs in here?" Acton asked as he carried Linus to the middle of the room.

She walked over to him. "No. When I adopted Mack and Tallulah, they were both outdoor dogs. Mack is a terrier and a fierce digger. Tallulah is a dachshund and likes to show Mack she can dig even better than him. They'd be bored to tears if they were indoors. And, anyway, with two cats and the rabbit, it would be too crowded in here. Especially with Linus," she explained. "The dogs stay in a large fenced-in area at the back of the house. I'm having a longer run built for them so that they can go all the way to the stables and still be safely inside the fence. They love being around the horses, so that should make them really happy."

She gestured to an area where a round table was positioned near a floor-to-ceiling paned window. "I'll put our snacks here. Linus is sound asleep so let's put him in the bassinet."

While she deposited the basket on the table, Acton looked around for the bassinet. He spotted the portable hooded bed sitting a few feet away from a small fireplace, where apparently someone had lit a fire earlier in the evening. Now the logs had mostly turned to a pile of glowing red embers.

With Stephanie following close on his heels, Acton carried Linus over to the bassinet.

"If you'll give me the carrier," she suggested, "I'll hold it while you lift him out and put him to bed."

"I think I can do that." Careful to keep the baby's head supported, he scooped up Linus from the padded seat and gently laid him on a sheet printed with bright yellow ducks.

The baby seemed to sense he was finally in his own bed and as he squirmed slightly against the soft mattress, Acton smiled with satisfaction.

"Aww, look at him. He's looks comfortable now."

"He should be," Stephanie agreed. "His diaper is dry and his tummy is full. He'll sleep for hours."

She reached over and covered the baby with a pale blue blanket, and as she tucked the fabric around his tiny shoulders, Acton wondered how it would feel to have a baby son of his own. How would it feel to have a woman like Stephanie give him a child?

The thought had him rubbing a forefinger over Linus's dark hair. It was fine and soft and curled slightly on the ends. The vulnerability of the baby awed him in a way that surprised him. He'd never thought of himself as a daddy. Yet this little guy put a whole set of ideas in his head.

Acton had always admired his parents. Not just because they'd been happily married for so many years, but because they were so devoted to their children. They'd raised Acton and his three siblings with firm discipline and a wealth of love. And even though his father hadn't always been a perfect dad, Acton doubted he could ever fill his boots. As for his mother, Acton was pretty sure he could look to the ends of the earth and not find a woman with Faye Donovan's patient and nurturing soul.

"What are you thinking, Acton?"

Stephanie's soft question pulled Acton out of his thoughts and he glanced at her. The tender concern he saw on her features speared him right in the heart, and for a moment he was too struck by the feeling to even speak.

Finally, he said, "I, uh, was just thinking about my dad—wondering if I could ever be half the man that he is. He and Mom raised four of us. And just looking at little Linus makes me realize what an incredible task that must've been for them. I'm not sure I could do it, much less do it as well as they have."

"Parenting is a scary prospect. Especially if you want to do it right." She motioned toward the table, where their coffee, cupcakes and cookies were waiting. "Let's go sit. I'd like to hear about your family."

Once they were seated at the table, Stephanie poured two cups of coffee and passed out the desserts they'd baked.

Acton held up one of the cupcakes frosted with pink buttercream frosting. "It's a little lopsided, but who cares? I'm hoping the people who attend will have their mind on donations rather than the food."

Stephanie bit into a cookie. "Oh, this is scrumptious, Acton! No need to go by the bakery. I pronounce you a good cookie-maker."

"Thanks, but you helped, remember." He looked at her and winked. "I'll have to tell Grandma Hatti about this. She'll be proud. Because she's the one who taught me about cooking and baking. I might even manage to talk her into coming to the fundraiser. That is, if her arthritis isn't acting up."

She finished the last of the cookie and reached for a cupcake. "You said there were four of you. I've met Gina, so who are the other two?"

He nodded. "My brothers. They're both older than me. Shawn is after Gina and then Danny."

"Do your brothers work on your family ranch?" she asked.

"They do. Shawn is like me—he works on the ranch full-time. He mostly deals with the cattle while I tend to the cattle and the horses. Danny helps out on the ranch, too, but not on a daily basis. He has an outside job as a sales manager at the Travis County livestock auction."

"So your parents have always been together?"

Nodding, he said, "All these years and they're still crazy about each other. Their long, happy marriage is great, but it's also kind of daunting. It's a lot to live up to. Could be that's why me or my brothers have never tried it. None of us likes failing at anything." He glanced at her. "What about you, Stephanie? Are your parents still together?"

She reached for her coffee. "Yes. But my father, David, wasn't always married to my mother, Marci. He was first married to Penny. She's Callum and Dillon's mother. When Marci married Dad she already had two sons, Steven and Wiley. He adopted both of the boys and then he and Marci went on to have me and my triplet sisters. So you see, it's sort of a convoluted family. But all eight of us siblings get along fairly well."

"Hmm. So the brothers I met in the kitchen are actually two half-brothers and a stepbrother?"

"That's right. All of the brothers are half or step to us girls. But that doesn't stop them from being bossy," she added with a tight grimace. "I'm still upset with them for the way they treated you."

He shrugged. "Don't worry about it. I don't figure I'll be rubbing elbows with any of them, anyway. Besides, they could tell by looking at me that I'm not good enough to be your real boyfriend."

A look of disappointment flashed across her face and Acton wondered what might have caused the reaction. Maybe it was lingering regret over her brothers' behavior. In any case, he'd much rather see her smiling.

"I wished you hadn't said that, Acton."

"Why?"

"You make it sound like—" She paused and shook her head. "You're putting me up on some kind of weird pedestal and cutting yourself down. It's not that way at all."

He made a mocking grunt. "You might think so, but I know better. Look around you, Stephanie. A guy like me in a place like this? No. I'm a rancher— a cowboy. I work in mud and manure. I'm like the guy who's mucking out your stables, not the one who's invited to come for a ride."

She reached over and flicked something off his shoulder.

"What's wrong?" he asked. "Do I have a piece of cookie dough on me?"

"No. I'm knocking that ridiculous chip off. It's getting too big for me to ignore."

She smiled at him and Acton had to smile back at her. No matter how hopeless this attraction for her seemed, he couldn't make it go away, or even dim it to anything less. He was beginning to want this woman…very much. And right behind his wanting came the stark fear of losing his heart.

Stephanie was in the process of getting dressed the next evening when a knock sounded on the door.

Fearing it might be Acton, who'd promised to pick her up and drive her to the fund-raiser later tonight, she hurried to the door, only to find Becky standing on the threshold.

"Becky, what are you doing?"

Her sister-in-law laughed. "What do you think? I'm babysitting Linus tonight, remember?"

She pushed the door wider so that Becky could enter. "Well, yes, I remember. And I'm still feeling very guilty that you're staying home with the kids while I'm out partying. On top of that, you and Callum are newlyweds and you should be celebrating Valentine's night together."

"You—partying? Ha! You're working a fund-raiser for the clinic. As for me and Callum, we're planning something special together for tomorrow night. Besides, I have two good reasons for spending the night at home. One, trying to corral the twins with a room full of dogs and cats would be disastrous. And two, Callum plans to use the gathering to talk business. That's not my idea of a romantic evening."

"Okay, I won't feel guilty anymore. But you didn't have to come for Linus. I was going to bring him and his things over to you."

Shaking her head, Becky followed Stephanie across the living room and down a short hallway to her bedroom. An array of glittery cocktail dresses was spread across the king-size bed, while in the middle of the dresses, Linus was lying on his belly, doing his best to paddle his arms and legs.

"You have enough to do with getting yourself ready," Becky told her. "By the way, the twins are excited to see Linus."

"Really? They can talk well enough to tell you that?"

"They're saying more words every day. I've taught them to say 'Linus.' Although it's coming out more like 'Nus' with the 'Li' missing."

Stephanie laughed. "How cute. Wouldn't it be wonderful if they could grow up as true cousins?"

Becky walked over to the bed. "It would. And who knows, that could possibly happen. Do you have his diaper bag packed?"

"I do. It's in the living room. Everything is in it, except for his bottles. They're still in the fridge."

"I'll get them," Becky told her, then made a slow perusal of the red dress Stephanie was wearing. The lacy sheath was body-hugging with long fitted sleeves and a boat neckline. "You look incredible in that red lace and those heels. I am so envious. You walk in those things like they're athletic shoes. I'd be teetering."

Laughing, Stephanie glanced down at the red high heels that fastened with a strap around her ankles. "I was going to ask you how I look. Is the dress appropriate? I don't want to be over-the-top, but I want to look like I'm going to a party instead of cleaning out kennels at the clinic."

"I'm giving you an A-plus. You look lovely. But

is that the way you're going to wear your hair—all frazzled out like that?"

Stephanie's hand automatically flew to her partially teased hair. "I was in the middle of doing my hair when you rang the doorbell. I'm going to wear it pinned up in curls on the crown. I had it that way last night and Acton liked it."

Becky smiled cleverly. "So you're trying to please Acton now? I don't think I'll tell Callum that just yet."

"I honestly don't care what you tell Callum," Stephanie said stiffly. "I'm still angry with all three of my brothers."

"Can't blame you for that. After you told me what they said to Acton, I'm honestly surprised he didn't try to bust all of them in the mouth."

Stephanie walked over to the dresser, where she'd laid out a comb and a stack of hairpins. "Acton is an easygoing guy. I'm grateful that he took it all in stride. Have I told you he's going to pick me up tonight and drive me to the fund-raiser?"

Becky walked up behind her and studied Stephanie's reflection in the mirror. "You didn't tell me. So is this supposed to be a date with you two? Has it come to that now?"

Stephanie shrugged. "We're not calling it a date. But it's the closest thing I've had to one in a long time."

"If that's the case, then you need to take extra

pains with your hair. I'm going to get Linus and get out of here so you can concentrate." She collected the baby from the bed, then on her way out, paused at the door. "Stephanie, I wouldn't worry. If Acton is the man I think he is, then all three of your brothers will be happy for you."

Turning away from the mirror, Stephanie looked gratefully at her sister-in-law. "Thanks, Becky. But like I told them, Acton and I are only friends—good friends."

Becky's smile was knowing. "I can't think of a better way to start a romance."

When Stephanie and Acton arrived at The Shoppes building, the parking area was already beginning to fill up with vehicles. Acton parked at the far end of the lot, then came around to help her out of the truck.

"Did you do gymnastics as a child?" he asked once she was standing on solid ground.

"No. Why?"

"Those heels. You'd have to be an acrobat to walk in them. But I'll say one thing, they're damned sexy." He flashed her a sizzling grin. "Everything about you tonight looks sexy."

No one had ever used that word to describe Stephanie. She'd been called pretty plenty of times, along with cute. But she'd never been called sexy. Hearing it from Acton's lips put a warm blush on her cheeks.

"Thank you, Acton. You look rather handsome yourself. I wasn't expecting you to get so dressed up."

He was wearing a dark, Western-cut suit with a white shirt. Black cowboy boots and a bolo tie with a silver-and-onyx slide completed the look that was masculine and classy at the same time.

He glanced down at himself. "I don't break out these clothes too often. But what the heck, it's Valentine's Day and we're going to a party. And speaking of Valentine's Day, I have a little something for you."

"For me?"

He opened the back door of the truck and pulled out a huge, beautiful bouquet of purple and yellow tulips arranged in an amber hobnail vase.

He said. "Considering the occasion, I should've probably gone with red and pink flowers. But I wanted you to have something different."

Stephanie was so touched by the unexpected gift that tears stung the back of her eyes.

He stepped closer and she accepted the bouquet from him. "What a lovely surprise, Acton! And the colors are gorgeous."

"My pleasure. I'm glad you like them."

Her gaze lifted from the tulips to scan his face and she noticed he'd left his hat in the truck. With his head bent slightly toward hers, the masculine scent of his hair swirled in her nostrils and acted on her senses like an aphrodisiac.

"I'd love to take the flowers in with me," she said,

while hoping her voice sounded steady. "But I'm afraid someone might confuse them as part of the decorations and they'd end up in the wrong hands."

"I'd hate for that to happen. Let's just leave them here. Since the night is cool they should be fine."

By the time he returned the bouquet back to the truck and locked the vehicle, Stephanie's knees were quivering and she latched a hand on his forearm to steady herself.

"Thank you, Acton, for the lovely flowers. Do you mind if I hang on to you while we walk to the building? I'm not used to these heels."

His eyes twinkling, he pressed a hand over hers. "I'm all yours."

All hers? For this one special night, Stephanie was going to let herself believe him.

Chapter Seven

The old Woolworth's five-and-dime building had been a part of downtown Rambling Rose for many years. Now it was little more than town history. In the past months, Fortune Brothers Construction had purchased and transformed the old structure into a group of elaborate units named The Shoppes at Rambling Rose. And with none of the businesses opened yet, Stephanie's brothers had offered the spacious lobby for the Paws and Claws fund-raiser.

Stephanie regarded their offer as a charitable act, but Acton was more inclined to believe their generosity had been a two-fold arrangement. Not only would the donation put them in a favorable light with the townspeople, but it also gave them a perfect opportunity to show off the impressive makeover of the building.

To be fair, that one awkward meeting in the Fame and Fortune kitchen was hardly enough for Acton to actually size up Stephanie's brothers. So he hardly had the right to belittle their motives. For Stephanie's sake, he hoped their intentions were heartfelt.

Now, as the two of them stepped inside the glass-enclosed lobby of The Shoppes, they both gazed in amazement at the elegant space. Beyond the Italian tiled floor and the artistic waterfall in the center of the space, yards of tulle in pink, red and white were draped from the ceiling, along with clusters of paper hearts. The dogs that were up for adoption were all wearing red sweaters, while the cat cages were festooned with paper hearts and balloons with enough helium to keep them floating out of the reach of their playful claws.

Love songs were playing over the impressive sound system, while along one wall, a dessert buffet had been set up, including the cookies and cupcakes that Stephanie and Acton had baked the night before.

"Wow! This looks nothing like the old building that I remember!" Acton exclaimed. "The room, the decorations—this is impressive!"

"It does look nice," Stephanie agreed. "But I'm more enthused about this huge crowd. And I see that Callum and Steven have already arrived."

Acton followed the direction of her gaze until he spotted the two men standing several feet away. Callum appeared to be in deep conversation with a man that served on the Rambling Rose city council. Steven turned his head just enough for him to catch sight of Stephanie and Acton. Even at a distance Acton could see the man's eyes narrow skeptically.

"I don't think Steven is too happy about seeing us together like this," Acton told her, while privately he was fighting the urge to walk over and tell the eldest Fortune brother to go to hell.

Unconcerned, she replied, "That's too bad. We're here together. Aren't we?"

Thankfully, the sweetness that radiated from Stephanie had a soothing effect on Acton and he told himself it didn't matter what her brothers thought of him. All that mattered was what she thought of him, and tonight she was looking at him with a warm, inviting glow in her eyes.

"We're definitely here together," he said. "Let's go mingle and see if we can talk some of these people into adopting a few pets."

The two had barely managed to move a few feet into the milling crowd when Dayna intercepted them.

"Is this turnout incredible or what?" she asked as she nibbled from the small plate she was carrying. "I honestly think most of the guests are here to see what Stephanie's brothers have done to this place.

If it wasn't full of dog and cat cages, it would look like a room taken right out of a palace."

"As long as people are donating money to Paws and Claws, that's the important thing," Stephanie said.

"Don't worry, Steph. The night is just getting started and I've already seen lots of money being dropped into the pot," Dayna assured her.

"That's good news," Stephanie replied, then flashed a glance in the direction of Callum and Steven. "You can bet I'm expecting my brothers to contribute to the cause. And if I don't see amounts involving at least four digits written on their checks, I'm going to disown them."

Acton whistled under his breath. "Sounds like you have high expectations."

"I do from my brothers. They can afford it."

"My brother donated a check with four numbers," Dayna said with a laugh. "But there was a decimal in the middle."

"Every donation is appreciated and welcome," Stephanie told her coworker. "No matter the amount."

Dayna turned a sage smile on Acton. "It's easy to forget that she's a Fortune," she said, then suddenly waved at someone across the room. "Excuse me, you two. My mom is signaling me. I'll catch up with you later."

Frowning thoughtfully, Stephanie watched Dayna

disappear into the crowd. "Sometimes she can say the weirdest things."

Acton said, "I understood what she was getting at. I feel the same way. You don't come across as anything like your high-rolling brothers."

She let out a short laugh. "Thank you. I think."

Acton's gaze made another trip around the room, which had been lavishly refurbished with plenty of plate glass and strategically placed lighting. From what Stephanie had told him, there were already several upscale retail businesses ready to move in. The change might be grand for some of the citizens of Rambling Rose, but Acton couldn't see it drawing in the regular, hardworking folks who'd originally founded the town.

"Judging by this building, I agree that your brothers could write a sizable check to Paws and Claws." He cast her a wry look. "I just hope you're not expecting four numbers without the decimal from me."

Her eyes widened with dismay. "Oh, no, Acton. You've already given more than enough. First your help baking and then your help hauling some of the animals over here. That means as much or more than money."

Shrugging, he wondered why it was so important to him to impress her. He sure as hell couldn't do it with money. But maybe, just maybe, she was different enough from her brothers not to care what was in his bank account.

"I didn't do that much. But I have been wondering about something. Where is Buddy? Isn't he going to be given the chance to be adopted? Or did Dr. Neil want to wait until his cast was removed?"

A smug smile came over her pretty face. "Dr. Neil took Buddy's cast off yesterday. But the dog didn't need to come to the party tonight to find himself a home. Someone has already made arrangements to adopt him."

"That's great news. After all Buddy has been through, I hope it's someone who appreciates him."

"It is." She smiled. "I confess, that someone is me," she told him. "Buddy is going to be my dog."

Acton wasn't surprised in the least. Stephanie was the nurturing sort and her heart was too big for her own good. It was no wonder that men had taken advantage of her in the past, he thought. And the idea that she'd been hurt in such a way sickened Acton to the core of his being. Obviously it had sickened her brothers, too. But that didn't give them the right to assume Acton was just another jerk out to get whatever he could from their sister.

"I should have known," Acton said to her. "So Buddy is going to have to learn how to dig holes like Mack and Tallulah."

She laughed and he noticed how the pearl drops she was wearing in her ears swung against her smooth neck. He'd never seen a real live seductress before, but he figured Stephanie looked very close to being one tonight. From the moment he'd picked her up at the Fame and Fortune Ranch, he'd been staring at her like a besotted buffoon.

"I'm sure they'll teach Buddy all about the art of digging," she said, then looped her arm through his. "Let's go see what we can find on the buffet table. I'm starving."

The party was still going on two hours later, although a large portion of guests had already departed with animals in tow. To Stephanie's delight, all of the animals, except for one young female cat, had found forever homes.

Grizabella was still sitting in a wire cage, watching people pass her by and, no doubt, wondering why she was the only animal left behind.

The gray-and-white feline was beautiful and sweet, but no one had seemed to want her because she was blind in one eye. The handicap didn't bother Grizabella in the least. She could run and play just as well as any of the two-eyed cats. It was the humans who wanted to put limitations on her.

Stephanie spoke softly to the cat, while stroking her little nose through the wire slats. "I promise you, Grizabella, I'll find you a good home. One where you'll be appreciated for the fine girl you are."

Stephanie hardly needed to take on another cat, especially since she'd signed on for Buddy. But she couldn't bear the thought of Grizabella being left behind.

"Has no one taken Grizabella yet?"

Stephanie looked around to see Acton had walked up behind her. He offered her one of the foam cups he was carrying.

"Thanks. I needed this." She took a careful sip of the hot coffee, then answered his question. "Unfortunately no. And it makes me want to cry, Acton. Just look how beautiful she is."

"She's as pretty as a June mornin'," he agreed.

Leaning toward the cage, he stuck a finger through the wire and wiggled it to attract Grizabella's attention. Instead of pawing at his finger, Grizabella decided she'd rather give it a loving swipe with her tongue.

Acton laughed. "Hey, I think she likes me."

"Of course, she likes you. She's a sweetheart."

He continued to waggle his finger and Grizabella rubbed her cheek against it.

"You know, I've always wanted a cat," he said after a moment. "I think the two of us would be great pals."

Stephanie was shocked. She'd recognized from the first day he'd brought Seymour to the clinic that, where animals were concerned, he had a big heart. But that didn't necessarily mean he was generous enough to take on an extra pet just because it needed a home.

"Really? You'd give a one-eyed cat a home?"

"I don't see Grizabella as a one-eyed cat. I see her as a pretty and loving kitty. My only concern is Seymour and that jealous streak of his."

He didn't see Grizabella as handicapped. Maybe it was silly of her, but suddenly she was seeing that sign around his neck that read Good.

"Oh, I think Seymour won't have a problem with Grizabella. In fact, I have a feeling that he'll like the company." She gave him an encouraging smile. "I'd be glad to come over and help you get the two of them acquainted."

"You'd do that?"

"Certainly." She glanced questioningly at the cat. "So? Is she going to be yours?"

"Sure. I couldn't tell either of you no. So Grizabella is going to the Diamond D to live with me."

Too happy to contain herself, Stephanie rose on the tips of her toes and kissed his cheek. "You're a wonderful man, Acton."

Grinning, he was about to reply, when voices suddenly rose from somewhere behind them. Both Stephanie and Acton turned to see Steven and Callum in what appeared to be a heated discussion with a tall woman dressed in a Navy blue, glen-plaid business suit. A curtain of straight dark hair hung against her back.

"Isn't that the mayor my brothers are talking to?" Stephanie asked.

Acton squinted at the trio. "Right. Ellie Hernandez. And from the sound of things, your brothers are disagreeing with her about something."

Slipping her hand into Acton's, Stephanie lowered her voice so that only he could hear. "Let's move over a few steps and maybe we can hear exactly what they're discussing."

Using the same hushed tone, he playfully scolded, "Stephanie, you want to eavesdrop!"

"So what? We're in a public place and those three aren't exactly trying to be discreet, are they?"

Acton glanced at the trio as Stephanie pulled him in front of a stack of empty animal crates. "Well, no," he answered. "Looks like they've forgotten they're at a public function."

Across the way, the young attractive mayor was waving her hand in a circular motion. "Yes, I agree," she said. "The renovations you've completed on this property are amazing. Everyone can see that. My problem is this—The Shoppes look more appropriate for Rodeo Drive in Hollywood than our little town of Rambling Rose!"

Scowling, Steven said, "As the mayor, you should be proud that your town can boast of such improvements. Don't you believe the people of Rambling Rose deserve to have nice businesses and buildings?"

The woman snorted. "I happen to believe if an election was held tomorrow, most of the citizens would vote to run Fortune Brothers Construction out of town on a rail!"

Callum chuckled. "Steven, I think Mayor Hernandez has been watching too many old Westerns. Maybe we should be worried about getting tarred and feathered, too, before they put us on the rail," he joked.

Stephanie cringed. "He's hardly winning any points with her," she whispered to Acton.

"From what I know about the lady, she's no pushover," Acton whispered back.

As if on cue, the mayor retorted, "I hardly think this is anything to joke about, Mr. Fortune. It's also obvious to me that neither of you understands what it means to be Texan. We don't take kindly to outsiders moving in and trying to change our towns, or our lifestyles."

Steven said, "I can't believe that any true Texan would be opposed to progress. And that's what my brothers and I are trying to do here. Make improvements to Rambling Rose."

"You're not being honest, Mr. Fortune. You're trying to make money. That's what you and your brothers are all about. And I don't like the idea of your profit coming at the expense of my citizens."

"Really, Mayor Hernandez, we're not vultures. We want what's good for the people of Rambling Rose just as much as you do," Callum said, attempting to assure her. "And the last I heard, capitalism isn't a crime. That's how this great country of ours was built."

"I've studied history, Mr. Fortuno," the mayor said in an icy voice. "Especially Texas history. The battle of the Alamo exemplifies how Texans fought and died for what they wanted. Maybe the both of you should take a lesson from that. Now if you'll excuse me, I have other people to see."

The mayor walked away and so did Stephanie's brothers. Once all three were out of sight, Acton whistled under his breath. "Man, oh, man, steam was coming out of her ears."

"She was seething, all right," Stephanie agreed. "This reminds me how glad I am that I'm not a part of Fortune Brothers Construction. I don't think I could sleep at night. I can already imagine what kind of obstacles the mayor is going to throw up when they start making plans for the hotel and all the other things they want to build around town."

"Well, Callum might joke about the mayor watching too many Westerns, but they need to realize if they get her riled up enough she might just turn into another Annie Oakley."

Regret turned down the corners of Stephanie's lips. "I wish my brothers could be…a little more Texan. Like you, Acton. Then I think they'd understand what people around here really want for their town."

"Hey, you two, I think Dr. Neil wants to start wrapping up this shindig."

They both looked around to see Carla popping a chocolate Hershey's Kiss into her mouth. The receptionist looked exceptionally pretty tonight, Stephanie thought. Her dress was blue velvet and her brown hair, which she normally wore in a bun, rested in soft curls upon her shoulders.

Carla was far more suitable for Acton, Stephanie thought. She came from a ranching family. The two of them had much more in common. And yet, Acton didn't seem to pay any more attention to Carla than he did the other women on the Paws and Claws staff—a fact that still amazed her. Why had he singled out Stephanie? Because he honestly thought she was special? Or because her last name was Fortune?

When are you going to get that out of your mind, Stephanie? Not everybody gives a damn about your last name. Not everyone cares about your money. And if that's what you think about Acton, you need to walk away from him right now.

Ignoring the mocking voice in her head, Stephanie said to Carla, "I think everyone has donated that's planning to. So it probably is time to get everything loaded and back to the clinic."

"I see Grizabella is the only animal left," Carla said, glancing in the direction of the cat cage. "Too bad no one wanted her."

Stephanie smiled proudly at Acton. "But someone did want her," she told Carla. "Acton is adopting her."

Surprised, Carla looked at him. "Really? I'm glad you felt sorry for her."

Acton frowned. "But I don't feel sorry for Grizabella. I don't believe she needs my sympathy. She needs my love."

Clearly embarrassed, Carla said, "Excuse me. I never thought of it that way. You're a nice guy, Acton."

She turned and walked away and Acton let out a long sigh. "Sometimes I can be a real jerk. I should've never said that to her. At least, not in that way. She meant well. It's just that it annoys the hell out of me when people dwell on the wrong instead of the right."

"I wouldn't worry about Carla. She'll think about what you said and in the long run it will help her. Now me, I'm the one who'd like to slither out of here without being seen. I can only hope the rest of the room didn't hear the things being said between my brothers and the mayor. But I have the feeling most of the guests did hear their conversation. My family is going to be the gossip around town," she said, then let out a caustic laugh. "What am I thinking? They already are the town gossip."

Draping his arm around her shoulders, he urged her over to Grizabella's cage. "Come on, forget all that. Let's tell Grizabella she's finished with that nerve-wracking cat room at the clinic. From now on, she's going to be a ranch cat."

Stephanie laughed and thought how she'd never met any man that made her feel so good—until Acton had walked into her life.

The hands on Acton's watch were nearing midnight when he finally pulled the truck to a stop in front of the massive Fortune estate.

After helping Stephanie out of the truck, he walked her to her private wing and stood to one side, holding the bouquet of tulips, while she unlocked the door.

"Would you like to come in for a few minutes?" she asked. "I can make coffee...or something."

Acton was sorely tempted to accept her offer, but tonight he couldn't trust himself. Tonight, something had happened to him and he couldn't yet figure out what it was or why it was making him feel so differently. He only knew that being alone with Stephanie might change everything between them and he wasn't sure if he, or she, was ready for that.

"Thanks, Stephanie, but I think I'd better get on home." He handed her the vase of flowers. "I don't want to leave Grizabella in the truck too long. She'll think she's being deserted."

"Oh, that's right. You have Grizabella. She was so quiet on the ride over here that I almost forgot about her."

She smiled tentatively at him and Acton inwardly groaned as his gaze focused on her moist lips.

"I, uh, had a great time tonight," he said. "And Paws and Claws raised more money than any of us expected. That's a good thing."

"I had a great time, too." She touched one of the purple tulips. "And I was given a lovely Valentine. Thank you for the bouquet, Acton. And thank you for wanting to love Grizabella. I'm learning you're a real softy."

He gave her a lopsided grin. "There's a lot you haven't learned about me...yet, that is."

She drew in a deep breath and Acton got the impression that she was nervous about something. Him? He hoped not. He wanted her to feel very much at home with him. He wanted her to feel like being with him was as right as him taking Grizabella.

"Really?" she asked. "Like what?"

"Like how much I've wanted to do this—for a very long time."

"This?"

His hands curved over her shoulders and the warmth radiating from her body urged him to draw her closer. "Taking you in my arms and kissing you."

She sucked in a breath, but he didn't wait to see if she was going to make any sort of reply. Instead, he pulled her into the circle of his arms and lowered his lips to hers.

Acton had meant to keep the kiss short and sweet.

He'd simply wanted a brief taste of her, just to let her know where his thoughts were headed.

But it didn't work out exactly that way. As soon as their lips made contact, some sort of explosion detonated inside him. And inside Stephanie, too, apparently. Before he recognized what was happening, their mouths were fused together and his hands were tugging her forward until the tulips were very nearly crushed between their bodies.

Kissing Stephanie was like dipping his tongue into a pot of wild honey. The smooth sweetness clung to his lips, making him want more and more.

It wasn't until he heard a tiny moan in her throat that reality returned. And even then it took a mountain of strength to tear his mouth from hers and set her back from him.

"I, uh, think I'd better be going, Stephanie."

"Going?"

She sounded just as dazed as Acton felt, and for a split second he wondered if he'd gone crazy. He wasn't built to ignore the passion in a woman's kiss. Everything inside his body was screaming at him to kiss her again, to take her into her fancy house and make hot, wild love to her.

But Stephanie wasn't just any woman. And he wasn't the same man who'd taken a woman to bed just because it felt good. No, somewhere in the past week, she'd changed him, and now all he wanted was to cherish and protect her.

Oh, damn.

Those were the things a husband wanted to do for his wife—for the woman he loved! The idea that Acton was falling that hard for Stephanie, rattled his senses.

"Yes. Going," he repeated huskily. "Tonight— at this moment—I think that's best for both of us." Bending his head, he brushed a kiss to the corner of her lips, then another one on her cheek.

Her hand latched on to his arm as though she didn't want to let him go. But then her eyes slowly opened and a tempting little smile curved her lips.

"Yes. Best for both of us. That's what I want, too," she whispered. "Good night, Acton."

She turned and entered the house and Acton stood there staring at the closed door, and wondered how long it was going to take his senses to come back to earth.

Chapter Eight

"Mom, do you have any sardines or tuna?"

Standing at the kitchen sink, Faye Donovan, a tall woman with short blond hair and a gentle face, turned away from the pot she was scrubbing to cast a concerned look at Acton.

"Son, are things getting so tight that you've run out of groceries and resorted to eating peanut butter and crackers?"

Acton laughed. "No, Mom. I have enough to buy myself a cabinet full of groceries. I just haven't taken the time to go to the supermarket. Dad has kept me and Shawn pretty tied up with that new cross fence we've been building."

"Yes, once your father makes up his mind to do something, he wants it done yesterday. But maybe that's a good thing. I never could stand procrastination. Especially in a man."

Was that what Acton was doing? He wondered. Three days had passed since the night of the Paws and Claws Valentine's party and he'd not seen or messaged Stephanie even once.

Oh, he'd wanted to. Everything inside him was aching to see her again. To kiss her and allow the passion he'd felt budding between them the other night to burst into full bloom. But he'd turned into a coward. What if he did make love to Stephanie? Where was that going to lead them? As far as he could see, it was going to lead to heartache. And then he'd end up being one more name on that list of no-accounts who'd already broken her heart.

Acton chugged down the last of the ice water he'd poured for himself. "The sardines and tuna aren't for me, Mom. I guess I forgot to tell you. I have a cat now. I adopted her the other night at the Valentine shindig."

Faye turned back to the saucepan soaking in the sink of sudsy water. "Oh, yes, I meant to tell you that I sent a donation to them through the mail. After wrestling around with that two-year-old colt all afternoon, your father was just too tired to get dressed up to go. To tell you the truth, I was a little disappointed. It was Valentine's Day and we haven't gone anywhere dressed up in a long time."

"Aww, Mom, that's awful." He walked over and wrapped an affectionate arm around her shoulders. "You should've let me know. You could've gone with me."

"It wouldn't have been the same. And, anyway, your father made it up to me. Look at this."

After wiping her hands on a dish towel, she lifted the right one and flashed a ruby-and-diamond ring at him.

"Isn't that something?"

Acton whistled. "I'll say. That must have cost Dad a couple of calves!"

"Oh, you!" She poked a finger in Acton's midsection. "A woman doesn't want a man who's always practical. She needs romance once in a while."

Would a ring from him put a smile on Stephanie's face? Not an engagement ring, but one that meant she was more than a friend? No. A ring would just complicate things, he thought. Besides, she'd probably laugh at any gemstone he could afford.

"I'll keep that in mind, Mom. Now what about the sardines or tuna? I'm desperate. Grizabella is hiding under the bed and the only way I can tempt her out is with fish. I've used every can I have."

Faye walked over and opened the door to a floor-to-ceiling pantry. "Was she a feral cat or something?"

"No. At Paws and Claws she didn't seem timid at

all. But when I got her home and she took one look at Seymour walking through the house, she was traumatized. Now I can't convince her that he's harmless."

She carried three cans of tuna over to where he stood next to the cabinet. "Well, I'm not sure this is going to convince her. But you're welcome to it. Maybe she just needs a female voice to coax her out. I'd come down and help, but Gina wants me to do some mending for her tonight."

A female voice. Yes, Acton knew exactly what female voice Grizabella needed to hear to calm her fears. But that meant inviting Stephanie over to his house. He wasn't sure he was ready for that.

Coward. Since when has a woman caused you to develop a yellow streak down your back? You're acting like an idiot!

"Thanks, Mom, but I'll manage somehow."

As he started out of the room, Faye called to him.

"Acton, speaking of the Valentine's party, I heard you were seen with a pretty young lady with the last name of Fortune."

"Who told you that?"

"Joyce Crandall. You know, the woman who plays piano at church."

"I've never said more than two words to her in my life. What is she? A busybody or something?"

"No. She just thought I might want to know that you're associating with the Fortunes. It's not like everyone in the county hasn't been talking about the rich family that's moved in and started taking over the town. Frankly, your father and I are a little surprised you haven't said anything to us about this young woman."

Acton should've known this was coming. Living in a small town, people talked—even when there was nothing to talk about. In this case, Joyce and every other guest at the Valentine party had probably noticed the way Acton had been glued to Stephanie's side the entire evening.

"Why should I have said anything? Stephanie is just a friend. A good friend. There's nothing more to tell."

Faye was unconvinced, which hardly surprised Acton. When it came to her sons, she'd always been able to read between the lines.

"So you two are just friends. Looks like I've been concerned about nothing."

Acton walked back to the center of the kitchen. "Concerned? Why would you be concerned that I'm friends with a member of the Fortune family?"

She grimaced, then made a helpless gesture with her hands. "I didn't mean it exactly like that. But there's been so much talk about the family and I remember reading about the trouble up in Austin with that bunch of Fortunes who have the tech business. His ex-wife was trying to kill him. She burned down part of their house and injured her own son."

Stephanie hadn't mentioned anything like this to Acton and he wasn't one to keep up with that sort of news. He did well to tune in to the market report when he drank his first cup of coffee in the morning. And the only reason he bothered with the market news was to keep account of cattle and hay prices.

He told his mother, "That has nothing to do with this family of Fortunes."

"Probably not," Faye agreed. "But I guess my concern is…well, none of you kids ever associated with a family who had that kind of drama connected to it. Or was worth the kind of money they're worth. They're just not your style, Acton. And I don't mean that in an insulting way. I mean it as a compliment. You're too good for them."

Acton groaned. "Oh, Mom, you're biased. And for your information, Stephanie isn't what you think. She's kind and sweet and very down-to-earth. She works as a vet assistant, for Pete's sake." He kissed her cheek and started out of the room. "I've got to go. Grizabella is under the bed." Pausing at the doorway, he added, "And don't worry about me. I'm not being sucked in by a diabolical family."

Groaning, she waved him toward the door. "Get out of here. Go charm your cat."

"Stephanie, are you feeling sick?"

The sound of Dr. Neil's voice interrupted her thoughts and she glanced around to see the veterinarian had finished removing a large cyst from a cat and was in the process of taking off his gloves. At some point during the surgical procedure Stephanie's mind must have wandered.

She blinked her eyes and mentally shook herself. "I'm fine, Dr. Neil. Did I do something wrong?"

The kind vet gave her a reassuring smile. "I don't remember you ever doing anything wrong, Stephanie. And you've never gotten sick at the sight of blood. But you look a little pale and strained. I hope you're not coming down with a virus. There are several strains running rampant around town right now."

She was coming down with something all right, and it was scaring the living daylights of her. Plain and simple, she was lovesick and she had no clue how to cure herself of the malady.

"I'm just a bit tired, that's all. Don't worry, Dr. Neil."

He gave her shoulder a kindly pat. "We've had a hell of day today," he said, then lowered his voice to a whisper. "And don't tell anyone, but you've worked circles around the other assistants."

The doctor's compliment put a smile on her face. No one, especially her brothers, understood how important her job was to her. Helping to make an animal healthy and happy was gratifying and rewarding to her. Just like being Linus's mother filled her with overwhelming love and protectiveness.

"Thank you, Dr. Neil. I'll keep that a secret." She

gestured to the black cat on the operating table. At the moment, he was still under anesthesia, but would soon be waking.

"Are you all finished with Chester?"

"All finished. Give him a shot of seven-day antibiotic and put him in recovery. As soon as he wakes up, he can go home. Ruby is probably going to burst into tears when she sees the hide cut off his back, but just reassure her that after a few days it will close up nicely. Oh, and send a bottle of antiseptic home with her to help keep down the bacteria. But no charge. The poor woman can't afford it. And just so you know, I haven't made any typos on her bill. I'm making adjustments on the cost of Chester's treatment."

Ruby, Chester's owner, was a willow-thin woman in her early seventies with graying auburn hair and thick tortoiseshell-frame glasses. From the woman's prior visits, Stephanie had learned Ruby was a widow. After her husband's death, she'd been forced to sell her home and move into a cheap rental house on the edge of town. However, that hadn't stopped Ruby from going around picking up stray cats and giving them a home, even when she struggled to feed herself.

"Yes, Dr. Neil. I'll take care of it."

After Stephanie transferred the cat to the recovery room, she collected a bottle of antiseptic from the supplies cabinet and made her way to the waiting area.

Before she walked over to give Ruby the news about Chester, she stopped by the checkout desk, where Sheri was studying a spreadsheet on the computer screen.

Stifling a yawn, she turned her attention to Stephanie. "Oh, what a day. You have a bill for Chester?"

"I do." She handed Sheri the sheet of paper with the itemized charges. "And I want you to put the charge to my account. I'll pay for it before I leave work this evening."

"Stephanie, don't be such a softy!" Sheri scolded. "You can't take care of every hard-luck person who walks in here!"

Stephanie glanced over her shoulder to where Ruby was reading one of the magazines left scattered around the waiting area.

"Dr. Neil is barely charging her anything. So I'll pick up the rest. She deserves help. And don't let on to Ruby about any of this. Just tell her that Dr. Neil didn't have to do that much to Chester." Sheri opened her mouth to object again, but Stephanie cut her off. "Just play along."

Sheri shrugged. "Okay, whatever you say," she said, then went on before Stephanie had a chance to walk away. "I've been meaning to tell you how gorgeous you looked the other night at the Valentine's party. Seeing you in your work clothes around here, I would've never imagined you in lace and high heels. You surprised me."

Even though Stephanie had grown up in a wealthy family and had often had to look the part at her parents' dinner parties, she'd never been the glamour-girl type. And since she'd moved to Rambling Rose, she'd purposely kept her image low-key. She didn't want to give the locals any reason to say she was trying to show off.

"Sometimes I surprise myself, Sheri."

"Well, having a guy like Acton Donovan at your side is like having a gorgeous accessory. You two looked mighty friendly, too."

Stephanie didn't have time for frivolous gossip. Especially when she figured Acton would soon be moving his fickle attention to some other woman around town. Maybe he already had, she thought dismally. Ever since he'd plastered that scorching kiss on her lips, she'd not seen or heard a word from him.

"We are mighty friendly," Stephanie replied stiffly. "But that's all."

Sheri laughed. "Steph, don't try to kid a kidder, or trick a trickster, or however that old saying goes. You've been going around all day with stars in your eyes. And who could blame you? If Acton looked at me the way he looks at you, I'd have to wear sunglasses even in the dark."

Stars in her eyes? Dr. Neil had already asked her if she was getting sick. Her emotions must really be getting out of hand.

"I think you need glasses, period," Stephanie told her, then quickly headed over to Ruby.

She had just given the woman an update about Chester's condition when she felt her cell phone vibrate in the pocket of her mustard-colored cardigan.

I need help with Grizabella. Can you come this evening?

After three days without a word from the man, he was asking for her help? Stephanie knew she should be annoyed with him. She should tell him to get one of his many girlfriends to help him with Grizabella. But she couldn't do that. Not when his message had her heart singing like a happy bird. It was ridiculous.

Without hesitation, she typed in a reply and punched the send arrow. I'll be over after work.

"You're smiling," Ruby said. "Must be good news."

Stephanie looked at the older woman, who was still sitting on the short couch. "I suppose it is good," she said, then added thoughtfully, "Would you mind if I asked you something personal, Ruby?"

"Honey, you can ask me anything."

"How long were you married?"

A fond smile creased her face. "Forty years. And that wasn't near enough time with my Stanley. When you're married to someone who's also your friend, time is precious. You're too young to appreciate that advice now, but later on you'll understand."

"So your advice is to marry someone you like," Stephanie said. "How did you know Stanley was the one?"

"His eyes. He looked at me with kindness. There has to be more than flames and sparks to make things last between a man and a woman."

Stephanie hadn't thought about it in exactly those terms, but she understood the advice Ruby was trying to convey. There had to be more than hot chemistry to make a relationship long-lasting. And perhaps that's where she'd gone wrong in the past. She'd let the thrill of a man's kiss cloud her judgment. Which meant, if Acton did kiss her again, she could enjoy it, but it would be a mistake to allow the passion to take control of her senses.

"I'll think about that, Ruby. Thank you for sharing it with me." She gave the woman an appreciative smile. "Now, I'll go see if Chester is awake. I'm sure he's going to be more than ready for you to take him home."

The Donovan Ranch was located north of Rambling Rose, an area of the countryside Stephanie hadn't yet seen since she'd moved to Texas. Now as she drove along a wide, graveled road, she was impressed with the beauty of sloping green pastures dotted with enormous live oaks and wide ponds full from the winter rains. Herds of black cows, many with calves at their sides, grazed on the grass that was managing to survive the cooler winter weather.

During one of their conversations, Acton had expressed to Stephanie just how much he loved the ranch and would never dream of living anywhere else. Now as she drove slowly through the property, she understood why he felt so devoted to the place. It was a pastoral paradise.

When Stephanie finally spotted the old farmhouse where Acton lived, twilight was spreading across the wide lawn and the two-story clapboard structure. She parked near the gate of a fence made of woven wire and cedar post, and was in the process of collecting Linus from the backseat of the car, when she heard a loud bark directly behind her.

Glancing over her shoulder, she saw Seymour racing toward her.

"Seymour! Hey, boy!"

As soon as the dog recognized her voice, he skidded to a halt and his bushy tail began to whirl in a happy circle.

Stephanie kneeled down and urged the dog to join her. "Come here, Seymour. Come here and let me look at you."

The dog trotted over to her and Stephanie smiled as she rubbed his furry head. If it hadn't been for Seymour, she doubted she and Acton would have ever met. The idea seemed unimaginable now.

After giving Seymour a final pat between the ears, she lifted Linus from his car seat. She made sure the baby was carefully covered from the cold, then gathered his diaper bag with her free hand and used her hip to shut the car door.

"Okay, Seymour. I'm ready. Let's go."

With a whine of approval, the dog took off in a proud trot toward the house. By the time Stephanie reached the front entrance, Seymour was already waiting at the door, his tail thumping excitedly against the board planks that made up the porch floor.

After knocking on the screen door, she glanced down at the dog. "Seymour, I don't see any bald spots on your pretty fur, so your scratching days must be over."

Seymour responded with a bark and she was laughing in response when Acton opened the door. The warm smile on his face welcomed her.

"Hi, Stephanie. Please, come in." He stepped past the door to join her on the porch and Seymour took the opportunity to dash through Acton's legs and straight into the house.

"Hello, Acton. Sorry I'm running so late. We had a very busy day at the clinic."

After the way they'd parted the other night, she'd thought it would be awkward to face him this evening. But as soon as he stepped close and their eyes met, everything felt familiar and right.

He looked at me with kindness.

Ruby's words echoed in her mind and she realized Acton often looked at her with kindness and so much more. Did that mean he was the one?

"No problem," he said. "I'm just glad you could make it. Let me carry Linus for you."

He reached for the baby and Stephanie handed him over. Immediately he peeked under the edge of the blanket at Linus's face.

"I'm glad you brought Linus with you. I've missed seeing the little guy. Just about as much as I've missed seeing you." He turned his smile away from the baby and directed it at her. "I forgot to give you directions. How did you find the place?"

"Dayna told me. She knows where everybody lives."

She followed him into the house and he closed the door behind them. Stephanie's gaze was immediately glued to his tall, lean body dressed in jeans and a black T-shirt that clung to his hard-as-steel abs.

Ever since he'd kissed her the night of the fundraiser, she'd not been able to forget how it had felt to be crushed against all that sinewy muscle. Nor had she forgotten the incredibly alluring taste of his mouth searching hers.

"Uh, you said you've missed me. If that's true, why haven't I heard from you before now?"

A sheepish look crossed his face. "I thought I should give you a breather."

She lifted her chin to a challenging angle. "Really? I thought you'd decided that I was such a terrible kisser you didn't want to waste your time with me anymore."

His jaw dropped. "Are you serious?"

"Yes, I guess I am," she admitted, while wondering where she'd found the nerve to bring up the subject. Most likely, Acton wasn't used to a woman questioning his actions, but Stephanie had decided it was time to learn just where things stood with them. "I mean, you took off the other night like a pack of wild dogs was on your heels. And then when I didn't hear from you, what was I supposed to think?"

Groaning ruefully, he stepped toward her. "It wasn't like what you're thinking, Steph. I was... I knew I had to get out of there or we, uh, or something might've happened that neither one of us was ready for."

Ready? For a long time now, she'd been ready for him to reach for her, to make love to her. But obviously he wasn't feeling that same urgent need. That should be enough to put a damper on her feelings, to show her that he wasn't looking for anything serious. Yet it wasn't enough to stop the longing that had been building inside her. Just looking at him made her think about things she'd never experienced before. He made her long for the things that she'd always wanted in her life. Yes, maybe her mind could recognize she was going too fast, too soon. But that wasn't what her heart was telling her.

She sighed. "I understand. It's just that a girl takes these things—like kissing—to heart, Acton."

A gentle smile suddenly crinkled the corners of his eyes. "You need to stop worrying. You're a fantastic kisser, Stephanie."

If any other man had said such a thing to her, she would've been horribly embarrassed, but with Acton, the words made her heart soar with joy. Oh, Lord, was she ever losing it.

She let out another long sigh, then reached for Linus. "Forgive me, Acton. I didn't mean to light into you like this. It was silly of me. And anyway, I came here to help you with Grizabella."

"You look tired. Sit down and relax for a few minutes. I'll hold Linus. Looks like he's asleep right now, anyway."

She glanced around the cozy room, with its tongue-and-groove walls, linoleum floors and multi-paned windows. A couch and armchair covered in a dark burgundy and brown patterned fabric were positioned along the outer wall, while directly across, two brown swivel rockers were separated by a wooden-tray floor lamp. The coffee table in front of the couch was cluttered with two coffee mugs and a glass filled with crushed ice and soda. Apparently he'd been eating a sandwich before she'd arrived. The crust of the bread was still lying on a paper towel.

"Sorry about the mess," he said. "I haven't had much time to clean."

"Don't apologize," she told him. "Your house looks lived in and that makes it comfortable."

She took a seat on the end of the couch and Acton joined her at the opposite end. As she watched him settle Linus comfortably against his chest, Stephanie was struck by how natural he looked with the baby in his arms. Whether he realized it or not, he was going to be a wonderful father someday—to some other woman's children. The mental image disturbed her far more than it should have.

He turned his head slightly and looked at her. "To be honest, Stephanie, I felt a bit guilty about asking you over this evening. You're so busy with the baby and work. But Grizabella has gone rogue on me and I knew you'd be the best person to help with her."

Since Stephanie hadn't heard from Acton since the night of the fund-raiser, she'd just assumed everything had gone well with Grizabella.

"Rogue?" She frowned with disbelief. "I can't believe she'd turn mean!"

"Not mean. But she's turned on me. I think she actually hates me now."

"I seriously doubt that. What did you do? Yell at her?"

"Yell? I've never talked so sweet to a female in my life." Clearly exasperated, he shook his head. "I thought bringing her home and making friends with her was going to be easy. But it's turned out to be a nightmare."

"Hmm. That is surprising. I thought she'd settle right in, too. What happened?"

"Like I told my mom, she took one look at Seymour and ran for the hills—or in this case, straight under my bed. I realize I probably shouldn't have let the dog in until Grizabella got used to her surroundings, but Seymour gets his feelings hurt if you look at him crossways. So I caved in and let him inside."

"Did the dog bark and try to chase her?"

"Not even a little. I was actually amazed that he behaved so well. But that doesn't do much good now. The only time Grizabella will poke her head out is when I set a bowl of tuna or sardines on the floor. I've already gone through a dozen or more cans!"

Stephanie laughed. "Acton, you're so funny. All you're doing is feeding her habit and teaching her to stay hidden. You have to earn her trust and show her it's okay to come out and join the land of the living."

He rolled his eyes. "Sure. That's easy for you to say. Can you show *me* how to do that?"

"I'll try. But I'd better warn you it's not something that happens in a matter of minutes. You might have to work on this for several days."

"Oh, great. That means I'll be sleeping with the smell of sardines for the next few weeks."

She chuckled. "I don't think it will be that bad."

They both fell silent after that and Stephanie was

beginning to wonder if he'd regretted asking her over when he finally asked, "So how have you been since the Valentine party?"

"Very busy. The clinic has been overrun with patients. But Linus is such a good baby. I hear these nightmare stories about babies crying with colic for the first three months of their lives. Thankfully, Linus sleeps and eats without any problems."

He gazed down at the baby. "Linus is too easygoing to get colic."

His assumption put an amused smile on her face. "How did you reach that conclusion?"

"Simple deduction. High-strung horses are usually the ones that suffer episodes of colic. I figure babies are pretty much the same." He glanced curiously at her. "Speaking of horses, did you ever work with large animals when you lived in Florida?"

"No. The vet I worked for was located in the city in a small-animal clinic. But I've always wanted the chance to work with large animals, too. Sometimes when an emergency arises, Dr. Neil will take the case. Not long ago I helped him treat a bull with an infected horn. That was fun."

Nodding, he said, "I remember. That was the day I brought Ryan and Elizabeth by the clinic—when they picked out the two cats to adopt," he said. "Carla said then that you were out back helping Dr. Neil with a bull. I figured that was something out of the ordinary."

She nodded. "It was. But who knows, Dr. Neil might decide to expand his practice someday to include large animals. Lord knows my brothers would only be too glad to construct a larger facility for the clinic."

"No doubt," he said. "Shawn and I stopped by the Crockett Café a couple of days ago and we heard plenty of talk about the new buildings going up. I think some of the old locals are expecting to see skyscrapers appear in the middle of Rambling Rose."

"I don't think anything like that is about to happen. Unless the new hotel they're planning turns out to be a high-rise building. But I'm hoping they think long and hard before they do something that extravagant. To be honest, one of the reasons I decided to move here to Rambling Rose with my brothers was because I thought small-town life would be a nice change from the city. I'd hate to see this place lose its rural charm."

"You and a lot more people," he agreed.

Wanting to change the subject, she shifted on the cushion and smiled at him. "So how have you been these past few days? Busy?"

"So busy we've hardly had time to look up. We've been building cross fence that goes for a couple of miles. Hard work, but it will be worth it. The new fence is going to make roundups much easier."

Impressed, she said, "So the Diamond D is that large?"

"By Texas standards it's a just a little patch of ground. But it's about all the four of us Donovan men can take care of." His gaze dropped to Linus and he gently traced his forefinger over the baby's cheek. After a couple moments he said, "I think I ought to tell you that my mother is concerned with the idea of me spending time with you."

Stephanie sat forward on the edge of the cushion and stared at him. "You mentioned me to your mother?"

He shook his head. "No. Someone who saw us together at the fund-raiser did."

A part of Stephanie was disappointed. If he'd been the one to tell his mother about her, it might have shown that she was becoming an important part of his life. On the other hand, it could be that he wasn't the type to discuss a girlfriend with his mother.

Stop it, Stephanie. Stop making excuses for the man. That sign around his neck doesn't read Good. It says Fun and Fickle.

Trying to shake away the sardonic voice in her head, she asked, "Why would your mother be concerned about me?"

He leveled a dry look at her. "For the same reason your brothers are concerned about me. We're not on equal footing. She thinks you'll hurt me."

"And my brothers believe you'll hurt me," she stated ruefully.

He grunted with amusement. "Yeah. Together we make a dangerous pair."

Unwittingly, she reached over and wrapped her hand around his. The contact brought his gaze around to hers, and as she studied his blue eyes, she realized she couldn't view him as something to fear. How could she fear something that made her so happy?

"It's not my plan to hurt you, Acton."

A dimple appeared in his left cheek. "I'm not planning on hurting you, either."

"So maybe our families should quit worrying about us."

"Or at least let us do the worrying," he added with a twinkle in his eyes.

His hand was warm, and for a moment she considered sliding across the cushions and snuggling up to his side. But she didn't want this evening to end with him running scared and her aching for something he wasn't ready to give.

Drawing her hand away, she focused on the messy coffee table. "Looks like you were eating when I arrived. Don't let me interrupt your meal."

Linus squirmed and Acton gently shifted the baby to his other side.

"Not at all. I'm finished. Would you like something to eat or drink? I have all kinds of cold cuts. Plus a pecan pie. I buy them from the bakery two at a time. Mom warns me that I'm going to get fat. She doesn't have a clue how much physical labor I do."

No matter how hard she tried, she couldn't imagine Acton with a roll of flab around his waistline. "No thanks. Maybe later, after we deal with Grizabella."

"I'm ready to take a go at her, if you are," he said.

Stephanie rose from the couch and picked up the diaper bag next to her feet. "Where should I put Linus's diaper bag? Will Seymour get into if I leave it on the couch?"

"With Seymour I can't make any kind of promises. Better let me put it on top of the fridge," he said.

Stephanie glanced around the room. "Speaking of Seymour, where did he get off to? He shot into the house like he couldn't wait to get in here and I've not seen him since."

"I think I know where we'll find him." Cradling Linus in one arm, he rose from the couch and jerked his head toward an open doorway on the opposite side of the room. "Follow me."

They left the living room and entered an open space where four doors intersected. Acton went directly forward and into a small kitchen decorated with red curtains, white-painted cabinets and a green Formica-and-chrome table with matching chairs. A clock in the shape of a colorful rooster hung on the wall behind the table.

"Does the rooster crow on the hour?" she asked.

He let out a good-natured groan. "No, thank goodness. I can hear Mom's real rooster all the way down here. I don't need two birds to tell me it's time to get up at four thirty in the morning."

She gazed around the cozy room. "This kitchen is adorable. I'll bet you have some memories of being here with your grandmother."

"Tons of them. She cooked all the time and my brothers and I knew if we begged hard enough she'd give us pie or something we shouldn't be eating before supper."

"Is this the way the house looked when you moved in?"

With his free hand, he placed the diaper bag on top of the fridge.

"The whole house is just like it was when Grandma Hatti moved out. It would hurt her feelings if I changed it."

"Why would you want to? It all looks fine to me. And this kitchen is just too cute."

He shrugged. "To be honest, it doesn't much matter to me how it's furnished as long as it's comfortable. But it hardly looks like a bachelor lives here."

"I imagine your grandmother appreciates you not turning it into a bachelor pad. Was this house where your grandparents always lived on the ranch?"

He nodded. "This house is more than a hundred years old. My great-grandfather built it when he first started the Diamond D. The newer house on the hill behind this one was built by my father after he and Mom got married."

"What happened to your grandfather?"

A shadow passed his face, but only for a moment. "One evening after work he sat down in his favorite chair, went to sleep and never woke up. Guess if I have a choice, that's the way I want to go."

He motioned for her to follow him and they left the kitchen and started across the hallway.

"So what do your brothers think about you moving in here?" Stephanie asked as she walked a step behind him. "Do they think they have just as much right to live here as you?"

He glanced over his shoulder at her. "They do have just as much right, but they're not interested. Shawn prefers the big house so he'll have someone cooking his meals and picking up after him. And Danny says when he gets a place of his own he wants it to be more modern."

"I see. So it didn't cause any friction between the three of you?"

As they reached another open doorway, he paused and looked at her. "No. Would something like that cause friction with your brothers?"

She let out a short laugh. "It hasn't always been easy merging four brothers from two different mothers. There's been some resentment and dissension along the way. But for the most part they get along. We all do, actually."

"Until you bring a strange cowboy into your kitchen, right?" he joked.

She pulled an impish face at him. "That's only happened once. But it could happen again," she suggested. "If the cowboy decides to help me do some more baking."

His eyebrows slowly lifted. "Maybe we ought to do the baking here. It would probably be safer."

She frowned. "You're not going to let that trio scare you away, are you?"

His lips twisted to a faint smile as he touched his forefinger to the tip of her nose. "No. In fact, I'm not going to let anything scare me away from you."

"Not even my kisses?"

His low, sexy chuckle sent a shiver down her spine.

"You get Grizabella out from under the bed and I'll show you how scared I am of your kisses."

Certain her stomach had suddenly been invaded by a thousand butterflies, she tried to make her smile provocative. "I just might hold you to that promise."

Chapter Nine

Inside Acton's bedroom, he carefully placed Linus in the middle of a queen-size bed, surrounded by pillows so there would be no chance of him rolling to the edge.

Stephanie covered the baby with a soft blanket and after making sure he was comfortable, she looked around the room. It was furnished with a varnished pine chest and dresser that matched the bed frame. Braided rugs covered part of the linoleum floor and white Priscilla curtains draped the double windows. She'd seen rooms like this in rural-living magazines, but never in person. She was struck by how homey and warm it felt.

"I'm guessing Grizabella must be under this bed," she said.

Acton nodded. "That's right. And just like I suspected, Seymour is waiting for her to come out." He nodded at the dog, who was lying at the foot of the bed, his nose resting on his paws. "When he's in the house, this is where he stays, watching for her to make a move. Would it be better if I took him outside?"

The moment he heard Acton say his name, the dog whined, but he never took his eyes off the fringe dangling at the bottom of the white bedspread.

"No," Stephanie answered. "Grizabella is going to have to get used to him. That's what caused all the problems in the first place."

Stephanie dropped to her hands and knees and peered under the bed. Grizabella was on the opposite side, hunched up next to the wall. Her one eye was as wide as a saucer as she stared fearfully at Stephanie.

"Grizabella," she said in a quiet, gentle tone. "Come here, girl. Everything is going to be all right. The dog is okay. He's not going to hurt you. And you don't want to live under the bed from now on."

The cat's ears twitched straight up, telling Stephanie that she'd recognized her voice. It was an encouraging sign, so she continued to coax the cat to her.

Finally, after several more minutes passed, Grizabella crawled over to Stephanie's hand and sniffed.

"That's right, pretty girl. You remember me, don't you?"

She rubbed the side of her face against Stephanie's fingers and after that it was short work to stroke her until she was calm enough to be picked up.

"Oh, thank God," Acton murmured under his breath so as not to excite the cat. "I thought you might use one of your magic spells to draw her out and you did."

"Grizabella has been traumatized, but she'll come out of it." She carried the cat over to Acton. "Here. You hold her now. She needs to get used to your smell and touch."

He took the cat in his arms and Stephanie thought he handled the cat with the same gentle expertise he used with Linus.

As his long fingers softly stroked the top of her head, he said, "Gosh, she's been hiding out for so long, I'd almost forgotten how pretty she is."

Unable to contain his curiosity, Seymour got up and came around to Acton. The minute he looked up at the cat and let out a whine, Grizabella arched her back and hissed. Acton managed to tighten his hold without scaring her even more.

"It's okay, girl," he said to Grizabella. "Seymour is really just a softy. He wouldn't hurt a flea if it was biting his tail."

Stephanie had to stifle a laugh. "That's not what I heard."

"Shh. She doesn't know that," Acton scolded. "Besides, his problem isn't with other animals. It's with people—namely, me."

Stephanie drew close enough to place her hand on Seymour's head, then, using a soft voice, attempted to introduce the two animals.

"I think it's working," Acton said after a few minutes. "I can feel Grizabella relaxing in my arms."

Stephanie continued to size up the two animals' behavior. "I believe you're right. The look she's giving Seymour now is more like curiosity rather than terror. And Seymour is clearly infatuated with her. He wants her to get down and play."

"I don't think she's feeling that friendly," Acton replied. "What if I take her in the kitchen and try to feed her? I still have a can of mackerel left."

"I'll go with you. Just in case of an emergency," she added.

"That doesn't sound encouraging."

Stephanie laughed at his wariness. "You're a rancher. You've been around animals all your life. You should know they're unpredictable."

"Yeah. I have scars on my body to prove just how unpredictable. I'll show them to you sometime. Just so you'll know I'm not lying."

"Uh, I believe you. For now," she added in a suggestive voice.

It was his turn to laugh and then he glanced at

Linus. "Will the baby be okay there if we both go to the kitchen?"

"Sure. He's perfectly safe. Plus I'll be just a few feet away. I can hear him if he so much as makes a peep."

"Good. Then, let's take this pair to the kitchen and give it a try."

Nearly a half hour later, the two animals had come to a truce and Seymour was lying on his belly patiently watching Grizabella eat the last of her mackerel. With only a few feet between the cat and dog and neither trying to make a dash for it, Stephanie and Acton decided a beautiful friendship was beginning to bud between the two.

"I thought they might become friends," she stated happily as she sat at the table, sipping coffee that Acton had made for her. "But I never believed it would happen this quickly. I thought I might have to make several trips over here to help get them acquainted."

Acton snapped his fingers. "Shoot. Now I'll have to think up another excuse to get you here again."

Stephanie leveled a wry look at him. "Why don't you just ask? Wouldn't that be simpler?"

A sheepish grin slanted his lips. "Yeah, I guess it would. Can you come over Saturday? I promised Ryan and Elizabeth that I'd take them to the park in town. But I was thinking we could have a little picnic here. I have an outdoor fireplace in the backyard.

I can build a fire and let the kids roast wieners and marshmallows. And if it's warm enough, we can walk them down to the pond. What do you think?"

Stephanie didn't know what to think. Being invited to another family outing with the kids was the last thing she'd expected from him.

"I realize it probably sounds boring to you," he went on. "But Elizabeth and Ryan have been hounding me about this for the past month and they would love your company. So would I."

For a man who was gun-shy of love and marriage, he was hardly acting like a playboy. Dayna and Sheri had both gossiped to her about a few of the women he'd dated during the past few years, and according to Stephanie's coworkers, Acton had dropped each woman after a brief fling. She didn't want to believe her friends were making up gossip, but when Stephanie was with him, he seemed anything but a womanizer. Was she stupid to think he might've put his roaming ways behind him? Or that he might not have been that much of a playboy in the first place?

Stephanie wasn't going to worry about answering that question. Risky or not, she wanted to be with the man.

"I think it sounds lovely, Acton. I can bring some things for the picnic. And don't worry, I'll get them from the deli instead of trying to make them," she said with a laugh.

She was surprised at the happy look that spread

over his face. It very nearly matched the joy that was bubbling over inside of her. It didn't matter if they had three children as chaperones. Acton wanted to spend time with her and in the end that's all that really mattered.

Chuckling, he said, "Don't worry about bringing any food. Having you and Linus here is what's important to me."

Just as she started to make a reply, Linus let out a whimper and Stephanie quickly rose to her feet and grabbed the diaper bag off the fridge.

"Linus calls. He's probably wet and hungry," she said.

To her surprise, Acton followed her into the bedroom, where they sat down on opposite sides of the bed.

"Why don't you let me change him?" he offered. "I know how to do it. I changed plenty of Elizabeth's and Ryan's diapers."

She cast him a doubtful glance. "That's hard to believe. You were still in your teens when those two were born. You were probably running around with your friends, playing sports and riding horses or something."

"True, I was doing all those things. But I still had time for my niece and nephew. And teenagers make good babysitters. At least, Gina always trusted me. She said Shawn didn't have the patience for kids and Danny wouldn't know which end of a bottle went into the baby's mouth. She said I had finesse with babies," he said proudly.

Stephanie laughed. "Like I have with animals?"

"Exactly."

She pulled a diaper out of the bag and handed it to him. "Then I would think you'd have some children of your own by now."

Shooting her a perplexed look, he reached for Linus. "I'm only twenty-five. I have lots of time to have babies. Besides, I told you the kind of women I've dated in the past. None of them were what I'd consider mother material."

Just like none of the men she'd dated were husband or father material, Stephanie thought dismally.

He removed Linus's diaper and rolled it up tightly. "Do you use wipes on him?"

Stephanie handed him a disposable wipe and a tube of protective ointment. "This seems to keep him from getting diaper rash. And thankfully, the women at the day care are wonderful about keeping him changed and dry."

He wiped the baby's bottom, then smeared a thin glaze of ointment onto his skin. All the while Linus kicked and cooed like he was enjoying every second of Acton's attention.

"There. He's all fixed and ready to go for another round." He propped the baby against his shoulder and gently rubbed his back. "Do you think he's hungry?"

"Maybe. Since he's not yelling for a bottle yet, I

was thinking I really should be going home, Acton. It's getting late and my brothers have no idea where I am."

He arched an eyebrow at her. "I've never heard you express any concerns about your brothers keeping up with your whereabouts. I'm thinking you might be using them as an excuse to leave. Right?"

She smiled sheepishly. "Okay. I confess. I'm guilty. That was just an excuse."

"Good. Because I'd really like for you to stay a little longer. Will you?"

How could she tell him no? Not when being with him felt so good.

"All right," she said, relenting to the persuasiveness of his tempting smile. "For a while longer, anyway."

Their gazes locked and Stephanie's heart thumped with anticipation. The light from the lamp behind him lit the blond curls scattered across his forehead to a rich, golden hue. Couple that with his tanned skin and sky-blue eyes, and his face was like a Technicolor dream. Almost too vibrant to be real.

"I did promise to kiss you if you got Grizabella to leave her hiding place under the bed," he murmured. "I need the chance to pay up."

Her heart began to pound, and as he leaned across the bed toward her, her breath stalled in her throat. When his face was inches from hers, she wet her lips in anticipation… And then Linus let out a frustrated cry, shattering the tense connection between them.

"On second thought, I guess he's hungry," she said, her voice husky. "Here's your chance to feed him."

For a moment the look on his face made her think he was going to ignore the baby's cries and kiss her anyway. But then he suddenly cleared his throat and reached for Linus and with a pang of regret, Stephanie realized the chance to feel his lips pressed to hers was over.

Twenty minutes later, the baby was full of formula and sound asleep. Acton laid him on the floor, atop an armchair cushion, and covered him with a blanket, then looked across to Stephanie. She'd taken off her ankle boots and now her bare feet were curled beneath her.

She looked tired, but beautiful, and though he should've felt guilty about keeping her here, he didn't. For the past three days, he'd been fighting an inner battle. One minute he'd convinced himself that he was walking down a losing path to think Stephanie could be more than a temporary girlfriend. And then there'd been moments where he hadn't given a damn about her money or social status.

"Well, the Texas sandman has done a number on him," Acton said. "He ought to sleep for a while."

"Texas sandman? Is that what you call him?"

Smiling, he eased down next to her on the couch and crossed his ankles out in front of him. "Mom used to sing that lullaby to us kids. It's all about the Texas sandman coming to visit and he puts you on a palomino pony with a saddle made of moonbeams and you ride over the Milky Way, beneath a blanket of stars."

"Oh, it sounds charming. Can you sing it?"

The only time Acton sang was in the shower, or on the back of a horse. Definitely not to a girl. "I don't remember exactly how the words go. Besides, you wouldn't want to hear me sing. But I can hum the melody for you. If you'd like."

She turned eagerly toward him. "I'd love it."

Taking her hand, he clasped it between his and began to hum the soft melody that he'd heard from the time he was a little boy. The enchanted look that came over her face had Acton feeling as though he was floating among those moonbeams. Or was it the touch of her hand that had sent him flying over the Milky Way?

Once he finished humming, she said softly, "That's beautiful, Acton. Really."

"Not as beautiful as you," he murmured.

Her smile was wobbly and he wondered if her heart could possibly be beating as wildly as his. It was thumping hard against his rib cage, and each beat begged him to pull her close, to kiss her until the room around them disappeared and they were cloaked in dark velvet.

Lifting his hand to her face, he stroked his fingertips gently across her forehead. "I don't have to go outside to see the stars. They're right here in your eyes."

"Isn't that kind of cheesy?" she asked.

"Probably. But I love cheese. Don't you?"

She chuckled. "All kinds."

Their gazes locked and her blue eyes conveyed a need that came close to stealing his breath. His hands cradled her face and he thought how touching her skin was like stroking satin. "Stephanie, you're so beautiful and special. All I want is to be close to you."

"Close. Yes, that's all I want, too."

His heart racing, he bent his head and gently touched his lips to hers. She responded instantly by slipping her arms around his neck and pressing her body against his.

Her eager reaction was all it took for Acton to deepen the kiss, and as he wrapped his arms around her, he was certain he'd never felt anything so delicate and warm and utterly precious.

Her lips were unbelievably soft and giving, and in a matter of seconds he was lost, his senses swirling faster and faster. Heat shot through his body like a bolt of lightning, and when her hands began to move up and down his arms, the sensation was like a pair of torches burning all the way through to his bones.

Hanging onto his control by a flimsy thread, he tried to rein it in. But before he could get a grip, her mouth opened and the tip of her tongue boldly pushed against his teeth. The intimate request broke the last of his restraint and he gladly let her inside. When their tongues began a slow dance, the contact caused fire to spread low in his loins.

For days now he'd thought of little more than kissing her again. Really kissing her. Yet now that he had her in his arms, he realized that kissing wasn't nearly enough to ease the ache inside him. And from the hungry way her mouth was clinging to his, it wasn't enough for her.

Pushed by the certainty, he cupped a hand around one breast and rubbed his thumb against the center. Her response was a tiny moan from deep in her throat, and the sound of her pleasure thrilled him. The idea that she could want him, even a fraction of how much he wanted her, was enough to rattle his senses. But his feelings didn't stop with the physical. No, his emotions were being sucked along, too, and the mixture was like a giant tidal wave washing over him, tugging him back and forth like a dangerous undercurrent.

The kiss went on for so long that Acton's lungs began to scream for a fresh load of oxygen. Yet the thought of deserting her lips, even for the sake of breathing, was torturous. And then her hands found their way beneath his T-shirt and pushed their way upward until her palms were lying flat against his chest.

The contact sent his head reeling even more and he was forced to tear his lips from hers and suck in a long, raspy breath.

"Stephanie, do you still think I don't want to kiss you?"

She pressed kisses over his chin and along his jaw until her lips hovered near his ear. "You've come close to convincing me that you do. But I think you need to show me more," she whispered.

She raked her fingers through his hair and he brought his lips back to hers. This time their mouths fused together in a kiss so deep and hot that the flames shot straight to his brain, then licked their way downward until the very soles of his feet were burning.

When their bodies listed to one side, he didn't try to stop the downward slide. By the time she was lying flat against the couch, all he wanted was to stretch out beside her, feel the whole length of her against him.

Without breaking the kiss, he fumbled with the buttons of her blouse. Once the fabric parted enough to reveal the top of one breast, he gently traced his fingertips over her flesh, then dipped them beneath the lacy cup of her bra.

The moment they came in contact with her nipple, a needy moan vibrated deep in her throat. Spurred by the sound, Acton teased the hard bud until the urge to taste it became too much to bear.

Lowering his head, he pulled the lace downward until the rosy pink nipple came into view.

With her hands on the back of his head, she guided his mouth to the heated point. Using his tongue, Acton circled the flesh, then drew it between his teeth. As he did, he felt Stephanie's fingers curling into his scalp and her leg slipping over his.

Desperate to explore more of her, he finished with the buttons on her shirt and pushed the tails away to expose her flat belly. His fingers slipped over the flesh and as he savored the incredible smoothness, his nostrils pulled in the fresh, flowery scent that clung to her clothes and skin.

The thought suddenly struck him that if he stayed on the couch all night with her wrapped in his arms, it wouldn't be long enough. If his lips could kiss hers a thousand times over and over, it would only whet his appetite for more. This desire he felt for her wasn't a one-and-done thing. It went far deeper than that and the realization caused him to lift his head and stare wondrously down at her.

"What's wrong, Acton?"

The blue pools of her eyes were filled with confusion and as Acton gazed into them, he was suddenly reminded of the night of the Valentine's party. He'd run from her kisses that night, because even then he'd recognized that what he was feeling wasn't like anything he'd experienced before. And now he knew for certain that whatever was growing between them was more than hot chemistry.

"Nothing is wrong," he murmured, then leaned slightly and pressed a kiss to her damp forehead. "You...this—it all feels wonderful to me. And I don't want it to stop. I want to make love to you, Stephanie. Right here. Right now."

"And what would be wrong with that?"

"Nothing. If I was sure that's what you really wanted. That you wouldn't regret it later."

Her eyebrows puckered together. "How do you know I'm not sure?"

"Because this—whatever it is—has happened between us rather quickly. You haven't had that much time to think about who I am and how I might fit in your life."

Her eyes suddenly filled with dark shadows, as she studied his face. "And you need time to figure out who I am and where I might fit in your life?"

He nodded, then cupped his hand around her chin and said, "That's what I'm thinking. But I get the feeling you believe I'm making excuses."

Sighing, she pushed herself to a sitting position, and with trembling fingers adjusted her bra and began to button her shirt. "No. I'm thinking you're making much more sense than me. I, uh, have always had a problem of following my feelings and worrying about the consequences later."

The sadness he saw on her face twisted something deep in his heart and Acton realized that no matter what happened in the future, he never wanted to cause Stephanie a moment of pain.

Leaning his head close to hers, he placed a kiss on her cheekbone. "Stephanie, I don't want to be like those guys who took advantage of your sweet, giving heart. When you make love to me—and I hope you do—I want it to be special. I want you to give yourself to me because deep down you know that you can trust me."

Moisture suddenly sprang to her eyes and threatened to spill onto her cheeks. The sight was like a hand squeezing his heart.

"I want it to be like that, too, Acton. Really."

A wry smile slanted his lips. "Then why are you crying?"

She shook her head. "Because I never expected to hear you say something like that to me."

His fingertips traced light circles on her cheek. "To be honest, Steph, I didn't know I could say that kind of thing to a woman. You're a first," he said wryly.

With a little moan, she hugged his neck, then before the sparks had a chance to start flying again, she rose to her feet and straightened her clothing.

"I think I'd better be going on home, Acton. It's getting late and I have to be up early."

In spite of all that talk about giving her time, he didn't want her to go. And the realization had him wondering what it would be like if they were married and she and Linus lived here with him. Instead of seeing her out to her car, he'd be taking her by the hand and leading her to the bedroom. Their bedroom. He'd wake up with her face on the pillow next to his. With her sitting across from him at the breakfast table. Maybe the monotony of married life wasn't what his brothers wanted for themselves, but Acton was beginning to think he could darned sure get used to it.

That is, as long as the woman at his side was Stephanie.

With that impossible dream swirling around in his head, Acton rose from the couch. "I'll carry Linus out to the car for you."

Chapter Ten

Saturday morning turned out to be one of those late February days in Texas that felt more like a day in May. As Stephanie carried Linus and his packed-to-the-brim diaper bag out to the car, the sun was shining warmly with just enough breeze to move the leaves on the live oaks.

During the drive to Acton's, the memory of her last visit to his house made a haunting circle through her head. Had he been thinking about her and how close they'd come to making love? The same way she'd been thinking about it? Every detail of those moments she'd spent in his arms were still achingly vivid and she couldn't wait to see him again, touch him again, even if it had to be in an innocent way.

When she arrived twenty minutes later, Elizabeth and Ryan were waiting for her at the front-yard gate. Chattering with excitement, both children greeted her with enthusiastic hugs, then promptly began to argue over which one of them could carry Linus's diaper bag into the house.

Thankfully, Acton appeared to remind the pair to behave or run the risk of being confined to the house for the rest of their stay. Which would've been a shame considering the nice weather.

As it turned out, it was warm enough for Stephanie to take Linus to the patio and join in on the fun of roasting wieners and marshmallows for their lunch.

After the meal, the five of them left the backyard and walked down a well-trodden path to a large pond partially shaded by a stand of willows. While she and Acton watched, the kids threw food to the fish, a task that kept them busy for a good half hour.

Once they walked back to the house, Acton got out a board game for the children and set it up on the coffee table in the living room. The four of them played, until an argument ensued over Elizabeth's claim that Ryan was cheating. Acton decided the best way to settle the issue was to end the game and turn on the television.

While the two kids became absorbed in a movie about a little boy searching for his lost dog, Stephanie and Acton sat on the couch and talked about their own childhoods.

"Did you always like horses and ranches?" she asked him. "Or was it something you simply fell into because you were born to a ranching family?"

"True, I was born into it. But I never wanted to be anything but a cowboy. Same for Shawn. In fact, when we were teenagers the two of us used to dream that one day we'd be rodeo stars and wear big shiny world-championship buckles." He grunted with self-directed humor. "We tried, but someone else got the buckles."

Intrigued, Stephanie asked, "What event did you do?"

"We both rode saddle broncs. It takes a lot of balance and finesse to be good at it and of the two of us, Shawn was better. But neither of us was championship material," he told her, then shrugged. "We both decided ranching was the safest way to make a living."

She shook her head with amazement. "I can't imagine getting on a bucking horse. Did you ever fall off and get stomped or kicked?"

He chuckled. "Plenty of times. It goes with the sport."

"And what did your parents say about you and your brother participating in such a dangerous event?"

"Surprisingly, it was Dad who disapproved. He

didn't forbid us to ride broncs, but he was hardly thrilled about the idea. Mom has always been the adventurous sort, far more than Dad, so she was all for it. She'd be in the stands watching, yelling and clapping us on."

Acton's mother hadn't worried about him riding a bucking horse, but she was concerned about him spending time with Stephanie. On first thought, the idea was ludicrous. The dangerous sport could have left Acton's body mangled. But sometimes a physical injury wasn't nearly as devastating as a crushed and hopeless spirit. And from Faye Donovan's viewpoint, she'd probably rather see her son wearing a cast on his arm instead of watching him try to piece a broken heart back together.

"It's nice to have a parent in your corner, rooting you on," she said wistfully.

Curiosity was in his eyes as he studied her face. "You say that as if you don't always get along well with your parents."

"Oh, no. I'm close to both of them," she quickly corrected him. "I honestly can't think of any major arguments I've had with Dad or Mother. But…" She paused then let out a sigh. "I'll be honest, with eight of us kids, sometimes I felt left out. Dad has always been driven with his work. He's in the gaming business. Video games, I should say."

"So that's how he acquired his wealth? Or did he inherit the money from his father?"

Stephanie practically cringed at the question. "The subject of Dad's father isn't something we talk about in the family. It's a pretty sore subject. You see, Dad's father, Julius Fortune, would never acknowledge David as his son. So, no, Dad's money came from years of hard work and determination."

Acton was clearly confused. "He wouldn't acknowledge his own son? Damn, that's tough."

Stephanie nodded. "Well, you see, Dad was the result of one of Julius's many affairs. To acknowledge him would've been the same as owning up to his sins."

Rubbing a thoughtful hand against his jaw, he looked over at Elizabeth and Ryan stretched out on the floor, both entranced by the lost dog trotting across the television screen. Then his gaze slipped over to Linus, who was sound asleep on the chair cushion. Was he thinking like Stephanie? That neither parent seemed to want the adorable baby? The idea was heartbreaking.

"I can't imagine my own father not wanting me or what that would do to a man's psyche," he said.

"It's a painful wound that Dad has tried to bury away and not talk about, but I figure it's colored the way he's raised us eight children."

His lips took on a wry slant. "Mom mentioned that she'd read about the Fortunes in Austin having family troubles. Something about their house burning and a son being injured. Are those your relatives?"

Grimacing, she nodded. "Yes. Although we don't really associate with them. Jerome Fortune, who goes by the name of Gerald Robinson, is my father's half-brother. From what I can gather, he's been just as much of a tomcat as their father Julius. Trust me, Acton, my father and my family aren't like the Austin Fortunes. I mean, we're far from perfect, but we certainly have not had the kind of drama that's gone on with the Fortune Robinsons. Is that why your mother is worried about you? She thinks all of us Fortunes are dysfunctional?"

Smiling now, Acton reached over and squeezed her hand. "She doesn't know you, Stephanie. Not yet. But when she does, she's going to love you."

Was he saying he intended to introduce her to his parents? She wasn't about to ask him. Not now. But the thought was enough to put a spark of hope in her heart.

It was nearing five o'clock that evening, when Gina arrived to pick up the children. As soon as Acton's sister entered the house, she promptly gave Stephanie a big hug, then went straight to where Linus was lying on the cushion.

"I was so hoping he would be here with you," Gina exclaimed as she bent over the baby. "Acton has told me how cute he is and he wasn't exaggerating. Look at that hair. And his eyes are so bright. You must be totally in love with him."

"I'm crazy in love with Linus." *Along with your brother.* The added thought came out of nowhere, shocking Stephanie with its connotations. Had she already fallen in love with Acton? Oh, Lord, if that was the case, then it was far too late to be worrying whether he was that one good man she'd been hoping to come into her life. Her fate was already sealed.

Gina glanced over her shoulder at Stephanie. "May I hold him?" she asked.

"Of course," Stephanie told her. "Linus loves being held."

Gina picked up the baby and, gently rocking him in her arms, began to meander slowly around the room.

After watching his sister for a moment, Acton gave Stephanie a conspiring wink. "Better be careful, sis," he warned Gina. "Holding Linus might put you in the mood to have another baby."

Laughing coyly, Gina said, "Who knows, maybe it will. Jack would definitely like to be a daddy again."

Picking up on the conversation, Elizabeth walked over and tugged on the leg of her mother's jeans. "Are we gonna take Linus home with us, Mommy?"

"No, honey. Linus belongs with Stephanie."

"But couldn't we keep him for a little while, then give him back?" the girl asked hopefully.

"It doesn't work that way, Lizzie," Gina told her daughter. "You wouldn't want me to give you away for a little while, would you?"

Tilting her head to one side, Elizabeth pondered her mother's question. "Well, if you gave me to Uncle Acton it would be okay. He lets us do fun stuff that you don't let us do."

Gina shot her brother a dry look. "Thanks, Acton, for making me look like a meanie."

Grinning, Acton held up his hands in an innocent gesture. "I'm just letting them be kids."

"Yeah, well, just wait 'til you have some of your own. It's going to be my chance for payback."

He didn't have a reply for that and Stephanie wondered what he was thinking. That it would be years and years before a child called him Daddy? If so, that meant she and Linus could hardly hope for him to make them a family of three.

You're putting the cart before the horse, Stephanie. You have no idea how long Linus will be your little baby, much less if Acton will ever hear wedding bells.

Stephanie tried to shake off the pessimistic voice in her head while across the room, Gina replaced Linus on the chair cushion and informed Elizabeth and Ryan it was time for them to go.

Once the children had collected their backpacks, Acton rose from the couch. "I'll walk out with you and the kids," he said to Gina.

Before they went out the door, Elizabeth and Ryan came over to the couch and gave Stephanie good-bye hugs.

"Will you come to our house sometime?" Ryan asked. "We want you to see Roscoe and Rosie."

"Yeah!" Elizabeth seconded. "The cats are happy 'cause Mommy lets them sleep on the foot of our beds. Only because their hair doesn't come out."

"She means as long as Roscoe and Rosie don't shed they get to sleep on the bed," Ryan drolly explained.

The girl wrinkled her nose at her brother. "That's just what I said, smarty!"

Groaning, Gina put a hand on each child's shoulder and ushered them toward the door. "Okay, kids, let's go before you give Stephanie a headache."

Stephanie waved a goodbye to the three of them and Acton followed his relatives out the door.

Less than two minutes later, she heard Gina's car drive away.

By the time Acton returned from outside, her heart was beating with anticipation. This would be the first time they'd been alone together since the night she'd helped him with Grizabella. Had he forgotten the kisses they'd shared? How close they'd come to making love? All day today he hadn't so much as hinted at what had occurred between them and Stephanie was beginning to wonder if he'd decided forgetting would be best for both of them.

"Well, they're on their way," Acton said. "The kids wanted me to tell you they had a good time."

Stephanie's nerves were suddenly so overwrought

that she jumped to her feet. "I'm, uh, glad. I really enjoyed them, too."

Picking up on her anxiousness, he asked, "What's wrong? You look like Grizabella when she first laid eyes on Seymour."

Her short laugh had a silly, breathless sound to it. "Nothing is wrong. I thought I'd go clean up your kitchen."

"I've already thrown the paper cups and plates in the garbage, so there's nothing to clean." A coy smile was on his face as he walked over and sandwiched one of her hands between the two of his. "And now that it's quiet and we're alone, I have something to show you."

Puzzled, she asked, "To show me? Where is this something? Should I bring Linus?"

After switching off the television, he walked over and collected Linus. "I'll bring Linus," he said. "You follow me."

They left the living room, but rather than head to the kitchen, he made an abrupt left, toward his bedroom. Throughout the day she'd noticed the door had remained closed and she'd assumed it was to keep the children from prowling though his personal belongings. Now she wondered if he was hiding something.

"Have you trapped a monster in here and it's going to jump out at us?" she teased. "I know it can't be Seymour and Grizabella. They're cuddled up together on a rug in the living room."

"Hmm. What a nasty imagination you have," he replied.

"I grew up with four brothers. I know what kind of tricks you guys like to play on us unsuspecting females."

Chuckling, he opened the door and gestured for her to precede him into the room.

The shades behind the white Priscilla curtains were closed, blocking out most of the late-afternoon sunlight to leave dusky shadows around the room.

Acton walked over to the nightstand and switched on a small lamp. A circle of soft light spread over the room and Stephanie's attention was immediately drawn to the dresser, where a blue printed vase held a bouquet of pink rosebuds. The sight of the flowers was surprising enough, but then she spotted the cradle near the foot of the bed and couldn't contain her loud gasp.

"Oh, my! A cradle! A real wooden cradle!" She rushed over to the small baby bed and ran her fingers over the smooth grains of the maple wood. Years of use had given it a soft patina and Stephanie could only wonder how many babies had once slept in it, and how many mothers had rocked their loved ones. "Where did you get this? It's obviously an antique, so I hate to think what you paid for it!"

Amazed, Stephanie looked over at him for an explanation and he came to stand next to her.

"I could tell you that I paid a small fortune for

it, just to impress you," he said. "But that would be lying. I didn't pay a cent. I brought it down from the attic. It's the cradle my mother used for all of us kids. My grandfather made it years ago, before his children were born."

Overwhelmed, her hand crept up to cover her open mouth. "And you want Linus to use it?"

"That's why I got it out of storage. While you're here with me, Linus needs a bed of his own," he answered, then asked, "Would you like for me to put him in it? Or would you rather do it?"

He'd been a busy man, Stephanie thought, as she noticed the inside of the cradle was all ready to use with a thick mattress made up neatly with pale yellow linens. The fact that Acton had gone to so much trouble, not only for her, but also for her baby, was enough to bring tears to her eyes.

"Oh, you put him in it, Acton, please," she said huskily.

He placed Linus in the bed and after tucking the cover around him, gently pushed the rocker into motion.

Linus gave them a drooling grin and waved his arms. His reaction caused both Stephanie and Acton to laugh.

"He likes it," Acton said in a hushed voice. "Thank goodness. It was going to be pretty disappointing if the thing had made him cry."

Still overwhelmed, Stephanie looked up to Acton

to see he was smiling down at Linus. "I can't believe you went to all this trouble, Acton. And why didn't you show it to me earlier?"

Shaking his head, he said, "It isn't trouble to do something for someone you care about. And I wanted to share this with you and only you."

She walked over to the dresser and touched a finger to one of the rosebuds. "I haven't noticed fresh flowers in your house before. Are these for Linus, too?"

Two long strides put him at her side. "No. I had someone else in mind when I got those." He rested his hands on the tops of her shoulders and began to gently knead them. "Someone with golden red hair and the prettiest blue eyes I've ever looked into."

Turning toward him, she slipped her arms around his waist and tilted her head back in order to look up at him.

"Acton, you…" She paused and tried to swallow the ball of emotion clogging her throat. "You didn't have to do these things to make me want you more."

His lips took on a wry twist as the back of his fingers grazed her cheek. "Is that what you think I'm doing? Trying to win your favors?"

Her cheeks suddenly flamed with heat. "No. I, uh, I guess it's hard for me to believe that you want to give to me instead of take."

Groaning, he framed her face with both hands, then bent his head and placed a soft kiss on her lips.

"You better believe it, Stephanie. Because I do want to give to you. Not riches—because I'm not a rich man. But I can give you me—if that's enough."

"Oh, Acton. You're all I want. Truly."

Tightening her hold on his waist, she pressed against him and he immediately brought his lips back down to hers.

Chapter Eleven

Acton's kiss was tender, evoking an emotion in Stephanie that filled her heart to overflowing. Her mouth and her hands clung to him, while everything inside her begged her to never let him go.

He continued to kiss her in that same gentle manner until the warm contact ignited a bright flame. Before Stephanie realized it, their mouths were fused together in a kiss so hot she was sure that every inch of her body was on fire.

When the need for oxygen finally tore them apart, they were both breathing hard, staring at each other with raw hunger.

"Acton, don't turn away from me. Not now," she whispered.

His hands came up to cradle her face. "I have no intentions of turning away. As long as I know this is what you want."

"Let me show how much," she whispered, her hands already reaching for the snaps on his Western shirt.

With very little effort, the fasteners popped apart and she pushed aside the wash-worn denim. His muscled chest was wide and warm, and so inviting that she couldn't stop herself from leaning forward and placing her lips on the smooth flesh.

He tasted salty and oh, so masculine, and as she moved her open mouth against his skin, she pulled the erotic scent of him deep into her nostrils.

"Stephanie." Her name came out on a whisper as his fingers thrust into her hair and slid against her scalp until they were loosely cradling the back of her head. "This is... You're torturing me."

Making slow circles across his chest, she came to one flat brown nipple and licked at it with her tongue. The contact pulled an anguished groan from his throat and she smiled against him.

"Do you want me to stop?" she asked, her voice thick and husky.

"No! I mean...yes! If you keep doing this, it's all going to end...before it ever begins," he said tightly.

Tilting her head back, she looked up to see his

features were strained, as though he was fighting to stay in control. The idea that she was arousing him to such heights amazed her, and filled her with the confidence to be the woman she'd always wanted to be. The kind of woman who could take a man's love and boldly give her all back to him.

"Then let me undress you." Even as she murmured the suggestion, she was pushing the shirt off his shoulders and down his arms until the sleeves stuck at his wrists. She fumbled with the cuffs, until the snaps came loose and she was able to pull the shirt over his hands and toss it to the floor.

"It's my turn now," he said, reaching for the hem of her magenta-colored sweater.

She held up her arms and he pulled the garment over her head, then tossed it backward in the direction of where his shirt had landed. With the glow of the lamp lighting her skin, he made a slow survey of the image she made in a lacy black bra and black skinny jeans.

Stephanie had always kept herself slim and fit, but she could hardly be called anything close to curvy or voluptuous. Now as Acton's gaze swept over her, she wondered what was going on in his head. Was she a disappointment to him?

Finally, he whispered, "You look incredible."

Stunned that such a word had come out of his mouth, her head swung back and forth. "I'm glad there's not much light in here. Otherwise, you'd see

I'm far from incredible. But I won't mind at all if you say it again."

His hands settled lightly on her shoulders, their warmth promising pleasures to come. "Oh, Stephanie, no matter what's happened in your past, you're wrong to doubt yourself."

The tenderness in his voice tightened her throat and filled her chest with a heavy ache of longing. "I want to be beautiful—for you, Acton."

"Honey, if you were any more beautiful I couldn't stand it," he murmured as his fingers slipped beneath the straps of her bra and slowly eased them off her shoulders. Slowly, the lace fell away from her breasts and he bent his head to brush his lips across one nipple and then the other.

The sensation was so light and teasing it had her aching for more. But just as she snared a hold on the back of his neck to anchor his head to her breasts, he suddenly stepped back and reached for the zipper on her jeans.

His eyes glittering, he said, "You have too many clothes on."

Her head swimming, all she could think about was having his hands on her flesh, his mouth on hers, and their bodies connected in the most basic way.

"So do you," she told him, her voice little more than a breathy whisper. "And I think we should do something about it. Don't you?"

His response was to ease her backward until her

upper body was lying across the bed and her legs were dangling against the mattress. Then his hands were on her jeans, easing them down her legs until the fabric bunched around her ankle boots.

He rapidly dealt with the footwear, then slipped the jeans and a pair of black panties over her feet. Once the garments had fallen to the floor, he turned his attention to removing the last of his clothing.

From her place on the bed, Stephanie watched through half-closed eyes as he tugged off his cowboy boots, then tossed his jeans and a pair of navy blue boxers to the floor behind him.

She'd expected him to look lean and fit, but she'd not been prepared for the wide expanse of his shoulders, the narrowness of his waist, or the hard, rigid indentions of his abdomen. His legs were long and corded with heavy muscle, as were his arms, and she didn't have to wonder if he was a physically powerful man. It was all there for her to see. Including his bold erection.

The sight of his naked body was all it took to create an ache deep in her feminine core and she realized she had never wanted any man as much as she wanted Acton at this very moment.

Turning toward her, he stepped between her legs and trailed his fingers down both of her thighs, then back up to the lower portion of her belly.

Groaning, she smiled at him. "Those hands of yours should come with a danger warning."

Growling with pleasure, he looped lazy circles over her skin, all the while moving downward until he reached the juncture between her thighs. By the time his finger slipped inside her, she was frantically arching her hips upward, searching for the pleasure only he could give her.

Over and over he stroked her, until she reached up to curl a hand at the back of his neck and yank him down to her for a kiss. His tongue instantly found its way between her teeth and he stroked the inside of her mouth with the same tormenting rhythm his finger was making in the heated folds of her womanhood.

The attack on her senses was too much for Stephanie to take and in a matter of seconds, she felt herself morphing into a beautiful bird, soaring into the wind and flying high above the clouds.

When she finally glided back to earth, Acton's face was hovered above hers and everything she'd ever wanted was mirrored in his blue eyes.

Her throat thick, she whispered, "You're not playing fair, Acton."

A smug smile tilted the corners of his lips. "All I want is to please you, Stephanie."

"Then please me more, Acton, and more," she begged.

He eased away from her and stood up, reaching for the nightstand. "I think I'd better find some protection."

"Wait!" The word popped before she could stop it and he looked at her with confusion.

"I'm sorry, Acton. That didn't come out right. I just wanted to say that I'm on the Pill. So if you're concerned about pregnancy…don't worry." Just to keep her periods regular, she could've told him. But there was no need for that much explanation. He didn't need to know it had been ages since she'd had sex.

The tense look on his face relaxed and then a smile brightened his face in the dimly lit room. "Oh. Okay. But still, I want to make sure we're both protected."

He glanced over to where Linus was lying quietly in his cradle. "No need to worry about Linus. He's already gone to sleep."

Stephanie held her arms invitingly up to him and he gladly joined her on the bed, then scooped her into his arms.

When he found her mouth, she wrapped her arms around him, drawing her body tightly to his. He was all heat and hard muscle and in a matter of seconds she was lost in a cyclone of swirling sensations.

Somewhere in the back of her mind, she sensed his hands were cupping her breasts, roaming across her back, down her legs, then back up to her rounded bottom. Each spot his fingers touched left her skin burning and tingling with pleasure and she knew with certainty that she could never get enough of this. Of him.

Once his hands had made a tantalizing tour of her body, he turned his attention to her breasts, kissing and nipping the nipples until they were rigid and throbbing. By the time, he finally rolled her to her back and poised himself above her, quickly sheathing himself in the condom he'd taken from the bedside table, Stephanie's insides were clawing and screaming to be connected to him. Yet when he did finally enter her, she wasn't prepared for the shock of pleasure that lanced through her like a white-hot arrow. It was breathtaking and all-consuming, and for the space of a heartbeat, she was too stunned to move or speak.

And then from somewhere above her, she heard him groan her name and the sound shattered her momentary paralysis.

"Acton," she murmured, her voice full of anguished need. "Make love to me. Please make love to me."

"Yes, sweet Stephanie. Oh, yes."

Bracing his weight with his hands on either side of her head, he began to move in a slow, enticing rhythm that led her brain straight into a mindless pool of desire. Robbed of all sensibility, her body took over and she met each thrust of his hips with reckless abandon.

Then just when she was thinking she could go on

making love to him forever, she felt his pace quicken
and his breathing grow harsh. Gripping his back, she
tried to hang on, to slow the runaway freight train
that was carrying them faster and faster toward their
ultimate destination.

But she couldn't stop it. With one final thrust, the
room around her began to whirl and she was suddenly lost, riding a wave of bliss that was taking her
all the way to the moon and back.

As soon as Acton had pulled Stephanie's sweater
over her head and she'd stood there before him with
such a look of self-doubt on her face, he'd known he
was in deep trouble.

At that moment, he'd wanted to do more than have
sex with Stephanie—he'd wanted to make love to
her. Real love. The kind that connected a man and a
woman together until the last breaths of their lives.

And now as she was lying curled up beside him
in the middle of the bed, the urge to protect her, to
keep her safely by his side, had grown to enormous
proportions. How had this happened? Why had he
allowed it to happen?

*Love isn't something you can control, Acton. It's
something that hits you even when you think you
don't want it, or need it. So now, good or bad, you'll
just have to learn to live with it.*

"It's not been dark for very long and we're here
in bed. This is shameful behavior, Acton."

The sound of Stephanie's drowsy voice broke through the taunting warning winding its way through his head and he gazed down at the crown of her head tucked beneath his chin.

"It's shameful, all right," he agreed. "A shame that it took us so long to get here."

Laughing softly, she turned in his arms so that she was facing him and as Acton looked into her glistening blue eyes, he knew his heart had never felt so full or content.

"Do you know what I feel like at this very moment?" she asked.

"Hungry?"

Another chuckle shook her chest, "No. I feel like a princess with the world at her feet."

His smile came from the depths of his heart. "Well, you have kissed a frog."

"And he turned into a handsome prince." She stretched her neck upward until she could press her lips to his. "That kiss is to make sure you don't turn back into a frog."

Certain that the tender feelings swelling his chest were exposed on his face, he buried it in her silky hair and tried to not to sound like he was being strangled. "Thank you for saving me from that fate."

Her sigh fanned the side of his neck as she slipped an arm around his waist. "Seymour deserves a special treat and I'm going to give him one."

"For what? Being a furry little beast?"

She gave his back a gentle pinch. "Seymour is a sweetheart. If it hadn't been for him having that scratching spell I might not have ever met you."

Amused, he lifted his head and gave her an impish look. "Hmm. You're right. I might just give him a T-bone steak for introducing the two of us."

The playful twinkle in her eyes dimmed as she traced a fingertip over his cheek and down to the corner of her lips. "Then you don't regret us? This?"

Making love to Stephanie had upended everything about the man he'd ever thought he was or would be. And no matter what happened in the future, he knew this time in her arms would play a part in shaping his life.

"I've been wanting us to be together, Stephanie. And you've given me so much. So much." Threading his fingers into her hair, he pressed a line of kisses over her cheek and down the length of her straight little nose before he settled on her lips. "No regrets, my darling. This is only the beginning for us."

"Yes, our sweet beginning." She'd breathed the words against his lips, and now opened her mouth to receive his kiss, wrapped an arm around his neck and snuggled her soft body next to his.

Desire stirred deep within him and the reaction had Acton wondering what was happening to him. The sweat hadn't yet dried on his body and he was already wanting to be back inside her.

With intentions of deepening the embrace, he

rolled her onto her back, but that was as far as he got before Linus let out a whimper.

At the same time, they turned their heads in the direction of the baby. As if on cue, Linus let out a hungry howl that said he wasn't to be ignored.

"I need to get him," she said. "It's time for his bottle."

She started to rise, but he put a hand on her shoulder. "You stay put. I'll tend to Linus. Tonight you're my princess, remember? And your prince wants to pamper you."

Acton climbed off the bed and was reaching for his jeans, when from the corner of his eye, he spotted Stephanie sliding off the bed to join him.

As she plucked her sweater and jeans from the floor, he turned to her. "What are you doing? Don't you trust me to take care of Linus?"

Shaking back her tousled red hair, she stepped over and placed a hand on his arm. "We're together now. And that's how we're going to take care of Linus—together."

In spite of the baby's angry cries, Acton took a moment to lean over and press a quick kiss to her lips.

She was too good for him, he thought. And sooner or later, she would realize she could do much better than a simple cowboy. But he'd already planted his boots in both stirrups. He had no choice but to ride to the bitter end.

Chapter Twelve

Stephanie laughed as Mack and Tallulah chased after the tennis ball she'd thrown toward the end of the long fenced run. With Tallulah's short dachshund legs, she had to work twice as hard to keep up with the terrier, but neither of the small dogs could beat Buddy to the ball.

Proud of his accomplishment, the bigger dog trotted back to Stephanie and dropped the prize at her feet.

"Buddy, I think we can safely pronounce your leg fit as a fiddle. But if you want to keep Mack and Tallulah as your friends, you're going to have to lag back and let them win some of the time."

The dog whined and Stephanie was fondly petting the back of his neck, when she heard footsteps behind her.

Turning, she was more than surprised to see her three brothers standing near the entrance of the chain-link enclosure. *Now what were they up to?* she wondered as she saw Steven motion for her to join them.

Giving the three dogs final pats on the head, Stephanie walked down the run to where her brothers continued to wait.

"What's wrong?" she asked as she got within hearing distance. "Has something happened?"

Steven was the one to answer. "No. We'd like to talk with you. And since you've been gone so much lately, we wanted to catch you while you're home."

Home. Strange how the last two and half weeks had changed her feelings about that one special word. Although her brothers didn't know it, the Fame and Fortune Ranch didn't feel like home to her anymore. Her suite of rooms, which were so lavishly furnished and supplied with anything and everything she could possibly need, didn't feel nearly as comfortable and inviting as Acton's old farmhouse.

Steven opened the gate to let her out of the dog run, then shut it carefully behind her.

Callum said, "Let's go sit by the pool and get comfortable."

Stephanie didn't have time to get comfortable.

She'd promised Acton that she and Linus would be over at his house by seven this evening.

"I can't get too comfortable. I have a date," she said.

Dillon cleared his throat and the awkward glances exchanged among the three brothers didn't go unnoticed by Stephanie.

"Okay, what is this about? You three look like kids caught with your hands in the cookie jar."

Callum pointed to a cushioned chaise lounge. "Sit down, Stephanie. We won't keep you long. We promise."

To keep the peace, she took a seat. Steven sat down in a chair opposite her, while Callum and Dillon chose to remain standing.

"Is something going on with Mom and Dad? Or our sisters?" Normally, Stephanie tried to talk with the family back in Fort Lauderdale on a weekly basis, but she'd been so busy these past few days that she'd not taken the time to call or text.

"No. They're all fine," Dillon assured her.

"It's you that we're worried about," Steven said. "You've been going out practically every night for the past two weeks and—"

Seeing where the conversation was headed, Stephanie held up a hand. "That is my business. Just like where you three go is your business. I don't try to butt into your lives, so why are you trying to butt into mine? It's ridiculous!"

"Ridiculous? Really?" Steven said, shooting the questions back at her. "How many times have we seen you locked away in your room, crying your heart out because some jerk called it quits?"

Stephanie couldn't believe how much she wanted to reach over and slap her brother's face.

"Listen, Steven, maybe you think you're trying to protect me, but what you're doing to me is worse than dealing with a no-account boyfriend! I need for the three of you to believe in me! To trust me to use good judgment—not just about men, but every important decision. Instead, you treat me like a silly teenager with her head in the clouds."

From the smirk on Steven's face, she could see her remarks had rolled off his back without making a dent in his mind-set. "Have you ever stopped to think that's what you're acting like?" he asked.

Callum sighed, then said, "Look, Stephanie, you're a Fortune. That makes things different for you."

She looked at him with disbelief. "Are you saying that makes me better than other people? Better than Acton?"

Callum shook his head. "That's not what I'm implying at all. It just means that there are some people out there who might want to take advantage of us—of you—because you are a Fortune. We just want you to take things slowly before you jump into a situation where you might get hurt."

In spite of her being a foster mother to Linus and her new newfound feelings for Acton, her brothers couldn't see that she was changing and evolving into a much stronger woman. They still saw her as gullible Stephanie, who'd never been able to pick a worthwhile man for herself. The idea cut her deeply.

Swallowing at the ball of emotion in her throat, she said, "So you think Acton is out to use me. Or he's after my money. Is that it?"

"Stephanie! We didn't say anything like that!" Dillon scolded."

"No. You didn't have to," she said bitterly. "It's pretty obvious that you're all afraid I'm getting hooked up with a loser—again."

"Look, Stephanie," Stephen spoke up, "We're not judging Acton. We don't even know him—yet. We just want you to take your time and use your head. Not just your heart."

Acton had opened her eyes and her heart, Stephanie thought. But trying to convince her brothers of that would be useless.

"Look, you three, I appreciate the fact that you want me to be happy. If that's the real purpose behind this meeting," she added crossly.

"What is that supposed to mean?" Steven asked, "What other motive would we have, except your happiness?"

"I'm not sure. Maybe all this high-rolling and wheeling and dealing you three have been doing around Rambling Rose has gone to your heads. Maybe you're afraid I might marry my cowboy and that would embarrass all of you!"

"Oh, Stephanie!" Callum rolled his eyes. "It's not that at all!"

Steven actually jumped to his feet. "Are you planning on marrying this Donovan guy?"

Was she already dreaming about becoming Acton's wife? Of being the mother of his children? Even if she was, she had no idea if Acton's future plans were headed in the same direction as hers. Yes, she'd spent every available night she could find with him, and during that time, their passion for each other hadn't dimmed. It had only grown hotter. But that didn't mean he was in love with her. Or that he wanted to make her his wife.

Yet even with the uncertainty of her future looming before her, Stephanie had never been so happy and she wasn't about to let her three meddling brothers spoil it for her.

Jumping to her feet, she said, "I'd never tell you three what my personal plans are. You'd only try to ruin them!"

She hurried toward the house, leaving her brothers staring worriedly after her.

In spite of the drizzly morning, Acton, Shawn and their dad were trying to finish building a section of fence when the last spool of barbed wire they'd been stretching reached the end.

"Well, that's it for now," his father said as he tossed the empty spool into the back of his pickup truck. "It's almost time for lunch, anyway. After I eat, I'll drive into Rambling Rose and pick up a few more spools of wire. You guys go do what you want until I get back."

The tall, lean man was in his midfifties, but looked and worked like a man twenty years younger. As Acton watched him step up into the truck and drive across the open pasture, he wondered if his mother had brought up the subject of Acton seeing Stephanie to his father. So far his dad hadn't mentioned a word to him, but that didn't mean he was unaware of his son's new girlfriend. Ramsey Donovan had always been the kind of father who thought it best to let his older children make their own decisions—and their own mistakes—in order to learn from them.

"I think I'll go back to the ranch house and eat with Mom and Dad," Shawn said. "I didn't bring any lunch with me, did you?"

"No. I'm going to drive into Rambling Rose and see if Stephanie can get away from Paws and Claws long enough to have lunch," he told his brother.

The other man grinned. "So it's gotten to the point where seeing her at night isn't enough for you."

Acton darted him an annoyed look. "What would you know about it, anyway?"

"Ha! I'm not blind, Acton. Neither is the rest of the family. We've been seeing Stephanie's car parked at your place. You two have been keeping some pretty late hours."

Acton tugged his hat down lower on his forehead and hoped it shaded the red blush creeping over his face.

"She'd rather come to my house than me go to hers."

Shawn's eyebrows arched with speculation. "Why? Because those snobbish brothers of hers don't want you around?"

Acton grimaced. "They're not snobs, Shawn. Not really. They're just concerned about their sister's happiness."

"How can you be so benevolent? You told me they treated you like a doormat that night you were helping Stephanie with the baking. Have you talked with them since then?"

"No. But I plan to. Soon. They don't understand what they're doing to their sister." It had taken him hours to calm her down from her brothers' so-called "advice" when she'd finally arrived at his place last night.

Shawn shook his head. "By disapproving of you? Hell, Acton. I wouldn't be talking to those guys—I'd be landing a few blows on their jaws."

Acton rolled his eyes. "That would really show what a good guy I am."

Shawn put a hand on Acton's shoulder and pushed him toward the old work truck they'd driven to this isolated part of the ranch. "You know what they say about good guys, Acton. They always wind up with the short end of the stick. Think about it."

Acton did think about it throughout the drive to Rambling Rose and even while he was sitting across from Stephanie in the fast-food restaurant. Making love to her had changed him in ways he'd never expected. Shawn would probably say she was making him soft and wimpy, but that really wasn't the case. Loving her had given him the ability to see things through her eyes and it had made the world a different place for him.

Loving her. Had he already fallen in love with Stephanie? Was that what was causing the emptiness he felt whenever he was away from her? Oh, Lord, he might as well admit, at least to himself, just how smitten he was with the redheaded beauty.

"I'm glad you could get away for lunch," he told her as he watched her bite into a cheeseburger. "You know I was thinking that for the exception of the Valentine fund-raiser, you and I haven't been out on the town on a regular kind of date. How would you like to go to dinner one night? To a special place— just you and me?"

"Without Linus?"

She looked crushed, but Acton didn't let her response put him off. "You deserve to treat yourself once in a while, Stephanie. Even parents hire babysitters and go out on occasion."

With a nod of acquiescence, she said, "Yes, you're right, Acton. I just feel…guilty about it, because I'm away from him during the day while I'm at work. And I hate to ask Becky to watch him. She has her hands full with her twins and then she'd tell Callum why I needed a sitter and he—"

"Wouldn't like it," Acton said grimly, finishing her thought. "Well, I can't make Callum like me, but I can fix the babysitter issue. Mom would be only too happy to watch the little guy."

Her mouth fell open. "I haven't even met your mother! Gina is the only member of your family that I've met."

"That's something I want to change…soon."

Her blue eyes wandered over his face as though she couldn't believe what he was saying.

He reached across the table and took her hand. "Would you like to meet my parents?"

A smile curved the corners of her lips. "I would love to meet your family, Acton. I just hope they approve of me spending time with their son."

"They will," he promised. "Just wait and see."

The muffled ring of a phone suddenly sounded from her purse and she frowned at the interruption.

"Excuse me, Acton, I should look at this. It could be the clinic."

He nodded his understanding and she took the call. The conversation was short, with Stephanie uttering only a few words. By the time she ended the call, her face was paper-white, her eyes wide. To say she looked stunned would be an understatement.

"Stephanie, what's happened?"

She looked over at him and he could see tears pooling in her eyes.

"That was Dr. Green," she said in a strained voice. "He had some news for me."

Acton frowned. "I'm sorry. Who is Dr. Green?"

"He's the head pediatrician at Rambling Rose Pediatric Center. He's the doctor who came to Laurel's aid when she first went into labor at the ribbon-cutting ceremony."

"Laurel—you're talking about Linus's biological mother?"

Nodding, she thrust the phone back into her purse. "I'm sorry, Acton. I can't eat. Would you mind if we get out of here? I'll explain when we get outside."

"No problem. Let's go."

Acton hurriedly gathered up the remainder of their meal and tossed it into the trash receptacle on the way out the door. Once they reached his truck, he helped her into the passenger seat, then took his place behind the steering wheel.

"Do you need to go see this Dr. Green?" he asked. "Is this something about Linus?"

Her expression sick, she said, "I don't need to see Dr. Green. But it is about Linus. And I—I feel like my whole world has just turned upside down, Acton. I don't know any other way to say it. Dr. Green says that Linus's father has been located and he's coming to Rambling Rose. I've known from the very start that it was a possibility that he or the mother might show up, but I... A part of me wanted to think that it might not happen. That I could end up being Linus's adopted mother."

Acton could understand why she felt her world was upended. He felt like someone had just whammed him in the head with a two-by-four. "Linus's father? But with the mother saying he was out of the picture I assumed the guy probably didn't want the baby. Looks like my assumption was wrong." Shaking his head, he suddenly backtracked. "But maybe I'm wrong in thinking he does want the baby. Just because he's coming to Rambling Rose doesn't mean he wants to be a full-time parent to little Linus. It might just mean that he's willing to help locate the mother."

Stephanie shook her head. "He'd hardly need to come to Rambling Rose for that reason, Acton. No, it's obvious. He's coming for his son—my little baby—at least, my temporary baby!"

By the time the last words came out of her mouth, she was sobbing and Acton was sure his heart was going to break for her as he reached across the console and dragged her into his arms.

"Don't cry, Stephanie. Everything will work out. Right now, you are Linus's legal foster mother and this man might not even be able to prove he is the father."

Sniffing, she drew her head back from his shoulder and used the back of her hand to wipe her teary eyes. "You're right, Acton. I can't fall apart now. I need to wait and see what this man is planning."

"Did Dr. Green know when he'd be arriving in Rambling Rose?"

She shook her head. "He's going to call me back as soon as he gets all the details."

Acton could only wonder what this was going to do to him and Stephanie. He knew, probably more than anyone, just how much Stephanie considered Linus to be her own baby. If this mystery man took him away from her, he wasn't sure she could deal with the heartache. He knew one thing for sure—he wanted to be with her, to reassure her that no matter what happened with Linus, he'd be there to support her.

Later that afternoon, between patients, Stephanie informed Dr. Neil that she needed to take a few minutes off to speak with Dr. Green at the pediatric center. The veterinarian was more than obliging and told Stephanie there was no need for her to hurry. Dayna could assist him until she returned.

On the short drive over to the new pediatric building, Stephanie prayed that the doctor could give her more details about Linus's father. Mainly, what the man's intentions might be. But deep down, she had the sickening feeling that this was the beginning of the end of her tenure as the baby's mother.

Thankfully, Dr. Green's afternoon schedule wasn't too hectic for him to spare a few minutes to speak with Stephanie.

When a nurse ushered her into his office, the fatherly man with a head full of white hair and matching beard left his executive chair and greeted her with a gentle pat on her shoulder.

"Have a seat, Stephanie," he said, gesturing to a comfortable chair in front of his desk. "I'm glad you came. I realize my news had to be jarring."

She attempted to swallow away the ball of fear that had been stuck in her throat ever since she and Acton had left the fast-food restaurant.

"I won't lie, Dr. Green. It has shaken me. I mean, it's always been in the back of my mind that Laurel might return for her son and I'd have to give him over. And I knew there had to be a father somewhere who might want his child. But the more I grew to love Linus, the more I let myself push those possibilities to the back of my mind."

"I understand, Stephanie," the doctor said with

empathy. "In your heart you've become the baby's mother."

Stephanie nodded glumly, then looked at him in question. "What does this man want? And how do we know he's actually the biological father?"

Folding his hands together on the desktop, the doctor said, "I've not spoken to him directly, but I think it's safe to assume he wants the child. He lives in Houston and I've spoken with social services there. The agency has ordered a DNA test on the man's behalf. Apparently he has some sort of letter proving he had a close relationship with Laurel."

Stephanie's head was swimming with questions, along with crushing images of seeing her baby whisked away by a stranger. Her brain refused to believe such a thing might happen, but her heart was telling her to prepare for the worst.

"A DNA test," she repeated in a hollow voice. "This man must feel certain that he's Linus's father."

With his white beard and hair and warm disposition, some of the children around Rambling Rose believed Dr. Green was actually Santa Claus. Now, as Stephanie looked to him for answers, she thought how wonderful it would be if he truly was Santa and could make her fondest wishes come true.

"It does sound that way," he agreed. "From what the woman with social services told me, this man has just now learned that Laurel had the baby and that Linus is here in Rambling Rose. As you might guess, he's very anxious to get the DNA results. So this evening when you pick up Linus at day care I need you to take him to the lab here in the clinic. I've already sent orders for a nurse to take a swab from his mouth. If we put a rush on it, we should see the results in a few days. Okay?"

On the inside, Stephanie felt like she was breaking into a thousand pieces, while on the outside she was gripping her hands together in her lap to keep them from shaking.

"Uh—yes, I'll take Linus by the lab. And then I guess we wait," she said as much to herself as to the doctor.

Dr. Green didn't immediately reply, and Stephanie looked across the desk to see he was regarding her with sympathy. The idea that he was already seeing the writing on the wall made her sick to her stomach.

"It's understandable that you've grown fond of Linus," he said. "But if this man does turn out to be Linus's father, then I think your heart will tell you what's right for the child."

Drawing in a breath, Stephanie called upon every ounce of inner strength she possessed to hold on to her composure.

"Have you heard anything about Laurel? Did this man know where to locate her?"

"She hasn't been located. But I was told this man might be able to help find her. Which would be a good thing. Don't you agree?"

Stephanie nodded. No matter how much she loved Linus, deep in her heart, she agreed that he deserved to have a real mother and father.

Rising to her feet, she said, "Thank you, Dr. Green, for taking the time to speak with me. I won't keep you any longer."

He joined her in front of the desk. "Anytime, Stephanie. I realize this whole situation is very unusual. As long as I've been a pediatrician I can't remember anything like this happening with a newborn. Especially here in Rambling Rose."

Bending her head, she fought against the tears glazing her eyes. "I'll be honest, Dr. Green, I was hoping to adopt Linus as my own. Now that—" She paused and drew in a shaky breath. "Well, it looks like that hope is over."

He took hold of her hand and gently patted the back of it. "Stephanie, you've been a very generous and loving foster mother for Linus. You should be proud of that. And you're still a very young woman. You'll have the opportunity to have babies of your own."

Yes, maybe, she thought. But Linus was already here. In her home, her arms, her life. She loved him. She didn't want to lose him.

Sniffing back her tears, she thanked the doctor again, then left his office before she broke down completely.

Thankfully, she managed to leave the pediatric

center without running into Becky. One look at her sister-in-law and she would have burst into a mess of hot tears.

When she returned to Paws and Claws, the waiting room was full of patients and the whole staff was too busy to ask her questions about leaving work in the middle of the afternoon.

Stephanie did her best to focus on her job, but Linus never left her mind for even a second, and by the time the clinic closed up for the evening, she was utterly exhausted.

As she left the building, she was thinking about her brothers and wondering how they were going to take the news about Linus, when she noticed Acton's truck was parked next to her vehicle.

Normally, the idea that he was waiting to see her would've sent her heart soaring with joy. This evening, she could hardly summon a smile.

"You look exhausted," he said as he met her on the sidewalk a few feet away from her parked car. "Has anything else happened about Linus?"

She let out a weary breath and he took her by the arm. "Let's go sit in your car. You can tell me there."

After they were comfortably seated in her little sedan, she said, "I went to see Dr. Green this afternoon. He informed me that I have to take Linus to the lab for a DNA swab."

"DNA! When?" Acton asked.

"This evening, when I pick him up from day care.

It seems this man from Houston believes he's Linus's father and he wants a test done as quickly as possible."

"Oh, God, that's not good."

Her eyes narrowed with speculation as she studied his face. "Not good? What does that mean? You've said before that Linus deserves a biological parent. And if you were Linus, wouldn't you be happy to know that at least one of your actual parents wanted you?"

He looked totally confused by her response. "Well, hell. Of course I would. But Linus is a baby. He doesn't know about that sort of thing right now. He only knows when someone holds him and loves him and feeds him. That someone is you."

"And you," she replied.

"That's right. And I'll just say it plainly—I don't want the little guy to be taken away. Real dad or no real dad. I realize that's probably selfish of me, but I can't help it."

By the time he'd finished, Stephanie was crying and she didn't bother to try to hide her tears. She was too tired, too afraid to do anything about stemming her overwrought emotions.

"You're not making me feel any better about this, Acton."

His expression turned to one of disbelief. "What does that mean? I don't want you to lose Linus any more than you do!"

"I know. But we need to be reasonable about this situation. Linus isn't my baby. Nor is he yours."

"Well, it sure as hell feels like he's yours—ours. And where was this guy when Linus was born? Why wasn't he with the woman he supposedly loved enough to make a child with?"

Stephanie had been asking herself the same questions. But the answers weren't going to change the facts. "There could be good reasons he wasn't around when Linus was born. Laurel might not have told him she was pregnant. She might have disappeared from his life before he had any idea she was going to have his child. Without any facts, we can't blame him for not being around when Linus was born."

He let out a heavy breath. "Nothing about this situation feels right, Stephanie."

"Whether it feels right or not, it's happening."

He reached over and gently touched the wet trail of tears on her face. "I'm sorry, Stephanie. I realize I'm not handling this very well. And that's making things worse for you."

She looked at him. "I understand how attached you've become to Linus."

Pain shadowed his eyes and though Stephanie wanted to him help him feel better, she couldn't. She was too crushed with her own pain to hardly know what she was saying.

He nodded. "Deep down...well, I know it would

be best for Linus to have his real dad. And probably best for you. It's just that right now it hurts to think of losing him."

She shook her head. "Yes, it hurts. But we no longer have a choice in the matter. Anyway, I need to go pick up Linus from day care and get the swab done before I head home."

Frowning with confusion, he asked, "Home? Aren't you coming to my house tonight? That's what we'd planned, remember?"

She looked at him blankly. Everything was barreling at her from all directions, tearing at her thoughts and emotions. She had to have space to collect herself. To think. "Yes, I remember. But things have changed since then. I need to speak with my brothers about Linus—"

His brows arched upward. "Your brothers? I'm the guy who's been Linus's stand-in dad. Doesn't that count for something?"

She blew out a frustrated breath. "Of course it does. But my brothers—"

"Yes, I see. You feel it's important that you be with them now," he interrupted, his voice stiff. "So go."

"You don't have to be so cold about it," she retorted.

"I'm not being cold. I'm being realistic. It's obvious you believe your brothers can help you with baby Linus much more than I can. And you're probably right. They have the clout and the means. All I have is my heart. And—well, none of that matters. I can see that now."

She glared at him. "That's not what I'm thinking! And I don't deserve this from you, Acton! Especially now!"

"You're right, Stephanie. You don't deserve it." His jaw tight, he opened the door and climbed out of the car.

"Where are you going?" she asked, stunned that he was leaving like this.

"You can handle this situation far better without me," he said flatly. "In fact, I figure your whole life will be better without me in it."

With that he slammed the door and went straight to his truck.

Numb with pain, Stephanie waited until he'd driven away before she started the car and left the parking lot.

As she drove to the pediatric center, she couldn't decide which was worse—the reality that everything she'd ever had with Acton had just ended, or that this might be the last time she'd be collecting her baby from day care.

Chapter Thirteen

Four days later, Stephanie stood in the bathroom and stared in shock at the result of the home-pregnancy test.

Positive.

It shouldn't be surprising. Her period was several days late and the mere thought of breakfast was enough to make her stomach feel like she was on a bobbing sailboat. Still, she was amazed that she'd gotten pregnant. She'd been taking her pills regularly and had never missed a one.

The only birth control that's foolproof is abstinence. The advice of her ob-gyn back in Fort Lauderdale had mostly drifted through one ear and out the other. Even when the doctor had been writing Stephanie's prescription, she'd warned her that having sex while on the Pill could produce a pregnancy. At that time, Stephanie's last boyfriend had ended their relationship because she'd refused to give him an interest-free loan to buy a fishing boat. Sex had been the last thing on her mind. All she'd wanted was something strong enough to keep her periods from popping up way too early. She'd had no way of knowing then that she'd eventually be falling into bed with a virile cowboy.

Now she was going to have Acton's baby. Oh, Lord, how ironic!

Overwhelmed, she placed a protective hand over the region of her womb and leaned heavily against the vanity. She'd not spoken to Acton since that evening they'd argued in the Paws and Claws parking lot. What was he going to think about this development? Being a daddy to Linus for a few hours at a time wasn't the same as being a full-time parent. Was he prepared for that much commitment?

Deep down, she believed Acton was a good man with good intentions. But he was only twenty-five and anyone who knew him said he was far from ready to settle down with a wife and children.

So why did you fall into bed with him, Stephanie? Why did you leap into his arms and let yourself dream about a future with him?

Because she loved him. Truly loved him, she answered the chastising voice in her head. But what good was love going to do her now? Acton thought she didn't need him. That she didn't want to include him in the important aspects of her life. How was she going to make him see that he was wrong?

A wave of nausea washed over her and she leaned over the sink and splashed cold water on her face in an effort to ease her heaving stomach.

It didn't matter how Acton reacted to the news that he was going to be a father, she firmly told herself. For years she'd wanted a baby and dreamed about being a mother. Now that she was actually pregnant, even under such dismal circumstances, she was happy that they'd created a child together.

Acton removed the saddle from the bay horse tied at the hitching post and carried it into the tack room. Right behind him, Shawn carried an armload of saddle blankets and bridles.

The two brothers had spent most of the morning riding the back pastures, checking on late calving cows. It was a job that Acton normally loved. Anytime he could spend a few hours on a horse, he was in heaven. But today he'd simply gone through the motions. But then, ever since he and Stephanie had parted ways, he'd been living on automatic pilot.

"I'm glad Dad is driving over to San Antonio this afternoon to see about buying that hay baler he's had his eye on," Shawn said. "If we work like hell while he's gone, we can finish the fence and surprise him."

With a mocking grunt, Acton lifted the saddle onto a wooden stand and jerked the fenders into place. "He'd be surprised, all right. He thinks we can't do anything right without him watching over our shoulders."

Frowning, Shawn hung the wet blankets on a hook to allow them to dry. "That's not true and you know it. What the hell is wrong with you, anyway? You haven't said more than a dozen words this morning and most of them have been sarcastic."

Closing his eyes, Acton lifted his hat from his head and combed fingers through is hair. "Sorry, Shawn," he said ruefully. "I hadn't realized I was being so surly. I've been—"

"A real jerk," Shawn interrupted as he walked over to where Acton stood. "What's up?"

Acton's nostrils flared as he sucked in a weary breath. "Nothing. I'm just not feeling well, that's all."

Unconvinced, Shawn shook his head. "Try again. You're not sick. You're miserable about something. And I have a feeling it's that Fortune woman. Acton, I tried to tell you—"

"Damn it, Shawn, I don't need to be preached at by you! Things are bad enough as it is and—"

Shawn interrupted. "What things? What's happened?"

Shaking his head with defeat, Acton sat down on

an upended feed bucket and quickly explained about Linus and how a man claiming to be his father has requested a DNA test.

"You think this man is legitimate?" Shawn asked.

Acton shrugged. "He must have good reason to believe he's the father. But I can't say for sure. Stephanie and I haven't spoken since the day she got the news. She'd rather be with her brothers. They're more capable of helping her deal with a crisis than me, apparently," he said sarcastically. "And you're right, Shawn, I should've listened to you and Mom. Stephanie will never see me as an equal. Or as a man who can take care of her."

"Aren't you being a little hard on yourself, Acton? And on her?"

"I'm just trying to be real, Shawn. And right now reality hurts like hell." He wiped a hand over his face, then stared blindly at the toes of his boots. "I'll admit that when we got the news about Linus I didn't handle things too well. But to be honest, Shawn, I was just as cut up as she was over the whole idea that someone might be going to be taking our baby away."

"Our baby?"

He didn't try to hide the pain in his eyes as he looked up at his brother. "I guess that sounds foolish to you. But Linus was beginning to feel like my son, too. Now he's—" Acton swallowed. "Well, it looks like there's a strong possibility he'll be going to go live with his real dad. And there's not a damned thing I can do to stop it."

"So the both of you were scared and hurting and you lashed out at each other. That's understandable. Have you thought about reaching out to her, trying to apologize? I'm not saying she's right and you're wrong, Acton, I'm just saying one of you has to extend an olive branch."

"I don't think she'll accept an olive branch or anything else from me," Acton said dully.

Shawn opened his mouth to reply at the same time Acton's phone dinged with an incoming text message.

"I'd better check this. It might be Dad." He pulled the phone from his pocket and was immediately shocked to see a message from Dillon Fortune. "What the hell?"

"What is it? Has Dad blown a tire or something?"

Acton gripped the phone as he tapped the screen to open the message. "No. It's from Stephanie's brother, Dillon." After rapidly scanning the short text, he said in a stunned voice, "He and his brothers are worried about her. They'd like for me to come speak with them."

"Seriously?"

Dazed, Acton rose from his seat on the bucket. "Yes. He says if I can get away, they'll be at their office in the work yard across from the Shoppes."

"Are you going?"

Groaning, Acton lifted his gaze to the dusty cobwebs hanging from the rafters of the tack room. "Yes. But I don't get any of this. They don't approve of me. At least, that's the feeling I get from them. So what could they want?"

"To hell with them!" Shawn boomed. "They need to know you don't approve of them!"

Shaking his head, Acton began unbuckling his chaps. "No, Shawn. This is not about me and them. Not now. It's about Stephanie and what's best for her. No matter what, I want her to be happy. Even if that means I have to step out of her life—permanently."

Shawn's eyes narrowed shrewdly and then his mouth fell open. "You really love this woman, don't you?"

Acton had been asking himself that very question for the past several days. Funny how it had taken a simple text from her brother to allow him to see the answer plain and clear.

"Yes. I do love her. Somehow I have to make her understand that."

Shawn gave his shoulder an affectionate squeeze. "You go show the Fortunes they're not dealing with a hayseed."

Even though horse manure was probably dried around the edges of his boots and dust had turned his black hat to brown, Acton didn't waste time changing into clean clothes. He drove straight to The Shoppes, where several pickup trucks and other work vehicles were parked around the modular building that served as the makeshift office of Fortune Brothers Construction.

Off to one side, three workers were loading scaffolds onto the back of a long, flatbed trailer, while a few feet away, a heating-and-cooling van braked to a halt. Dust billowed from the wheels as the driver jumped out and hurried into the office.

Acton followed at a slower pace, and after placing a brief knock on the door, he stepped inside a long room furnished with a desk at each end and a grouping of comfortable furniture in between.

All three of Stephanie's brothers were present, along with the man who'd jumped out of the van. All turned to look at Acton and then the man behind one of the desks the one he remembered as Steven, rose and walked over to greet him.

"Hello, Mr. Donovan. We're glad you could come."

He reached out to shake hands and Acton politely complied. "Hello, Mr. Fortune."

He inclined his head toward the two men walking over to join them. "I imagine you remember Dillon and Callum."

Dillon was dressed in jeans, boots and a plaid Western shirt. He looked much like the natives of Rambling Rose, while Callum and Steven were both in khakis and ties and appeared as though they'd be more comfortable in a high-rise office in downtown Houston.

Acton shook hands with the other two men and Steven gestured toward the couch and armchairs. "Let's sit."

While the four men took their seats, the van guy grabbed a handful of papers from one of the desks and discreetly let himself out of the office.

"I'm sure you're wondering what this is about," Callum said.

Acton tried not to grimace. "You three haven't exactly invited me to be friends. So, yeah, I'm wondering."

To Acton's surprise, Dillon appeared regretful. "I can't speak for my brothers, but I'm sorry about that, Acton. It's not that we had anything against you personally. It's more like we, uh, we worry about Stephanie. She's been hurt too many times."

"So why worry now? Stephanie has ended things with me. She's apparently seen things your way."

Steven was stunned. "We didn't tell her to end things with you! In fact, she hasn't mentioned anything about the two of you. When did this happen?"

So, Acton thought sickly, he wasn't important enough to Stephanie for her to mention him, even as an afterthought.

Acton said, "The day the doctor ordered her to take Linus in for a DNA swab."

Callum nodded with sudden dawning. "I'm beginning to see. She was very distraught that night. We thought it was all about Linus."

"She was heartbroken," Acton said in a clipped tone. "Over Linus, not me. So now you don't need to worry about Stephanie any longer. She's free to date anyone she wants."

The brothers exchanged troubled glances before Steven leveled a pointed look at Acton. "Is that what you want? To step out of Stephanie's life?"

"Hell no!" he retorted, then cleared his throat and said, "I mean, I want Stephanie to be happy. That's what's important to me. I, uh, well… I wish that she still cared about me. Because my feelings for her are very serious. Maybe she didn't understand that. Or maybe she did understand and it didn't matter to her. I was seeing me and her and Linus as a family. But now that Linus might be going away, I guess everything is over."

The brothers kept looking at each other as if they were totally confused.

It was Steven who finally said, "We've made a mistake about you, Acton. We thought you were probably just playing Stephanie along. She's beautiful and rich and unfortunately a bit gullible."

"So you three think," Acton said, his voice brittle. "I happen to think she's very smart and special. And her heart is bigger than her head."

"Look," Callum said, "we don't know what was said between you two, but we do know that Stephanie is in a bad way. And we believe you might be able to help."

"How? Before I left to come over here, I tried texting her. So far she's ignored my message. I figure she'll keep on ignoring me."

Dillon said, "Eric Johnson, Linus's father, and a social worker will be coming to the ranch this evening to collect Linus. We don't have to tell you that once the baby is gone, Stephanie is going to be crushed."

Acton felt as if he'd been punched. "You mean the test results are back? The man actually is Linus's father?"

Callum nodded. "The test has determined that Eric is the father."

Acton mulled over the jarring news. Stephanie's heart must be tearing right down the middle, he thought sickly.

Steven cast him a hopeful glance. "We thought you might try to see Steph tomorrow. After she's had tonight to pull herself together."

Acton scooted to the edge of the chair. "What makes you think she'd want to see me tomorrow? Or even agree to see me?"

Callum was the one to answer. "Before this matter with Linus's father came up, Stephanie was happier than we'd ever seen her. We all agree that part of that happiness had to do with you. If you say you're serious about our sister, then we ask that you don't give up on her. She needs you now…more than ever."

This was the last thing Acton had expected to hear from Stephanie's brothers, and though it made him feel somewhat better, he still had a multitude of doubts.

"I'm not sure how forgiving Stephanie might be," Acton said. "But I promise you, I'm not giving up."

At Paws and Claws, Stephanie was in the recovery room, checking on recuperating patients, when Dayna stuck her head in the door.

"Do you have time for one more patient?" she asked.

"Dr. Neil left the building about five minutes ago," Stephanie answered.

"I know. He stopped by the front desk on his way out. But you're still here. And a woman has come in with her cat. She says he's limping on his front paw."

Stephanie glanced at her watch as she walked over to where Dayna stood. "It's still a half hour before we close the doors. I suppose I could have a look."

"That's what I thought you'd say." Dayna shot her a coy grin, then turned to leave. "I'll put them in Exam Room 3."

Sensing Dayna was holding something back, Stephanie called out. "Wait, Dayna! Just who is this woman?"

Her smile even wider, Dayna glanced over her shoulder at Stephanie. "Faye Donovan."

Acton's mother? Wait—could he have sent her on his behalf? No! That was a ridiculous thought. Acton would never let anyone do his talking for him. Even so, how was she going to face Faye Donovan? This child she was carrying was going to be the woman's grandchild. What would she think if she knew?

Dayna suddenly stepped closer. "You look pale, Stephanie. Are you okay? I can tell Mrs. Donovan to come back tomorrow."

Putting the meeting off wouldn't help Stephanie. It would only cause the cat to suffer longer than need be.

Squaring her shoulders, she said, "Don't do that. I'm okay—just a bit tired. We've had a very busy day."

Dayna blew out a weary breath as she turned to leave. "You telling me. I'm going to be seeing cats and dogs in my sleep."

With Dayna gone, Stephanie smoothed a hand over her hair, then straightened the white lab coat she was wearing over her moss green blouse. This wasn't the way she'd envisioned meeting Acton's mother, but now that he'd apparently walked out of Stephanie's life, she supposed it hardly mattered where she met the woman.

Down the long hallway, Stephanie rapped her knuckles on the door of Exam Room 3, then stepped inside. Standing next to the examination table was a tall, slim woman with short blond hair. Somewhere in her fifties, she had soft, pretty features that faintly resembled Acton's sister, Gina. She was dressed casually in jeans, cowboy boots and a denim jacket. But it was the gentle smile on her face that caught Stephanie's attention.

"Hello. I'm Stephanie Fortune," she introduced herself.

The woman offered her hand. "I'm Faye Donovan."

Stephanie shook her hand, while hoping she didn't look as nervous as she felt. "It's nice to meet you."

"Please, just call me Faye. All my friends do."

Was she implying she wanted them to be friends? Oh Lord, just how much did Faye know about her son's relationship with Stephanie? Didn't she know it was over between them? Except that it couldn't ever be over entirely, Stephanie thought sickly. Not with the baby coming.

Clearing her throat, she said, "All right. And please, call me Stephanie."

"Thanks, I will." Smiling again, Faye gestured to the cat carrier. "Samson seems to have something wrong with his paw. I tried to look at it myself, but he's not the most cooperative cat on the ranch."

"Dr. Neil has already left for the day," Stephanie explained. "But I'll see what I can do for him. If that's okay."

"That would be great," Faye said brightly. "Samson is an outdoor cat and he loves to roam and get into mischief. I'm thinking he might have stepped on a mesquite thorn."

"That's possible," Stephanie agreed, while Faye unlatched the door on the carrier. "Is he friendly with strangers?"

"The only thing I've ever seen Samson bite is another cat," Faye answered. "I can't predict how he'll react to you. But Acton says you're a genius with animals, so I'm sure you won't have a problem."

Yes, Acton had praised her work as a veterinarian assistant. But as a woman, she wasn't sure what he was thinking or feeling.

"I hope you're right," Stephanie replied.

Thankfully, it didn't take long for the large, black tomcat to cozy up to Stephanie and she quickly went about examining all four feet.

"Are you sure Samson was limping earlier?" Stephanie asked a few minutes later as she stroked the cat's back. "He appears to be walking up and down the exam table just fine and I don't find a thing wrong with any of his pads."

Stephanie didn't miss the sheepish expression stealing across Faye's face.

"Samson always was a little faker," she said. "He'll do anything for attention."

"I guess he's decided he's over his lameness now," Stephanie replied.

Faye's chuckle was riddled with guilt. "I'm sorry, Stephanie. You've caught me red handed. There's nothing wrong with Samson. I just used him as an excuse to see you."

Stephanie had already come to that conclusion. Still it was a surprise to hear Faye admit it.

"To see me? Why?"

Shaking her head, Faye said, "In spite of how this looks, I'm actually not an interfering mother. But this one time, it's just that I can see—the whole family can see—that Acton is in a bad way. He's not behaving like himself, at all. And I thought you might want to know. To talk with him. Maybe?"

These past few days since she and Acton had quarreled had been some of the worst of Stephanie's life. To think that Acton might be hurting, too, jarred her already ragged senses. "So he told you we argued?"

"No. The last time Acton mentioned you was when he asked me about having you over for dinner one night soon. I happily agreed. And then a day or two later, his mood just completely changed. He became a complete grouch, with hardly a word for anyone. His father and I didn't have to wonder what was wrong. We knew something must have gone wrong between the two of you."

The pain in Stephanie's chest was smothering her and she had to look away from Faye's perceptive gaze before she could speak. "I haven't heard from

Acton in the past few days. I think he's decided I'm not right for him."

Faye sighed. "And what about what you've decided? Do you feel the same way? That he's not right for you?"

The question caused Stephanie's gaze to swing back to Faye's concerned face. "No! I mean, I thought we were perfect for each other. And then...this thing with Linus's father happened and, well, now everything is just...awful."

Faye stepped forward and gently patted Stephanie's arm. "I'm sorry, Stephanie. God knows I didn't come here to upset you. I understand you have enough problems without my interference."

She had problems, all right, Stephanie thought glumly. Far more than Faye could know. "Then you know about Linus?"

Faye nodded. "Acton has talked a lot about you and the baby. When he told us about the father coming we could see he was crushed about the whole thing."

"Yes. So am I."

A moment of awkward silence passed and then Faye said, "I understand that you're probably thinking Acton isn't ready to settle down. It's no secret that he's dated plenty of women. I'm sure you've been told that. But until he met you he was never serious about any of them. Whatever you're thinking, Stephanie, he's a good, hard-working man. And he loves children. That's all I'm going to say. Except that I hope you two can patch things up, because I have a feeling you and I could be great friends."

With tears stinging the back of her eyes, Stephanie did her best to smile. "Thank you, Faye. I won't forget what you've said."

But in the end would it make any difference? Stephanie didn't know. The only thing she knew for certain was that Acton had chosen to walk away from her, and in the next few hours Linus would be out of her life. Those two realities were almost more than she could bear.

That evening, Stephanie and Linus, along with her three brothers, were in the great room of the Fame and Fortune Ranch house, waiting for Eric Johnson to arrive.

In the past days since Stephanie had spoken with child services and set up the meeting with Linus's father, Steven had taken it upon himself to research the man's background. He was thirty-five, a native of the Houston area and a wealthy businessman who owned a trucking firm that operated nationwide. He was currently single and from what information Steven had gathered, he'd been dating Linus's mother. But something had obviously gone awry between the two of them and Laurel had ended things abruptly.

Two days ago, Stephanie had spoken over the phone to the social worker dealing with Linus's case and the woman had explained that Eric had provided the agency with a letter that Laurel had written to him. He'd also produced signed documents from friends who knew both Laurel and Eric, stating that the two had been in a real relationship. The information had been enough to warrant a DNA test. And now he was coming to collect his son. His baby.

Each time those words tried to enter Stephanie's brain, she fought them like a tigress protecting her cubs. No matter what kind of papers Eric had provided, or what the lab test said, as far as she was concerned, Linus had been her baby for more than two months now. Everything inside her screamed that he belonged with her.

"Stephanie, are you okay? Would you like for me to put Linus in his bassinet?"

She looked around to see that Steven had come to stand next to the rocker, where she clung to Linus and hummed the Texas sandman lullaby to him.

Oh, God, if she could only turn back to all those times she and Acton and Linus had been together as a family. Her heart had been full then. Now it was nothing but a ragged ball of pain.

Acton is in a bad way. He's not behaving like himself at all. Faye's words drifted through her mind, causing the pain in her heart to intensify.

"No," she said hoarsely. "I want to hold him. This might be the last time."

He was studying her with a worried look when the doorbell suddenly rang. Stephanie flinched.

"I'll answer it," Callum offered.

When he returned to the great room, he was followed by a tall young man with light brown hair and a middle-aged woman wearing a plain dark suit.

Dillon and Steven promptly walked over to join them, while Stephanie remained frozen in the rocker, her fingers clenched to Linus's blanket.

She could hear her brothers introducing themselves, and then a few more pleasantries were exchanged before the man stepped away from the group and began walking toward her.

He was dressed in an expensive-looking sports jacket, dark slacks and a pair of Italian loafers. By the casual way he wore the clothing, Stephanie could tell he was a man who was accustomed to having the best of things.

He came to a stop a few feet in front of her chair and the knots that were already tying her stomach twisted even tighter. "You must be Stephanie," he said. "I'm Eric Johnson. Nice to meet you."

With Linus in her arms, she rose from the rocker and extended a hand to him. "Yes, I'm Stephanie," she said automatically. "It's nice to meet you, Mr. Johnson."

His gaze immediately dropped to Linus and a bright smile spread across his face. "So this is my son. I've been waiting for this moment and now that it's here, I, uh, well, I'm blown away. He's incredible!"

Her throat was clamped so tight she had to swallow twice before she could utter a reply. "Linus is a very special little guy."

His gaze was full of awe as he continued to look down at Linus. "Dr. Green has shared all his medical history, but you're the person who can tell me about his personality. Does he cry much?"

Since she'd learned of Eric Johnson's existence, she'd thought of him only as a shadowy figure who'd be taking Linus away from her. She'd not pictured him as a father seeing his baby for the first time. She'd not imagined him wanting this baby as much as she wanted him. She could see now how misguided her thinking had been.

Drawing in a bracing breath, she said, "Linus is a very good baby. If he cries it's usually because he's hungry or wants his diaper changed. He never has a tummy ache and only spits up on occasion. He loves his bottle and usually wakes just once in the night around two."

Eric extended his arms toward the baby. "If you don't mind, I'd really like to hold him."

"Of course." Her response sounded brittle, but he was too busy plucking Linus from her arms to notice.

Feeling as though she was about to crack into a million pieces, Stephanie watched him carefully position Linus in the crook of his arm.

"My son," he said with a wealth of tenderness. "You and I have lots of catching up to do."

I guess it would be best for Linus to have his real dad. And probably best for you.

As she watched a look of awe come over Eric Johnson's face, Acton's words drifted through her mind, haunting her with the truth. Even in Stephanie's distraught state of mind she could see this moment was monumental for him, and despite the pain she was feeling, she realized she couldn't resent the man for wanting his own child.

"Excuse me," she told him. "I need to speak with my brothers."

Leaving father and son, she walked across the room to her brothers and the social worker. The woman's features were haggard, her shoulders slumped. No doubt, the consequences of a stressful job, Stephanie concluded.

"I'm Margaret Malloy," she said, politely introducing herself to Stephanie. "I want to thank you, especially, for making this transfer easy for everyone concerned."

Easy? There wasn't anything easy about having her heart ripped out of her chest, Stephanie thought. But there was no point in piling her misery on this woman. It wasn't Margaret Malloy's fault that this series of events had touched all their lives.

"I want what's best for Linus," she said simply.

Sensing Stephanie's frazzled emotions, the agent

gave her an empathetic smile. "I'll go take a look at the baby and give you a few minutes alone with your brothers."

After the woman excused herself and walked away, Steven took one look at Stephanie's face and wrapped an arm around her shoulders. "Stay strong, honey. You'll get through this."

"Sure," she said stiffly. "I'll get through."

"You should take comfort in the fact that Eric appears to be a good guy," Callum said to her. "And he truly wants his son."

"What about Laurel?" Stephanie asked. "Has he heard from her?"

"No. But he has a few ideas about where she might've gone," Steven said. "He's already talked to the authorities about her."

"Hell of a way for a man to find out he's a father," Dillon said, lowering his voice so that only the four of them could hear. "Getting a letter from his ex-girlfriend telling him she was carrying his baby."

Steven said, "Yeah, that was bad enough. But he had no idea where she or his unborn child had gone to. It wasn't until he saw a news article about a woman going into labor in Rambling Rose, then later leaving the baby at the pediatric center and disappearing into the wild blue. He considered it a long shot that the story might be about Laurel, but he decided to look into it. I'm not sure how I'd handle that kind of shock to the senses."

Stephanie's eyes burned with unshed tears. "It's pretty obvious he's not going to change his mind and decide to leave Linus here with me."

Callum shook his head. "Sorry, honey. No chance of that happening. He's walking on air."

Drawing in a shuddering breath, she said, "I have Linus's things all packed. I'll go get them."

"I'll help you," Steven told her.

As soon as they returned from Stephanie's suite with Linus's belongings, Eric and the agent were ready to leave.

Thankfully, he was thoughtful enough to allow Stephanie a moment alone with Linus and she carried the baby to a private spot in the room.

"My sweet little boy, I love you so," she whispered as she smoothed a finger over his soft hair. "I have to tell you goodbye now. If Acton was here he'd tell you goodbye, too."

As though he understood, the baby let out a short cry and boxed the air with his little fist.

Smiling through her tears, she bent and placed a kiss on his forehead and drew in his baby scent one last time. Then, squaring her shoulders, she carried him back to his waiting father.

"Please keep me updated on how he's doing," she told him through the tightness in her throat.

"I will," he promised. "And thanks again for taking such good care of my son."

Seeing Stephanie was about to break apart, Callum quickly ushered the three toward the foyer. "I'll see you out," he told them.

Stephanie watched until Linus and his father disappeared. By then, Steven was at her side, patting her hand in an effort to console her.

"Linus has his father in his life now," he said. "Just concentrate on that good thought."

A real parent. In a little more than eight months she and Acton were going to be real parents. They just weren't going to be parents together.

Dillon stepped forward and peered closely at her face. "Stephanie? Are you okay? You look white."

As she looked helplessly at both brothers, her stomach roiled in protest.

"I—I'm sorry! I'm going to be sick!"

She raced to the nearest bathroom and as she threw up over the commode, she thought about Acton and how she was going to face him with the news about their baby.

Chapter Fourteen

Linus is now in Houston with his father. Get it together. Stephanie needs you.

Acton had been trying to force a few bites of breakfast down his throat this morning, when the text message from Dillon had arrived. And he'd had to read it several times over before the reality of it had finally sunk into his weary brain.

Linus was truly gone and he couldn't begin to imagine the pain that Stephanie must be going through. He wanted to console her. To take away all the hurt she was feeling. But did she really need him now? Would she forgive him for walking away? For not understanding?

These past few days without her, he'd been trying to convince himself that she was better off without him. That she'd be better off with a man who could give her all the things she was accustomed to having in her life. Things that he could never give her.

But now as he drove through the rain toward the Fame and Fortune Ranch, he desperately wanted to believe that his love would be enough for her.

After a fitful night, with hardly any sleep, Stephanie was in such an awful state, she was forced to call Paws and Claws and tell them she was too sick to make it into work. It was the first time she'd ever missed work for any reason and she felt guilty about it. But her brothers had convinced her she was right. She couldn't face work after going through the trauma of losing Linus.

What were her brothers going to think when they learned that not all of her misery was over Linus? That she was pregnant by the cowboy they'd feared would break her heart?

Oh, God, could it get any worse?

Finding no answers in the spring rain collecting in puddles on the walkway, she turned away from the window of her private suite in the ranch house and sat down on the couch.

After switching on a large, flat-screen TV attached to the opposite wall, she punched through dozens of channels before pushing the off button. She couldn't focus on anything. Her thoughts continued to vacillate between Linus and Acton.

Was the baby okay? Was Eric Johnson holding him, loving him? Was he doing all the things that Linus needed to be happy and healthy?

Her heart felt heavy, and she heaved out a sigh as she tried to accept the fact that she couldn't do anything about Linus now. But it was a different matter with Acton. Somehow she was going to have to find the strength to face him and tell him about the coming baby. Whether he had any deep feelings for her or not, he had a right to know that the two of them had created a child.

Eventually her pets must have sensed she needed comforting. Violet, the Siamese, curled up by her side, while, Daisy, the yellow tabby, settled herself in Stephanie's lap. Even Orville hopped over and snuggled his furry body next to her bare feet.

"Well, guys, at least you three love me. But it's going to be awfully quiet around here without Linus and Acton."

Violet let out a coarse meow and then another. Stephanie was stroking the cat and trying to blink away another stream of tears, when the doorbell rang.

The unexpected sound jolted her. Who could that be? Her brothers had left for the construction site earlier this morning and Becky and the twins were on their way to the pediatric center.

Easing away from the pets, Stephanie went to the front door and peeked out the peephole.

Acton!

Rain was dripping off the brim of his brown hat and the shoulders of his khaki Western shirt were splotched with wet spots. What was he doing here?

Her heart thumping fast, she opened the door and discovered her tongue had momentarily become glued to the roof of her mouth.

"Acton. What…why are you here?" she finally asked.

He gestured to the folded quilt and a plastic container jammed beneath one arm. "Your brothers told me you weren't feeling well. I thought you might need a little TLC. This is my grandmother's chicken soup and a favorite quilt of mine. It has dogs and cats on it, so I thought it might cheer you."

None of what he was saying sounded like a man who wanted to end things, Stephanie thought. And when she looked into his eyes, she was mystified to see there was no anger or accusation flashing back at her. What did any of this mean?

Totally confused, she asked, "My brothers? You've talked to them?"

His smile took on a wry slant. "I have."

She gestured for him to come in, and after he'd walked to the middle of the room, she shut the door and leaned her back against it.

"So you know that Linus is gone?" Even as she

asked the question, fresh tears sprang to her eyes. She promptly dashed them away with the back of her hand. "I'm sorry. I can't seem to stop crying."

"Yes, I know about Linus. I can only imagine the pain you're feeling right now. I'm really sorry, Stephanie. I know how much you cared about Linus. To tell you the truth, I'm missing the little guy pretty bad myself, too." He walked over to the window and placed the container of soup and the quilt on the table.

Questions swirled in Stephanie's head as she moved slowly toward him. "It's been awful, Acton. Just awful. Not just because I lost Linus, but…because I lost you."

His expression solemn, he shook his head. "I messaged you yesterday asking if we could talk. You never responded."

A few minutes after Faye Donovan had left the clinic, Stephanie had discovered Acton had sent a text message earlier that morning. Her first instinct had been to call him. But the timing had been all wrong.

She sighed. "I didn't respond because I…had to go home—to pack up all of Linus's things and get him ready to leave with his father. It wasn't a good time for us to talk."

Damn it. If only he'd known. He'd been a class A idiot. "I'm really sorry. I had no idea." He'd stop kicking himself eventually. Maybe in a year. "And now?" he asked gently.

Fearing another burst of tears was about to flood her eyes, she turned and walked over to the opposite side of the room. Standing near the fireplace, she stared out the window at the falling rain.

"We do have a lot to talk about," she said quietly.

At the sound of his footsteps, she glanced around to see him walking toward her and the look of yearning on his face caused her heart raced with anticipation and hope.

Stopping an arm's length away from her, he said, "And the first thing I need to say is that I'm sorry. Truly sorry."

Moisture filled her eyes as she met his gaze. "Oh, Acton, after we argued that day at Paws and Claws, and I'd had time to calm down and think more clearly I felt ashamed and guilty and stupid. Yes, I was knocked sideways over the news about Linus, but that was no excuse for shutting you out. And I'm sorry about that. You were right all along. Linus should be with his real father. That's the most important thing."

He moved a step closer and Stephanie was suddenly overwhelmed by his rugged face and familiar scent. She was going to have his baby and she wanted it, and him, more than she wanted anything in her life.

"You don't need to apologize to me, Stephanie. I

was the one who handled things badly. But that was because I wanted to be the one to comfort you—help you deal with losing Linus."

"I realize that now. But that day I wasn't thinking clearly, Acton. And then afterwards, when reality began to set in…well, I thought I'd blown everything between us." Her gaze somberly searched his face. "I think…the big problem is that I haven't been completely honest with you."

"You haven't? About what?"

"My feelings for you. I should have told you long before all of this happened with Linus that I love you. That I've been in love with you almost from the very start."

A mixture of amazement and doubt washed over his face. "Love? You love me? Why didn't you tell me?"

Her gaze dropped to the pearl snap in the middle of his chest. "Because a guy like you—you're not ready for marriage. And I was afraid it would make you run from me."

"Who says I'm not ready?"

She looked guiltily up at him. "Well, most everyone who knows you has told me that you—"

"That I'm a playboy?" he interrupted with a frown. "That I don't have a serious thought in my head? Well, they're wrong, Stephanie. Maybe on the outside that's what people think they see, but they don't know what's going on in here." He tapped the region of his heart. "I've been committed to our relationship from the very beginning, Stephanie. I love you, too, sweetheart. More than you'll ever know."

Hope bubbled inside her, but before she could truly let her heart celebrate, she had to tell him about the baby.

Biting down on her lip, she carefully studied his face. "You say that now, Acton, but you might feel differently when I tell you the rest."

Curious, he arched his eyebrows. "The rest? Your love comes with a condition?"

She smiled. Because when she thought about Acton's baby, that's the way it made her feel—happy. Oh, so happy.

"No. It comes with an addition. I'm pregnant, Acton. I'm going to have your baby."

His eyes grew wide. "Pregnant? You, me… We're going to have a baby?"

She nodded and, holding her breath, waited for his reaction.

It came with a smile that spread from ear to ear. "Oh, Stephanie! Wow! A baby for us! This is…amazing!"

"I realize it's unexpected and I haven't confirmed it with the doctor, but I've already taken a home-pregnancy test. And morning sickness is hitting me as soon as I lift my head off the pillow. I'm not sure how it happened exactly. But I think my pills are too weak, or you're too virile. Take your pick."

Suddenly he was laughing and hugging her tightly against him. "We're going to have a baby and you love me. The only way I could be any happier is if you agree to be by my side for the rest of our lives."

Leaning her head back, she smiled up at him. "Again, before I answer I have a condition."

"Okay, lay it on me. I'm guessing you're eventually going to want a giant wedding with twelve bridesmaids and me in a tuxedo."

She laughed. "The wedding doesn't have to be that big! As far as I'm concerned I'd be happy if we eloped to Las Vegas."

His blue eyes twinkled. "Hey, now that's a thought," he said, then asked, "So what is the condition?"

"That we make our home on the Diamond D— in your grandparents' farmhouse. Do you think you can make room for me, our baby and six more animals?"

Mystified, he gestured to their luxurious surroundings. "I can make room for all of you and more. But, Stephanie, what about this place? It's so grand and—"

"Yes, it's grand. But my home is with you—in the little house where we first made love. I want our children to be raised on the Diamond D, just like you." Her smile was full of love. "And don't worry about this place. My triplet sisters are planning to move to Rambling Rose soon to help with the restaurant. This part of the house will be perfect for them. And your house will be perfect for me. What do you think?"

"I came over here determined to fight for the woman I love. Now I'm thinking I'm the happiest man in the world." Dropping his head, he placed a long, sweet kiss on her lips. "I want us to get engaged soon, Stephanie. As soon as I can find the perfect ring. What do you say?"

"I say yes!"

Cradling her face in his hands, he rubbed his thumbs over her cheeks. "I do have one important question, though," he said. "Do you think Seymour and Grizabella will be willing to share their home with all your furry friends?"

Smiling cleverly, she brought her lips back to his. "Seymour and Grizabella will be glad to share. Remember, I can put special spells on animals."

Groaning, he pulled her tightly into his arms. "Mmm. And you've put one on me that's going to last a lifetime."

* * * * *

MILLS & BOON

Coming next month

THE PRINCE AND THE WEDDING PLANNER
Jennifer Faye

Bianca shook her head. With him gazing into her eyes, her heart had leapt into her throat. Was that desire reflected in his eyes? The prince desired her? Her heart tumbled in her chest.

She didn't know how long they stood there staring into each other's eyes. It was like Leo had a gravitational force around him and she was being drawn in. Though she knew letting anything happen between them would be a mistake—compounding all of the other uncertainties in her life—she remained rooted to the spot in front of him.

Her heart raced as she found herself getting lost in his dark gaze. Her fingers tingled with the urge to reach out to him—

Someone cleared their throat. Loudly. Annoyingly.

And in that second, the connection dissipated. Bianca blinked and glanced away. Heat rushed to her face. She was grateful she didn't have to speak because she didn't trust her tongue to work correctly.

Leo cleared his throat. "Yes, Michael. What is it?"

"You are needed, sir. The call from Canada."

Leo sighed. "I'll be right there." Once the man moved on, Leo turned his full attention to her. "I'm sorry. I've been expecting this call all day."

"I understand. You have important business to attend to."

Reality had come crashing in on them. And none too soon. He was a royal prince. She was a wedding planner with an uncertain heritage. They did not belong together.

"About this…" As his voice trailed off, he looked at her with confusion reflected in his eyes.

He wasn't the only one to be confused. Her heart had betrayed her mind in wanting what it could not have. And now that her feet were once again planted firmly on the ground, she couldn't forget that she was here to do a job. That needed to be her focus. Not getting swept up in some fairytale.

"It's okay," she said. "You have important work to do."

"You're not upset about ending the evening so soon?"

She shook her head. "Not at all. I understand that business must come first."

As he escorted her back to the palace, he didn't offer her his arm. And she made sure to keep a reasonable distance between them. Because as much as nothing had happened between them, something most definitely had almost happened.

Continue reading
THE PRINCE AND THE WEDDING PLANNER
Jennifer Faye

Available next month
www.millsandboon.co.uk

COMING SOON!

LET'S TALK
Romance

For exclusive extracts, competitions
and special offers, find us online:

 facebook.com/millsandboon

@MillsandBoon

@MillsandBoonUK

Get in touch on 01413 063232

For all the latest titles coming soon, visit
millsandboon.co.uk/nextmonth

MILLS & BOON

THE HEART OF ROMANCE

A ROMANCE FOR EVERY KIND OF READER

MODERN
Prepare to be swept off your feet by sophisticated, sexy and seductive heroes, in some of the world's most glamourous and romantic locations, where power and passion collide.
8 stories per month.

HISTORICAL
Escape with historical heroes from time gone by. Whether your passion is for wicked Regency Rakes, muscled Vikings or rugged Highlanders, awaken the romance of the past.
6 stories per month.

MEDICAL
Set your pulse racing with dedicated, delectable doctors in the high-pressure world of medicine, where emotions run high and passion, comfort and love are the best medicine.
6 stories per month.

Celebrate true love with tender stories of heartfelt romance, from the rush of falling in love to the joy a new baby can bring, and a focus on the emotional heart of a relationship.
8 stories per month.

Indulge in secrets and scandal, intense drama and plenty of sizzling hot action with powerful and passionate heroes who have it all: wealth, status, good looks…everything but the right woman.
6 stories per month.

HEROES
Experience all the excitement of a gripping thriller, with an intense romance at its heart. Resourceful, true-to-life women and strong, fearless men face danger and desire - a killer combination!
8 stories per month.

DARE
Sensual love stories featuring smart, sassy heroines you'd want as best friend, and compelling intense heroes who are worthy of them.
4 stories per month.

To see which titles are coming soon, please visit

millsandboon.co.uk/nextmonth